SISTAHGIRL
PUBLISHING CO.

VOODOOLOVE

SONIA CAULTON

A Novel

A SistahGirl Publishing

Request for permission to make copies or any part of the work should be mailed to Permissions Departments SistahGirl Publishing Co. P.O. Box 250593 Atlanta, Georgia 30325.

Library of Congress Cataloging-in Publication Data
99-095010
Voodoo Love: a novel/ Sonia Caulton.-1st SistahGirl ed.
ISBN 0-9655545-1-1
I Title. II Series

Printed in the United States of America
SistahGirl 1999

God's Praise

Giving honor and glory to God for his mercy and grace when I thought I couldn't make it through the desert where my faith and strength was tested two years ago. God, publicly, I repent for my constant doubt in you and your word because I did not understand your plan and purpose for my life. Although I blamed you because I could not understand why me, you stood by me and carried me when I refused to take another step and you loved me when I forsaked you and walked away. You continued to show me love and to show me your purpose while I tried to find another way. God, once again, after it's all said and done, you are worthy to be praised for you are "The Great I Am."

Acknowledgements

Friends are needed while traveling through the wilderness of life because they feel your pain and catch a hold of your vision when no one else understands. I will like to thank my mother, Constance Caulton, and my best friends, Carol "Peaches" Carter, Debbie Toombs, Timika and Kenya Caulton, and Ronald "Ron" Barner.

And special thanks to all the Black Bookstores that made room for me on their shelves.

To my precious son,
Nigel Isaiah Walton
Whose my strength, weakness, love and joy.
Because of him, I pray for wisdom and insight to be the best mother and friend he needs in life.
Because of him, I love and forgive those who have hurt me.
Because of him, I sacrifice my own wants for his needs.
Because of him, I have to continue the race when I want to give up.
Because of him, I understand the purpose and plan God has for my life.
Because of him.

CHAPTER ONE

If it wasn't for the cracking of the television waking Darika out of her much needed sleep, she probably would have slept through the night without knowing Keith hadn't made it home again for the fourth time in two weeks. But the tenth or twelfth time of their marriage. She looked at the huge wooden clock across the room that read four thirty a.m., and rolled her eyes back into her head and sighed out of frustration as she hit her pillow with an open hand. She slung the king sized silk comforter off her body and jumped to her feet while staring at the empty space where Keith should be sleeping. "This is it," she said, while shaking her head and placing her hand on her hips. "I've had enough of this shit. He thinks he doesn't have to come home? Well then, he can just pack his things and get the hell out. I know for sure I'm not going anywhere. And if he thinks I am, he better think again. This house is mine. And I know for a fact any court will award it to me with no problem—on the grounds of adultery and mental cruelty. Who does he think he is?"

She immediately picked up the phone to call his office but she knew he wasn't there but then again she was hoping that he was. She would give anything right now to hear lie one hundredth and ten about him falling asleep at his desk while working on a major project. "I'm trying to come up with this powerful design, baby," she mimicked him to say. But she didn't even waste her time dialing the number. Her heart wouldn't be able to stand it if the phone just rang. So she called his best friend and partner, Matthew Slack. Although Darika knew he would lie for Keith, she called him anyway. If it wasn't for him, she and her husband wouldn't be going through this type of mess. It was Slack who was introducing him to other women.

Slack's wife, Juanita answered the phone sounding half asleep.

"Hello, Juanita," Darika said, calmly.

Not recognizing Darika's voice Juanita asked with annoyance, "Who is this?"

"This is Darika, girl, I'm so sorry to be calling your house at this time of morning but is Slack home?"

"Yeah, he just walked in here," she said.

"May I speak to'im?"

"Hello," Slack answered very skeptically. Darika had heard from Keith how afraid he gets when the phone rang during the middle of the night. She was sure she had made him shit on himself as he tried to figure out what woman had found out his home number.

Darika's calm attitude had changed to snappy and irate. "Slack, where is Keith?"

"Hey, Darika," he said, pleasantly trying to calm her before she started cursing him out. He knew from the past once she was started there was no stopping her. "Just got in from working the Stein project myself." He yawned. "Boy I'm tired."

"Don't play with me, Slack," she said, with both hands or her hips and the phone tucked tightly between her chin and shoulder. "Where is my husband and I don't want to hear any lies." Not giving him time to say a word she answered for him. "He's with

2

one of his bitches isn't he? I'm going to leave his ass this time. I'm not joking. I've had just about all I'm gon' take from that man. I just thought you would want to know that so now you can fix him up with all of your little sluts. If Juanita doesn't have the sense to leave yo'sorry ass, she'll be putting up with yo'shit from now until."

"Yeah, Darika, you know Keith is trying to bring in all the money these days," he said, trying to play their conversation off and keep his temper down.

Darika knew he couldn't respond the way he wanted to because Juanita was lying beside him and he didn't want her to know Darika was calling about Keith not making it home yet.

"Jaunita is sleeping so good I don't want to wake her with this talk about business so let me go into the next room here. Yeah, we were at the office working on that big Stein project. Didn't Keith tell you that's where the money is? You'll be getting that nice down payment on the private school you want to start building once this project goes through," he told her.

What private school, Darika thought, she had no idea in hell what he was talking about. He was taking it overboard now. "What are you talking about, where is my damn husband?"

Once he got into the guest room, his head began to spin, fire shot through his nostrils as he muttered through his teeth with anger. "Don't you ever call my house at this time of morning looking for Keith or any damn body else. He ain't over here and that's all I'm gon' tell you. And as far as what my wife put up with that ain't none of your damn business. If you worry about your own business, you would be better off and you wouldn't be having to call me at four in the damn morning."

"Go to hell." She slammed down the phone and out of frustration, she dropped her head in her hands. There was no holding back. Her tears began to fall with one blink of an eye. Her heart was beating so fast she thought it was going to jump out of her chest onto the floor. She placed her hand between her breast and took two deep breaths. But that didn't do any good. Her heart was still racing like a horse and her hands were shaking. She couldn't understand why Keith was doing this to her. She rubbed her hands across her short black hair and then looked at them to see how much hair had came out this time. Keith had her under so much stress she was losing weight and hair like a person with AIDS. There was no need of her dieting, not while she was married to Keith and he was doing whatever the hell he wanted to with who-ever the hell he wanted to. She fell back on the bed and sighed while trying to calm her nerves. She thought of a rose garden, some-thing her therapist told her would relax her mind whenever she felt overwhelmed with bullshit. But that didn't work either; Keith was in the rose garden with another woman. She had heard her heart beat like this before—when she knew her husband was somewhere he had no place being— like in another woman's bed. "I'm so damn tired of him and this mess he's pulling I could just scream." She through up her hands. "I give up— I don't care who knows. Irene Tate, big elephant ass and Cassandra Odum, skinny stick- man-looking ass can talk all day long about Keith leaving me for another woman. I don't care anymore. I would rather have my sanity any day over wondering what in the hell I did to make this man run to another woman and where he is when he's not with me. I'm thirty-five years old. I don't need to be going through this mess. He can give me a damn divorce today and I wouldn't care. No woman should have to go through this. I gave this man all my love and he wants to stay out all damn night like he's single. If you don't love me, then leave."

Her voice began to crack and her hands began to shake uncon-trollably as her temple's pound with pain. Her temples felt like some-one had punched her in them. She paced the floor while staring at his side of the bed and cursing him underneath her breath. Her voice was strong and deep so it carried. There was no need of her trying not to wake her mother who was in the next room. Her mother knew the deal with Keith. He was no good. Darika threw on her robe and stormed toward the heavy oakwood bedroom door, slinging it open as if it was plastic. Her feet stomped through the halls of the hardwood floor, six bedroom, seven hundred thousand-dollar mansion looking for Keith. She ran to every bedroom in the house praying to God he was asleep in one of them; but he wasn't, just as she had expected. A lump developed in her throat and her racing heart stopped beating for at least a second or two. She then ran downstairs to the garage, praying with all her heart he was slumped over the steering wheel of his car, too drunk to have made it into the house last night, but his car wasn't even there. She slammed the door and slid down the kitchen wall onto the floor. She wanted to die. There was not enough strength in her body to go on living like this. She silently prayed to God to just kill her right there, because the pain she was feeling was killing her slowly and she would rather die instantly. She looked at the knife on the counter top and contemplated on jabbing it into her stomach or grabbing the gun out of the hall closet and shooting herself in the head with it. Death would be the only way to end the pain she was feeling, she thought. She could imagine the look on Keith's face when he came home after being with another woman and found her laying on the kitchen floor dead. She was sure he would take the blame and wish he were dead instead but then she heard a voice tell her, "Wake up fool. Once you're dead, his bitch would be there to comfort him and they would no longer have to sneak around." She quickly erased the thought and began to think on the seven years they had been married. And for the first time she could admit to herself they weren't the best seven years. She was Keith's fool and not his wife.

There was no one for Darika to turn to. Her mother knew of her painful marriage but Darika was tired of talking to her about it. She was beginning to hate Keith and plotting to have someone kill him if God didn't do it first. Darika didn't like her mother thinking in that sense. But the love a mother has for her child is understandable and if that child is being hurt that mother would do anything to come to her defense. Darika didn't want to see her own mother roasting with anger about a situation she wasn't willing to change. And as far as her friends, she was much too embarrassed to call any of them because they were tired of listening to her cry about the same drama. A cheating husband. Her best friend, Cookie told her not to come crying on her shoulders if she wasn't going to leave Keith. But she did anyway when she thought he was fooling around with Gail Baylor, one of the television news anchor women. Darika thought Cookie was being cruel. Friends are supposed to be there for one another no matter if the advice given is taken or not. Cookie never would have given John a divorce if he didn't insist on it. Darika recalled her begging him over the phone not to leave her. She was willing to forgive him and work things out with him when she found out he had been screwing one of his employees, a woman named Velma from the projects. Cookie is still bitter from that but who wouldn't be after having their husband leave them for a woman less than who his wife was. Cookie still shouldn't want everyone else to leave their husband just because hers left her. Come to find out Gail and Slack were seeing each other instead of her and Keith. Juanita had caught them at the airport coming in together from New York. Darika had made it her business to let Cookie know that.

When Darika confides in her friends, she doesn't mean for them to become personally involved and voice their opinions about what they think she should do. She doesn't really want their advice to be truthful. She just needs an ear that will listen to her vent. When she's ready to leave Keith, she'll leave him, like now. She's a woman fed up. Of course she's been fed up before, and she's told everyone she was leaving and didn't. And they had the nerve to stop talking to her and called her stupid. If she was stupid for not leaving her husband and giving him another chance, then stupid she was going to be because she loved that man. A marriage isn't meant for a person to walk away from it in a day when it took years to develop. Her friends told her to get out of it while she could four years ago and take the house and collect alimony but she couldn't when she'd rather be married to the man. She loved Keith and leaving him has never been easy. Just like it isn't now but she has made up her mind. He's a good husband and a wonderful man in spite of his cheating. When there was no explanation of why she would lock herself up in the room, crying three days straight uncontrollably and sometimes going off in a rage of breaking every thing in sight when things didn't go her way, Keith advised her to seek help. And he stood by her until she did. She was diagnosed as a bi-polar depressor and border line manic. She had heard some women husbands actually leave them when they have out breaks. For two years she carried on before being diagnosed and Keith put up with it. He had read up on her symptoms and diagnosed her before she had ever agreed to seek help. And he blamed himself for it. And when it was discovered she couldn't give him the children he wanted, he didn't leave her for a woman who could. He stayed with her. He has been her backbone and her laughter when she didn't feel she could smile. He's everything she wants in a man that's why she married him. But then again he's everything that she hates.

Darika sat with her head in her hands crying while trying to figure out why Keith was doing her the way that he was. She admits she had allowed Keith to run over her. She was stupid just like her friends believed she was. But she was no different from them or any other woman that loved her husband. She didn't want a divorce from him because he had laid between some lonely, cheap trick's legs who didn't know the first thing about getting her own man. The mistake she made was letting them know he was cheating and it was hurting her. If she would have been cool about it like Camille Cosby or Hillary Clinton, and not show any hurt nothing would have been said. At least not to her anyway.

Darika considered herself to be a good wife, someone who stood by her husband no matter what. Meaning, when he cheated, she loved him anyway. No she couldn't sing the song of a wife that had died to her life so that he could live his. Meaning, she gave nothing up for him. She didn't stop teaching because he needed her to answer the phones of his business and she didn't have a house full of kids like he wanted. And she didn't work in the textile mill twelve hours a day to help ends meet. Hell no, she wasn't a good cook but he knew that before he married her. Of course she was a little careless with the money. She over spent and everytime someone in her family called to borrow some of it she took out the check book. But Keith makes over five hundred thousand dollars a year, a couple of hundred dollars shouldn't be a worry. No, she didn't want sex every time his dick got hard and he came rubbing on her. She had a right to turn him down. Where does it say just because a woman's husband wants sex she has to want it also? She was his wife, not a whore off the streets. So hell yeah, she told him if he was hurting her and sometimes made him get up. She didn't care if he got mad or not.

They had arguments like any other couple and she said things she didn't mean and he said things he didn't mean but later they apologized and laughed about it. Although she hated to wear that dental floss for panties and that cheap looking stuff from Fredericks of Hollywood he enjoyed seeing her in, she wore it anyway just to keep him happy. So why wasn't he happy with her? Why was he sleeping in some other woman's bed at 5:30 a.m.? She asked herself as she looked at the clock on the wall. Then it hit her. A statement Belinda had made one afternoon while they were having lunch. Her voice played in Darika's head. "If you could give that man some babies, you wouldn't have to worry about another woman— you'll be all the woman he needs." Darika knew this but there was nothing she could do about it; she was barren from endometriosis at the age of twenty-two. She screamed to the top of her lungs while shaking her fist up at the heavens and blaming God.

Darika needed a clue to who this other woman was—what she looked like or where she lived. She had a feeling she was a younger woman. Because every woman she's caught him with had been a young woman in her early twenties. The babies that were fascinated by his money and that would swing off the chandlers like he wanted them to. She jumped up from the floor and ran down to the basement to his study. She was sure to find a picture or her name or number written down on a piece of paper somewhere. Keith had never been careless with his cheating it was always the women he chose that had exposed their affair. But there's a first time for everything. Maybe today he slipped up and lost track of the game. Darika had never been the type of woman to snoop around for anything that might hurt her and a number and a name of another woman scribbled on a piece of paper would have done just that. Why else would a woman's name be on a piece of paper beside her number if Keith had no intentions on calling her and they sneak around until they were exposed. While her girlfriends' were searching through their husbands' pockets and finding strips of paper with a name and a number, she was thinking Keith wouldn't dare fool around. Because she didn't want to think he would have, she had caught him time after time and he had apologized and promised her he would never do it again.

She spotted his sports jacket hanging on the back of his chair so she rushed over to it and began looking through the pockets. There was nothing. She also searched through his briefcase, desk drawers, and under the cushioning of the leather sofa and still found nothing. She sighed out of frustration as she flopped down at his desk. She didn't know anything more about this lady other than she wears cheap perfume that stuck to Keith's skin like sweat, and red lipstick that's either on his collar or lips and she had good pussy because he didn't make it home last night.

Whether she knew who this other woman was or not she was sure the woman had seen her and knew everything about her. It was in a mistresses nature to know about the woman who couldn't keep her husband at home and happy. All of them had been curious about Darika in the past. They were curious to know if she was just as beautiful as they were. Darika figured this other woman was no different. She had probably parked her car at the corner of their house and followed her for a day. Just to see if her appearance or character had anything to do with why Keith was lying in her bed every night instead of his own. The thought made her sick and weak; she dropped her head out of embarrassment and began to fight the battle all over again. The same battle she had fought from a childhood up until now. At the age of thirty-five she still considered her dark beautiful flawless skin to be a curse. A curse that had held her back and caused her to be overlooked. A curse she couldn't do anything about. She blamed it for the reason her husband didn't love her and people didn't like her. Darika was attractive in the eyes of many including her husband's but her complex about her dark skin tone made her think differently. And she felt the women thought the same and they did. They thought she was far from his type although she was his wife. They couldn't understand how in the hell she had landed a man as sexy and handsome as Keith. After all she was dark as deep dark chocolate with short hair, thick lips, beady eyes, wide hips and a big butt when they were high-yellow with European features just as his. And it killed Darika. She had told Keith how when she was growing up, the children used to call her blacky and her teachers always overlooked her for any of the leading roles in the school

9

play because she was dark skin. And she had never had a boy-friend in high school or college because they thought she was ugly. She feels Keith shows her up when he dates beautiful light skinned women.

No one knew Darika carried such a burden of low self-esteem around with her. They didn't know that she associated herself with everything of elegance and beauty because she didn't feel she was. It was hidden very well. She walked around with her head up high her nose in the air and her lip turned up at anyone she didn't feel was up to her standards. But when no one was looking she hurt from rejection and kept herself close to her husband's side. She felt Keith was the one thing to make her look beautiful.

There were unopened bills lying on his desk. She was sure one of them would tell her about this other woman. She picked up his personal monthly credit card statement and phone bill. That's how her girlfriend, Belinda Fisher found out about her husband's un-dercover whore. The eight hundred dollar phone bill and the can-celed checks from where he had been paying her rent told all. Darika's heart began to pound as she ripped opened the envelope. With her knowing there was another woman was enough for her to have a heart attack but knowing Keith has been taking care of her is enough to kill her. There was no doubt in her mind Keith was taking good care of her; he sure as hell had the money too. Besides what woman in her right mind would sacrifice her morals by fooling around with a married man and not make him pay a little money. But today's single women didn't know the first thing about morals, when they are lonely, in desperate need of a man and black men are scarce. Love isn't their motive for having a man. It's whatever he has to offer and they don't give a damn if he's married or not. Bills need to be paid, the children need new shoes, and if a married man has the money to do it, a lonely woman would subject herself to shit to get it. That's all these damn songs that come on the radio sing about today the big secret of one woman sleeping with another woman's man. Ain't nothing cute about that shit, Darika thought. A man can have a wedding band on his finger as big as a halo and "I'm happily married," stamped across his face and a woman would still approach him. "Who in the hell is she," Darika screamed. She no longer blamed Keith for his infidelity but the women, who she was sure had approached him first.

This other woman had not only seen Darika but Darika had seen her also. Darika was sure they knew each other and had spoken once or twice while in passing. Half of the women that meet their husband's whores know them or have seen them somewhere or another. Darika figured this other woman had seen her and Keith together and she had set out to get him. Either she's a woman that works very close to him. Someone like that Bridget Nelson, the young twenty-six year old he hired a year ago, the sales clerk at her favorite clothing boutique she's dragged him in on occasional Saturdays. Or maybe she's the bank teller who greets him with a smile and calls him by his first name every Friday he goes to make a deposit. She noticed how they all look at him, batting their eyes and gliding their tongue across their lips as if they could just sex him right there in front of her and all the customers. When she was younger and she and Keith were just dating, having women look at him used to make her feel envied but now this shit has to stop. He's married with a band on his finger.

When Belinda had finally come face to face with the woman her husband had been seeing for two years, she was shocked to know she was the caterer of the company she had always used to cater her parties. And this same lady had been to their home a number of times and sat at her table and ate her food while at the same time sleeping with her husband. Three months ago Darika and Keith celebrated their seventh year wedding anniversary and Darika now bet anything on her life the other woman was there. She was just one of the women who laughed in her face as she overheard their friends telling them how proud they were of them for making it to seven years. She knew seven years meant nothing to Keith because he was unhappy at home, laying between her legs every night and paying her rent. She laughed at the comments.

Now as Darika looked back on that night, she remembered a couple of women there that she had never seen before. When they introduced themselves to her, they said they were colleagues and clients. None of them wore a wedding ring and they were beautiful women but she thought nothing of it. They said they were colleagues and clients and that's exactly what she thought they were, so why were they at her anniversary party? It was supposed to be for their close friends and family. They weren't friends of hers.

Her eyes scanned the charges and she screamed, "Mama," as she read seven thousand dollars in the now due box. She knew Keith hadn't spent that much money on himself. She tried to catch her breath; she had stopped breathing. There were charges for women clothing from Sak's Fifth Ave, and Bloomingdales that totaled up to four thousand dollars. Five hundred dollars were charges for a weekend in Vermont at the ski lodge and that was for the hotel alone. Plane tickets to and from D.C. to Atlanta that totaled up to three thousand dollars for just the month of January alone. She threw the bill down on the desk and picked up the five hundred dollar phone bill that had several numbers from Atlanta. None of the numbers she knew. There were a couple of calls to his best friend's John and Alfred, but the other hundred and fifty calls she couldn't recognize.

She immediately picked up the phone to call one of the numbers praying to God she would answer. The phone rang about two times before a chipper older white woman answered with a New York accent. Darika slammed down the phone and fell back in the chair while grasping for air. Feeling as if her heart had jumped out of her chest onto the desk. "He's fooling around with some old white bitch in Atlanta," she cried to her mother as she entered the office. "You low-down bastard . . . you're sleeping with some old white bitch," she then said, as she looked at his picture on the desk and busted out crying.

Her mother walked over to her and placed her arm around her shoulders. "Baby, it'll be all right."

"He didn't come home last night, mama," she said. "What did I ever do in my life to deserve this, why does God hate me so much to put me through this? There's nothing worse than loving a man and him not loving you back. And this man is my husband. He's never loved me and I was just too damn blind to see it. I tried to make him love me with putting up with his shit for years and did nothing but make him hate me all the more. I can't give him no babies. Hell, I don't even fuck'im."

"Darika, shut yo'mouth, chile. Don't you go blaming my God for that man being low-down. You shouldn't have married him in the first place."

"I thought he loved my ugly black ass."

"Chile, if you don't close yo'mouth— you are beautiful."

"No, I'm not. You never thought so when I was a child. You and everybody else but my daddy used to make fun of this black skin of mine. And he didn't make fun of it because I was as black as him. What made me think Keith wanted me?"

"Are you out of your mind?" Rita asked. "I'm not listening to no'mo of this mess you talkin." She turned to walk out of the room.

"I want to die." Darika cried out.

"Girl, you are talkin foolish. I thought you were much stronger than this . . . block it out. I couldn't lose all I had for some other woman and neither can you. It'll be all right. You're beautiful. Maybe when you were little I called you ugly once or twice but I didn't mean it. I called all my children ugly when y'all got on my nerves. I know that's no excuse but I was a young mother with five children. I was always frustrated about something. Look at you now, you've blossomed into a beautiful woman."

"Why is he in love with another woman?"

"That's not love— he's fucking."

Darika looked at her mother surprisingly.

"I don't want you to go messing up what you got. Keith, has provided for you well. I'm proud to rub in Anna Mae and Deloise's face about what you have. I don't like Denise's ugly husband either he's arrogant but he's a provider and that's something you don't mess with because you can't find another man that can take care of you the way Keith can."

"Mama, I have a master's in teaching I can get a job."

"You want'a work?" Her mother asked her in disbelief.

"I'm divorcing him. This is something you should be encouraging me to do, mama."

"Do you even know who this other lady is?"

"It doesn't matter. She's some old white woman in Atlanta.

Her number is all on the phone bill." She handed her mother the phone bill.

"Where is the phone?" Rita asked, as she looked over the bill.

"For what?"

"Chile, I've been doing this for seventeen years since I've been married to yo'daddy. You gon' mess up a good thing and I'm gon' show you how to keep it. Now call out them numbers to me. You know I don't have my glasses." Darika called out the numbers and Rita dialed them. She looked at her mother wondered for the eighty time in her life why she didn't get her complexion or looks instead of her daddy's, who she hated so much. "Hello, Is Mr. Keith Jones there—he's not," she responded and looked over at Darika.

"No, is he supposed to be here?" The woman asked.

"Well, this is the number he gave me and told me if I had any problems to contact him here. I'm his mother and secretary."

"Nice to meet you. He talks so much about you. He and my daughter are dating you know—"

"Dating. Your daughter. Who is she, I never met her?"

"Well, you should have. She's an intern at the firm. Andrea is her name."

"Yeah, the intern, Andrea I know her."

"That bitch," Darika whispered. "Give me that phone."

Her mother nodded and rushed off the phone. "It was nice talking to you. I guess I'll page'im now." She slammed the phone down and rolled her eyes at Darika. "Have you lost your mind?"

"So he's fucking the little twenty-four-year-old intern that has been to my house sat at my table ate my food, slept at my house and has been fucking my husband. No wonder we can't have a baby because he enjoys fucking them. So he's screwing the half-breed." Darika slammed her fist on the desk. "And I'm gon'beat that bitch's ass."

CHAPTER TWO

Darika circled the block twice before pulling into Andrea's driveway. Keith's car was parked in it. She didn't want them to look out the window when she rang the door bell and notice her car. She didn't want Keith to go running out the back door, so she parked in a neighbor's driveway instead and walked across the street. With her heart beating as fast as it was earlier that morning, she knocked on the door softly. Andrea sprang open the door without looking through the peep hole. What a dense, Darika thought but she didn't give a damn. It was to her benefit. By the looks of her sandy brown curls scattered over her head, she had been rolling around in the hay with someone's cowboy. Darika warned her to be quiet before she had even thought about calling out Keith's name to warn him. The smell of breakfast filled the large condo that Keith had purchased for his interns every summer. His style was all about the room from what Darika could tell. It was decorated a lot differently and more expensive from the last intern that had lived there last summer. African art on the walls and the same contemporary furniture he tried talking Darika into getting for their den. The same exact color as a matter of fact and the huge big screen television just like he has at home. Andrea's eyes swelled up with tears as Darika scanned the room but not one fell.

"Where is my husband?" Darika asked sternly. Andrea pointed to the bedroom. "How dare you come to my house, laugh in my face, and all the while, you were sleeping with my husband."

"Iiiiiiii," she stammered.

"Bitch, please. Go into the kitchen and get me the biggest knife you have and if you so much as blink, or one of those tears fall, and you decide to scream, I'll kill you."

And like a fool Andrea brought her the biggest, sharpest knife she had with her eyes as dry as the Sahara Desert. Darika snatched it out of her hands and cut right into the cream oversized sofa and chairs as if she was cutting into flesh. Andrea was too terrified to scream or cry. She hoped she wouldn't be next.

Trying to catch her breath Darika told her. "You stay here I need to talk to my husband."

Andrea nodded and stood at attention as Darika walked into the bedroom with the knife in a stabbing position. She was expecting to see Keith lying in the bed but instead he was in the shower. She heard him singing Al Green's "Love Will Make." And of course, out of passion, love will make a fed up woman stab a lying cheating husband right in the heart. She snatched opened the shower curtain and ran the sharp knife down his arm. He screamed from the pain and so did Andrea after hearing him scream. She rushed into the bathroom but was quickly warned off by Darika jabbing the knife at her.

"What in the hell are you doing here?" Keith asked Darika.

"To kill yo'ass. So this is where you've been laying your head these days, ah, nigga?" Darika asked him. "While you decide if you want to be married or not, I've put up with you and this mess long enough. I want a divorce and I want the house. You have a place to stay."

"You're not getting my house. I'll burn it down before you get it," he said, as he grabbed a towel and pressed it against his arm to stop the bleeding and the pain. The cut seemed deep enough for him to get stitches.

"So you want to show-off in front of your lil' bitch here," she said, as she raised up the knife to stab him again.

"Don't do that," he screamed like a bitch.

"I'm through with you, Keith. You can't keep doing me like this."

"Doing you like what?" He slowly stepped out of the shower creeping against the bathroom wall afraid of her driving the sharp knife threw his heart.

"What is this, Keith?" She asked as she picked up the empty condom wrapper lying next to the bed. "I'm tired of you lying to me."

"You have no damn business following me," he yelled, as he snatched up his underwear and pants.

"I'm your wife and you are not at home, what do you mean? You brought this woman to my house."

"We were not seeing each other then."

"Come home and get your things and you can come back to her." She threw the knife on the bed and turned around to walk out the door. Andrea ran to the other side of the room to stay clear of her. Darika stopped and took one last look at her while trying to hold back her tears. "Bitch, you think you've done something haven't you? Yes, you got my husband but you won't have him for long I'll pray to my God for that." Darika walked out the front door slamming it behind her with tears rolling down her cheeks.

The divorce papers were filed a day later by Darika on the grounds of adultery and mental cruelty. Although she didn't want it after she had time to think about what she was about to give up, she had to go through with it anyway. She had told her mother, Cookie and Belinda about the empty condom wrapper she had found on the floor at Andrea's and they pressured her into calling her attorney ASAP. To them the empty comdom wrapper meant Keith had slept with Andrea. Darika knew this without finding the wrapper because the bed was a mess and Andrea's hair was scat-

tered all over her head. Because she knew they would give her hell
if she ever decided to stay with him or even be friends with him,
she filed for the divorce. Keith begged her to forgive him as he has
always done but with the advice of Cookie to hang the phone up
in his face every time he called and to even call the police on him
if he came to the house, Darika did just that.

By no means did Keith leave Darika for another woman. He
just did what she asked and that was for him to pack his clothes
and get out. He wished they could have worked things out and not
have gone through this unnecessary divorce but Darika has her
mind made up for some reason to believe she's going to get half.
And Keith has made up in his mind that she's not getting shit no
matter how wrong he has been in the past and the present. He
never would have packed his things and gotten out of his house
where he's paid the mortgage for the last four years if he knew she
was for real about filing for a divorce. He would have put her out.
He thought by him moving out, it would have given her sometime
to think and cool off. And she let her damn mama and those other
gossiping vultures talk her into filing for a divorce and putting out
a restraining order against him. He couldn't believe she had the
nerve to call the police on him when he had gone over to try and
talk to her.

He wasn't in love with Andrea and the sex wasn't all that. She
was there, she was pretty, she didn't nag him about every damn
thing and she thought she might be pregnant. He was finally going
to be a father. He had thought about telling her to have an abortion but now that Darika has filed for a divorce it really doesn't
matter. On occasions Darika crossed his mind because he loved
her and had for seven years but he did whatever it took to get over
the thought. And it didn't take much either. All he had to think
about was her calling the police to escort him off of his own property. And there were no more thoughts of her.

Andrea was eight years younger than Keith and she had no
clue about living life but Keith had taken on the job to teach her
and she was willing to learn. There was hope in teaching a young
woman how to respect and love her man than it was teaching an

older woman who was already set in her ways. Andrea looked up to Keith for all of his accomplishments and wisdom when Darika gave less than a damn. For a long time Keith felt he was nothing more to Darika than a handsome status trophy. She loved showing off to the world, because she thought of herself as a reject because of her dark skin.

Every night this week Keith had planned to cook dinner for Andrea because he hadn't been spending any time with her lately because of work. That was the mistake he had made with Darika in the past. He had rushed home from work to prepare Chicken Cacciatori, asparagus and a Caesar salad by candlelight. He had even hired a saxophonist to come and play for them as they ate.

Women didn't only fall in love with Keith because of his sex or his good looks, which both of those were a plus along with the affection and romance he gave them. They fell in love with him because he knew how to make them feel like a woman with one stroke of the hair, just the right words and a caring heart. He caused the woman to grow tired of being the mistress, the other woman that he saw after work or late at night. With a man as good as he was, they wanted all of the luxuries Darika had, his last name, his warmth in bed every night instead of on occasions, and the chance to give him the son he wanted. And then the extras: the beautiful house in the suburbs, the Mercedes, and the access to the checking and savings accounts. He was different toward Darika than he was with the women he had affairs with. He was able to stimulate a woman's soul and bring joy to her heart something he couldn't do with Darika because of her difficulty with loving and being loved. Darika had only had the pleasure of experiencing his romanticism once and that was during the beginning of their marriage. After she complained the whole time Keith was trying to take their love and marriage to another level, he vowed to never be that way with her again. And he hasn't.

There was no perfect wine in the winery to fit the mood so Keith figured he could run over to his own special vineyard and select Andrea's favorite before she got home. Darika wasn't at home which was a blessing to him; he could sneak in and sneak out without running into her. He ran down to his cellar and grabbed two bottles of his four-year-old red wine. Just as he ran back up the stairs Darika was standing at the top of them waiting on him. "Damn," he muttered.

"You got some damn nerve coming in here getting wine for you and that bitch to drink. I got all the nerve to call the police."

"Don't do that."

"Why don't you get it all and take it with you because this house is going to be mine when the divorce is final and whatever is in it, will be also. But I don't want that damn wine I'll throw it in the trash."

He grinned and shook his head. "I thought you weren't here. Where is your car anyway?"

"Don't you worry about it—I had to sell it to pay the mortgage."

"The mortgage is only seven thousand dollars. That was an eighty thousand dollar car you were driving. What happened to the rest of the money?"

"I need money to live. It takes four thousand alone to pay for the utilities in this house. How long are you going to carry on like some drifting young middle-aged crisis whore?"

"Darika, who are we kidding, there's no love between us and it hasn't been for a long time. You didn't have to sell your car. I've paid the mortgage up to three months until the divorce is final and I'm awarded the house. I have a great attorney. You can't afford this house and there's no need for you to lose it. The alimony I'll be awarded to pay you will only cover half of it."

"How do you figure, niggah?"

"There you go turning ghetto on me again. I need to be going now."

"You are a niggah to have done me the way that you have. Only niggahs leave their wives for some young child."

"You got that all wrong. Only men who are unhappy leave their wives."

"She's turned you against me hasn't she?"

"No, and don't blame her. Our marriage has been nothing but a show for those damn people at the Emerald. She has nothing to do with it."

"I love you," she cried.

"Maybe you do, but you have the damnest way of showing it. Have you ever asked yourself why I fool around? Has it ever dawned on you that you might be the reason? No. While everyone is giving advice, have any of them told you to look at yourself?"

"You're rubbing it in my face because you don't want me."

"What?" He looked at his watch and walked up the stairs. "Look I'm out of here I need to be going."

"Keith," she said, as he brushed pass her. "Keith, don't leave," she pleaded with him, as he walked out of the door.

Watching her cry was never easy for him when he knew it was him who had caused her pain. He loved Darika but there needed to be a change for them and the separation was the only way to bring it about. He had no intentions on divorcing her although she had filed for it. He had his attorney sitting on the papers he received from her attorney until he and Darika decided to work things out which he knew they would do soon. She loved him too much to divorce him.

Dinner was getting cold, the wine was chilled, and the saxophonist played for Keith as he sat waiting on Andrea who hadn't returned any of his pages or answered her cell phone. Keith was worried but not worried enough to go looking for her. He put the food in plastic containers and placed it into the refrigerator, popped up the wine poured him and the saxophonist a glass and flipped on his television. Andrea better have a good explanation of where she was at eleven o'clock at night when she got off work at five thirty. Better yet he didn't need an explanation he was going to take his shower, do his sit-ups and go to bed. He paid the saxophonist and showed him out and there was Andrea pulling into the driveway. Keith didn't bother waiting on her. He slammed the door shut and walked upstairs to the shower.

"Hello," she muttered, as Keith stepped out of the shower but he didn't say a word. "What is your problem, you're not speaking tonight?" She asked, as she got undressed. Turning around for him to unzip her blouse. "Are you giving me the silent treatment because I'm just now coming home or because I didn't call?"

Keith still said nothing. He dried his wet tan body bone dry and his thick black pubic hairs fluffy.

"Andrea, I don't sweat over small stuff like that."

"That's the problem, you don't care. Tell me the truth am I just a scapegoat until you and your bitchy wife get over y'alls' little argument? I'm tired of this. For three weeks you've been here, and you haven't. Every time that bitch calls, you run to her aid. Yes, I didn't come home or call deliberately because you do it everytime you're with her. I've never loved a man the way that I've loved you and I probably never will. It's something about the voodoo that you use to keep a woman in love with you. And as soon as she falls into your trap you mess over her. I'll never have you to myself as long as she's around so who am I kidding. You have that same spell on Darika. And the love she has for you won't let you go. Here I am, this young girl excited about being fucked by the older rich man who could give less than a damn about me."

"Is this what this is all about, Darika? You've never known me to run to her defense when she calls here. When I'm not here, I'm at the office and you know that. I realized I haven't been spending a lot of time with you so I made it a point to romance you and cook dinner by candlelight all this week, but you didn't show up until now. And you are talking about shit I have no clue about. By any chance, do you think I left Darika for you? Hell no. I don't owe you an explanation about anything. I'm away from Darika because I needed to be. And you're young. I don't expect you to understand."

"No woman would ever understand you and your self -centered ways. You love no one but yourself, Keith. For so long I envied Darika thinking she had a prize and she has nothing but trouble. I'm not pregnant my period came down today."

He looked at her and smiled not showing that he was a little disappointed he was looking forward to finally being a father. "That's good. We didn't need a child together anyway."

"I'm getting from under your spell before I'm just like Darika— old, screwed up, with no other arms to run to. I'm turning in my two week resignation and I'm moving out."

"Fine." He put on his silk pajama pants and got down on the

floor to do his fifty sit- ups.

"Is that all you have to say?" She asked while standing over him. "Is fine?"

"10,11,12,13," he counted, as he rolled his body back and forward. "You've said everything. I have nothing else to say."

She rolled her eyes and walked out of the room so that he wouldn't see her cry.

Now that Andrea had moved out Keith had no intentions of running back to Darika. He didn't want her to know things between them didn't work out. Which she had told him in the beginning they wouldn't and he knew this. Andrea was still young, although she was willing to grow with his teachings about life and love. Just like he had told her in the beginning, he'd never left Darika for her so it didn't bother him if it didn't work, but he didn't feel like hearing Darika rub it in his face.

Darika sat at a table in Marllows restaurant eating bread sticks and drinking sweet tea while waiting for her cousin Phyllis to arrive. She was the only person that would understand what Darika was going through without calling her stupid for wanting Keith back and wishing Keith was dead for hurting her the way that he was. Although her mother had gone through the cheating husbands' syndrome and fought many women several times over her father, she still couldn't understand why Darika had put up with Keith's shit for so many years. Phyllis had called to say she would be a couple of minutes late getting off from work. Darika tried not to go through the whole basket of bread sticks before Phyllis arrived but she was so hungry she couldn't help it. Months without eating a decent meal for crying and praying Keith would come to his senses and come back to her, had her finally stuffing her face like a cow.

As she buttered her uncounted piece of bread and watched the door for Phyllis, her eyes met a memory of a bitch she will never forget as long as she lives. Her hands griped the bread and knife as her stomach knotted up into a big ball and her eyes and facial expression screamed out bitch die. They stared each other down.

After five years of praying she was dead, Natalie Lovelace stood at the hostess station with what looked like her husband and two kids. She seemed very happy. And there Darika was very sad because she was still going through the same bull Natalie nearly stomped her to death about some years ago.

During their second year of marriage as Darika and Keith were trying to battle out their differences as all newly married couples do, Natalie entered their lives as Keith's personal accountant. Darika knew from Keith's past hiring Natalie was a mistake. He was a flirt and she was beautiful and single. Darika tried not to let her insecurities show but it was hard. Her husband was spending more time at the office than at home and so was Natalie. Darika began popping up at the office unannounced and catching Natalie hovering over Keith like a bitch in heat and him sitting back enjoying her breast rub up against his head. Darika didn't act a fool like she should have. She just started spending more time at the office and Natalie began to hate her for it. She began rolling her eyes at Darika and not speaking to her on purpose but Darika made her speak anyway by saying hello as she kissed Keith.

Darika didn't have to let Keith know she knew about the affair between them because Natalie did. And all hell broke loose. Keith was trying to end the six-month affair when Natalie followed Darika to the beauty salon and thought she would convince her to leave Keith or else. Keith had told her, Darika wouldn't give him a divorce.

Just as Darika stepped out of her car to walk into the beauty salon, Natalie stopped her.

"May I speak with you?" Natalie asked Darika.

Her approach had shocked the hell out of Darika. She wasn't believing her eyes. Here is this woman who she knew was sleeping with her husband wanting to talk. About what? When they were in the office together she couldn't even look Darika in the face and she wanted to talk. Darika stopped just as she asked because she knew Natalie was about to shed some light on the situation between her and Keith. Not that it would matter. Keith was her husband and she wasn't leaving him. Darika looked into Natalie's eyes without a smile or a blink and asked her. "What is it? "I'm in a hurry and I'm late for my appointment."

Natalie was cocky for a woman who was messing around with a married man. She actually had the nerve to confront his wife about their affair. "I guess you know Keith and I are involved and have been for some months now." She gloated as she told Darika how they had rented hotel rooms and sometimes fucked on the desk in his office.

"Okay, what's your point?" Darika asked her. "He's not leaving me and I'm not leaving him if that's what you want to know."

"He doesn't love you bitch," Natalie snapped.

"Is that what he told you or is that what you want to believe?" Darika asked her. "Your affair doesn't have anything to do with me, Natalie. Keith is still my husband and I'm still his wife whether you two fuck or not. Foremost you are way out of line for following me and confronting me with this bullshit. I know you want my husband. All of you lonely bitches do. But what goes on between you and him and any other woman he might see is between y'all. Baby, Keith doesn't love you. If he did, he would be with you right now and you wouldn't have to be wasting your Saturday following me around and you two wouldn't be sneaking around. I hold the check book whether I fuck him or not. You have to fuck him to get the bills paid and the extra money. Do you understand? Don't you ever in your life come around me again with this type of mess."

Darika wasn't surprised at all at how Natalie stood speechless after she had put her in check. She had always had that ability to make any person feel low with words or a stare and she had done it again with Natalie. She couldn't wait to pull out her cell phone and call Keith and tell him what had just happened. His bitch had the nerve to confront her about him. Natalie wasn't saying a word and she wasn't moving. She was a very pretty lady and Darika could understand why Keith liked her but she couldn't understand why she couldn't get her own man and leave hers alone.

"So is there anything else you would like to talk to me about?" Darika asked her.

Natalie didn't say anything. She was too embarrassed at how Darika had talked to her. Keith had told her how Darika's quick and firing tongue made him want to choke her to death and now she felt like doing the same.

"Well, it was nice talking to you but I need to be going." Darika turned and walked across the street. Halfway to the front door of the salon something told her to look over her shoulder but it was too late. Natalie had already run up behind her and pushed her face down into the street and began stomping her. The ladies in the beauty salon had run out to get Natalie off of Darika but the damage was already done. She had fractured two of Darika's ribs and chipped her front tooth. Darika remembered lying in the middle of the street crying in great pain until the ambulance came.

For years she had watched her mother and Aunt Beady fight women over their cheating husbands not knowing today she would have to do the same. But Darika didn't get a chance to lay one lick on Natalie as her mother and aunt did on their husbands' mistresses. She filed assault and battery charges against Natalie but because her father was a friend of the judge that had presided over their case she had only gotten a slap on the hand.

Darika and Keith had never heard of her since then. But every year around Keith's birthday he receives an unsigned birthday card. He throws them away because he believes they are from Natalie. His apologies to Darika for what Natalie had done, meant nothing to her but she still couldn't leave him.

Natalie walked toward Darika's table with her two kids that looked just like her. Darika wasn't believing what she was seeing. She hoped Natalie wasn't walking over to her. She hoped she was just going to walk passed her but there she was standing at her table. She and Darika stared into each other eyes just as they did four years ago.

"Hello, Darika," she said, and smiled.

Darika grabbed her purse from under the chair and muttered just low enough so the kids wouldn't hear her. "Go to hell." And walked out of the restaurant.

Every time Darika called her attorney about the status of the divorce he was never in his office to give her an update and he wouldn't return any of her calls. When Cookie and her mother would ask her the status of the divorce, her attorney never returning any of her calls had become her excuse. When in fact, she didn't want the divorce anymore. She was calling her attorney to drop it but she would never leave the message with his secretary. She wanted to speak with him personally. She was lonely and she was desperately missing Keith. She had time to cool off and think things over and now she wanted him home.

Trying to teach tenth graders U.S. history was a nightmare. She'd rather be selling bean pies in the hot scorching sun. The children were nothing like they used to be and getting up at six thirty every morning to be at work at seven thirty wasn't her idea of the good life. When she left the class room seven years ago, she vowed to never step foot in a class room again. But of course, never say never. She only has access to one of the checking accounts and that was basically for the mortgage and it's utilities. Keith had closed the other three accounts. Being single again was not the thing for her. There weren't any men knocking down her door just as she thought there wouldn't be. When she did have a man, at least she knew she had one with money whether she had to share him with other women or not.

She's struggling and things are different now. She was now coming home to an empty bed, and quiet house. Her girlfriends figured by now, three months later, she should be over Keith and on with her life. But it's not that easy when all her thoughts of Keith were about him being with and loving another woman. And a high-yellow one at that. Maybe if she was dark like her, maybe if any of the women were dark she wouldn't feel so bad. With Keith fooling around with nothing but light skinned women when his wife is dark as night, to Darika— that's like Keith telling her she's not good enough or pretty enough for him. But yet she's his wife. It's the same with a skinny man married to a fat lady, but yet he fools around with nothing but skinny- looking stick women. He's trying to tell his wife she needs to lose weight, something she could do. But if Keith is telling her she needs to change her complexion from dark to light, she can't do that. As a child she's tried, by taking a bath in bleach, and it broke her out real damn bad too and as a teenager she'd used bleach cream. That did nothing.

No matter how much Darika tried to hide it, word was she

and Keith were no longer married. It wasn't hard to figure out who had made it everyones' business to know. Irene and Cassandra were the gossipers of the country club and the church. Silly of Darika to think no one would find out. When Beatrice Simpson and Dawn Cook, had walked up to her after church three Sundays ago apologizing for Keith leaving her for his twenty-four year old white intern, Darika said nothing but could have died. They've never said two words to her since she's been going to the Emerald so why were they apologizing about her husband and his affair. The part about the woman being white was a lie anyway but Darika didn't bother telling them differently. That's how Irene and Cassandra had reported it and it really didn't matter. Beatrice was just happy someone was in her situation, because her husband had left her for a white woman. Afraid of who else might know her business, Darika stopped going to the church.

Damn what everyone else might think, Darika thought as she drove over to Keith's office after leaving the restaurant. She didn't care, she wanted her husband back from this woman. She barged into his office and ordered Pam to let Keith know she was there to see him. Slack walked out of his office and looked at her as if she had no right to be there. But he spoke.

"Hello, Darika," he said, and handed Pam a memo to type.

"Hello, Slack."

If Darika didn't know he was just as whorish as Keith, she would have thought he wanted Keith for himself the way he stayed in their business. Slack opposed their marriage from the beginning because he didn't think Darika was right for Keith. Darika couldn't determine why other than he didn't think she was pretty enough. She had never done or said two words out the way to him but he disliked her.

Pam didn't care too much for her either. While she sat in the lobby waiting on Keith to come out of his office, Pam didn't look her way. She just continued to type and sing along with some song on the radio. She was another one that stayed in their business. Every time they would have an argument Pam would have an attitude with Darika as if she was in the wrong whether she knew the whole story or not. Darika believed she hated her so much because she had a thing for Keith. But Darika knew she was one woman he wouldn't fuck with a blindfold. Pam was overweight and wore tons of red clay for make up. Fat women weren't Keith's style.

Pam used Keith as her confidant and always used the advice he gave her. One night while she was arguing with her husband he hit her upside the head with his fist because she spit on him. She went crying to Keith as if she did nothing to deserve that hit and he gave her the money to divorce him and the fool did it with no hesitations because Keith told her. She was a brainwashed fool for Keith. If he asked her to swim the English Channel, she would do it with no questions asked. She never did like Darika and Darika had no idea why. She knew about all the women Keith had ever fooled around with and she never told Darika about one of them. She was the one to book him rooms and flights from here to there with the sluts. And she wonders why her marriage didn't work.

Keith gave Darika the okay to come into his office. When she walked through the work area of office, all the eyes of his employees followed her until she disappeared down the hall. Darika was embarrassed by their stares. She felt they knew too much of their business also, because Keith didn't make any of his affairs a secret. The women came in and out of the office as if they worked there. Some of his employees had even covered for him by telling Darika lies when she would call looking for him on a late night he was supposed to be at the firm.

"We need to talk before we go another month carrying on like stubborn children," Darika said, and sat down on the sofa. "Since you don't want to fight for us, I will. It's worth it, Keith. I know that you are enjoying the little young piece of pussy you have cuddled under you every night, but I love you and I'm your wife. I was there when you had nothing and I'm still going to be there when you have nothing once again. We've been through a lot together and we've always come out stronger. I don't know what she has on you but I want you to get some sense about this and shake it off and come home. You don't want the divorce any more than I do so make a decision: your wife or your whore."

He leaned back in his black leather swivel chair and sighed relieved Darika had come back for him. With no one, he was missing her.

"Well, if you put it like that, my wife." They both smiled and hugged.

"So what are you going to tell her?" Darika asked.

"What else but I'm going home to my wife."

"I love you," she cried and laid her head on his chest.

"I love you, too, baby."

CHAPTER THREE

The way Darika figured it, she should have left Keith a long time ago if she knew he was going to make such a drastic change for the better. Their marriage had sparks and passion like it had never before. She guess him leaving and finding out there was no other woman that loved him and was going to put up with his shit the way she had for seven years, made him realize she was the only woman for him. For the past couple of months they've been spending more time than a little together and they haven't had any arguments. It was strange to Darika being they've argued almost every day of their marriage before he had gone to live with Andrea. Darika felt very secure in her marriage. In other words, there has been no sign or threat of another woman trying to steal her husband. This has made her life heaven while her family and friends made it hell, because she had taking Keith back. Once again she was called stupid by them but this time, it didn't bother her. Where were they when she was lonely and about to lose every damn thing she owned? Darika couldn't understand her mother's anger. She was the main one telling her not to leave him, when she thought of the money she was no longer going to be receiving from him every month to help her pay her car note. She cursed Darika out so bad after she called and told her they were back together Darika cried for her to stop. She told her that she deserved every low-down thing Keith was going to do to her and she was the stupidest out of all of her children. Rita was still pissed with Keith for having to let her car go back. Darika tried to come to his defense and tell her mother how much he had changed but she wasn't hearing it. His history was much more like the present. She believed a dog could never change his spots as far as she was concerned. Darika felt if she had forgiven him for his cheating why couldn't everyone else. He cheated on her and she was the one married to him.

Darika knew Phyllis understood exactly why she had taken Keith back; she was in the same situation.

"Cuz, the hell with what everybody else is saying. Keith is yo'man and he loves you. If a man realizes his mistakes and tries to fix them, he's a changed man as far as I'm concerned," Phyllis said, sitting in a daze while twisting her thin braids around her finger. "It's yo'family that will screw things up for you. They claim to want to see you happy, but they don't. Just remember misery loves company."

"It's yo'family that's going to stick with you when that man is gone," Phyllis', best friend Yolanda said, as she sipped her tea. "The worse thing you could have done was to go back to him." She looked around the room and over her shoulders to make sure Keith wasn't standing behind her. "He's not here, is he?"

Darika shook her head no and sighed as she fell back into her chair. She was tired of people thinking they could put their two cents into her life even if she didn't ask them to. She knew what she was doing and Keith had changed. The nerve of Yolanda trying to give her advice as if she knew her like that. Darika had only met her once or twice and they've never really had a conversation other than today. So how in the hell could she voice her opinion about her going back to her husband, Darika thought.

"Believe me, a man is not worth having if he's going to take you through hell by fooling around and mistreating you."

"Luanda, what do you know, you don't even have a man and haven't in some time now." Phyllis and Darika gave each other a high five, smacked their lips and rolled their eyes to the top of their head. What in the hell could she tell them about a man.

"And to be truthful, I wouldn't want one if he treated me the way y'all men treat y'all. I'm happy with Yolanda Denise Gibbs. There is no man out there that could bring me the happiness I can't bring myself."

"When you need that satisfaction of a man's touch and warmth, who in the hell do you turn to? Hell yeah, my man has fooled around and I have caught him, but I'm not leaving him for nobody. Girl, a cheating man is better than no man at all."

Darika didn't agree with Phyllis she just turned her head and remembered the time in her life she felt the same. And it got her no where.

"When you are lonely, you have your man to turn to. Why let him go and this other woman reap the benefits of him? See, you should be tired of that mess you talking, because whether you believe it or not, a man is going to be a man and cheating is just apart of his nature."

Darika still didn't agree. But this time she thought she would hip Phyllis on the facts of why a woman can't leave a no-win situation even if the man told her it was predestine that she'd lose. "I didn't stay with Keith because I needed a man or because I felt it was in his nature to cheat; I stayed with him and I came back to him because I love that man. He keeps me alive with his presence and laughter. We've been through so much I just couldn't turn away and not give it another chance to breathe and grow—"

"Tell me that you don't trust him." Yolanda pleaded with her. "You could never trust him."

"No, she can't I can tell you that much. I don't trust Stanley and I let him know that," Phyllis said.

"So why are you with him?" Yolanda asked.

Phyllis chuckled out of embarrassment. "Girl, I need a man. I'm just one of those women who can't be alone. I'm gon' be honest with you. And I know what you are going to say, I need to love myself and I do, but I need to love a man also. I know that there's another woman right now in Stanley's life, but as long as he's taking care of home I can't complain. If and when you get a man, believe it or not, you are going to have to share him whether you want to or not, ain't that right, Cuz?"

Darika nodded. She for one, didn't want to share her husband with any other woman. But the women wanted to share him with her.

"Then I'll just be by myself. Because I be damn if my man is going to be sleeping in another woman's bed."

"Don't you have children, don't you need some extra help?"

"I have three and what I can't provide for them they don't need. I'm a nurse and I make pretty decent money. I'm not going to bring a man into my life or my children's life just for his finances." She took another sip of her tea. "That's the problem with people today. Loving someone for all the wrong reason's."

"Voodoo Love will make you do that— don't get me wrong I love Stanley."

"And I love Keith," Darika chimed in. "I wouldn't be with him today if I didn't love him."

"I have three kids by Stanley, and as long as he has those three voodoo spells over me I ain't going nowhere. I don't care who thinks I'm stupid. Times are hard these days and a woman can't do it on her own. I'm so damn tired of you Superwomen thinking ya'll can. Yeah, my man fools around and I know this, but I ain't going nowhere—not right now anyway. Not until those children are old enough to take care of themselves and it won't be all on me."

"Darika, where is Keith right now?" Phyllis asked her.

"He's at his office," Darika said with confidence. "Would you like for me to call him?"

They all laughed but the question put doubt in Darika's mind along with other things. She hadn't heard from Keith at all today and normally since they've been back together, she hears from him at least three times a day. He should have been home an hour ago. Darika hoped he wasn't up to his old ways. When she spoke with Juanita earlier, she was upset about some one calling the house during the middle of the night and hanging up. Which means to Darika, if Slack is fooling around most likely Keith is also. They do things in pairs. Darika tried not to seem worried. She jumped up from the table and began setting it for dinner so that she could hurry up and get that talking, no man having, Yolanda the hell up out of her house. Who in the hell told Phyllis to bring her anyway. Just like a lonely bitch to come in and put doubt in a happy woman's heart about her man.

"He has really changed Yolanda," Darika said, out of the blue as she put the wine glasses on the table. "I know you and my family don't believe it, but I do and that's all that matters. Those other women meant nothing. Where are they now?" She turned off the pots on the stove and took the chicken out of the oven. She now understood why Belinda Fisher's husband never wanted her to sit around a table full of bitter cackling hens because they will destroy a happy home with their bitterness.

"Those women are somewhere thanking God they weren't the fool married to that cheating nut."

"Get her out of my house," Darika said, forcing herself to laugh the comment off. That was her husband she was calling a nut and she didn't know him or her like that.

Darika kept looking at the clock on the microwave wondering when in the hell they were going home. She hoped Phyllis wasn't trying to stick around to borrow any money because she didn't have any to give her. Keith made her promise not to be a money tree for her family. Phyllis was good for borrowing from Darika and never pay her back.

It's been four hours already and they've eaten, drank a whole bottle of wine and she and Phyllis reminisced about their childhood. So why weren't they making their way toward the door? She wouldn't mind one bit if they ate and ran because she had things to do. A husband to find. It was 10:30 p.m. and Keith hadn't walk through that door yet. She tried not to look worried. She didn't want Yolanda in her business any more than she already was. Darika excused herself to go upstairs to call Keith at his office. There was no answer. She then paged him and called his cell phone and still no answer. She was no longer worried, she was pissed by now and didn't give a damn if it showed. They have to get their asses up and go home now. I need to go and find this man. He's not going to do this to me once again. It hasn't even been three full months and he's already not coming home. She walked back downstairs to tell them goodnight and to her surprise they had their purses on their shoulders ready to walk toward the front door.

"Y'all are leaving so soon?" She asked.

"Yeah, girl," Phyllis said, reaching into her purse very evasively, grabbing a business card and cupping it in the palm of her hand. "We have to get up early in the morning and I know Stanley is looking cross eyed because I ain't home yet. We enjoyed the dinner, girl."

"We're going to have to do this more often," Yolanda said.

"I enjoyed y'all. But Yolanda the next time, you come over here bring yourself a man," Darika told her.

"Girl, I ain't thinking about you," Yolanda said, and laughed.

While Yolanda and Darika weren't looking, Phyllis slid the card underneath the sterling silver vase on the sofa table.

Darika walked them to the door and hugged them tightly. Within a second she ran to the kitchen, grabbed her purse and keys and she was on her way to Keith's office. It took her less than fifteen minutes to get to downtown to the office building on the corner of Penn Ave. His car was no where insight. At this point she was beginning to regret coming back and she too thought she deserved everything he dished out to her, because she was stupid. Once she realized she was wasting her time because Keith had better sense to bring his business to his office, she jumped into her car without a destination but a mission to find Keith. She decided to drive through the parking lots of the downtown hotels and even called two or three of them on her cell phone to see if a Keith or Anthony Jones had checked in. Anthony was his middle name. She attempted to call his cell phone and home to see if he had made it in but still no answer. Her mission was in vain because she had no idea where to look. And then she thought if she did catch him she couldn't say anything because that would prove her family and Yolanda right. She headed back down Jefferson to Grandson, making a right onto Kingsley, waiting for the light to turn green when she spotted a white 1998 Porch speeding across Harrison and Grandson to the expressway. She screamed. "What the hell," and pressed her foot down on the accelerator, running straight through the red light, and dodging on-coming cars. Keith did not notice Darika blowing her horn or flashing her lights his music was blasting sky high and he was too busy talking to the lady on the passenger side. Darika tried following the speeding Porch, but her BMW 525i didn't have the get-up. She couldn't make out who the lady was, but as long as she knew she was a lady that's all she needed to know to confront him. There was a woman in the car. She flew through her second red light just a car away from pulling up beside Keith when flashing blue lights and a police siren caused her to slow down and pull over. "Damn! Damn! Damn!" she screamed, while beating the steering wheel as she watched Keith drive onto the highway. She got out of the car. The policeman was a brotha so she was sure he wouldn't give her a ticket or take her to jail for almost making several people wreck.

"Officer, please let me explain."

"I didn't tell you to get out of the car," he yelled. "Get back in."

"Excuse me. Why are you yelling at me?"

"Get back in the car and hand me your license, insurance and registration."

Darika slid through the half-cracked car door, reached into her glove compartment for her insurance card and registration. She looked straight ahead waiting for the officer to walk up to her car. She felt if she was white he wouldn't be talking to her like she's a criminal. To her it was the black officer that was on the power trip. She hated the way they came up to the school with their chest sticking out to handle fourteen and seventeen year olds who had gotten into trouble over the weekend. Police Chief Elderage Collins was a good friend of hers; and his son used to be a student at her school. He was going to hear from her first thing tomorrow morning.

"You know I have all the right to take your butt in—"

"Officer, I can explain."

"Did I ask you to speak?"

She looked at his badge number and name tag and memorized it as she handed him her information. She had made it up in her mind to turn him in. "I know Chief Elderage Collins wouldn't condone you speaking to me like this. I'm a good friend of his you know." Which she was lying. Chief Collins hated her black ass. She once heard he referred to her as.

"Good," he said, sounding annoyed because of her name dropping. "I don't care if you know Jesus personally you broke the law. You ran two lights back there Mrs. Darika Jones," he said, reading her names from her license.

"You're right, I shouldn't throw around the people I know."

Chief Collins would probably arrest her himself if he knew she had ran two lights. It was because of her, his son wasn't able to march during graduation with the rest of his classmates. He only needed half a credit which he had to get in summer school.

"As I was trying to tell you earlier, I didn't mean to run those lights but . . " She began to cry for his sympathy but he wasn't moved.

"But what."

"I'm a little embarrassed to say, but I was trying to flag my husband down. He had another woman in the car."

"You what?" He chuckled and sighed. "Now if you would have told me you had diarrhea and you didn't want to get it on the upholstery I would have probably let you slide, or even if you would have told me you left your iron on and you thought your house was burning. But something like you saw your husband with another woman." He shook his head and proceeded to write her out a ticket. "I'm supposed to take your license but I'm not," he said, as he handed her the ticket and her information back.

"Thank you," she snapped, and threw the ticket in the glove compartment with everything else.

When she got into the house, Keith had just stepped out of the shower and he was down in the kitchen with a towel wrapped around his waist drinking two raw eggs. Drinking raw eggs and doing a hundred sit-ups and push-ups was his nightly ritual. She slammed the door which startled him.

"What's up baby," he said, after cringing at the taste of the eggs and not noticing the angry look on her face. "Where have you been at this time of night?"

She looked at him and rolled her eyes and flopped down at the table. She was in a no-win situation. He made her promise him that she would trust him and she wouldn't follow him around. If she told him she was out following him and she saw the woman in his car, he might think she was lying when she told him she trusted him. "I got a ticket."

"Damn. " he said, and kissed her on the forehead. "How did you do that?"

"Speeding."

"What did I tell you about that? I went to the gym tonight and guess who I saw? Cookie. Her boyfriend had her car so I had to take her home tonight."

Darika's heart sank to her feet and the temperature of her armpits rised and they began to itch from her nervousness. Now that she thinks about it that lady did look like Cookie with her long braids blowing in the wind. A wave of relief came over her and she smiled. Thank God for once she listened to him and he was right when he told her to just be quiet.

"She said for you to call her tomorrow morning because she didn't know that you and I were back together. She seemed a bit surprised." He smiled.

"I thought I told her when I spoke to her last week."

"No, you didn't. You told everybody on my side of the family," he chuckled. "I can't believe in just a couple of months out of her marriage and she already has a boyfriend. And you women say us men move fast." He shook his head and walked up the stairs.

The phone rang. It was her cousin Phyllis.

"Hi, girl." Darika said. "What's up?"

"Look up under the flower arrangement, on the table, behind the sofa. I left you something."

"What?" Darika walked into the den and looked under the vase and picked up the business card and read it out loud.

"Don't be talking so loud so he can hear you. That woman will help you a lot. She sure as hell has helped me."

"I don't need my palm read," Darika said, and laughed.

"No, but you do need other things. She does more than read palms. After Stanley left me the first time and I lost every thing, I vowed to myself it would never happen again. That lady has really helped me."

"Madam Ruth." Darika said, as she read her name off the card and laughed.

"Yes, she'll help you too if you ever need her. She put a spell so tight on Stanley he came to me crying to take him back. And she promised me he would never leave me again and he hasn't. As far as him fooling around, he doesn't. I was just talking shit for, Yolanda. You know she wants to be right at something. She wants to know that there is somebody else as miserable as she is."

Darika laughed. "I kinda figured that. But Phyllis I don't mess with voodoo, girl. I've seen too many people's lives destroyed because of it and no one really benefits from it."

"He's got it on you sort of speaking; he's benefiting."

"I don't know."

"Well, if you ever need help, call her."

"Thank you for the advice."

"Always, that's what family is for."

"Well, I need to be going. I'll talk to you later."

"Hey, Cuz?" She asked just before Darika got ready to hang up the phone. "Let me borrow five hundred dollars until next week."

CHAPTER FOUR

merald Point was the only elite black country club in Washington. There were some exceptional white members: those white women who were brought in by marriage to a black man, who claimed to be so much for the black man and his injustice's. But yet he still thought he had a statue of beauty on his arm because his wife was lighter than any black person in the room. Every black person who was somebody and successful, from politicians to doctors, from attorneys to athletes, with a college education and a member of some Greek sorority or fraternity, were members for a small fee of twenty thousand dollars a year per person. Even people who didn't live in Washington but visited on a regular basis were members. It was a luxury only designed for the rich in mind. The Emerald was paradise to most of the men and women and a reward and reminder of how far they have come. Sitting secluded behind fields of green trees, on forty acres of green land, surrounded by a man made lake, was the beautiful peach and cream stucco mansion. There were casinos, green golf courses, two tennis courts, a gym, aerobics classes twice a day, breakfast, lunch, brunch and dinner served by some of the world's best chefs. Blacks who only thought white people with money had it so good would be surprised and proud at how well the brothas and sistahs of Emerald Point lived. They were educated entrepreneur millionaires or damn near close to it, with thousands in their banking accounts and in stocks. They lived in mansions in all white suburbs. Some had even built their on private communities where all of their rich friends lived. They vacationed in other countries for months at a time, and sistahs renting diamonds for one night affairs along with wearing thousand dollar gowns specially designed for them. But with all the success of the people, there were still some back stabbing, prejudices and jealousy going on among the well to do overcomers. Business deals made under the table to eliminate the middle-man who had his heart set on making thousands from the deal but didn't find out he wouldn't until after the deal was final, marital affairs for the hell of it, and light skinned blacks turning their noses up at dark skinned blacks. But the root of the jealousy was, who had the most money to spend. Who had the most power? Emerald Point was like a Soap Opera, except for all the characters were black.

Out of the three hundred members they all knew each other or had heard a rumor or two about one another or had even spread a couple of them. There wasn't a person no one knew nothing about and if there was, the club's gossipers Cassandra, Irene and Darlene Hicks would get a rumor started just to find out the things they didn't know. For instance, everyone knew Colleen Benton's third child was Kenneth Dirks and not her husband's. He just didn't know it and still doesn't till this day. The new members Ron and Scott, doctors from Atlanta, thought they had everyone fooled by showing up at the Gala with women, but most people knew they were gay, once married, and now lived together. Funny how news travel from Atlanta to D.C. Irene had suspected Erma Black and Vernon Caldwell were having an affair but she had no concrete evidence so she pretended as if she knew and drilled Erma until she told her everything. Somehow Vernon's wife found out about the affair by a phone call during the middle of the night. Love affairs between married couples were common at the Emerald. But no one was ever killed or divorced as a result of them unless the husband was too embarrassed to have a forgiving heart after knowing another man had laid between his wife's legs. Or he just wanted to get out of the marriage anyway, because he had someone else or his wife knew she would receive alimony.

At one time becoming a member of the Emerald was the hardest thing to do after they did the extensive background check along with five interviews. But now it seems like anyone with twenty thousand dollars could walk through the doors and say they want to join. God knows Audrey and Benson Raison shouldn't have gotten a membership. They are ghetto with a capital "G." Darika noticed them sitting at their favorite table by the bar getting drunk and kicking off their shoes as they challenged everyone to a game of bid whist. By no means did they exemplify elegance and prestige which is apart of the Emerald's code of conduct. Darika wanted to know where Irene and Cassandra where when they were interviewed because those two alley cats would have never docked the doors of the Emerald. It was a decision made over their heads by Clint Black and Ralph Pettis, the presidents of the board, who love money. The Benson's had won the thirty million dollar lottery in Florida and they always donate a hundred thousand dollars a year to the charity Karen Pettis was over. She's Ralph's wife and he made them members because of her.

There were six wings to the Emerald and each one was named after either a fraternity or sorority or an important person that had a wing donated in his or her name. The Thurgood Marshall's study was a room strictly for men. No woman has ever gone in there. Rumor has it, that there are several rooms men use for the expensive call girls they slip through the back door. Darika didn't know how true it was, she had heard some women mention it.

William Hudson, a neurologist from New York, founded the prestigious country club twenty-five years ago after several blacks applied at the all-white country club, The Swain Lake, where he attended. He along with all the other wealthy Whites and Jews weren't standing for blacks being members of the same club they attended. It was against the club's policy to allow blacks as members so they denied their application, not caring who they were and how rich they were. When several well-known black attorneys and doctors were turned down, they had threatened to sue the club if they didn't change their policy so that they could become a member. So to keep that from happening William donated five million dollars for the building of the Emerald. He was quoted as saying, "If blacks were allowed to join the club they would want to have bar-b-ques on the front lawn and would want to add chittlings to the menu." Blacks were disturbed by his comment and some even boycotted his family's department stores. Most blacks quickly joined the Emerald because of the status that came with being apart of the elite country club founded by the wealth Hudson family. Others still applied at The Swain Lake country club because they needed a sense of importance by being around wealthy professional white folkes.

It was the night Darika had been waiting on to show off her red satin thousand dollar dress and her new look. Her strenuous two hours of exercise every night and eating little of nothing had shrunk her hips and butt to a perfect size ten. She looked the same, less a couple of inches, and long black weave that made her look a couple years younger than thirty-five. Cassandra and Irene didn't know she and Keith were back together so tonight they will see. She strolled down the long spiral staircase into the ballroom with her arm clinging to Keith's, thinking she was the luckiest lady alive. She had one of Emerald Point's finest and sexiest men next to Collin Wolf, the surgeon, General Harold Newby, Richard Clifford, the investment banker from New York and William Ford, D.C.'s Mayor. Everyone spoke to Keith as if she wasn't standing beside him. They noticed her weight loss but they wouldn't dare say a word on how good she looked. Some of them were still upset with her because they didn't receive an invitation to the cocktail party she had two weeks ago. Even though they hated her, they still liked coming to her elegant parties. To them she was arrogant and she needed attention that they weren't willing to give her, so they dealt with her out of a long handled spoon just so they could receive an invitation to all of her parties she had throughout the year. They didn't carry on too much of a conversation with her because she had a tendency to make people feel really small with her smart quick tongue. She loved to boast and brag. She squeezed Keith's arm a little tighter because she noticed no one was saying hello to her. She was doing exactly what he had told her to do before they left home and that was to smile more and frown less.

Keith knew why the people weren't speaking and so did she but tonight she decided to play dumb. People weren't saying hello to her not because of her dark skin as she would say it, but because of her attitude. What's a damn smile for tonight? She was arrogant but yet she had low self-esteem. She never smiled, she didn't speak unless she was spoken to, and she walked around with this snooty frown on her face that made anyone afraid to speak to her, even if she wasn't snooty in her heart. The frown alone made people stop and think before saying hello. Plenty of people had come up to him and asked jokingly what he had done to make her upset with the world and he would laugh it off and apologize for her nasty attitude. Something he was tired of doing.

Keith was well known and liked even if he tried not to be and everyone showed him much love and respect as he walked down the stairs into the ballroom in his black tuxedo. Darika was pissed because she's his wife and he should have acknowledged her as being so even if these assholes didn't. She couldn't wait until they got home so she could curse him out for embarrassing her the way he was. He waved and nodded his head randomly at those who spoke to him. In her opinion he shouldn't have said shit to them. They weren't speaking to his wife and she was right beside him.

Women wanted him and they enjoyed flirting with him because they knew he would flirt back. If there was ever going to be a black Ken doll, they would have to model it after Keith. He was the perfect man. He had been featured in several top magazines that had talked about his success as being a millionaire with two successful architectural firms in D.C. and Atlanta. He shook the hands of the men and hugged the women as if he were running for office. He was a people person. But none of the women in the club could ever say they had slept with him although plenty of them wanted to. He was sexy, rich and his pigeon-toed walk told them he had good sex. Sleeping with any of the women at the Emerald was too close to home because Darika knew everyone there. And plus an affair was never a secret there and he didn't want anyone knowing his business. As if they didn't know he had cheated on Darika before.

Hundreds of people turned out for the fifth annual Save the Inner City Youth fund raiser Gala. Yet most of them weren't really aware of the violence and poverty in the inner cities but they still came out to give their support. It was a tax write off and their way of giving back to the community by purchasing the two hundred fifty dollar dinners. Five years ago, Andrew Washington, the president of the club, orchestrated the event after he decided he would run for Mayor of the city. Throwing the fund raiser would surely attract inner city voters and would look good as part of his campaign aid. He still didn't win.

Darika was sure she was going to have on the prettiest red dress in the room. It was specially designed to drop off her shoulders with a satin crisscross bodice and the popular A line cut around the seams. She wasn't noticed as she wanted to be but Keith was as usual. She finally felt a stare as they waited to be escorted to their table and she slowly turned toward the direction in which it was coming from. And there she was, Marissa Lyons admiring Keith as if he was a fine piece of art. Darika watched her with fury in her eyes until she noticed and turned away. She wasn't even embarrassed by her cover being blown, she just simply smiled at Darika and turned to talk to the lady next to her. If Darika had a knife, she would have cut her eyes out and donated them to someone who wouldn't take them for granted by looking at another woman's husband while she's standing right beside him. Marissa had always had a thing for Keith and it was known. There was no way of her hiding it. She was one of the fake women that had come to their seventh year wedding anniversary and laughed in Darika's face as if they were the best of friends while trying to get her husband into bed. She practically did everything but fuck

Keith in front of everyone. There was no alcohol or anything friendly by the way she was dancing all over Keith. A woman that wraps her leg around a man's waist while they are dancing is simply saying in layman's terms "I want to fuck you, damn your wife and my husband standing over there watching." It ate Darika up inside and all Keith could do was laugh. But Darika knew he would have fucked her if she didn't make it so obvious. Or maybe they've already done it, and that one time Keith cleaned his tracks. Anger and curiosity hit Darika like a lighting bolt and she pulled on Keith's arm.

"Yes, baby?" He asked her, while looking straight into her eyes and she looking into his.

"I'll ask you when we get home." Because this wasn't the time or the place.

Marissa still had her sight glued on Keith as Darika watched her out of the corner of her eye helplessly. There was nothing she could do to her at least not now but damn her to hell in her thoughts.

The hostess announced Keith and Darika and they were escorted to their table. Darika nearly fainted when she realized who they were sharing a table with, Roderick and Evelyn Moore, and Charles and Tina James. She looked at Keith and he looked at her just as surprised. It had to be a joke. They couldn't stand each other, at least they couldn't stand Keith, but hated Darika. She was the one that had acted a fool by cursing them out, getting personal with their wives and made Keith pull his money out of the deal right at closing. It was a deal that was supposed to bring them a lot of money but Darika realized it was going to bring them a lot of money, but not her husband. Keith showed them that he was the bigger man by saying hello and shaking Roderick and Charles's hand. Not a word parted from their wives' lips nor Darika's. Eyes began to roll like marbles as the women huffed and puffed out smoke of anger.

But that didn't last for long when Beverly Hayman walked into the room, and then their anger was deterred toward her. She walked down the stairs with elegance and grace in her diamond studded champagne colored dress that clung to her body like a stocking. Evelyn and Tina turned up their lips and looked at each other.

"All bow down, Queen Elizabeth just entered the room," Tina said.

"Who does she think she is?" Evelyn chimed in.

They had their reasons why they didn't like her but Darika didn't. She didn't know anything about Beverly other than she was a designer, owned a boutique in the Gallery and she was married to a millionaire. Darika's dislike for Beverly came when she saw her carrying on a conversation with her biggest enemies Cassandra and Irene. And she didn't care for those two because she didn't think they liked her because she was shades darker than them. Why else would they have never said hello to her or even invited her to their monthly luncheons? It was because of her dark skin and their prejudice against it, she blamed. As she blamed every time she was rejected or disliked.

All eyes watched Beverly as her husband seated her at the table with all the other millionaires' wives that welcomed her with a smile. The men sat at one end of the table and the women sat at another laughing and talking about their day at the spa. Darika watched them with envy, knowing rightfully she and Keith should have been sitting at the table also. If she had anything to do with it they would have, but Keith had purchased the two hundred and fifty dollar tickets without her knowing instead of the four hundred dollar ones which also embarrassed the hell out of her. He was good and cursed out when they get home tonight, she thought. Any other time he has talked to the "back biting MFs" he called them as he explained to Darika why he refused to buy the millionaires tickets. So why tonight did he chose to be so righteous when the millionaires are sitting with the millionaires and everyone under them are sitting where they need to be. He has even played golf, gone sailing and fishing with them on occasional Saturday's, and held in-depth conversations over glasses of cognac while smoking a fine cigar in the Thurgood Marshall's study. She didn't hear him calling them "Mfs" then. But now he talks about they're not black enough for him. Darika sighed and rolled her eyes at the thought of their conversation on the way to the Gala. Just like him they were college graduates, spoke correct English, drove fancy cars, lived in beautiful mansions and had plenty of money in their accounts, but Keith would visit the projects from time to time. Hell, he should. He still had some relatives living in them. Juanita, noticed Darika staring over at the table so she waved and motioned for her to come over. Darika never left Keith's side fast enough.

She and Juanita hugged as if they hadn't seen each other in years when they had just spoke to each other a couple of nights ago, each feeling very pleased she had no drama to deal with from their husbands being with another woman. Darika didn't mean to make it noticeable but she did when Cassandra spoke to her and her mouth fell open in surprise.

"Are you surprised I spoke?" She asked Darika. "Not as surprised as I am that you can smile." Cassandra looked like money. She was a beautiful woman about in her late 50s' with a head full of natural colored gray curly hair, cut close to her head, with beautiful flawless peanut butter toned skin; wide face and ears that stook out from her head. Once she didn't like someone, no one did. She was messy.

The other women nodded their heads to agree with Cassandra. None of them had ever seen Darika smile or had ever seen her talking to anyone outside her cocktail parties. "I've never seen you smile before," Charlene said, "Every time I see you you're either rolling your eyes or frowning."

"Not me," Darika said. "Every time I see you, you look the other way to keep from speaking."

The women laughed including Charlene because they knew Darika was telling the truth. Charlene did not like her.

"So when are you having another one of your parties?" Cassandra asked her.

"Soon."

It was Darika's basic instinct that told her to look over her shoulder. It was an instinct that only a woman who had a cheating husband possessed when another woman is trying to come up on her husband. Once again, Marissa was all over Keith and he was loving every minute of it, even if he tried not to. Darika didn't mean to make her frustration noticeable but Cassandra had picked up on it.

"He's your husband; go and handle your business, chile."

Darika walked over to the punch bowl where they were standing. Both of them looked at her as if she had caught them with their pants down.

"Baby, Marissa was just telling me Israel would be a beautiful place for us to visit this summer."

"I don't need for her to tell me were to go on my vacation I'm going to Italy. We are going to Italy—me and my husband," she said, looking at Marissa who got the hint to get the hell on while she still could.

Keith didn't know where all of that came from but he was used to Darika being jealous if she saw him carrying on a childish conversation with another woman. "Now what was that all about?" He asked.

"What do you think?"

Her jealousy had him fed up."I don't know—you tell me." He walked off leaving her standing alone.

First Marissa and now Andrea. Darika had no idea she would have to face her demons tonight. If so she would have come better prepared with her armor of security, that her husband was truly remorseful for his past and he would not be tempted to go back no matter what. Darika's heart and mind has been at ease for these last five months, and she knew where her husband was every minute of the day. Either he was at work or sitting in front of the television with her by his side. Or he was down in the cellar making wine. Now not even a year later she's reminded that he had broken her heart and the woman still loved him and he might still love her.

Andrea spotted Keith the minute she walked into the door and he spotted her. As their eyes met, Darika watched both of them and she fought her tears. By Keith's expression, Andrea should have been able to tell something was wrong; he didn't smile back at her when she smiled and he had turned his back toward her to continued his conversation with Slack. He knew Darika was going to cut the fool if she saw her and he wanted to prevent that. He looked out of the corner of his eye for Darika but he didn't see her standing at the bar watching his every move. He choked on his cognac when he heard Andrea's voice and a tap on his shoulder. He sighed and turned around.

"Hello handsome." She threw her arms around him and hugged him like a long lost friend who truly missed him.

He pulled away to notice Darika storming across the room toward them. "Damn," he whispered.

"What's wrong? Why I haven't heard from you?"

"Here comes Darika. We are still married."

"How are you doing, Andrea?" Slack jumped in front of Keith and asked her.

"You are what?"

"Baby," Keith called Darika while trying to keep from shiting on himself.

"You just don't get enough, do you? I should have stabbed you instead," Darika told her.

"Hello, Darika, I'm just saying hello—to be truthful I thought you two were divorced."

"That's what you wanted isn't it . . . . you leave my husband alone. What are you doing here anyway? This club isn't for sluts like you. These are dignified people here with class."

"Darika, this is not the place or the time," Keith warned her just in case she thought about getting loud.

"You don't tell me," she snapped at him. "Your little whore walks in here and hugs you like nothing has happened and I'm supposed to accept it. No, what I want to know is how did she get in here?"

She smirked. "Keith, tell her."

Darika looked at him waiting for an answer. "What is she talking about, Kenneth? I know you did not—"

"Well. I," he stammered.

"Why are you bitching, Darika? You got'im. I could have had him if I would have kept the baby."

"What in the hell. "

"What baby, slut."

"Call me what you want, but before I packed my bags and left his ass I was eight weeks pregnant with his child."

"You are out of your damn mind. No, you were not," Darika cried.

By this time, Keith had grabbed Andrea by the arm and pulled her over to the side. "Andrea, why don't you do the best thing for both of us and just leave. You shouldn't be here anyway."

"Why shouldn't I? You are still with her, Keith? But I thought —I had an abortion for you."

"No, don't put that on me. I will not let you do that. You knew I was married and there was a possibility of me going back that's why you had an abortion but you said your period came on."

"But you said you were leaving her."

"You had no business telling her that."

Darika became frustrated and stormed up the stairs to the outside.

"I'm married and I'm happy. Please, just don't come around here anymore." He had planned to have her membership revoked first thing tomorrow morning.

"But you said— you used me, didn't you? I hope you know, Keith payback is hell, I wish you dead."

He chuckled and he had even felt like the devil she was making him out to be. "And you don't think you are going to get pay back for sleeping with another woman's husband? Think again."

"I'm getting now."

"Keith, man, go ahead and handle your business," Slack walked over and told him. "I got this."

"Do not leave me, Keith," she yelled as he ran up the stairs to catch Darika.

"What in the hell is wrong with you?" Slack asked Andrea through his clenched teeth.

Just as he got outside the valet was helping Darika into the car and she sped off into the night.

"Damn! Get me a cab, please," he ordered the valet.

He ran into the house screaming out her name trying to explain but she had locked herself inside the bedroom without a thought of coming out to listen to him.

For the next couple of days silence permeated their house, as they walked around rolling eyes and daring the one to bump into the other. Keith had given up on every effort to apologize. By now he couldn't understand what Darika was so upset about. Andrea meant nothing to him. And Darika had stopped looking for an apology. She didn't even care if it was true or not about Andrea being pregnant by Keith. To her an apology doesn't mean a hill of beans if he's going to continue to do the same thing that's going to cause her pain and him to apologize. Usually Darika's eyes would be puffy and red from crying all night but not this time she smiled inside and walked around the house singing The Spinners. "It takes a Fool to Learn That Love don't Love Nobody."

She had finally gotten the picture of Keith's definition of love.

CHAPTER FIVE

aking Jones and Slack architect firm a multi million-dollar company, ranking twenty among the top architect firms in America didn't come easy just as it wasn't easy to keep it there. Late nights on the drafting board and hard work would always be the motto for the company's success.

The work week was finally over and all Keith thought about was jumping into his car, driving as fast as he could across town to his beautiful home, taking a warm shower and flopping down in his favorite chair with a glass of cognac, watching television until he dozed off to sleep. If Darika had made any planes for them tonight, she was in for a rude awaking because he wasn't going anywhere. He didn't give a damn about who invited them over for dinner, what play was in town, or what new restaurant she had heard about, he wasn't going anywhere. Maybe he should agree to adopting a child, maybe then she would get off his back about always spending time with her and dragging him with her every time she wanted to go somewhere. Then he thought that after she adopts one child, she would want to adopt another. Hell, no, he thought. One child is all he wanted at the age of thirty-seven and he had two more months before that day.

It was a path he had never taken before since they had been married. And as long as he could remember he had never been faithful to any woman and he was somewhat embarrassed by it. His mother had always told him he would grow up to be just like his father and he thought she meant he would father children all over the city and never take care of them, or he wouldn't amount to anything, so he promised himself he wouldn't be like him but little did he know the power of his mother's tongue had cursed him to be an unfaithful man who needed love from more than one woman.

Keith was determined to do right by Darika even if it killed him; he owed her that much. He was tired of being unfaithful like his father was to his mother. While growing up, his mother used to beat him because he reminded her so much of his father and he never knew how other than their resemblance. But it was when he grew older when he discovered he had the ability just like his father did to cause a woman to fall in love with him and hurt her without even trying. Keith didn't like seeing Darika unhappy and crying because of him but it just happened that way. Being faithful to one woman, his wife, someone he had promised to God to cherish and love was not an easy task. And he wasn't going to even lie about that. Beautiful women just walked up to him so boldly and free as if he wasn't married even though he would tell him he was. And having Slack as a friend didn't make it any better when he always introduced him to beautiful women.

By far did Keith need Slack's help to land a woman. His golden tan complexion, high cheek bones, tight muscular body that was built for holding on to, hazelnut brown eyes, wavy black hair, 6'2" height, shoulders of a commanding officer's, and his well-proportioned pecs that caused his chest to protrude through any shirt he wore had women dazzled and mezmorized over him. Who said light skinned brothas were out of style for the 90's? Not Keith

Jones. He's the type of man that never goes out of style no matter what complexion he is. Many women think he should be on a runway or the cover of Ebony Man Magazine he was just that handsome. He walked on the tip of his toes which alone caused women knees to buckle and their legs to cross. It says a lot about a man when he walks into a room and all the women eyes would follow his every move while a tingle of chills would tease their throbbing love as they imagined what it would be like to sleep with him for just one night. Men would ask themselves, "What is it that he has and they don't?" And the answer would be on any woman's face that laid eyes on him. Charisma.

But Keith hasn't touched another woman since he and Darika have been back together, but that doesn't stop her from accusing him of doing so. If a beautiful woman passed them on the street and he didn't look, she would accuse him of having eyes in the back of his head. That's because she knows he has an addiction to women like a person has an addiction to crack. When Keith is trying to do right, temptation always calls on him like a thief in the night to do wrong but this time he was going to fight it.

He grabbed his briefcase and headed for the door when Slack came out of his office to stop him.

"Hold up my man, I know you ain't about to go home on this Friday night."

Keith nodded his head. "Yep." And tried to walk around Slack.

"Hold up, what's at home but a nagging woman who probably thinks you are already out sleeping around. I flew some of the finest, I mean finest women from Atlanta for me and my partner. What'cha say about that?"

"No. I'm going to that big fancy home where I pay a seven thousand-dollar house note. I hardly spend anytime in because I'm always with you at this office. I've learned how to tune Darika out so her nagging doesn't bother me. I'm going to take me a shower and fix myself a glass of my finest cognac, sit in front of my television and fall asleep."

"I told you she has something on you cause you've changed. We don't hang any more you're all about work, work, work. You don't talk about any women anymore and none of them call the office, you haven't even asked me to lie for you since you've been back with Darika. I saw whats'er name the other day beautiful girl . . . fine. Yep, she's fine."

"Who?"

"You know her. The one with the big lips— tight body— works out all the time, Judy, the flight attendant. She said that she's been paging you and you've changed the pager number. I said damn what has she put on my part'na. He's a changed man."

"Me going home tonight has nothing to do with Darika. Can't a brotha be tired and you not think he's whipped?

"No, because I know my brotha he acts nothing like the way you are acting. I tell you what I know this root doctor from Mississippi she can tell you what type of spell Darika has working on you." They both chuckled. "But on the real note I need you man. I told, Dana, that I had a friend for her girl. She's a gynecologist. Dana, said she's nice looking you will like her."

"O,I will?"

"Help a brotha out will'ya?"

They heard the elevator and then a knock at the door. For the last time Slack pleaded with Keith to stay and he still refused. Slack opened the door and the two women walked in looking beautiful and smelling like fresh roses on a dewy morning. If a fly was in the room, it could have found a perfect landing spot in Keith's mouth as it hung open when he saw the two women. He didn't mean to look so doggish with his drooling but he was too busy trying to figure out which one was for him. He knew which one he wanted. The slim light skinned one in the black knit T-strap dress with the red nail toe polish and the small braids that looked like black string. To him she looked far too sexy to be a doctor. Weren't doctors supposed to look like his friend Rhonda who wore glasses, ruffled shirts and pants that were always above her ankles?

Slack introduced them.

"Dana, Tammy, this is my partner in business and in crime, Keith Jones.

Both of the women said hello in unison while admiring God's best creation yet. Sexy, sexy, sexy ran through their minds. Dana wished she would have met him instead of Slack because Keith was cuter and sexier. Slack wasn't all that bad and he wasn't all that good. He was tall, brown skin, big pretty eyes with long eye lashes and a beautiful smile, but he was skinny to the point of being bony, married and with nasty attitude. So this is Keith the one he talks so much about, she thought. Damn he's fine.

Tammy tried not to let her eyes rest on Keith standing in front of her but she hoped they were telling him how pleased she was that he was going to be her date. Now she could lay her curiosity to rest because he was finer than any blind date she had ever flown an hour and a half to see.

"Well, it looks like I'm going to be escorting you two lovely ladies alone tonight."

"And why is that? Why isn't he going?" Dana asked.

"Yeah, Keith, why aren't you going?" Tammy asked, and smiled. She was hoping he would get her point, and change his mind.

"Don't pay any attention to this man," Keith said jokingly putting his firm arm around Slack's neck. "He's also my partner who lies. I couldn't dare let him escort you two beautiful women alone." He picked up each of their hands and planted his wet lips on them.

On the way to the restaurant, Keith and Tammy became better acquainted as they talked about their lives, their family, careers and past relationships. Tammy had just gotten out of a four-year relationship with a man she's still in love with Keith could tell by the conversation and he told her he was in one and they were living together. He could tell by the expression on her face she was disappointed and had no idea. Dana didn't tell her because Slack didn't bother telling Dana. As always, he didn't care if she knew or not that's just the way it was when he was involved. After they talked about their past and present relationships, there was silence between them and the drive seemed long. Slack and Dana had gone on ahead of them. Keith knew they had no plans on coming to the restaurant although they said they were. They just didn't want Tammy tagging along with them so he threw her off on Keith.

When they pulled up to the restaurant's valet parking, Tammy opened her own door which didn't surprise Keith at all, but embarrassed him. The way she had described her ex-boyfriend he could tell she didn't know what a lady should be treated like but know one knew she wasn't his lady. He ran to open up the restaurant door for her but she had reached for it and they nearly slapped each others hand for the handle. There was no wait and Slack and Dana hadn't made it yet so Keith requested that he and Tammy be seated. He wasn't worried about any of Darika's friends spotting him because she had none and he knew she wouldn't be popping up she hates to eat alone.

Keith was pleased she allowed him to pull out her chair for her. They sat across from one another not saying a word but occupied by their surroundings. Keith looked at her from time to time and she was worth looking at. She had a pretty sugar brown complexion and Keith was sure she tasted the same. She felt him staring at her but she was too embarrassed to look at him so she kept her face buried in the menu hoping Dana would come so that she could curse her out for wasting her time. She was sure Keith thought of her as being desperate that's why she flew a thousand and something miles to meet a man who was involved. So she thought it was best that she correct him.

"I had no idea you were involved and in love Dana didn't tell me that. But I wish she would have it surely would have saved me a lot of time."

He chuckled. "Look at it this way, you got a chance to get out of Atlanta and have yourself a free dinner."

"I can buy my own dinner thank you. If it was a fancy dinner I wanted, I could have stayed in Atlanta and gone to the Sun Dial."

"But you would have been alone," he chuckled. "Your girl would have been here with a man and you said you don't have a man so what would have been so fun about eating dinner at a fancy restaurant if you had to do it alone."

She just stared at him because little did he know she had been her own date plenty of nights. "Well, tell me this, you told me you were involved but you didn't tell me if you were in love or not."

Keith smiled and made sure he told the waitress to add double cognac with no ice. Tammy didn't drink so she ordered a sweet tea.

"Well, are you?"

"Yes I'm in love I'm married to her."

"Married I thought she was just a girlfriend." She looked at his hand. "Then where is the wedding band."

"It's right here," he said patting his shirt pocket. "I took it off while I was at the gym today and I forgot to put it back on. By no means was I trying to hide the fact."

"Why didn't you tell me sooner?"

"I didn't think it mattered since you and I are just having dinner together. I didn't think you were interested in me."

"I was."

"I understand. Some women can't deal with a married man."

"I didn't say I couldn't deal with it. So are you faithful?"

"I try to be."

"Are there any children?"

"No, she can't have any."

"Do you want any?"

"Of course I do. What man doesn't want a son to carry on his name?"

The waitress came back with their drinks and Keith couldn't wait to take a sip. Tammy added five sweet-n-lows to her tea before tasting it and added another after taking a sip to discover it wasn't sweet enough.

"Slack is married and he's being unfaithful and if y'all are as close as he say y'all are I know you've been unfaithful in the past."

"And you are right but it's nothing to be proud of. She and I separated for awhile because of it."

"And you are happy now?"

"I tend to be," he told her and took another sip of his drink.

"You tend to be," she replied.

"You know how you women can be sometimes, nagging a brotha about the simplest things. When that happens, I rather be alone."

She nodded and he motioned for the waitress. They placed their orders.

Tammy became jealous of Darika and she didn't even know her. She wanted to know what she had done to get a man as good as Keith who was faithful, loving and successful. And she couldn't even bare him the son he longed for. Right away she thought if she was in Darika's shoes she would keep her career but she would give him all the babies he wanted. Taking her out to dinner didn't mean he was unfaithful she just told him that because she had nothing else better to say. A man as fine as him couldn't be anything but unfaithful because women threw themselves at him all the time. It is because of his loyalty to his friend why she is sitting in a restaurant across the table from him not because he thought she was beautiful and a doctor as all other men do. Good men do exist, she thought and sighed silently.

"Why are all the good men taken?" She asked him and dropped her fork in her plate.

"I wouldn't say all of the good men are taken."

"You are. Does she realize what she has, if not let me be the first to tell her. A very sexy, handsome man that loves her."

"Sometimes Tammy, I just don't know if she knows that I love her but I guess from my past it's hell for her trying to believe that I do. She accuses me and I don't do anything. Like tonight when I go home some eyes are going to be rolling and maybe even a frying pan or some of my clothes out the door."

They both laughed at the thought.

"I didn't wear my pager on purpose tonight I just wanted to have a drink and not be bothered but I just so happen to have a beautiful woman join me. Now if she was to walk through that door right now, she would swear we were sleeping together even if we both told her we weren't."

"She's lucky and insecure."

"Is that what it is? But I love her She needs me."

"And how is that?"

"In a lot of ways. Nine years we've been together."

"That sounds so beautiful to hear. But I know I'll never be able to tell someone how long I've been married. I'm never going to get married."

"Why not? Is it by choice?"

"Nope, the men today aren't trying to hear that marriage thang."

"Yes they are."

She smiled. "Like I said you being married doesn't matter to me."

"A brotha is trying to do the right things these days. If you would have caught me some years ago it would have been on."

"But I didn't."

"You in Atlanta and me in D.C., that would have been hard. So what do you want to do after this, maybe some jazz or a movie."

"I'll have to take a rain check I'm a little bit tired."

"How could you come to D.C. and be tired?"

"I've been to D.C. before it's just that I work ten hour days, six days a week for one of the public clinics and I hardly get any rest."

"So your man couldn't compete with your job."

She laughed "No, to be truthful he became saved and according to the bible we were unequally yoked so he had to break it off. For the life of me I couldn't understand that one but now I do."

"I'm glad. See you are what they call temptation. The man couldn't try to live for the Lawd and try to fight you and your sex off."

She laughed out loud before realizing where she was.

"And I bet you have great sex," he said, and then laughed and later apologized. "I shouldn't have said that, I'm way out of line."

She looked into his eyes and smiled. "I've been told."

"What, that I can be out of line?"

"No, that I have good sex."

There was a pause as both of them stared into each other eyes.

"Well, I guess we better be going," Keith said, while pulling out a hundred dollar bill. He had learned from before as long as Darika is around never pay for anything with a credit card especially a restaurant he didn't take her to.

The waitress brought over the check and Keith told her to keep the change. He pulled out Tammy's chair and opened the door for her.

On their way to her hotel, they had become even more familiar with each other as if they were rushing it so they wouldn't have to take up any time doing it when they got into the room. They both knew what would happen if he went up to the room and believe it or not, Keith didn't want anything to happen. He had made it this far with keeping his demons under control and he was going to continue. He parked his car in front of the hotel door so that he would have to come back down and he walked her up to her room.

When he got to her door, he read the room number out loud to himself. "Room 563." And he opened the door for her.

"Why don't you come in?" She asked him.

"Not tonight. I need to be heading home."

"Just for a little while," she said, and stood in front of him with her nose nearly touching his. "I enjoyed hearing about your childhood."

"You know as well as I do if I come in that room we are not going to do any talking. And we don't need for our emotions to become involved right now."

"And they don't have too. I'm a grown woman don't talk to me like I'm some child or some woman that might get mixed signals. I know you are married."

He smiled and kissed her on the cheek. "Get yourself some sleep."

She walked into the room out of embarrassment and slammed the door behind her.

His watch read twelve o'clock p.m.. He placed his key into the lock and turned it slowly gently pushing open the door and tiptoed in the dark house.

"Ouch," he moaned after hitting his leg on the table.

"Why don't you cut on some light," Darika calmly said, as she flicked on the lamp.

"Baby, what are you doing sitting down here in the dark." He lifted up his pants leg to find the chair had caused a red mark to appear on his leg.

"The same reason you are tip-toeing through it. Is there someone you are hiding from? You called at six thirty and said you were on your way home what happened?"

"Just got a little tied up went out for a drink with Slack, talked a little shit to'im—well talked a lot and lost track of time."

There was no way she was going to fall for it. She rolled her eyes and stuffed her bottom lip into her mouth and sighed. "You are lying and I'm not putting up with it this time. You claim when you are not home you are at the office with that skinny rod iron pole, Slack who doesn't give a damn about Juanita and think you are stupid for giving a damn about me. Tell me this Keith, does he have that much influence on you that he can bring one of his lonely whores around and you jump at the chance to sleep with one'im."

"I don't have time for this bullshit. Slack has nothing to do with why I'm late. I went because I wanted to. I don't have to come home and sit up under you like I'm your damn pet. That's your damn problem always assuming about another woman. Hell yes, I had drinks tonight and a woman joined me—and you know what Darika I told this woman how much I loved you and I wouldn't do anything to hurt you. Yeah, I admit in the past I've messed up but I haven't since we've been back together."

She laughed sarcastically. "You are not only stupid but you think I am."

"I don't need this." He turned around and grabbed the door knob.

"Don't you walk out of that door, Keith!"

Slam.

Since he was so stupid and he thought her to be also, he jumped into his car and headed downtown to the Ritz Carlton and road the elevator to room 563 without thinking twice about Darika. He let out a deep breath and gave the door one hard knock before Tammy answered smiling as if she knew Darika would cause him to run back. She held out her hand and guided him in.

By the break of day, he walked through the same doors he stormed out of in a rage. He was expecting to see Darika lying on the sofa but she was still asleep in the bedroom. He stood at the bottom of the stairs contemplating on whether to walk up them and deal with the consequences or just go into one of the guest bedrooms. He knew there was an argument waiting on him if he did either one so he prepared himself for the argument where she was. He slowly walked up the whined rod iron staircase like a scared teenaged boy who had broken curfew looking down at his Italian shoes he had bought him when they went to Spain.

The squeak from the hinges of the door and the sunlight creeping through the half-open curtains of their bedroom woke Darika. She opened one eye and noticed a fed up look on Keith's face and knew now wasn't a good time to curse him out like she had planned. There was no telling what he might say and she didn't want to hear it. She sat up in bed and watched him get undressed not saying a word and him not looking at her at all. She knew if there was another woman she sure as hell had chased him to her.

"Where have you been?" She finally asked.

"Out—thinking," he said, looking at her with big piercing brown eyes.

She waited for him to walk into the bathroom to take a shower before she began to cry.

Slack was in the doghouse with Juanita after missing her birthday because he was in Atlanta visiting Dana. He had become attached to her and had even thought about leaving Juanita if she wasn't pregnant. Although the night was meant for him and his wife to be alone, he asked for Keith and Darika to join them. He and Keith talked in their normal code of business which was their cover up for talking about what was going on in their lives outside of their lives with their wives. Keith had the ability to interpret Mr. Hopewell called and was upset that he hadn't gotten him those sketches to Tammy, is very upset with him because he hadn't called her or come to Atlanta to visit after he told her he would. The two had played this game so many times they were pros. Darika tried to join in on their conversation because she really thought they were talking about business but Slack spoke over her which infuriated her. She waited for Juanita and Keith to leave the room before she leaned over to ask him. "Why aren't you with one of your women?"

Her question caught Slack by surprise and it showed. "One of my women," he responded. "What are you talking about, Darika?

"You didn't think I knew, did you? My husband tells me everything so don't you ever talk over me again."

Juanita and Keith walked back into the room with plates and a bottle of her favorite dessert wine from Keith's own wine cellar. She cut the cake in large chunks and placed it on the plates. Music played in the background but no one paid it any attention. Keith and Slack began to speak in codes again and he asked him about the comment Darika had made. Before Keith could respond by telling him he hadn't told Darika any such thing, Darika began to talk over both of them.

"Juanita, you are a loving sistah because like me you put up with a lot of shit."

"Darika, don't start that women's lib shit in here," Keith told her.

"You don't deserve it." She looked Juanita in her eyes with a slight smirk making it hard for her to determine whether she was serious or not so she agreed with an Amen.

Slack and Keith dropped their forks and sat with their mouths wide open because they knew she was serious. Slack had always told Keith that Darika was crazy but he had no idea she was crazy enough to come into his home and tell his wife what she deserved not while he was sitting there and not while his wife was eight months pregnant.

Sweat beads formed across Keith's forehead and his heart began to race with anticipation of what Darika was about to say next. He knew anything she was going to say was coming straight from the heart she hadn't had any alcohol to blame. "Darika, I personally don't want to hear this shit tonight."

"Let us women talk. Go ahead and talk sistah. Men always think they can put a sock in our mouth's because they might pay the bills. You are right I don't deserve this."

"Juanita," Slack asked, as he stood up and put his hands on his hips to give her a look to shut the hell up but Darika paid him no attention. "Don't hurt yourself by trying to jump on Darika's bandwagon.".

"Bandwagon," Darika replied. "You know what I'm talking about, Slack and so does Keith he's been your alibi plenty of weekends."

"Darika, this isn't the place," Keith leaned forward and told her.

"Slack, you have a beautiful wife and she seems to care a lot about you. She doesn't deserve to have an unfaithful man like you in her life. She's tried for years to give you a baby and now that she's giving you one you want to fuck up."

"What the hell—" Slack asked as he shifted his weight to his left leg and looked at Keith for an explanation.

"O'shit," Keith muttered through his teeth and fell back in his chair. "No, the hell you're not. Let's go."

"No, Keith," she yelled. "I can't sit here and act like I don't know when I know he's seeing some other woman behind her back. Girl, you know at one point Keith was sleeping with every woman in Washington and I left his ass that's what you're going to have to do to Slack leave him. I couldn't give Keith a baby so he thought he would go out and get some other woman pregnant. I'm sure Slack told you about the woman coming to our front door asking for child support."

"Darika, shut the hell up."

Juanita looked at Slack with tears running down her face for an explanation. And when he couldn't give her one she turned to Keith.

"Keith, man what is going on? What is she trying to do?" Slack asked him.

Keith looked at Darika for an answer because he sure as hell didn't know. She had always joked and said she would tell Juanita but Keith never took her seriously. He thought she knew that fucking up a man's marriage could get her killed without any questions asked.

"I knew it. All those weekends you told me you were going out of town you lied. Slack, how could you do this to me? We've been together for fifteen years. I'm your wife and you're supposed to love me. For years I've put up with this shit and you've told me it would get better."

"Baby, I don't know what the hell—"

"Don't lie. You and this nigga here," she said pointing at Keith. "have been fooling around for years and I just happen to get some sense and leave Keith but if I caught him again I'm killing him."

Juanita ran out of the room crying and Slack rushed toward Darika with his fist balled ready to put it right to her mouth but

Keith jumped in front of him. "What in the hell is wrong with you you're not about to hit my wife are you?"

"This bitch must be crazy coming in my house destroying my fucking marriage. You and I go way back."

"But I'm his wife and I come before you."

She jumped up from her chair and looked him dead stiff in his big black pupils that were surrounded by a yellow background that should have been white. She had paralyzed him; he couldn't move if he wanted to hit her. "You think you want to hit me?" She asked him. "Go ahead and yell and tell Juanita what color suit you want to be buried in because muthafucka if you hit me you are going to die tonight and I got *my* husband here to prove it was in self-defense when I kill yo'ass."

Slack slowly lowered his fist to his side while looking at Keith and shaking his head in disbelief that Keith didn't knock the hell out of Darika for him.

"Keith man, go ahead and get your wife out of here before I whip this bitch's ass."

If he believed it or not, Keith felt like doing the same. He got up trying not to let his embarrassment show and placed Darika's purse on her shoulder and he shoved her toward the door. He couldn't look at Slack but yet he tried to apologize to him. It was much too late. Slack had already lost respect for him and didn't care to deal with him anymore after that night even if they were partners of one of the most successful architect firms in D.C. and Atlanta Slack wanted out. It was sad to think a friendship of fifteen years had gone down the drain and maybe his marriage after he had pushed them both out of his house and slammed the door behind them without a goodby. Keith didn't think about what he should have done until he tried calling Slack the next day and the day after that but he would never return his calls. For two weeks Slack didn't come in to work and it was then when Keith received a letter in the mail from Slack telling him he was selling his half of the firms. Their friendship had ended. Keith took the blame for having such a bitchy wife and not stepping up to the plate to defend his best friend and his marriage. After all he had lied to Juanita once before and she believed him so why didn't he again?

Keith handed Slack 2.7million dollars to buy his half of the company in D.C. and Atlanta.

CHAPTER SIX

Keith sat back in his favorite purple recliner wearing only his silk boxer's and T-shirt while staring up at the vaulted ceiling waiting for Darika to walk through the front door. He was holding in his hand some of his old college pictures that she had blacken out the faces of all the women. Women she didn't know if he had slept with or not, women he was only friends with fifteen years ago. In anger he began cursing to the top of his lungs wishing she was there so he could curse her. She had no right going through his things. He never accused her of fooling around with Mark, her so-called friend who calls the house every other day claiming he's checking up on her. For all he knew, they could have been sleeping together in his bed while he's at work. Nevertheless, she claims he's so gay. Gay my ass, Keith thought. He knew the truth about a woman and her so-called gay friend. And Darika's was no different,but Keith doesn't let stuff like that bother him. He trusted Darika. He was just sorry she didn't trust him. "Mark this, Mark that," is all she talked about. It used to be her mother and Cookie that gave her advice now it's Mark. Keith wished they would get together so that someone else besides him could deal with her jealousy, depression and low self-esteem.

All of Darika's belongings sat packed at the front door in plastic bags and boxes so that she could grab them and leave. Keith was fed up. Damn, when a woman is fed up, how about when a man is? Fed up with being accused and cussed out about nothing. When he's trying to do right, he's blamed for doing wrong. The pictures weren't the only thing to set Keith off to pack up her things and neither was last night's episode,but those and many other incidents just like them from ten years ago till today was the blame for her ticket out the door and papers to be filed for a divorce. Her insecurity had run him crazy. This time he didn't need a three month break from her, he needed a divorce. And he wasn't making the mistake of moving out of his house either. She was moving out and not coming back.

The phone rang and he immediately answered, hoping it was Darika so that he could tell her to hurry home and get her things because he had something to do and he wanted to be there when she came. Instead of it being clown number one, Darika, it was clown number two and three, her mother and sister screaming at him as if he were a child. "Damn,"he muttered. He thought about hanging up on them but he wanted to hear what they had to say. He wanted to hear what lie Darika had told them this time.

"You low-down bastard, don't you hang up this phone" Rita warned him.

"Mrs. Summers," he sighed. "I don't have time for this today."

"Not today hell, that is my daughter you are up there mistreating and I'm tired of it."

"And so am I." Denise chimed in. "Who do you think you are sleeping around on her with every woman in D.C. and thinking she's supposed to put up with that shit?"

"She ain't putting up with nothing from you no mo'," Rita

screamed. "I hope she divorce your ass this time because if she don't, I'm gon' beat her ass. You think my daughter need you. Well, she don't. Since she's been married to you, you've caused her nothing but problems. You're the reason she's up there depressed and talking about killin herself all the time. You and those nasty bitches you sleep around with. They got some type of root on her and so do you. Because God knows, I don't know why she hasn't left you before now."

"That's right." Denise added.

"It never fails, every time Darika and I argue she runs to her mama like a child. Mrs. Summers, every since we've been married, you've been in our marriage."

"You're a damn lie," she screamed. "And I will not let you put the blame on me. That is my child and if she's hurting, I'm hurting. You let your damn fat mama put her input in the marriage. She tells you what to do and you do it. Why can't my child do what I tell her to do? When yo'mama told you to take Darika's name off of that insurance policy as beneficiary, you did it. And Darika is your wife."

"Now why would you want to talk about my mother, Mrs. Summers. She's never done anything to you."

"No, but her son has. You are up there running my daughter crazy and I don't like it. And yo'mama know you are doing it too, but her fat ass don't ever say nothing."

"I just want a divorce from, Darika," Keith told her.

"She wants a divorce from you too," Denise screamed. "She don't want to be married to you no more than you want to be married to her. She said you don't satisfy her no way."

Keith laughed at the comment. "It's all clear to me now. Now I see why she's so crazy."

"Hold up, you hold it right there nigga. Who do you think you're calling crazy? I'll show you crazy. You are the one who's crazy and you made her crazy."

"No, you made her crazy and got her thinking because she's not as light as you and Denise, she's ugly and don't nobody want her. She's always had a chance to go but you, along with her own crazy mind, told her to stay so that I could take care of her," he chuckled. "Now who's the crazy one. If someone was mistreating me, damn how much he's taking care of me. I'll leave. That's why Mr. Summers fooled around on you. Because of your crazy way of thinking."

"No, you didn't nigga."

"That's why your daughter is so ghetto because you are."

"Mama, let me get at him'im."

"Nawh, baby I got this one. You don't bring my dead husband in this. If he was alive today, he'd put a bullet so deep in yo'ass—putting our baby through this mess."

"Mrs. Summers, you've taken up enough of my time for today. I need to be going. Good bye."

"You better not hang up this phone I'm not finished with you yet."

"Bye. I have nothing else to say."

"You better not—"

Click. Keith hung up the phone and fell back in his chair and took a deep breath.

Their marriage not working out wasn't all his fault. Darika was crazy and insecure. She accused him of fooling around just because her girlfriend's husband was cheating. If anything it was Darika who drove him to another woman along with her mother, who was always in their marriage giving advice that wasn't needed nor asked for. A normal young married couple had a sex life. It wasn't a problem with him satisfying Darika, he doesn't know what the hell Denise is talking about. Hell it was the other way around. She couldn't satisfy him. Every time they made love, she complained the whole time "Don't bend my legs back, you're hurting me, ouchhhhh." He thought he was on top of a child instead of a grown woman. Before he married her, she would try to fuck his brains out. It was after they got married things changed. He used to beg her for sex, and beg her to cook and clean the damn house. She didn't work anywhere because her mother told her she shouldn't. Before he married her, she was a school teacher that didn't believe in a man taking care of her and afterwards, she sat at home getting depressed and locking herself up in the bedroom for two and three days at a time and turning off the telephone like she was hiding from someone. That's when he should have left her because he saw that she was crazy then. While her mother was giving advice, she should have advised her to get help. She wasn't a good wife anyway, he thought, she was never the supportive type who had her husband's back. That's why Keith can't let her walk out of that court room with half. Everything he had accomplished in his career wasn't because of her support but her constant doubt in him that he would make his firm what it is today. Some people would wonder from her doubt in him alone how did he stay married to her as long as he did. His answer. He was voodooed. Her never having faith in him made him fight and strive to become a millionaire, with two successful architect firms. He looked for her support and her encouragement each time he would fall, but she could never give it to him. She was too busy with her own life. Which was a life that never made any sense to him anyway because she always allowed her dark skin to hinder it.

Keith had never been so angry to where he wanted to hit a woman, but Darika brought that side of him to surface more than once these days. He admits to not being faithful during their marriage, but he hasn't done anything lately for her to feel insecure. She hasn't found out about anything. And besides with his busy work schedule, he hardly has time to fool around with her let alone with another woman. He has to rebuild the clientele she destroyed when she thought she would tell Juanita some mess about Slack cheating. Slack took half of the clients with him when he left.

Last night it took everything in Keith not to kill Darika that's why it's best for the both of them to go their separate ways before he does. With the taste for a glass of cognac and him relaxing in front of the television, Darika met him at the door screaming. "You low-down muthafucka." She slapped him as hard as she could before he could see her hand coming. The slap was so intense that her hand burned with pain.

"See you're fucking up now. What is your problem?" He yelled while rubbing the redness from his golden-toned face. His heart was beating fast.

"No, you tell me what in the hell is this?" She helding up a piece of paper that had a name and a number on it. "I'm tired of your shit, Keith. If you don't want me, tell me so that I can pack my shit up and leave. I'm not going to sit here and let you sleep with another bitch right under my nose."

With the muscles in his jaws contracting and the veins in his neck and temple bulging, Keith had to make himself smile through all of his anger to keep from knocking the hell out of her. He remembered the last time, she went crazy and started beating him she hadn't taken her medicine. "Baby calm down,"he said, placing his hands on her shoulders. "Have you taken your medicine today?"

"Get your hands off of me. I want to know who does this number belong to," she said, waving the small piece of paper in his face.

He actually didn't know what she was talking about. Leaving another woman's number lying around wasn't like him. She had to be snooping in order to find something such as this small piece of paper. He thought, about what woman she could be talking about. He didn't have Tammy's new number and Chantel's number was at the office, so what was she talking about?

"Baby what are you talking about?"

"Who in the hell is Cathleen Wright and what are you doing with her number?"

He thought. "I don't know a Cathleen Wright."

"You're a damn lie because you wrote down her name and number," she cried. "This is your handwriting." She read off the number and handed it to him. "Who is she?"

He looked at the piece of paper and it all came back to him. It was a number he wrote down two or three weeks ago. "No, the hell you didn't. I know you didn't call her. Cathleen Wright, is a new client over the High Point Mall project. I've been trying to land that contract for months now. Remember I told you about her. Her husband Charles Wright, CEO and owner of the Wright's Group out of New York. Their building two new office buildings here and an apartment complex and they want the firm to design the property. Tell me you did not call her."

Darika's face became tight like stretched spandex across the butt of a big woman. Those were the same words Mrs. Wright tried telling her but she wouldn't listen. Darika cursed her out anyway.

"This contract is worth 3.5million dollars and she's white. You know I don't want a damn white woman," he cried. "Tell me you did not call her, Darika." He slammed his hand against the wall causing it and the pictures on it to shake. "What in the hell are you doing going through my things anyway? If you called her, God, so help me. You betta not have called her," he warned Darika while balling up the piece of paper and throwing it at her. He knew that his warning was too late Darika had already done the damage.

He ran upstairs to his office to look up Mrs. Wright's number in his Rolodex. Hopefully she didn't curse her out too bad. He didn't know if he should call her acting like he had no idea Darika had called her or if he just should apologize right off the back. He looked at his watch and dialed her work number before she left the office for the day but hung up after the first rang. He had to get what he was going to say to her down pack. His mind was so clouded he couldn't think straight. He sat staring at the phone angry at the fact he was going through this type of shit. But he fell to realize he had brought it on himself.

He walked back down to the living room and stood over her with a hard angry face. "There's no need for you to cry so shut the hell up."

Darika looked up at him wiping her face with her hands. "I'm sorry, Keith."

He had heard those words once too many times for the same shit but this time he had enough. "Save it, Darika."

She jumped up off the sofa and began to kiss him. Making love to him when she's fucked up before has always changed his mind. "I'm so sorry baby, please forgive me. I just—"

"You just what—"

She forced her tongue down his throat and ripped open his shirt. Which was his favorite shirt. "Shit," he said, as he pushed her back on the sofa and looked down at his torn shirt, and buttons that were scattered over the floor. "Look what you've done."

She grinned. "I bought it."

"You're crazy as hell and I'm tired of it."

"Make love to me, Keith," she asked him, as she unzipped his pants and placed her hands in his underwear and began rubbing his sex. It became rock-hard.

"No, You are going to call my client and apologize to her for calling her and acting a damn fool. You had no business going through my things."

"After we make love, I promise."

"No. I want you to do it now," he ordered her, while handing her the phone and the phone number.

"Keith, I just don't want to lose you. I thought you were fooling around with her," she said, as she slowly got down on her knees, unbutton his pants and snatched them down to his ankles and began to bring him pleasure and joy.

"Darika stop it," he whispered and moaned. His eyes rolled back in his head and his knees began to buckle to where he nearly lost his balance for the joyous feeling. He rubbed his heavy hands through her Black colored hair and moaned for the warmth of her mouth that caressed his sex. Although he was telling her to stop, she didn't until his body began to jerk and she could taste his sweet creamy nectar. He flopped down on the sofa feeling weak, drained and satisfied. Darika sat beside him with her head on his hairy chest pleased that she could make him forget he was angry with her. Her giving him head was one of his life's pleasures but it hadn't made him forget he was angry. She doesn't do it often enough. It was only a temporary high, something for the moment. She was still going to call his client and apologize.

He looked down at her lying on his chest like an innocent child and he knew she was far from innocent. Ever since they've been back together, he's had nothing but problems with her calling his female clients and accusing them of fooling around with him. He could deal with her going through his things and asking him his whereabouts but fucking up his clientele wasn't getting. If she knows her man like she says she did, she would know he hasn't tipped out on her since last month when he had the one night stand at the Ritz and used her Visa to pay for it. Keith looked at her and shook his head.

The phone rang and Keith pushed her off of him as if she was a rag doll. He prayed that it was Mrs. Wright. He was ready to get it over with. If he lost her as a client and she never referred him to another one of her friends, he deserved it because he was told by his mother and Slack, Darika would be the fall of him.

"Hello," he answered in a deep professional voice.

"Hello, Mr. Jones?"

"Yes." His heart began to pound at the sound of Mrs. Wright's voice.

"Hi, this is Cathleen Wright."

"Hello, Mrs. Wright, how are you?" He looked at Darika and rolled his eyes as he struggled to pull up his pants. "I thought that we would talk again Thursday?"

"I thought so to until I received a phone call today."

"A phone call—a phone call from who?" He asked and looked at Darika as if he could kill her.

"So I guess you don't know?" She asked him sounding annoyed.

Keith thought it would be best if he acted as if he didn't know. "Know about what?"

She sighed. "Well, today your wife—so she called herself . ."

"Yes."

"She called me today and when my secretary wouldn't put the call through to me she used some awful words which caused her to cry. It seems that her main concern was our relationship. I tried telling her you were designing some property for my husband and I. And do you know she," Cathleen sighed. "Told me that I was a lying back stabbing bitch."

He sat silent trying to figure out what to say next.

"Mr. Jones?"

"Yes, Mrs. Wright, I'm still here. I'm very sorry that happened—I apologize. Sometimes Darika can be very jealous and make an ass of herself."

Darika looked at him and rolled her eyes.

"No, try insecure. If I didn't like you . . . "

Keith let out a silent sigh of relief. "Thank you. I apologize once again and I think Darika should apologize to you as well. If you would please hold on, while I call her to the phone." He handed Darika the phone but she wouldn't take it. He yelled out her name as if she was in the next room. "Darika, I have a call for you. Here she is Mrs. Wright." He placed the phone to Darika's ear and popped her as hard as he could on her leg and ordered her to speak.

"Hello."

"Darika."

She gave him back the phone and whispered. "I don't want to speak to her."

"Yes you do. You owe her an apology." He handed the phone back to her and demanded her to speak.

"Yes."

"Hello, Darika, this is Mrs. Wright you called me today."

"Yes, ma'am, and I'm very sorry. I thought you were someone else. I acted way out of character and I apologize. Please, don't blame Keith for my behavior." She began to cry. "I love Keith and I don't want to lose him. I just thought—"

Mrs. Wright began to feel sorry for her. "Please, don't cry."

Keith knew her tears weren't sincere so he snatched the phone from her and rolled his eyes. "Mrs. Wright are we still scheduled for Thursday."

"Sure. And call me Cathleen."

"I'll see you Thursday, Cathleen.."

"Bye, bye. And you have a nice day."

He hung up the phone and stared at Darika as she sat with her head in her hands crying. "Stop it. You're not fooling anyone. By the time I get in tomorrow, I want you to have your shit packed and gone."

"Are you kidding me? I told you I was sorry."

"I don't care I'm tired now."

"Pack my bags," she replied. "This is my house just as much as it's yours. If anybody leave, it's going to be you. It's not that serious."

"I don't want you anymore. I don't want a woman who's insecure and jealous of everyone I associate with. Let's face it, we are never going to make it like this. Lately, all we've done was argue about some other woman that doesn't exsist."

"Who is she?"

"What, you don't have a clue, do you? You don't have a clue that I'm tired of somebody watching my back every minute. If I'm not with you, you think I'm with another woman. It's no one, Darika. I just don't want you anymore. This craziness is driving me crazy . . . I want out. I can't keep apologizing for the past and trying to make up for it. I said I was sorry but yet you still hold it against me. Some people grow apart and we have. It's best that you pack your things and leave."

"Are you just speaking for tonight or what?"

"Darika, I want a divorce." He walked out of the room feeling relieved it was finally over. But she didn't. She felt she had been done wrong. He didn't have to tell her he was leaving her for another woman she already knew and she couldn't deal with it. She picked up the five-pound crystal Lenox vase and charged at him. As hard as she could, she hit him in the back of the head with the vase. And stood back waiting for him to fall. The blow nearly knocked him down to his knees but he caught his balance by holding onto the wall. Darika then jumped on his back and began to bite him on the side of his face and beat him in the head with her fist. With his body he pushed her into the wall nearly knocking the wind out of her and forgetting she was a woman. He then grabbed her by her neck with his strong hand and reared his hand back as far as he could to slap the devil out of her, when realized she was his wife and he was better than his father. He loosened his grip from her neck and she fell to the ground crying uncontrollably gasping for air. He stood over her with tears in his eyes and he apologized. "I'm sorry."

"You nearly killed me," she said, choking and looking up at him.

"I don't know what came over me. I've never hit you or any other woman before. I'm sorry." He picked up her weak body as if it was a feather and grabbed her purse and keys and carried her outside placing her on the ground.

"What are you doing?" She asked.

He dropped her purse and keys beside her. "Only one of us can live in this house until the divorce is final."

"Are you out of your damn mind? You nearly choked me to death. Somebody call the police," she screamed. He tried to kill me."

He walked back into the house gracefully. Without looking back.

CHAPTER SEVEN

Eleven thirty a.m. had rolled around and still no sign of Darika after Keith put her out last night. She should be in school today but there was no telling with her and Keith didn't bother calling to see. Worried about what she might do to his house when she comes home and find her clothes packed, he didn't go into the office today. Her temper was quick and she was liable to do anything like slashing his clothes and furniture and busting out the windows of his house if he wasn't there to put a foot to her ass first. He had thought about sitting her things on the outside and changing all the locks but he knew that would only cause a scene. Which it was already going to be a scene once she finds them waiting on her at the front door.

Cathleen called him to say they needed to move their meeting from Thursday to today since she had a previous engagement she could not break for tomorrow. Keith was skeptical about leaving home knowing Darika might come by on her lunch hour but his meeting with Cathleen was worth 3.5 million. Keith got dressed and headed to Marllows, the Italian restaurant she had suggested they meet for lunch. If any damage was done to his house, he knew just where to find Darika. He had no problem with pressing charges against her.

Just as Darika was on her way to talk things out with Keith she saw him driving down the street. She blew her horn for him to stop but he didn't hear her so she busted a U turn in the middle of the road while trying to flag him down. He drove very fast in the small white sports car which made it very difficult for Darika to catch up to him. The people in front of her drove like snails. She jumped between and around the cars to try and catch up to him but there was no way without her getting a ticket. So she decided to follow him until he stopped at his destination. He pulled into Marllows and she pulled in behind him. Ordinarily she would act a fool because she knew he had to be meeting a woman there but this time she didn't care. To keep her cover from being blown she sat in the back parking lot and watched him walk into the restaurant alone. She knew the woman had to be waiting on him inside. Not once did she think he was there for a business meeting her mind wouldn't let her go that far. Her husband was a whore and had always been. Work was the last thing on his mind.

Keith spotted Cathleen sitting at a table in the middle of the restaurant waiting on him. Her appearance caused him to look twice at her. She was actually sexy in her tight fitting jeans, showing off her small ass which for a white woman it had roundness like a sistah and her costly breast protruded through her cream sweater top that sat above her navel. But in all her sexiness Keith could never imagine being with her. She was white and white women did nothing for him.

"Hello." Keith said, extending his hand out to hers but she stood up to hug him.

"Hi."

"You look very relaxed today if I would have known . . ." Keith said, and sat down.

"I just felt like being free today, that's why I asked if we could have lunch first before jumping right into business."

"Will Charles be joining us today?"

"No, The High Point project belongs to me so he's letting me make the decisions. He's just writing the checks." She signaled for a waitress.

"That's great. So I take it he trust you would make the right decisions with his money."

"I always do."

They both laughed.

Darika cringed while her stomach turned inside out as she sat across the room peeping over her menu at her husband and this white woman who seemed like they were talking about something other than business. By the way Cathleen's breast were laying on the table and her blouse slightly open for Keith to get a sneak peek, Darika knew her assumption was correct. From what she could see, Cathleen wanted Keith, and by his response of laughter, he wanted her too. Bullshit if a white woman can do nothing for him, if she opens up her legs he'll lie between them. Darika still didn't react even after she thought about how they tried to make her think there was nothing going on between them because Cathleen was a happily married woman and white. Even after Keith for so many years claimed he never found white women attractive she couldn't tell today. Not the way he was sitting all up in her face. Anyway their meeting was supposed to be on Thursday and here today is Wednesday, Darika thought and took a sip of her water. She still wouldn't react.

Keith looked around the room because he had the strangest feeling someone was watching him. The restaurant was crowded with white and black people and there was no telling who was watching him with hate for sitting with a prize in some eyes and a white bitch in others. But the sad thing about it he wasn't with her like they thought, he was only sitting with her for business, but those on the outside looking in would never know.

"Are you looking for someone?" Cathleen asked him.

"No. I'm just looking around."

"You seem a little uneasy. Have you've ever been in public

with a white woman before?"

"Sure but she's always been accompanied by a white man. In my business I have a lot of lunch dates with white women and white men but never with a white woman alone."

"Do you find white women attractive?" She asked him.

"All women are attractive," he answered.

"My sister lives in California and she says the black men there would rather date white women before dating black."

Keith thought they must be out of their minds. Black was the only thing he desired.

"I see a couple of interracial relationships here but I don't think anything of them. Charles hates them, believe it or not, a man with so much money shouldn't worry about petty things such as interracial couples."

"Very true."

"It was rumor his daughter was screwing one," she said and laughed.

"One of what?"

"A black man."

"I guess Charles nearly died? A black man inside his daughter."

Her tongue slid across her top thin lip. "Is that how you describe making love. A man being inside of a woman?"

"No . . . I was just say."

"I bet you didn't know Charles wanted to hire a white company for the job but I insisted on hiring you. You do know you have the contract don't you?"

"I do?"

"Yes, that was decided months ago when I first saw you . . . I mean your work. Charles insisted on that I reconsider but I insisted on your company. I know that you've heard my husband doesn't care too much about black people but yet he gives thousands of dollars to their political campaigns and their different charities."

"So why me?"

"He would have settled for a firm owned by a black woman before giving it to a black man. But I felt black women are just like white men they have every thing handed to them."

"Do you think?" Keith asked her, and took a sip of his sweet tea.

"Yeah, they're spoiled."

"That's not true. Black women work hard to get where they are today."

"Maybe so, but I can't tell. But what I can tell is that you are a hard worker and I like you. In. more. ways. than. one," she said, in very slow motion.

Keith was flattered but not impressed. White women did nothing for him but turn his stomach. They had flat asses, small hips, skinny lips, long dog like hair, and cat looking eyes. Since this thing with black men and white women became so popular he's had dozens of white women approach him, but he simply say no. Something they hardly hear. "White women just don't turn me on." Maybe he was paranoid, but he could of sworn he felt the same stare fall upon his back. He turned around quickly to catch it but he didn't see anyone.

"Are you looking for someone again."

"No, some ones looking for me, I believe."

She chuckled. "A black man and a white woman together has always drawn attention to themselves. Keith I'm here to help you if you will allow me. There's more where that 3.5million dollar contract comes from."

Cathleen was a thirty something white woman who was married to an old billionaire who she had no interest in, other than for his money. Black men have always been in her bed.

"Where are you getting at Cathleen?" Keith sighed and asked.

"I have a room just around the corner at the Ritz, what do you say?"

He chuckled. "You want me to sleep with you?"

"More than once." She ran her thin hands through her thick blond hair and through it over to the side. "I would say I'm worth 3.5million dollars of it."

Damn, Keith thought. Keith couldn't do it even if he wanted to. But he needed to either sleep with her or lose the contract in other words.

"And like I said before, there's more where that comes from. You'll be receiving more work than you can handle from New York to Miami."

"I'm married and so are you." Being married meant nothing to Keith but it was his only scapegoat from having to sleep with her. He couldn't feel it. It wouldn't even rise. With all the talk of sex his mind couldn't even paint the picture. That's what he gets for being a whore all of his life. Now it has caught up with him. To do or not to do for 3.5million.

"You've cheated on your wife before or she never would have called me acting that way. And as far as my husband, he'll never know. He's into his money. O'yeah the meeting is still on for to-morrow he'll be here then. So what do you say? This will be our little secret."

"Cathleen."

"Why is it so hard to decide? You are getting the best of both worlds a contract that will pull your company out of the red for this year and many contracts after that and sex."

Keith didn't say anything. He squeezed his fist and bit down on his bottom lip while thinking how the money could help him.

"I get it. You're just not attracted to me right?"

He didn't want to hurt her feelings so he lied. "No, that's not it."

"Then what is it? Why are you making it so hard? I've wanted you since the first night I laid eyes on you at the fight against AIDS charity ball. You didn't notice me but I noticed you."

Although he was going against every thing he believed, he couldn't afford to be righteous when money was at stake. He had it figured out. He would just get really drunk, blank her pale skin tone out, and imagine she was black, and Toni Braxton.

"Do we take your car or mine?" He asked.

She smiled and ran her hand through her hair once again. "I'll just follow you there if you don't mind."

"Sure."

Darika noticed their lunch hadn't been touched and they were leaving. Something was up and it wasn't business. She waited before following them so they wouldn't see her. She watched them from the window, paid for her tea and ran outside to catch them. They were already down the street when she caught up to them. She drove a car behind Keith who was driving behind Cathleen. Darika wondered where they were going but no longer had to wonder when they turned into the parking lot of the Ritz. Darika's heart sank and a tear came to her eye. Enough was enough she was turning her back on Keith for good. Her heart could not stand anymore pain from him.

Cathleen checked into the room first and Keith later followed her after making sure no one noticed they were together. He was ready to get it over with. This was the first time he wished Darika was following him and came knocking on the door. Cathleen had gotten undress to her panties and bra while fixing herself a drink. Keith looked at everything but her; the pictures on the wall had more color than she did.

"I'm fixing drinks would you like one?" She asked.

"O.J. and Gin." That was the only way he was going to get a hard on. Gin did it every time.

"O.J. where is he?" She asked and laughed. When she saw that Keith didn't find her joke funny she felt embarrassed, so as usual she ran her fingers through her hair. "Don't mind me, I'm just acting silly." She handed Keith his drink and he gulped it down and handed her the glass for another one.

"What's wrong, are you trying to get drunk?" She grabbed his limp penis and began rubbing it.

"Just having a hard time," he said.

"Don't worry about it." She unzipped his pants and pulled out the penis she wanted so bad and gave him just the help he needed to rise to the occasion.

For a hundred dollars, the front desk clerk gave Darika the room number of the executive suite on the tenth floor, which was under the name of Cathleen Wright. Darika thought about going up there and beating her ass and dragging Keith out of there, but she thought of a better idea instead. She remembered Cathleen's office number so she called it again. This time she insisted on speaking with Charles Wright, her husband.

"I'm sorry, ma'am he's not available. I can take your name

and number and have his secretary give you a call back later. She's out to lunch right now."

"I don't want to speak with her. I want to speak with him."

"What is it in reference to?" She asked, with annoyance in her voice.

Darika sighed. "His wife."

"Hold please." She placed Darika on hold and clicked over. When she clicked back over, Charles was on the other line.

"Charles Wright, how may I help you?"

"I know you don't know where your wife is right now, but I do, because she's at the downtown Ritz in room 1020 screwing my husband."

"This is nonsense. Who is this?"

"And he's a Black man." Darika disconnected the call and grinned with pure satisfaction.

CHAPTER EIGHT

"Dr. McClinton, I'm not crazy . ." she told him, as she sat on his sofa looking down at her hands. Lying down on the sofa seemed too much like something a crazy person would do so she insisted on sitting up. "I know there's another woman. It has always been. I was just too stupid not to leave him."

"Have you seen this other woman?"

"Sort of kinda, but I don't know if they are sleeping together or not. She's some rich white woman. I followed them to the hotel the other day but I called her husband on them before they could do anything. A woman always have that feeling when there's another woman and I've had that feeling more than once. He's leaving me for her." She began to cry. "I love Keith and I don't know what I'll do if he leaves me this time."

"Do you think you might kill yourself or just fall into a depression?" He asked and crossed his legs. "I thought you told me some weeks ago you had prepared yourself for him to leave. You knew of this woman weeks before you called her or saw them together. How did you manage to get out of bed this morning or did you feel like staying there?"

"Yes, but I pulled myself out to come here."

"And why is that, you've been depressed before and you've never come."

"I needed to talk to someone. Although I pay you, but you listen without voicing your opinion."

"You don't like opinions, Darika?" Dr. McClinton asked her, as he sat comfortably in an upright position with his legs crossed and a yellow legal pad resting on his lap and a number two pencil in his hand.

"Like my daddy always said, opinions are just like assholes—everybody has one. But of course everyone thinks you're supposed to follow theirs. My girlfriend, Cookie sure as hell think I'm supposed to take her advice every time she speaks. She doesn't take my advice and she's with that bum Antonio, who's no good himself and she wants to talk about my husband."

"I've never heard you mention her before."

"Yeah, she's my best friend. She has a low self-esteem problem. That's who needs to be in here talking to you instead of me."

He gave her a look through the top of his glasses.

"Well we both need to be in here."

Darika had only been seeing him for two months and the sessions were not as bad as she had imagine. Although he was one of the most unorthodox therapist, she has ever seen or heard of, she liked him. He was a pale skinned, tall, lanky white man with a recessive hair line that nearly caused him to be bald. He looked more malnourished than skinny or maybe that's mildly putting it. The truth of the matter is, he looked like he had full-blown AIDS. After all, he was gay. Darika could tell by the rainbow flag coffee mug that sat on his desk and his office that looked more like a gallery than a psychiatrist office. The walls were a cranberry red covered with pictures of naked men leaping through gardens and playing in the rain. There were also sculptures of naked men sitting in each corner that always seemed like they were staring at her.

"She's over weight and just recently went through a divorce—her husband, low- down bastard went and remarried some skinny pencil that doesn't look like anything God could have created. But because she was skinny he fell in love with her. It nearly killed Cookie. Just like I know Keith's whore is some light skin bitch with long hair. All my life I've had men to look over me for someone lighter and I've had people not to like me only because my skin was darker than theirs."

"Why do you think people dislike you, Darika?"

"I don't expect you to understand because you're white. I've dealt with this problem all my life. It's my dark skin, Dr. McClinton. See white people are not the only one's that don't like black people, black people don't like black people. They think I'm evil and unattractive."

"Who does?"

"Some black people. But let me put blame where blame is due it was the white man who made blacks think black was evil. I'm what you call black."

"Black," he responded. "I thought your race was now called African-American."

"I'm speaking of my skin tone." She went into a day dream as she thought about the first day she met Keith at the gas station. "I'm not going to lie, I needed him; he made me feel beautiful. The beauty I didn't have on my own he gave me." She chuckled and sighed. "I can't believe I'm telling you all of this."

"Why?"

"You might really think I'm crazy."

"Not at all."

"We would walk into a room together and people would just stop and stare, wondering what that tall handsome light-skin man doing with that ugly black woman. And then they would think again, she had to be beautiful to him or he wouldn't be with her."

"Now what is he?"

"He's handsome: light skin, tall sexy. He looks half white;

some people think he is."

"So you yourself think light skin is beautiful?"

"I think all blacks are beautiful, not just light skin."

"So where did you get your skin tone?"

"My damn daddy. You know as a kid none of the little boys wanted me as their dance partner and as a teenager I can count on my fingers the number of boyfriends I had. None. I know I shouldn't be with Keith but I can't let him go. But now I have no choice, he's leaving me for another woman." She looked at her watch and sighed while trying to hold back her tears. "It's almost time for us to wrap this session up I've enjoyed it as I always do."

"I'm curious to know, have you ever fooled around, Darika?"

She gaped at him very amazed he would ask such a question she had to wonder where it had come from.

"Off the record, yes, but he never found out about it. I had my tracks covered."

"So why didn't you come last week?"

"I was tied up. I had a student parent meeting and it lasted a little longer than I anticipated. Don't worry you still get your hundred and fifty dollars. I should have gone into the business of psychology. God knows I'll never lack any clients. Half of the world needs to seek therapy. I know half of my teachers and students do." She reached into her purse for her mirror to fix her make-up.

"Have you been taking your medicine."

She looked at him out of the corner of her eye as she lined her lips with a fresh coat of Ruby Red lipstick. "That medicine is for crazy people and I'm not crazy, so the answer to your question is no."

"No, you're not crazy, but you do have a disorder."

"No, I do not, and my mother and sister has it because of that bitch Bell Ruth.She's not going to have me thinking I'm crazy when I'm not and neither are you. Yes, I cried and locked myself up in the room but I was trying to deal with Keith and all his women. That was my way of dealing with that. Once I realized, he's going to cheat I haven't been depressed."

"What does Bell Ruth have to do with anything you are bi-polar and you need your medication on a regular basis."

"Bell Ruth, has a lot to do with it. Let me ask you something Dr. McClinton, do you know anything about voodoo?"

He nodded his head. "I know a little."

"Well, this disorder I, my mother and sister have it's not a hereditary disorder. It's a spell that this lady name Bell Ruth, who my daddy used to fool around with for many years, casted on my mother and her children because my daddy wouldn't leave us for her. Did Carla tell you we had two brothers that drenched their clothes in gasoline and set themselves afire."

"No," he said, and pushed his glasses up on his nose. "She never even told me she had brothers."

"They were twins. They were the first to be diagnosed with depression but my mother didn't know anything about the disease. She just thought it was my brothers way of trying to get attention."

"How old were they?"

"Twelve. They were supposed to be the boys Bell Ruth would have had for my daddy but she couldn't conceive or carry a pregnancy to full term. You know that's why I think I can't conceive. She put the curse on me; she took my uterus. She's the reason I have endometriosis"

Dr. McClinton looked at her like she was crazy. He was wondering if not taking her medicine had her talking about voodoo and curses.

"And at the same time she was trying to become pregnant my mother became pregnant with the boys which brought my daddy closer to her because that's all he wanted. Someone to carry on the Summers' name. He eventually broke up with Ruth and she hated him for that and casted a spell on my family that would destroy us all."

A moment of silence stood between them as Darika took long drags from her cigarette and Dr. McClinton sat in disbelief while writing down his observation. He had heard of voodoo but he never believed in it or had ever seen anyone it had affected. He thought spells and curses were all in a person's mind and it was surly in Darika's. Just as her thinking people don't like her because she's "*black.*"

Darika mashed her cigarette into the ashtray waiting for him to respond with a question but he continued to write. His silence made her feel awkward and somewhat nervous so she lit another one and watched his pencil fly across the paper. She could tell by the look on his face that he didn't believe her and he thought she was just as crazy as the medicine she was taking. Stella, his secretary beeped into the office to tell him the hospital was on the line two. He jumped up from his chair, forgetting Darika was sitting on the sofa, and dashed over to the phone with speed. His mother was very ill with cancer and she was expected to die any day now. Darika sat with her legs and arms crossed with her third cigarette dangling from between her lips, looking out the big oval shaped window at the high-rise buildings of downtown Washington. She was upset with herself that she had turned back to smoking again. Five months ago she had promised herself she would never touch another cigarette but sometimes situations cause change. Like most people eat or drink when they become depressed, she smoked a pack of cigarettes a day. No one knew she smoked, not even Keith. She only did it outside and she would carry gum and breath spray in her purse and would wash her hands really well with plenty of soap so that the smell couldn't be detected. She had been smoking since she was sixteen. Depression and anger was the only reason she reached under her car seat where she hid the half pack of Capri's five months ago. And within three hours she had smoked them and went out for more.

Without warning, tears rolled down Darika's face onto her navy silk blouse. She felt she was falling apart and Keith was the blame. He was the blame for her sitting in a physiatric office telling a white man all her problems, how she and other people thought of her as being evil and ugly; he was the blame she couldn't stop smoking even when she wanted to, and he was the blame for their marriage going to hell. She tried to wipe the tears away as fast as they fell but she couldn't, so she stopped trying. She didn't want Dr. McClinton to notice her weeping like a child, so while he had his back turned she grabbed her purse and walked out of the office.

The empty and out of control feeling that had come over her she had never felt before and it was scary. She walked over to the water cooler to get a drink of water and perhaps sit down for awhile to regain her balance, but the feeling still hoovered over her like a dark cloud. So against her will she reached into her purse and grabbed the Prozac pills and popped two of them into her mouth and washed them down with water. It took seconds for them to do what they had to do and put her back in control again. She walked out to her car and stood outside it while she collected her thoughts and smoked a cigarette. Dr. Mark McClinton was also her secret no one knew about. She nearly cursed Carla for a slow walking mule for suggesting she go and see him. She thought she was implying she was crazy. But she only knew staying in bed for two weeks at a time, eating everything in sight, and crying uncontrollably wasn't normal. She had been down the same road and being bi-polar depressed was the reason her brain was un chemical balanced.

With a brand new sense of pride about her situation, Darika drove across town to Cookie's house to tell her the good news. They hardly talk anymore since Cookie's new boyfriend Antonio came into the picture and started taking up most of her time. Cookie was the only person she could talk to about Keith and not worry about her telling anyone how stupid she was for staying with him. They were best friends and had been since third grade. They considered themselves sisters because neither one of them got alone with their blood sisters. She was there when Cookie went through her nasty divorce, they were each others' support when winds and tides strong enough to knock them down rolled into their lives. And God knows they had seen enough of those in their lives.

"I'm leaving Keith, girl," she said, beaming with excitement as she flopped down into the rod iron chair. She tried to light a cigarette but the spring wind kept blowing the match out.

"When did you start smoking? What we did when we were sixteen was only a peer pressure thing. How long have you been doing this?"

Darika didn't mean for her to know she still smoked. She

was unaware she had taken the cigarette out. It was a mistake. "I just started and it's only to clam my nerves. But getting back to Keith, I don't want it anymore, girl."

Cookie rolled her eyes up in her head and sighed silently. She had heard those words once too many times and this time she chose not to believe them or comment. As far as she was concerned, Darika never should have gone back in the first place. She was a fool for going back.

"Hellooo, Did you hear me? It's over. I packed my things last night"

"Do you know they haven't decided who they are going to hire for the Promotions and Sale position. God knows I could use that extra three thousand dollars a year. Word is they are going to give it to Becky Stein some Jewish girl that works in the mail room. No experience just white," Cookie said with her face glued to Wednesday in her daily planner. She wasn't looking at Darika because she was trying to ignore her but because she was on a diet for the fifth time in six months and her stomach was growling and Darika was stuffing chunks of lemon pound cake in her mouth. If she looked at her, she was sure she was going to grab a piece of the cake and shove it into her mouth and blow her diet. And she would have to start all over again next Monday.

"She's Jewish not white."

"Jewish, White, they're all the same to me. Both are sneaky."

"Keith couldn't believe I asked for a divorce."

"Antonio is taking me and Zoria to meet his mother in New York," Gloria said, trying to ignore Darika.

"Why are you ignoring me?"

"You've noticed—good, so lets not talk about it because I don't want to hear it today. Darika, you know you are not going anywhere and so does Keith so stop lying to yourself." She looked Darika in the eyes and glanced over at her piece of cake.

"I'm for real this time. And if you were any type of friend no matter how many times I say I'm leaving and I go back you are supposed to still give me your support. You're right I shouldn't have gone back but I did. But this time you have my word. I'm tired of his shit now."

"About time. So did he put you out or you left on your own?" She asked as, she sipped on her unsweeten tea looking at Darika as if she already knew the answer.

"No, I left on my own. Cookie, girl, I'm tired of him cheating."

"Who's number did you find and did you call her?"

"Her name is Cathleen and hell, yeah I called her." Darika spoke, matter of factly. She wouldn't tell her she was white though.

"So what did she say?"

"She told me they weren't sleeping together but I didn't believe her I still packed my bags and left."

"Good for you because Keith is going to keep dogging you if you keep letting him. This time you have to mean what you say in order for him to take you seriously. I don't care how many times he calls you do not return his calls and if he so happens to catch you at home— wait a minute, where are you staying?"

"At a hotel."

"If he catches you at home, act real dry toward him and do not tell'im that you miss him. Let that nigga know that you've moved on with your life. And sex. I don't care how horny you get do not call him. Get yourself a toy—dildo preferred. If it's over, it's over. That's what I had to tell myself when I realized John and I just weren't gon' make it. It was over."

"I can't help but wonder what she looks like." As if she didn't already know. It was taking every thing in her not to tell Cookie she was white, skinny, with big breast. Cookie has never called Keith and just gone off for all the things he's done to Darika, but this time she just might. She can't stand for a brotha to be with a white woman when there are so many sistahs available.

"Who gives a damn. Don't worry about that, Darika. Don't even worry about how he makes love to her."

Darika plastered her hands over her eyes at the thought. "I wasn't until you brought it up."

"Let's talk about something else he disgust me. Girl, do you know that nigga hasn't sent me my money for this month. This makes the third month in a row he hasn't sent child support and hasn't even called to tell me anything. You see he's trying to make a joke out of the situation," she said, while using her hand as a sun visor over her eyes. Darika knew this was her chance to do what she has always wanted since John left her— make him suffer by putting him in jail for failure to pay child support. "Nobody told him to go out and get remarried and have another baby. She already has two and he has one that needs to be taken care of also and then they just had another baby. I don't care about anybody else's mouth he has to feed, I just care about my child Zoria. I didn't want to do it but I see I'm going to have to, and that's go to the white man to get that Negro to pay me my money. I'm letting him pay me pennies compared to what the white man would have him pay me. I didn't ask him for much and he can't pay that. I bet it's that wife of his. I can't stand that bitch. She's the reason he hasn't been over to see Zoria in months and he hasn't even called her. Do you know he didn't even call her on her birthday? His daughter."

"Why don't you go by his house. You know where he lives don't you, and y'all talk."

"Me and his wife don't get along at all. She thinks I want him back which I don't. Out of the ten years we were married I can't look back at one good time we had. So hell no, I don't want him back and I don't want to talk."

"Don't take this the wrong way because I can't stand John just like you can't but he loves Zoria and he's probably just having a hard time. Last I heard the business was suffering after that law suit."

"What do you call that if you are not trying to take up for him? I don't want to hear it. He needs to pay me something. I'm having a hard damn time myself. Bills need to be paid. Mortgage has to be paid every month. Zoria is a growing child and she needs food, and clothes. I don't care nothing about his hard times, what about mine? I'm going to the white man. He'll make'im pay. You are a typical black woman, always trying to give those bastards a chance. He makes hundreds and thousands a year."

Darika didn't blame her for being angry but she didn't want her to do anything that might hurt Zoria.

"Wait before you do that, Sis."

"I'm thinking about letting Antonio move in, what do you think? He's always over here. There's no need of him paying rent for an apartment he's never at. He loves Zoria and it doesn't look like he's going anywhere soon. His ex-wife has him paying child support out the ass and she left him with credit card bills he didn't even use. He's in just as much debt as I'm in. Besides he asked me and I told him I had to think about it. So what'd you think?"

"No, No, No," Darika said, nodding her head and putting out her cigarette.

"Why? I need the help." Cookie's natural was newly trimmed and the Soft Shine gave it a beautiful shine as the sun beamed down on it. She was the only woman Darika knew could pull a boyish hair cut off and not look like a dyke or a militant.

"I'll give you the money."

"Girl, you can't give me money you don't have. That's Keith's money and just as soon as you file those divorce papers it's coming out of your account." That's why Darika had her own money in her own account just in case something like this would happen. She learned from last time

Antonio walked outside with his arms open and a beer in his hand. "I want a hug," he said, while grinning. Darika rolled her eyes at him and sat back down. She couldn't understand what Cookie saw in him. He looked like a ball of dirt with a head and legs nothing was attractive about him. He was a mechanic and he was always dirty. Darika bet he didn't know the meaning of a bath tub full of water.

"Hi, baby. Darika, is out here trying to convince me that she's leaving Keith again."

"O'really, you're leaving this time, Darika?"

Darika's nostrils began to flare out to her ears and wrinkles from frowning appeared on her forehead. She hated the very sight of Antonio and she couldn't believe Cookie has been discussing her business with him. She could have reached over the table and slapped Cookie dead in her fat mouth for talking so much. "Cookie, have you lost your mind, don't tell him my business."

"What business, he already knows how Keith dogs you out

and you keep talking about leaving him." Cookie said, as she and Antonio chuckled.

"I wonder how he knows. I understand he's your man and all but some things you just don't tell him, like my business. What we talk about is between us."

"Why are you trippen?"

"Baby, she's right. Darika, I'm sorry. I thought we were all family I would never tell anyone your business—I'm glad you are leaving the bastard you were too good for him anyway. He'd bragged to me about some woman he had been seeing—"

"What woman?" Darika asked.

"I forgot her name."

"Why are you just now telling me this?"

"Yeah, why are you just now telling her?"

"Baby, you know me I'm not a shit starter and it wasn't my place. But now that it's over between them I can tell her."

Darika began to cry so Cookie put her arms around her to comfort her.

"You know a man like him will never get what's coming to'im unless he dies."

Cookie and Darika looked at him and didn't say a word.

"He reminds me of my sister's husband; he fooled around on her like Keith has done you and she used to always pray to God to take care of her revenge so God finally heard her cry and he did. He was found shot to death in his car."

"What, you never told me about that." Cookie said, as she eased her hips back down in her chair.

"No, because it never came up. He had done her wrong but she won in the end because she got the half a million in life insurance and the house and a chance to get her a new man. And they never found out who killed him."

"Well, I don't pray those types of prayers."

"Why not?"

"I don't wish death on anyone."

"Girl," Cookie chuckled. "I wish John dead every day but not because of any insurance money just for what he did to me. If he died today, Zoria would be entitled to $250,000 that I know."

"You're her mother and you would be over the money." Antonio told her.

"Yeah, you're right. God knows I need it."

"At what expense?" Darika asked her.

"What do you mean at what expense?"

"You don't get it do you?"

Antonio looked at Darika and took a big gulp of the beer.

"His sister's husband wasn't killed by random and neither would John be . . . what Antonio is trying to tell you, is that you could pay someone to kill John."

Antonio began to laugh as Cookie joined in. "Darika, girl, you have a wild imagination. How did you get that idea out of this conversation?"

"Antonio, am I right?" Darika asked him.

Cookie looked at him and waited for an answer. "As a matter of fact Darika, you are right you're smarter than I thought you were. Now leave that nigga and stay gon'."

"What, oh nooooooo . . . " Cookie singed. "Tony, you must be crazy I was thinking a tree might fall on him or a car accident. Having someone kill him no."

"It won't be traced back to you or anyone else."

"Neither will this conversation so lets end it."

Darika hoped Cookie would now look at him through another pair of glasses other than the blinders she's been wearing. Darika had always told her he was crooked and up to no good but now she was beginning to think the samething.

"Cookie, two hundred fifty thousand dollars, you need it."

"Don't listen to him, girl."

"I'm not."

Antonio fell back in his chair and shrugged his shoulders. It would take some time to get Cookie to see his side.

CHAPTER NINE

It goes without saying that a man shall reap what he sow. And the pain he will feel will stab him deeper than any pain he had ever inflicted.

Keith's brother Kelvin had put the thought in Keith's head of Darika being with another man. Keith hadn't heard from her in two weeks and her clothes were still waiting on her at the front door. The vision of her enrapt with someone else had his heart and mind in tatters. Keith was now convinced that Darika had been lying to him about her out of town trips to chaperone her Beta club students. Now he wondered about the debate team and her supposed late night work at school to catch up on supposed work. It was obvious. He had been played. The fact that he felt chumped shocked him and left him speechless. Darika of all people was creeping and he didn't even recognize it.

While she rambled through his things and accused him of sleeping with his secretary and the lady down at the bank, she was doing the sleeping with God knows who. And then it dawned on him. Was she sleeping with Mark the whole time that young nigga was calling the house and she was claiming he's gay and they were friends?

Keith didn't think anything of it when he called the school about a month ago and Angela told him Darika hadn't been in at all that day. He remembered now that she had left the house dressed as if she were going to work. Then he was too caught up in his own life to put the thought of another man pass her. Now it hit him like a ton of divorce court law books. Now he knew the truth.

Lord knows Keith didn't mind her packing her bags and leaving him but to cheat on him and let another man lie between her legs. Possibly there was another man making Darika happy the way he used to and it was killing him. For the first time he felt the pain she must have felt when she realized there was another woman in his life. But then again, Keith thought, he was the man and men didn't hold up too well to being cheated on. He was the husband sharing his wife with another man. His and Dariks's pain couldn't be compared. The women he had flings with had meant nothing to him. None of them were worth leaving her over, even as Darika insisted she wanted out because of his cheating. He never got caught up in the love his mistresses had for him. As far as he was concerned, they were only there to past time, to substitute for the wife he wish he had.

Now that the shoe was on the other foot and Darika was the one cheating, he couldn't deal. A man's wife is his prize on a pedestal, the forbidden fruit that all other men had better not look at, dream of, and especially not touch. Once that sanctity was broken, she was tainted. From the pain Keith felt for the first time in years, he thought of Darika as still his wife.

The dancing and singing around the house, the long auburn colored weave she wore that cost $1200, the switch from bloomers to thong bikini, the thigh high tight skirts and the smile she kept on her face even while she slept told him nothing about another man being in the picture. He thought her change in attitude was her way of proving to herself and him that at the age of thirty-seven she could still be sexy.

Keith sat across the street from the school in his car waiting for her to leave for the day. It was five o'clock and her car was the only car in the parking lot. The janitors had even gone home. Keith felt kind of silly for spying but he had to know if there was really someone else. Kelvin was ready to bet his life that there was. And if he was right, Keith wouldn't be the one to tell him. He didn't want his brother knowing his wife had cheated on him.

The suspense of who this other man could be was killing him. He watched every car drive by and he watched for the doors of the school to open; maybe the man was already in there with her. Finally around five- thirty a black convertible Sabb with tinted windows drove up. The car looked familiar but Keith couldn't place it. He slid down in his seat so the man wouldn't recognize him. A tall slender man, with a bald head, wearing tan linen slacks and a white linen shirt, stepped out of the car. He looked somewhat young and inexperienced to be having an affair with his wife. He looked like Mr. Brown, the twenty-six year old eleventh grade history teacher. Damn. Keith knew him as Mr. Brown, by his last name, but Darika called him Corey. He had come over to their house several weekends claiming Darika was helping him write his thesis. Keith had left him and Darika alone while he was at the office working. That had just happened a month ago. Fire covered Keith's eyes and his stomach began to boil along with his temper. Corey looked around as if he was making sure no one was looking and walked up to the school door. Darika opened it smiling just before they kissed and hugged. Keith's heart fell to his feet and he took a deep breath as he realized once again he had been played. He felt the rage of a jealous husband who wanted no other man to look at nor touch his wife. The jealousy and love he thought he had lost for her came to the forefront of his heart. There he was now standing in the shoes of Axel Cohen the businessman convicted to life in prison after his rage drove him to kill his wife and one of his construction workers after catching them together in his sauna. Keith had just finished designing the Bradford Point Mall project for him when he was shipped off to prison. Just by watching Darika kiss another man he could see how a man could snap and act out a rage of passion and love while pulling the trigger or slitting throats. Darika was the bum in bed when they did make love and now another man was enjoying Keith's same pleasure. He sighed and thanked God he didn't have a gun because the both of them would be dead.

When they walked out of the school, they were holding hands and laughing. To Keith it was a laughter after good sex. He wondered if they had a quicky in her office on top of her desk. Her laugh seemed so warm and innocent as if she enjoyed it. He couldn't remember the last time he whispered in her ear and she giggled like a shy school girl. And now there was another man making her laugh. Keith wondered what could he have said to her. "You look sexy today." Something he hadn't told her since they got back together. For the first time in years he noticed how beautiful she was. Nothing about her had changed. She was sexy as hell and her dark skin still had the young radiant glow it had when he had first laid eyes on her at the Rock and Pop Cafe in Houston. Her smile was soft and tender which made her lips look succulent and tasty. Her short petite frame was diminutive as if it belonged to a twenty-five-year old. Keith was wanting Darika like never before.

They pulled into the parking lot of Marllows restaurant and he drove up behind them. He had taken a couple of his clients there for lunch before. The parking lot was half full which meant he couldn't make a scene that would bring attention to himself as the betrayed husband. He didn't want to look like the fool, although Darika had played him as one. He watched them walk in together with their hands around each other's waist. He had no idea Darika's walk had so much elegance and confidence until now as she walked with another man. Her short sexy legs moved with an arrogance across the parking lot as if she was a model on a run way. He gave them time to be seated before walking in behind them. The hostess tried to stop him at the door to seat him but he walked passed her to the corner booth where Darika and Corey were laughing. He discretely slid into their booth and notice Corey's hand between Darika's legs. His appearance startled them both.

"O'hell," Corey said, as he snatched his hand from between Darika's legs.

"Keith," Darika stammered while pulling her skirt down.

Keith looked at them with deadly eyes and whispered. "And

you're damn right. What's going on here?"

"What'd you mean?" Darika asked.

"Don't play with me Darika. You know damn well what I mean."

"What are you doing here, Keith?" Darika asked him through clenched teeth when she noticed they had a small audience.

"No, you don't ask any question. I do all the damn question asking. Now the question is what are you doing here with him and why in the hell is his hands between your legs? You are my wife."

"So I'm your wife now?"

"Hell no! Slip of the tongue."

"Are you following me?"

The question caught him off guard. "Yeah. No. You had this man in my house and the whole time you were fucking him under my nose." He thought of Corey sitting in his favorite chair while drinking his cognac and smoking one of his imported cigars. He had allowed him to not knowing he was fucking his wife. He had seen her nude. Keith looked at Darika's body and dropped his head. He couldn't let her see his hurt so he cried inside. "He's one of your teachers, Darika."

"It's just like you sleeping with your secretary for all of these years."

"What? Pam's married. So how does it feel Mr. Brown to be fucking the boss?"

"I love, Darika."

"You what?" Keith tried reaching over Darika to grab Corey's thick neck. "How in the hell are you going to stand there and tell me that you love my wife."

"You've fucked her over and now that she's with someone else you want to claim her as your wife. She's told me how you used to stay out all night. What you didn't have time to handle at home because you were busy fucking around she came to me and I handled it. I took care of her. I'm the man." Corey jumped up from the booth holding his arms open inviting Keith to try and grab at him now. He was going to knock the hell out of Keith. "It's over between you two brotha so let it go. Give her the divorce she's been asking for."

"Divorce. You'll get it no problem. I don't want you." Without thinking Keith stood in Corey's face daring him to every look at Darika again.

"Old man you don't want none of this."

"Old." Keith exclaimed. He was far from old and he damn sure didn't look it.

"Sit down you two. Corey, sit down," Darika ordered him. "Both of you are carrying on like children. Keith, you made me do this so take the blame. I loved you but you were in love with some other woman. I was your wife."

"Darika, you have to be out of your damn mind if you think I'm going to take the blame for you opening up your legs for another man. I've never blamed you for me screwing around although you were the blame. You made me unhappy with the crazy shit you used to do. Following me, looking through my things."

"Is every thing okay over here?" The manger asked as he walked over.

Darika answered. "Yes, just a misunderstanding." Keith and Corey stood toe to toe eye balling each other and not saying a word.

The manager then walked over to them. "Is every thing okay?"

"Yeah, my wife and I were just about to leave. Com'on Darika." Keith said, and grabbed Darika's arm but she wouldn't move. "Darika, either you are going to come with me or I have to carry you out of here. Now let's go."

Darika slowly got up from the booth and grabbed her purse and Keith pushed her toward the door and informed Corey of some valuable information. "This is my wife and she will always be no matter how good you fuck her."

"Darika, call me," Corey yelled. "I'll kill you, Keith, man if you hurt her."

Keith threw Darika in the car as if she was a rag doll and slammed the door. Corey stood watching them as Keith pressed his foot down on the accelerator and drove off in anger. Being stopped by the police as he drove 55 in a 35 mph speed zone was the least of his worries. If they gave him a ticket, he would only have Judge Beasley, Johnson, or Pinkett pull it for him they were close friends of his they were members of the same country club. He began beating the steering wheel and gripping it so that he wouldn't reach over and push her head through the window.

"Take me to my car."

"No, I'm going to take you to get your things from out of my house and then I'll take you to get your car."

"You had no right."

"Like hell I didn't. I had all the right in the world. You attacked me because you thought Cathleen Wright and I were sleeping together."

"You were . . . I saw you two laughing at Marllows and checking into a hotel."

So that explained why he felt like he was being watched. "You were there. That was a business meeting."

"Didn't look like it to me. How and why you two ended up at the Ritz?"

"So you're the anonymous lady that tipped her husband off?" He wanted to thank her but it didn't matter now. He had caught her with another man. "Do you realize you 're sleeping with one of your teachers. He's almost young enough to be your son. Is it the fact that you can't have children, so you want to sleep with one."

"Age doesn't matter. You screwed Andrea, she was young enough to be your daughter."

"Is that what this is all about? He's one of your teachers and that matters. If anyone ever finds out about it, sistah, just kiss your job good-by. So who in the hell is Mark?"

"He's another man I'm fucking."

Keith looked at her out of the corner of his eyes. "But you said he was gay."

"I lied. I can do the same thing you can but I can do it better. You had no clue until you decided to follow me. Keith I don't need you anymore and it hurts you like hell. Face it, your ego is shattered. Your wife who you thought couldn't get no other man was fucking around on you."

"Shut the hell up you slut."

"So I'm a slut now?"

"How could you do this to me?" He asked.

"The pretty boy Keith, ain't as handsome as he used to be. His wife chose a young thing over his thing," she chuckled. "and you thought I was so ugly that you had to go and sleep with all the light skin women that came your way. Tell me how does it feel to have been made a fool of, and it happened right under your nose."

Keith pressed his foot on the breaks. "Now I'm telling you once again to shut the hell up." He had turned red

"In your own house. In your own bed. My mama and Cookie will get a kick out of this one. Now you see what it feels like. But aren't you just curious about how long it's been going on? As long as you've been sleeping with Andrea, Marissa Cathleen and who ever else you've been screwing. I wasn't going to take it lying down this time. Remember love don't love nobody."

Before both of them had realized what had happened, Keith's hand flew from the steering wheel and pushed her head into the window without any excessive force but the pain was felt by both of them.

"You didn't have to hit me. You had no right," she cried, while holding her head.

"You didn't have to talk to me like that either," he said, as he pulled over on the side of the road. "There were others, Darika? Mark was calling my house. You're boasting about doing it under my nose. In my bed. Who else did you sleep with, so that I can knock the hell out of you again? Andrea, and Marissa has nothing to do with this. I haven't seen those two women since God knows when you messed that up. But you gave me what I deserved and I'm going to be smarter than you and leave. I don't have to put up with this shit. You lost out. You've needed me for all of these years, I never needed you. You'll hear from my attorney first thing Monday morning I want a divorce and I don't want to see you or even hear from you. The next time we'll see each other is in court.

"I want the house."

He looked at her and shook his head in disgust "You ain't getting shit I'll burn it down before you see any parts of it.

She saw the seriousness in his eyes. "You low-down bastard." She jumped on top of his head and began beating him.

When they pulled into the driveway, they both jumped out of the car as if they could go another round. Keith had a cut above his left eye from Darika's ring. She had a knot the size of a plum on the side of her head from when he pushed her into the window, and her lip was bleeding from his back hand slap after she slapped him as hard as she could. Kelvin was lying on the sofa with his two-year mistress Cidney. They both jumped off the sofa when Darika and Keith walked into the house. Keith looked as bad as Darika did. It was their second fight that night.

"What happened?" Kelvin asked. "Were y'all in an accident?"

"There's your shit. Get it and get out," Keith told Darika as he huffed and puffed with anger. "Anything that you find missing you'll find it at the women's shelter,"

"I got my own, brotha, you want find me at no shelter. I prepared myself for this."

"What in the hell is going on?" Kelvin asked again. He ran into the bathroom downstairs to get his brother a towel to wipe the blood from his face.

"You were right. She was screwing one of her teachers," he told Kelvin and walked up the stairs to put a bandage over his eye.

"Male or female?" He asked.

"Don't you worry about that," Darika advised Kelvin.

Cidney handed her a cold towel for the knot on her head and her swollen lip.

"Don't you give her shit," Kelvin said, as he snatch the towel away from Darika's hand and threw it across the room.

"One of the youngest teachers in the school," Keith yelled from upstairs. "She was screwing him."

"You slut. Get your shit and leave," Kelvin ordered her.

Darika looked at him and rolled her eyes. She knew not to say a word to Kelvin out of the way. His type was quick tempered and the beating he might put on her might just be severely. With Keith being angry with her he would probably stand back and watch without saying a word. She had seen the types of beatings his wife had gotten from her quick tongue. Darika and Kelvin hated each other with a passion.

Keith walked back down the stairs slipping his shirt over his head carefully, trying not to hit his eye. "And what make it so bad, the nigga has been in my house. And this nigga over here," he said, pointing at Darika. "Bragging about how she played me for a fool and was sleeping with the nigga in my bed." He dropped his head and thought about what she had said and pulled the 45 caliber pistol out of his pocket and pointed it at her.

Cindey screamed and Darika began to cry pleading with him to put the gun away.

"I'll kill you," He warned her.

"Bro, put the gun up. This is crazy. Just let her get her things and get out of here. It ain't worth it."

"I'm going to kill him too."

"Please, Keith don't do this," Cindey cried. "You have to think. You two were married and y'all have had problems and you've gotten over them. You've hurt her and now she has hurt you but not intently. You know Darika loves you. Sleeping with this other man was her way of getting your attention."

Kelvin looked at Cidney and muttered. "Shut the hell up."

She rolled her eyes at him. "She never thought you cared about her, she always had that doubt in the back of her mind with you fooling around. Killing her because you now feel her pain is not the way. Please, don't do this. Think."

"Bro, listen to her."

Keith thought about what Cidney had said and he sighed as he lowered the gun from Darika's head back into his pocket. Darika grabbed up what she could and ran outside screaming and Cidney ran behind her.

"Give me the keys, bro. I'll take her home." Keith handed Kelvin the keys and dropped his head. "Go upstairs and get you some rest and we will talk in the morning."

"Yeap," Keith nodded. Before walking up the stairs, he walked over to the bar and grabbed his bottle of Hennessy and walked up to his bedroom with his head hanging low. Kelvin watched him feeling his pain. He had just gone through the same thing two weeks ago.

"Get your ass in the car," he ordered Darika as he walked outside with one of her bags she had left behind.

"But she still has some more things she need to get, baby."

"Forget them we'll mail'im to her."

Darika slowly walked to the passenger side of the car looking back at Cidney as if that was going to be Cindey's last time seeing her alive. She waved good-bye to Cindey and thanked her for saving her life.

On two wheels, Kelvin took her back to the school and dropped her off. He was in such a rush to get her out of his sight, he helped her get her things out of the car by dumping them onto the ground. Darika was afraid of who might drive by and see them, so she quickly picked them up as fast as he dumped them. After all her clothes were out of the car, Kelvin speeded off into the night.

CHAPTER TEN

"Jabari, get your ass up. I'm only going to tell you one'mo time before I come in there and get you up myself," Beverly yelled from her bedroom as she neatly placed her shoes back into their shoe box. "And that was my last time telling you then."

He knew she meant business so he pulled his long slender body from his full size bed and sat on the edge of it waiting for her to bust through his closed door.

"I don't like the fact you sleep more than me anyway. You flunk out of school and think you are going to come here and sleep all day, brotha you better think again. Did you go looking for a job today? You do know you got to get the hell out of here. I've gotten used to not raising a child or a grown man," she said, flipping through the unopened envelops from solicitors. "I send you to college and your ass flunk out like some fool. Hell, you had already spent two extra years there then you decide you want to drop out."

"Damn, and I got to hear this shit from yo'ass," he mumbled, and pulled his long dreadlocks back off his round yellow face.

"So how was your luck with finding a job today?" She asked him as she busted through his door.

"It was so-so," he said, looking down at the floor.

"So-so," she repeated. "What do you mean so-so, either you have prospects or you don't. Jabari, don't lie to me."

"I'm not lying. Am I gon'have to hear this every day?"

She looked around his room that looked like a cyclone had gone through it and rolled her eyes to the back of her head before giving him an answer. "As long as you are in my house yes. You will hear every thing I have to say and if you don't like it, get out." Clean and dirty clothes scattered all over the floor and hanging over the back of his desk chair told her he hadn't grown up a bit since he's gone off to college. He was still as nasty as he was when he was a teenager and she used to clean up behind him. She stepped into the room and nearly broke her neck as she slid across rap and video game magazines buried underneath clothes on the floor. Several pairs of his size eleven sneakers sitting under his bed caused the room to smell like a garbage dump. Poster of sports figures plastered the egg-shell colored walls with red thumb tacks. She felt like telling him right then to pack his things and get out. He had made her once clean kept guest room into a pigpen.

"Man, you are tripping."

"Not enough. Clean up this room, and now." She slammed his door and stormed back across the hall to her room.

She was angry with herself and him. She was the blame for him turning out to be a self-centered, irresponsible, mama's boy. If she wouldn't have listened to her mother about him growing up to hate her because she beat his ass every time he got out of line, he would probably be a lot more responsible than he is now. No matter how hard she tried to give him the best, he couldn't even show her his appreciation by graduating from college and making something of himself. He insisted on dropping out of school to become some rapper.

She flopped down in the oversized purple chair in the lounge area of her bedroom and took one sip of wine and let out a sigh of relief. Wine was the only thing that could relax her mind after a hard day's work of color coordinating, sketching designs for seasons in advance, meeting the demands of store buyers and setting up fashion shows. Who said owning your own business was easy, she thought, when there are deadlines to be met, decisions to be made, and long work hours. There was more stress working for herself than working for anyone else. Nevertheless, there were rewards for her hard work and accomplishments. Vogue and the Cosmopolitan fashion editors had given her a great fashion review in the New York Times after her fashion show last night. They called her "An extraordinary fashion designer with class and elegance that was sure to go far." The review had made her day after so many had doubted her ability as a black fashion designer to last no more than a season. She had thought about cutting out the review and mailing it to several people who had advised her to find another profession. Yet she would only be dancing to their music if she had done that and their music was not her taste. She was on top of the world now and as far as she could tell life was beautiful there. Orders came in today by the dozens and she was right beside her ten staffs of amateur designers and shippers to pack up the orders. She had signed several contracts with Bloomingdales, Neiman Marcus, Saks Fifth Avenue, Marshall Fields and Nordstorms to carry her designs. For several years she fought for recognition in the large dominated white industry and now she was there. She jumped up from the chair and danced around the room to the sweet music of success that played in her mind.

As she got undress to do her daily chorus, she took off her clothes piece by piece, she stood in the mirror admiring her petite lean caramel toned body and she was pleased with what she saw. Each day she comes home from the studio she would get undressed in front of the mirror with a glass of wine and music from the seventies in the background. She stood gazing at herself as if she was the perfect Mona Lisa. She cupped her perfect breast that still stood at attention after one child and at the age of thirty-seven. The thought of losing her breast to cancer came over her and she said a silent prayer for the Lord to protect them. The deadly disease seemed to have already attacked three women in her family, her grandmother, aunt Rose, and her cousin Brenda. Beverly did her monthly mammogram after each months period and she visits her doctor every six months. She never felt so much fear as she does when she's lying on the doctor's table and watching his stern face as he pressed down on her breast and studies her x-rays while making sure there are no lumps. Her butt was still round and tight. She could look down and see the hairs on her vagina without sucking in her stomach. She did have a small pouch for a gut but it wasn't as big as her behind so it was hardly noticeable. For thirty-seven she had the body of a twenty-year-old and she was pleased. She just wished she had the energy of a young woman. She threw on her jogging pants and a T-shirt and headed downstairs to prepare dinner.

She hated cooking and slaving over a hot stove. However, she had to do it to keep her husband happy or more like to keep the arguments to a minimum. If she could have gotten away with it, she would buy a freezer full of Mrs. Swanson's TV dinners and cold cuts for sandwiches and tell him to fend for himself. Knowing him he would need for her to put the frozen dinners in the oven for him or place the meat on the bread. He acts like he cannot do anything for himself. And it's only the fault of his mother who has spoiled him rotten. And that will be the same thing some woman says about her if she doesn't make her son get out and stand on his own two feet. She dumped the hamburger in a skillet to brown it, grabbed a box of Hamburger Helper from the pantry and whipped it up within fifteen minutes, chopped up some lettuce and tomatoes for a salad and baked some Brown'n Serve rolls. It took nothing to please her husband he would eat anything she cooked. Unlike some of her girlfriends husbands who want them to cook a big Sunday dinners every night, Gene was pleased with whatever. There were dishes scattered in the sink from no one other than Jabari who she doesn't allow to wash them afraid she might catch "Jackman Poison."

She stared at her reflection in the kitchen window and nearly went crazy at what she saw. Her hair looked a mess. She wondered if anyone noticed last night, she sure as hell didn't or she would have put on a hat. She flew that hussy to New York to fuck up her head, she thought. It was cut too close to her scalp. Anyone could see what she was thinking, because they could see her brain. "That's what you get for messing with family." She pulled the small hand held mirror from the drawer and ran to the bathroom. And turned her back toward the bathroom mirror while she used the hand held mirror to scan her head. "What in the hell did she do to my head?" She screamed. Brenda, her cousin and sometimes beautician, for this very same reason had cut her hair entirely too short after she told her not to. The style in the magazine wasn't that short, she thought, while trying to comb her hair with her fingernails that sanked into her scalp. Steam formed from her ears and nostrils. She ran back into the kitchen and picked up the phone to call Brenda. They had fallen out once before when she cut Beverly's hair too short and they didn't speak for months so Beverly was prepared for them to fall out again.

She dialed the number in anger.

"Cuts R'Us, Brenda speaking how may I help you?"

"You did it again. And I flew your ass to New York to make a fool of me."

"Beverly, what are you talking about, girl? What have I done now?"

"You think because you don't have no hair everybody else shouldn't have any. Last night I looked like a fool in front of all those people and I didn't know it. Now how in the hell am I supposed to be in CiCi's wedding with the shortest hair of all the other weave wearing bridesmaids? The wedding is in four weeks and my hair doesn't grow like grass so it's still going to look like it is today. You know what I look like, a damn man with processed hair."

She was over exaggerating but that was the only way she could get her point across.

"You cut my hair too short and it's not even in the style I asked you to cut it in—you did your version and fucked my head up."

"I didn't hear you complaining last night."

"Because I didn't notice. Cousin or no cousin you did a shabby job."

"I'm not going to even let you bother me today. I have a shop full of people and I don't want them to hear me curse you out," she muttered through her teeth. "What do you want me to do, weave you some tomorrow."

"Hell no, I don't want you to cash the check I wrote you for this mess."

She laughed. "Now you are talking stupid. That check is already deposited in my bank."

"Well, pay me back. Brenda, I kid you not. I'm not satisfied."

"You're never satisfied. I cut hair. I don't create miracles. If you wanted your hair just like the chic in the book, you should have gone to her beautician. Don't call me talking no mess, Beverly. You received the services and you didn't complain then and I don't want to hear it now. You can come in tomorrow and let me weave it to achieve it or you can shut-up and work with what you got." She yelled and all her customers began looking into her mouth hanging on her every word.

"Cousin or no cousin I am a paying customer and you are not going to talk to me like that. I tell you what. I tell you what, you keep that money but, sistah, you won't get another dime out of me because I won't step foot up in your shop ever again."

"Fine because I don't need a complaining person like you in here anyway. You know what, you make my ass itch, Beverly."

"And you make mine too, with your no doing hair ass." Beverly slammed the phone down and began pacing the kitchen floor while cursing under her breath. She was furious. She flopped down so hard at the kitchen table she hurt her tailbone.

After she had promised herself and him he was not to eat any of the food she had bought, she yelled for Jabari to come and eat dinner anyway. He did look a little malnourished when she was talking to him in his bedroom. She stared at him as he charged down the stairs into the kitchen like a raging bull. He gave her a smile and began to fix his plate. Amazed at how much he looked like his sorry low-down daddy, who couldn't understand the meaning of no from a thirteen-year old girl, she rolled her eyes at him. She tried to suppress the thought of his father forcing her shorts down, and forcing himself inside her, but looking at Jabari reminded her of that summer day she was raped. Jabari had all of his features the 6 feet tall frame with light skin, slanted eyes and broad shoulders. Beverly hoped Jabari was nothing like him in character or she was really in trouble.

"Baby, how do you think mama's hair look?"

He had his face buried down in his plate not looking up at her. "It's cool."

"You haven't even look at it."

He slowly raised his face from his plate and fell back in his seat and stared at her hair. "It's cool. Cousin Brenda, did it didn't she?"

"Yes, don't you think it's too short?"

"Mom, you've always had short hair."

"I did not until she cut it all off. You know she has something against me. I truly believe she's jealous of me. She's been that way since we were kids."

He sighed and ran his hand over his black dreadlocks. Let his mother tell it there was always someone jealous of her even when she was struggling just like everyone else and had nothing.

"My mama could afford to buy me designer clothes; hers couldn't, so she would push me down to get mines dirty. I'm married, she's not. I have one child, she has three."

"And don't forget you're rich."

"Don't be funny with me, boy. She's struggling to keep that shop open and I've sent her customers upon customers and she messes up my head. Now what type of mess is that?"

Jabari shrugged his shoulders.

Eugene walks through the door. "What's up gang?"

"Do you see a gang in here?" She asked him and rolled her eyes so hard that they hurt.

"Well, excuse me. Hello, Beverly. What's up, Jab?"

"Mom's bitching about her hair."

"Watch your mouth before I slap you in it." She has been giving him that warning since he's moved back into the house two weeks ago. "I'm the only one that can curse in this house. What's wrong with you, have you lost yo' mind?"

"No, we're both adults and besides it's nothing but a word. Shit, damn, ass."

"Keep being smart if you want to, boy and you'll find you and your shit outside."

He shrugged his shoulders and resumed his position over his plate. He knew his mother was crazy and he could only go so far with her.

Eugene laughed. "He's right Beverly. It's nothing but a word."

She looked at him and rolled her eyes once again. She was still pissed with him for not saying anything to Jabari for dropping out of college and allowing him to move back into the house. After thirteen years, he had no business still trying to be Jabari's friend. Now was the time for him to be his daddy and put his foot in his ass for being stupid.

"Your hair looks nice, baby," Eugene said, as he kissed her on the forehead.

"No, it doesn't, Gene," she snapped.

"And you're right," he said, smiling and shaking his head because no matter what he said she would never agree. He had come to realize just because he would say the sky was blue, she would argue it was red.

After thirteen years, snappy annoyed remarks and eye rolling was an accepted gesture from Beverly toward Gene every time he says or goes to say a word. She had done it so much she didn't realize their friends began to notice and they had brought it to her attention. What she felt toward him was deeper than the small things. He would say to irk her. She hated he wasn't the man she wanted him to be. A man who didn't let the world along with her push him over. She had very little respect and love for him as a husband. Obligations caused her to stay married to him after all he had done for her and Jabari.

His appearance that has always been a factor caused problems. For many of women it wouldn't matter as long as he treats them with respect and takes care of home, but for Beverly it was an issue. Gene was husky, with a small afro,a gut that wouldn't

disappear and he wore wide frame glasses. His appearance reminded her of someone in the seventies. She tries to tell him to
change with the time but he refuses. He's the first black person
she's known to make millions and not look it. If it wasn't for her,
making him trade that damn Oldsmobile in for a Jaguar, he would
still be driving it.

Of course she realized over the years, he had to gain a couple
of pounds and become more boring than he already was. She at
least thought she would love him for it. It's sad to say she has no
more love for him than she did when he asked her to marry him
thirteen years ago. She asks herself plenty of times why she had
even said yes when she looks at how unhappy she is with him
now. Then she looks at the beautiful house, the cars, and her career, and she knows she wouldn't be where she is today if she had
said no. Jabari would have never had the chance to flunk out of
college because she wouldn't have had the money to send him.

Gene's money played a major role in making her life better.
She was a twenty- five-year-old single parent raising a twelve-
year old boy, living from pay check to pay check on a bank teller's
salary. The men she loved were just as broke as she was and they
weren't trying to marry her. So when Gene walked into the bank
where she worked and asked her out to dinner she refused because of what she hates about him today. After pulling up his
account and realizing he could possible help her pay her rent for
that month, she accepted and one thing led to another. A year
later she had a wedding for a princess, a wedding in which she
thought she would dream of having.

Nothing about him made her want to jump on him and wrap
her legs around his waist the minute he walked through the door.
Nothing about him struck a match to her ass and brought out the
hot side she knew she had as she fantasized about being with
other men.

Another woman she never worried about although she knew
there was some lonely woman out there willing to love him the
way she didn't. There was no doubt in her mind Eugene loved her
and wouldn't dare think of anyone else besides Lynn Whitfield
and Oprah Whinfrey, women he couldn't possible have. Plenty of

times she has wished there was another woman in the picture. It would surly give her a break from having to have sex with him or having him always wanting to be under her.

Beverly has admitted to herself that she had married Gene for all the wrong reasons and she was staying married to him for the same. While most of her friends are divorced and on their second marriage, she ain't trying to be in their situation. She couldn't hang with the Jones when it comes to divorce, not that she doesn't believe in it, but she ain't no fool. All the years she's been married to Gene she has never wanted for anything. The minute they were married he allowed her to stay at home and be a full time wife and mother, he put her through college, gave her money to start her career and bought her a beautiful home in the suburbs of D.C.

She watched Gene and Jabari hover over their plates like lions over their prey and she decided she would rather be doing something better. She walked upstairs to take a hot bath and relax her mind. The warm bottle of wine sitting on her vanity she grabbed it and took it in the bathroom with her. She made sure she locked the door behind her because she didn't want Gene barging in trying to join her. Tonight she didn't feel like being bothered; she just wanted to be alone. She dimmed the bathroom lights and cut on the radio to 104.7, Motion of Love. Teddy Pendergrass *Turn Off the Lights* was just going off and she hated she had missed it. That was her song. It was that song she had sex in her aunts backyard. Jared, A.K.A. "The Love Doctor" had come on and his voice sent chills up her spine and between her legs. She had never seen him before, but she could imagine him to be sexy and fine with a voice so deep and comforting. It was a voice she would love to whisper in her ear as he lay on top of her asking "Whose is it?" The water was warm and she had no bubble bath but the Love Doctor's voice made her body melt into the water and break it's roughness. She was enjoying herself. She had drink three glass of wine and the music was playing nonstop. She was in the mood for love. Wine always put her in the mood that was the only way she would initiate sex or even enjoy it with Gene; she had to be intoxicated. Thirteen years they've been married and she has never enjoyed one night of sex with him. She can't remember the last time she had an orgasm. Gene has sucked her toes, flipped her over and rubbed her down, still no gratification. She had felt deprived. Masturbating was the only thing that gave her the satisfication she needed. And she enjoyed it more than having Gene touch her. She sank deeper in the water with her legs open when she heard Gene softly knocking at the door. She sighed and cracked the door halfway to stare at him standing in his boxers. It was nothing sexy about him.

"Can daddy come in?" He asked. Without saying a word she reluctantly opened the door. She went to step back in the tub when he grabbed her and began to kiss her wet body. He loved her breast they are what made her sexy to him. Her body began to melt with passion but his kisses had nothing to do with it. It was the wine. She pulled down his underwear, pushed him over to the chase lounge and straddled over him while placing his sex inside her. Her feet were glued to the wall as if suction cups were on the bottom of them. And her hips began to rock till her wetness met his. She was tired and felt even more intoxicated. She slowly rose and stepped back into the luke warm water to wash the sweat from her body and the wetness from between her legs. Gene sat drained and panting like an animal as she walked out staring at him from the corner of her eye. She knew he would want seconds as soon as he could get it up again so she threw on panties, a long night gown and jumped into bed. She pretended to be sleep when he walked into the bedroom. She dozed off without a warning.

Beverly couldn't keep her eyes open thanks to Gene who kept trying to get on top of her every hour on the hour last night. She could have said yes but she wasn't in the mood. She had a deadline to meet for her spring collection of fine raw silks and cottons. There was a growing demand for her product. Orders needed to be filled to go out but being understaffed she couldn't get them out as fast as the stores needed them. Earl, her gay assistant put pressure on their distributors to produce the orders and ship them out ASAP.

Beverly Haymans were on wedding gowns, men suits and women fashions. They were sold only in specialty stores such as

Neiman Marcus, Sak's, Marshall Fields, Nordstorm and Bloomingdales in five cities. She never thought she would be as large as she is today. Designing was only a hobby she never really had interest in until she was fired as Chief teller. Then she swore never to work for anyone else again. It was her husband who believed in her designs and convinced her she should put her talent to work for her. He put up $60,000 for her to set up, and orders rolled in after she put on her first fashion show.

There was a phone call. It was her mother, Ella yelling about her calling Brenda and getting her upset. She put her mother on hold and told Earl she had to take the call in privacy. She knew she was going to have to get her mother told and she didn't want Earl to hear her do it. She waited for Earl to walk out of the door before she clenched her teeth together and whispered in the phone.

"What is your problem?".

"Do you have me on that speaker phone?" Ella asked.

"No, mama."

"Well, you really made Brenda upset with you. She called me almost in tears." Beverly rolled her eyes to the top of her head and sighed. She could give a damn she was almost in tears when she realized her hair was cut too short. "Beverly, you can't just be calling her up cursing her out like that she's going through a lot these days; she's about to lose that shop, boogie man is giving her problems. They are talking about kicking him out of school for good and her car is about to get repossessed if she doesn't catch up on the payments. She can't help she gets scissor- happy sometimes. Hell, I told you she couldn't do hair along time ago, but you didn't pay me any attention. Her mama called me cursing you out because Brenda called her upset. And I had to curse her out because don't nobody talk about my chile but me. So now me and my sistah ain't talking because of you. I don't even know if she's still going to play BINGO with me tonight or not. I need to call her and ask."

"They'll get over it."

"I don't know, Bev, they were pretty upset. You know Lucy is still pist with you because you didn't buy the bar-b- que for the family reunion last year. She couldn't understand why you and

Gene didn't just put the money up so that all the family could come instead of asking everybody to send fifty dollars."

"The hell with Aunt Lucy and her daughter. She cut off all of my hair."

"Well, baby, you didn't have much hair anyway."

"Mama, I know what I had but now I don't have nothing but scalp."

"All right, if you say so." Her mother knew from the past once Beverly's mind was made up about something no one could change it. She sighed. "I'm getting ready to go to the doctor for my mammogram God knows I pray that they don't find nothing."

"They won't." Beverly prayed because she knew if her mother was diagnose with the disease there was a great chance of her being diagnose with it also one day. She waited for her mother to bring up the argument she and Gene had this morning. She knew he had called her and told her all about how she cursed him out for not letting her get any sleep.

"Eugene, called me this morning." Beverly sighed and dropped her pen. She was really pist now. "He's so sweet and when you blow up at him for no reason you hurt his feelings. Baby, you have a good husband women only wish they had a man as good as Gene."

"Mama, I don't need you or anybody else to tell me about my husband or marriage. And I sure as hell don't appreciate him call-ing you."

"He didn't mean any harm he just can't understand why you didn't want to sleep with him."

"What? Did he tell you that? I open my legs every damn time he wants to lay between them and one night I say no he runs and tell you, my mama, as if I'm some child. And the same damn thing with Aunt Lucy."

"Bev, that's nothing for you to tighten up your ass about. Like I said he meant no harm. Why don't you talk to the man instead of always fussing at him like he's your chile."

"How do you know what I do with my husband?"

"I'm ya'mama. I know you got an attitude," she chuckled and began to cough and choke.

"No disrespect, mama, but how do you know me, you never raised me."

"So you still want to hold that against me, don't you, chile?"

"I have work to do, mama, so let me get off this phone."

"Why do you even call me mama, if you don't think of me as one, Bev? If you want me to feel guilty for running out on you, I do. I should have taken you with me but yo' daddy wouldn't let me. You're just not going to let me live it dow,n are you? Bev, I left you with your daddy because he loved you, not me."

"Yes he did. Daddy was a good man to you."

"We didn't even sleep in the same bed. Why do you think he slept on the sofa every night?"

"Because you were sleeping with his cousin."

"Your daddy never loved me, Beverly. He only married me because I was pregnant with you."

"Do you know what you did to him when you left him for Willi. You want to tell me about how good a husband I have when daddy did every thing for you. You stabbed him in the back by sleeping with his cousin."

"We were drunk things got out of hand."

"No excuse. You fooled around on him every chance you got. I remember seeing you get out of the car with Lonnie Benson when you were supposed to be at Aunt Lucy's. Men called the house every night just disrespecting daddy as if you weren't married to him."

"What went on between me and your daddy is none of your business and I would like it if you would stay out of it. All I'm going to tell you is don't ruin your marriage with that damn attitude you have."

Sarcastically Beverly laughed aloud. "That's none of your concern."

"I hope you don't think he won't fool around. Hell if Bill Cosby did it, so will Eugene Hayman."

"And if he does I wouldn't care." She tried to make herself believe.

"You say that now but just wait until some other woman get your goldmine and treat him like the priceless jewel he is. You'll be sorry."

" I resent you telling me anything. I try so hard but I just can't find it in my heart to forgive you. My daddy loved you so much he blew off his head when you left'im."

"No, he didn't."

"Yes the hell he did. You won't even take the blame."

"Take the blame for what?" Ella yelled. "For years you and everybody else made me the reason for the bastard killing hisself. Yeah I fooled around and he allowed it, because he didn't want me to leave him."

"Why would you leave him he was taking good care of you and he loved you."

"He was a sissy; he and Billie Payne were doing whatever sissy do in Billie's dead mama's house. I know she turned in her grave. I know because I saw'im."

Bye, mama, you are out of yo'mind. My daddy was not gay and I won't let you lie on him. He wouldn't sleep with you be-cause—"

"He was gay, if that's the word y'all call'im today. He was messing with some of his students buying them clothes and sneak-ers to let him play with their little weinies."

"Mama, go to hell and burn there for the lies you are telling." If she could, she would have sent her there today instead of wait-ing for the Lord to take her.

"You want to know why yo'cousin Mike is walking around in women clothing— ask'im. You're daddy touched all over'im. He was a sick bastard. He only killed himself because a student had turned him in."

"I hate you."Beverly said, in slow motion and slammed down the phone and fell back in her chair. Her heart raced and her stom-ach had felt like someone had punched her in it, she was shaking like a leaf on a tree. Her daddy couldn't have been so sick to mess with his own students and he couldn't have been gay. She picked up the phone to call Mike but there was no answer. She knew there was no truth to what her mother had said about her father but she wanted to hear it from Mike.

The sight of watching her father cry and drink himself into a slumber after her mother told him she didn't love him anymore was like having someone jab at her skin with a sharp dagger. She had never seen him cry before until he read the letter Ella had left behind telling him she was leaving him for his first cousin, Willie Cook. Beverly hated her with a passion for hurting her father but he still loved her. Just when Beverly thought her father was moving on with his life an accident happened and he died instantly. Rumor was he had killed himself but Beverly knew it wasn't true she knew her father and knew he would never take his own life. He was a church-going man and he believed in heaven and hell and that, if he had done something such as kill himself, he was going straight to hell. When Beverly left him to go outside and play that day, he was cleaning the gun just as she had seen him do plenty of Saturdays. She remember standing in his bedroom doorway watching him shine it up when she told him how she wished she was old enough to take that gun and go and shoot her mother and Willie with it. Her father didn't hesitate to tell her that wasn't a nice thing to say but he laughed at the idea. It was her turn to jump rope when she heard the shot. Silence fell upon the loud block and everyone gazed at her front door waiting for her father to walk out. Mr. Walker and Jo Jo Jackson jumped up from their card game and ran into her house. She ran behind them but they wouldn't let her past the first stair after they discovered her father lying on the bed shaking with blood gushing from his head.

The day of his funeral Ella showed up in a tight black dress with Willie by her side. No one could believe they had the nerve to walk into the church together let alone show their faces at all. After Aunt Pat and Delois, James's sisters had jumped over more than three pews to beat Ella down, she wished she would have never shown her face either. Beverly laughed from the inside but cried out for them to stop. After seeing her mothers face swell up, as the heels of their shoes tapped dance on it. Beverly didn't know that would be her last time seeing her father's side of the family. Her mother had shipped her to Lagrange, Georgia to live with her Mudear because Willie didn't want her around. And her life became hell. At the age of ten she was raped by her fifteen-year-old cousin, Bug. No one believed her when she tried to explain why there was blood in her panties. She was beaten for telling such a lie. Mudear had put her on a bus back to Harlem where she didn't have a chance. Her mother abused her just for living and at thirteen Willie's, nineteen-year-old brother, Malcom raped her. And killed himself two months after Jabari was born to keep from going to jail.

Beverly hid her pregnancy through that summer by wearing coats and big shirts. She was afraid to tell anyone what had happened. She thought she would be labeled a liar just as her Mudear had called her. It wasn't until Bug raped Rev. Washington's daughter, Patricia, two years later that Mudear called her to apologize, but her apology couldn't bring back Beverly's virginity or childhood. Also, it couldn't keep Malcom from sneaking into her room laying on top of her at night. He felt since no one believed her when she told them about Bug raping her they wouldn't believe her if she had told he had done it also.

After Beverly gave birth to Jabari in the middle of the bathroom floor, Ella came rushing in and nearly fainted. The cry of the baby woke her out of her sleep. Beverly tried to explain as Ella's hands choked her neck and called her a liar. She moved her back to Georgia to live with her sister, Lucy. It wasn't until Lucy called the police and they questioned James before the truth came out. Later that night he was found hanging from his ceiling by his belt. His letter told all; he had raped Beverly.

CHAPTER ELEVEN

All of the women gathered around the male strippers like vultures around raw flesh. They rubbed their hands across their baby- oiled chests getting hot and some even wet by the way they were smiling and their eyes rolling back into their heads. There was something about a bachelorette party with all the alcohol one could drink and men stripping down to nothing but their bare asses that brought out the freak in most middle-aged, middle class, professional women especially the house wives. Most of the women haven't seen much excitement like this since Buck was a calf way back when they enjoyed having sex with their husbands. The male waiters felt like the sex objects they were as hands slapped their tight asses and reached for their hard genitals that bulged through their leopard skin bikinis. Masculinity was on the young bucks side because they were too sexy for the word. They aroused the older women with their tight bodies and their black bow ties hugging their strong black necks. By the look on their faces, they were actually surprised the women were so forward, at least women who looked like they had it all, beauty, a shit load of money, and husbands that worshiped the ground they stood on. When they walked in to serve the women, they didn't think twice that the stuck up women would give them a second look. But if the men knew how to read between the lines they would realize they are just what the women want— ordinary men with sex appeal. Young men they wouldn't mind taking care of for a change.

Beverly was just as hot as all the other women that danced around the club but she sat reserved in a half-lit corner booth sipping on her fourth glass of wine. She hated the fact Patricia Oliver was video taping the party. A bachelorette party wasn't supposed to be captured on video tape. Anything a woman can't hold as a memory in her mind she doesn't need. What if that tape fell into the hands of their husbands, he wouldn't appreciate seeing his drunk wife dancing with one leg on the shoulder of a naked man.

Beverly wanted to join in on the fun and run her hand across a firm chest and push her ass into a man's pelvis but she didn't want to give the other ladies anything to talk about. They were watching her and waiting for her to slip up. They wanted to know if she was as happy as she pretends to be. And if she was she wouldn't be dancing up on a naked man. Although all the women were married to men they claimed made them happy at some point, they were envious of Beverly and her marriage. Gene treated her like something more than a woman who needed the credit cards to make her happy. Beverly was the one that got a new car every two years without the threat of suicide or divorce, her anniversary gifts were trips around the world instead of shopping sprees, and Gene spent time with her without her begging him too. While her girlfriends cursed about the other woman, Beverly consoled them. She was sure there was no other woman in Gene's life. Sex for a diamond, she didn't have to. All she had to say was she wanted a new ring and it was hers. She spent as much money as she wanted without him watching over her spending or cutting up her credit cards. The backstabbing eyes watching her meant nothing because naked men with rods for dicks dancing around nude really did nothing for her. It was her alcohol that caused her to drool over them and the lack of sex appeal in her husband. If she wasn't buzzed, watching them would be just like sleeping with Gene. She got nothing out of it.

Of course she found some of the men to be sexy, but that was before they had taken off their bikinis. Her eyes danced upon one of the waiters every now and then but she would turn her head as soon as he caught her staring. She was embarrassed but intrigued by the fantasy of going to the Ritz Carlton with him for that night and making love to him nonstop and never talking to him again in her life. The thought made her body temperature rise and her legs cross. It was only a thought which she had several times before tonight with some of the men at the Emerald that tried hitting on her.

Cheating and therapy was the answer all the women had found to be the solution to their troubled marriages and lives. Beverly wasn't in a troubled marriage but she was unhappy with it. She couldn't see herself talking to a total stranger about why she doesn't love her husband and hates for him to touch her so therapy wasn't the answer for her. Some of the women at the party had at least been divorced once or twice with the threat of their third one. Divorce and getting half was the in thing for them. It was the advice they gave each other without even thinking twice. Two days from now CiCi will be doing her third walk down the isles of the church. However, she was acting like she was new to the game. Her groom, William DuBois was a doctor who had been married twice already himself and both of his wives still attend the Emerald with their new husbands. For some reason he seems to believe he's found his soul mate in CiCi and they are going to be in the marriage for the long haul but yet he still made her sign a prenuptial. And she signed it.

Darlene, Cici's best friend and maid of honor slid into the booth with Beverly. She had gone all out of her way just as she does everything to throw this party. If it's nothing no one would talk about weeks later, she won't be apart of it. And everyone would talk about this party after Patricia talking ass shows them the tape.

Beverly looked her up and down without realizing it and smiled to keep from laughing. Darlene was a tacky dresser for her husband to have so much long money let her put it. From what Beverly heard, it was his family that has all the money, which meant none of it was his own hard-earned money. Beverly had gone to Darlene's house on several occasions and she can't see why in the hell she even bragged on it. It's no castle. Darlene spent money on things that really doesn't matter like this bachelorette party that only twenty women out of the fifty she invited came to. She and CiCi are the most disliked women at the Emerald so that's one of the reasons why no one showed up. The women Beverly called to meet her at the party refused to come. They didn't care if they were going to have a stripper for every woman and the strippers had bodies of Malik Yoba and faces of Blair Underwood. Beverly only came to get out of the house from Gene and to keep from killing Jabari for wasting her money on his silly ass. It didn't take Darlene long to do what she does best once she scanned the dance floor. With a smile on her face she muttered between her teeth. "Will you look at Rita, if she used some of that energy at home Troy wouldn't be sleeping with everyone in D.C.. She and Katherine both act like they've never seen freedom. You know Katherine's husband asked her for a divorce a couple of months ago."

"I didn't know that," Beverly muttered. "I thought they had such a good marriage. They're always together."

"You and me both but you can't believe everything you hear and half of what you see. You know how it is. Hey girl," Darlene said, and waved at Katherine after she caught her staring at her. "you look good tonight, Kat. I heard she was devastated but I can't tell, can you? If one of these little young boys don't be careful, she might be taking one home to that five-hundred thousand dollar house she won in the divorce. Said Steve cried."

Beverly chuckled. "How do you know so much?"

"Word gets around. You know Jackie's, little boy got kicked out of school for cursing out a teacher? He's a bad ass. I told my little boy not to hang around him anymore."

"Why did you do that?"

"Chile— I don't want my son carrying a bad name because of'im."

"Hello, ladies," Gail Baylor, said in the same professional voice she uses to give the news every night. She was the head anchorwoman on channel 2 news and the prettiest. All the other women including the white women had nothing on her. She was tall, not too thin, with long jet black fine hair, caramel brown complexion, thick black eye brows and elegance. Beverly and Darlene was surprised to see her out.

"What are you doing out? Aren't you supposed to still be honeymooning?" Darlene asked. "I can't believe that husband of yours let you out of his sight or did he just get tired of you already."

"No sweety, I'm married to that man the rest of my life. I don't need a honeymoon to stay cooped up under him. And him getting tired of me, think again." She took a deep breath and sniffed and rubbed her nose for the third time in two minutes.

"Do you have a cold? If so, get from over here. I can't be getting sick. I'm in a wedding in a couple of days."

Gail looked at Darlene and rolled her eyes. "How are you doing Beverly? I haven't had a chance to thank you for the beautiful bridesmaid dresses and my wedding gown. You did a wonderful job. Everyone said how beautiful they were."

"Thank you."

Darlene and Gail directed their attention toward the front of the club where they noticed Darika standing there looking lost.

"Who invited her?" Gail asked.

"Who?" Beverly looked around Darlene to see whom they were talking about. "Isn't she married to the sexy architect? I forget his name."

"Keith Jones," Gail added.

"Not anymore, he's divorcing her," Darlene informed them and then waved at Darika.

"Then I need to be getting a divorce," Gail said, and chuckled. "He's a millionaire and sexy."

"Who invited her?" Beverly asked.

"She's a friend of Balinda Fisher, and Balinda is CiCi's cousin, so Balinda invited her and she isn't even here. She's the one that told me Keith asked Darika for a divorce."

"About time because she's crazy."

"Who are you telling, but everyone wants to go to her parties."

"I don't—I don't like her. She thought I was fooling around with her husband and she came up to the station acting a fool and nearly made me lose my job."

"Girl, you are kidding. How long ago was this?"

"Some years ago."

"Yeah, Balinda told me how she acts a fool over that man."

"She just know who's gon' let her get a way with it," Beverly said and smacked her lips. "I will cut the fool back on her."

"Not with that one you won't," Darlene and Gail said.

"Ah, that's what you think."

"Well, ladies I have to be leaving y'all. I see a couple of women here I haven't spoken to yet. I'll be seeing y'all around."

"Are you coming to the wedding?"

"Wouldn't miss it for the world."

The minute she walked off Darlene began.

"You know why she was doing all of that sniffing and rubbing her nose, don't you? That man got her on that stuff. I heard she didn't want to marry him but she had to because he knew too much about her and she was afraid he might tell it all."

"What is it that he knows, Darlene?"

"He knows why she really sweats the way she does and it has nothing to do with the lights of the cameras. She's on that stuff. She's doing coke,girl. He got a spell of voodoo love on her all right and it ain't nothing she can do about it if she doesn't want her secret revealed. I heard she's not happy with that man. So that explains why she's here and not at home with him. For one thing, they have nothing in common. They're more like Whitney Houston and Bobby Brown, Marie Presley and Michael Jackson— all of them are rich but their character just don't match. This man she's married to—hell I don't even know his name, that's how different they are. He's a mechanic and a backyard one at that. I heard she met him in the grocery store but I don't know how true that is but—"

Beverly had heard the same thing but she didn't want to go into it with Darlene so she changed the subject. "So how is Paul?"

"He couldn't be doing better. No, we couldn't be doing better." She too was into her second marriage. Word had it it wasn't working out but Beverly wanted to hear it come from her. Those damn kids of hers who were so spoiled and controlled her were running the man away.

"What about Gene?"

"He's wonderful."

"Hello ladies."

"Hey, Odessia." Beverly jumped up to hug her. Odessia wasn't a really close friend of hers but they spoke every time they saw each other and Beverly liked her. People often told her she could be Halle Barry's sister and that was no lie. She was just as pretty and sexy. Odessia wasn't mixed, she was all the way black, just had a high yellow daddy and mama. Her hair was cut close to her head and her natural curls seemed like pin curls as they lay on her scalp. Beverly knew she was forty if not damn near but know one could tell if she didn't tell them. Darlene slid over so that she could sit down.

"I'm glad you could make it, although we haven't seen you at the Saturday lunches lately."

"Well, I've only heard from one of you since my surgery. A sistah ain't good for a phone call no more. Thank you, Beverly, for calling me."

"That's what sistahood is about— reaching out to my fellow sistah when she's in need," Beverly said, and took a sip of her wine.

"I thought all my sisters understood that. We're just not here to meet on Saturdays for lunch and sit around and brag about which one of your husbands is the richest and how smart our children are."

"I have a family you know. My children and husband require time," Darlene said. She would never take the blame for anything.

"Well, I wouldn't know anything about that."

"I have a child and a husband also but I knew I had a sistah who was going through a trying time in her life and she needed my support. She needed all of our support."

Darlene sighed. "So how are you feeling now, Odessia?"

"I'm feeling great. I've realized that I can't put my trust in people no matter how much they tell me their going to be there for me. And I've also realized I have a lot of things to be graceful for that's how I pulled myself out of that slump I was in. I've had a wonderful life these forty-one years."

"Forty-one," Beverly replied. "You look great."

"What's so wonderful about your life? You've never been married and you can't have children."

"Darlene, it's more to life than being married and having children. Watch what you're saying."

"That's okay, Bev, I expected Darlene to say something like that. Anyway, I thought my life would be over after the hysterectomy but my life is just beginning. I had to go through something in life so traumatizing as a hysterectomy to realize I have other things to be graceful for other than a uterus. Children are not important to me because out of the forty-one years I've never tried to have any. I could have gotten pregnant at one time in my life if I wanted children but I really didn't care for them much. And marriage, it will come in due time. All of my life I've waited on that perfect man and I haven't gotten him yet. Not to say that he won't come I've wasted a lot of time waiting on him. Life goes on and some things with which you have to be content. You've been married twice and from the talks of things if you don't watch it you might be looking for husband number three."

"Those are lies you are telling. My husband and I are doing fine."

"Whatever."

"I'm glad to see that you're out and about, Dessia. Now I can get you to help me construct the Fall Festival for the children of the Woodmore Homes."

"I don't know about that but we'll talk." They laughed.

"Move so that I can get out," Darlene ordered Odessia.

"Are you upset, Darlene?" Odessia asked, while scooting out of the booth.

"I don't appreciate you trying to put my business in the streets because your life is hell." She rolled her eyes to the point of no return and walked off. Odessia and Beverly began to laugh.

"She's a nut."

"Who are you telling?" Beverly looked at her watch and realized she needed to be getting home. Not that she had a child to put to bed or a husband to cook dinner for or a job to go to tomorrow morning she was actually getting bored. She hugged Odessia goodnight and waved goodbye to some of the other women she associated with and walked toward the door. The waiter she had been staring at all night bumped into her while she dug in her purse for her keys.

"Excuse me," he said, and smiled. Beverly smiled back and kept on walking. Temptation was there but she couldn't give in to it even if she wanted to.

When Beverly got in, she stopped by Jabari's room to check on him. She hadn't done that since he was a baby. She stood over him feeling very proud of how handsome he had become because God knows as he was growing up she was worried. She woke him.

"Baby, wake up."

"Mama, I'm asleep. Get out of here." He threw the pillow over his head and buried his face into his sheets.

"Wake up baby." She couldn't remember the last time she called him baby. "Mama wants to talk to you." Or the last time they had a one on one conversation without her cursing him out about something.

"In the morning. I'm sleep."

She was tired of playing with him "Jabari, wake up," she said, with a stern commanding voice.

He struggled to open his eyes. "What's going on?"

"You would tell mama if someone ever touched you in a way that it would make you feel uncomfortable, wouldn't you?"

"It depends."

"Jabari, what are you talking about? It depends on what? No one has any business touching you."

"Ma, I'm twenty-two years old. Tangy, can touch me all she wants; she wants me you know that? It's because she works for you is why she won't give me any play but if I was any ole'niggah on the street. . ."

"What did I tell you about that word? I'm not talking about that type of touch, Jabari. I'm talking about someone molesting you."

"Hell nawh! I'll killa a niggah over some bullshit like that."

"Watch your mouth before I punch you in it."

"Mama, chill, everybody curses in front of their parents these are the 90s and I'm grown."

"Don't make me knock hell out of you boy."

"Who touched somebody? Anyway."

"Nobody, I'm just trying to make sure nobody touched you as a child and you just didn't tell me."

"The nigga ain't dead. I know that's how cousin Mike turned fruity, I'm far from fruity, mom."

"I know you better be."

"Now can I go back to bed, now that we know no one has touched me?"

"Yes." She kissed him on his forehead.

CHAPTER TWELVE

Turning forty had Keith feeling stressed and old. To him he wasn't the young blackanova he used to be some odd years ago when he could pull any woman he wanted. Now he finds out light skin brothas are out and dark skin is in. And women are just not falling for the same lines they used to when a brotha could buy them a drink and flatter them with his personality. Now they want to see the money along with a ring for marriage. At Keith's age he felt he was too old to be trying to start over and remarry and he damn sure wasn't going to take care of a woman. He hated turning old, and getting gray hair or even gaining the chance of having prostate cancer. Last month he had gone for his yearly exam and he was fine. He hoped it stayed that way for the rest of his life. He would just give up on sex and women altogether if he had to use a machine to rise to the occasion. So far he has done well about not losing any hair or his teeth. On occasions he still had twenty-five year old women trying to talk to him but he had turn them down. A younger woman is not apart of his agenda these days. He had discovered along

time ago when he was fooling around with Andrea they are looking for a father figure and not a man. And they don't know anything about pleasing a man sexually.

He stood in the mirror combing through his natural wavy hair
looking for gray strands that told his age but he didn't see any.
Thank God, or he probably would have hit the floor. For the first
time in ten years, he didn't get up to do his five miles run; he had
slept in and he didn't feel guilty for it. Even if he wanted too, he
couldn't pull himself out of bed. He was forced against his will to
sleep in and lay staring up at the ceiling. When he sat on the edge
of the bed and placed his feet on the floor, he couldn't stand. He
thought about his life and became depressed. He wished he was
dead. He was now single and going through a divorce after ten
years. There was no one other than his family to leave all of his
accomplishments to because he had no children. He had loved
Darika that much to have given up something he wanted more
than all his money and success. And she stabbed him and left him
for dead. Keith couldn't understand what he was going through.
One day he's feeling fine about the situation and the next day he's
thinking about it and getting depressed.

If this was the type of depression that had Darika prisoner of
her own life and happiness, he could finally relate because it was
trying to attack his being. Today he just felt like being alone and
not answering his phone. Yesterday his employees gave him a
surprise birthday luncheon and he nearly cursed them all out for
doing so. There was no need for him to celebrate a birthday he
was turning old and he was alone.

Somehow he managed to pull himself out of bed after laying
there for three hours trying to force himself to sleep. He got dressed
and drove himself around with no destination. He stopped at his
barber, and ordered him to cut his hair close to his scalp, and to
remove all of his facial hair. The new look made him look five
years younger than twenty-five. He smiled at himself in the mirror
and tipped his barber fifteen dollars. He then had gone to the car
dealership and gotten himself a black Range Rover and had his
Porche painted purple. Most mid- life crisis' men favorite color is
red but Keith thought he would be different. He had never been a

depressed type of person. He had life figured out and nothing about it could get him down so he had to be going through some type of mid-life crisis, the way he figured it. He had toned down his conservative look from the slacks, the Polo button- shirt, and the Cole Hann loafers to black Versace jeans, a white T-shirt to match, and black Gucci loafers. With his new look he was beginning to feel a little bit better. In fact, he was feeling a lot better. He had tipped the sales person forty dollars for hooking him up with his new look.

He now had an appetite so he drove to Marllows feeling very confident that he was still the handsome Keith Jones he used to be. The young waitress was pleased to escort him to his seat. She even tried smiling at him but Keith paid her no attention because she was white and young. Keith followed her to his table in the corner. While looking straight ahead as she led the way, he nearly knocked Beverly down as she was walking toward the door.

"Excuse me," he said, looking down into her eyes and smiling. She must have come to his chest in height.

"Knock me down next time why don't you," She told him and laughed. "I know I'm short but not that short."

"You should be a little bit taller and people wouldn't walk all over you." He told her and laughed.

"You're not a giant yourself."

"I'm just taller than you."

They both laughed.

She looked closely at him trying to figure out where she had seen him before. "You know you look so familiar," The hair cut and his shave and the jeans and T-shirt threw her off.

Keith knew who she was; she was the drop dead sexy woman in that tight- fitting dress he saw at the Gala a couple of years ago. He was surprised she didn't know who he was, or was she just pretending not to know. So he pretended not to know who she was. "So do you," he said, walking over to his table as he pulled her along and sat her down.

"Yes, I know you, you designed Sarita and Carl's house. You did such a beautiful job. You still attend the Emerald don't you?"

"Yes, but I hardly ever go. I'm very busy."

She looked down at his hand and noticed a ring print on his wedding finger. "Having lunch alone?"

Keith nodded and she gave him a strange look for no reason at all. She wasn't even aware of her expression.

"Is something wrong with that, didn't you eat alone?"

"No, I met some of my friendgirls here. We go to lunch together every now and then. Where is your wife?"

He chuckled. "You haven't heard, we're divorced."

"What do you mean I haven't heard?" she snapped. "Was I supposed to?"

"I just know how the people are at the Emerald, very nosey and gossipers."

"I didn't know who you were let alone if you were divorced or not and I'm not nosey, nor do I gossip. I couldn't care less about your life." She was getting huffy with him insinuating she has time to dig in his business.

"Why are you getting an attitude if that's not your character? Don't worry about it but I just know how news travel."

"How is your husband, Gene Hayman, I believe his name is? The computer programmer."

"He's fine, thank you."

"That's great." The waitress brought him a glass of water and a menu.

"You're right, news does travel around the Emerald and sometimes I don't believe it until I hear it from the horses mouth. And since you've said it pretty much and your actions show it I believe it. Have you ever heard you are arrogant and rude?"

He chuckled and took a sip of his sweet tea. " Well, you know what, Beverly, my daddy has always told me opinions are just like assholes. Everybody has one. No, but thank you for informing me."

"Have a nice day. Mr. Jones."

"So you do know my name." She looked at him and rolled her eyes before walking off.

Keith was finally going to celebrate his birthday. It wasn't at the place he perferred but it would do as long as his brother was buying the drinks. Kelvin had persuaded him to join him at the strip club downtown where they could get free table dances all night and all the chicken wings they could eat. Since Keith's been out of college, he hasn't stepped foot in a strip joint but tonight will be his first in thirteen years. He was excited, but not about seeing naked women he couldn't touch, stand on top of his table, dancing around nude and enticing his nature to have one of them. Keith was excited about having his life back and being able to change it. As he drove around town today, for the first time in his life he had a chance to look at his life for what it was really worth outside of all of his success. And it was worth nothing. He was unhappy and he never loved Darika like a man should his wife or he never would have fooled around on her. He stayed with her as long as he did because he felt sorry for the life she had to live with thinking every one hated her because she was dark skin. He wanted to be the one man to make her feel beautiful and loved, but he couldn't because he didn't love her. Keith thought he could make it right for her but instead he had entrapped himself to be obligated in making her happy. She cheated on him and it was good that she did because he never would have left her completely alone if she wouldn't have. Keith was impressed by his observation of his life. He couldn't understand why people go out and pay a psychiatrist to tell them things about themselves that they already know if they just take the time out to analyze their lives.

Keith turned up his Michale Franks' CD, poured himself another glass of cognac and jumped into the shower. He heard his door bell rang through the intercom in his bathroom. He grabbed his towel and wrapped it around his wet body and ran down the stairs to the door. He was expecting his brother. He sprang open the door and to his surprise it was his next door neighbor, Wanda Hendricks.

"Hello,"

"Hi," she said, while sizing him up. "I'm sorry, were you expecting me to be someone else?"

"Yeah, I thought you were my brother." He looked down at his towel and felt embarassed. "Excuse me."

"No problem at all. It seems like another fuse has blown over at my place and I was just wonder if you had some candles or a flash light."

"Sure. Come in and make yourself at home while I look for them." Keith closed the door behind her and walked into the kitchen. He hardly saw Wanda with her being in and out of town every other week on work. She's been his next door neighbor for the last four years and they've never really said any words except for "hello" and "good-by." And they said those many words when Darika wasn't around. Darika accused Wanda of wanting Keith because she was single and needed a man to help her raise her three sons.

"Your house is just as beautiful in person as it is in the magazines," Wanda yelled into the kitchen. "Did you hire someone to do the decorating or did your wife do it?"

"I did it." He gathered up most of the candles Darika had in the kitchen drawer. But he had no idea where the flash light was.

She laughed. "Then you have wonderful taste."

"Thank you."

She acknowledged the music playing. "Michale Franks, St. Elmo's Fire. I love him."

"He's one of the best," Keith yelled.

"For a white guy." She spotted his drink on the coffee table. "What are you drinking?"

"A VO Supreme cognac. You're more than welcome to help yourself to a glass if you want. The glasses are behind the bar." He remembered he had left the flash light in the laundry room after he finished fixing the dryer last week so he ran down to the laundry room to get it.

"I think I will. I haven't had a drink in four years since my divorce was final. I almost forgot what good cognac taste like."

Keith ran back up with the flash light.

"I think these should be enough candles for you until you get that fuse fixed. I can fix it for you if you would like. Just give me a couple of minutes to run upstairs and put on me some clothes."

"Thank you, if it's no trouble."

"None at all."

Keith ran upstairs to throw on a pair of shorts and a T-shirt. When he walked back downstairs Wanda was playing a game of chess. "What do you know about chess?"

"May I tell you, I know a lot about chess. Now fix me another one of those drinks while I show you."

"Show me? Nobody shows Keith Jones anything about chess I'm a master." He poured both of them a drink and took a seat across from her waiting his turn to show her a thing or two.

They had played three matches and gone through a whole bottle of cognac before Keith realized he should have met Kelvin an hour ago. Chess was his game and once he started playing it was hell trying to tear him away. He strategically studied the board before making his next move.

"Would you please make a move."

"Hold up, don't rush me." He continued to take his time.

"I can't believe I'm sitting here with you," she said, looking very amazed at how handsome he was.

"Why not?" He asked before he made his move. "Check."

"You are the one who helped me get through my divorce whether you know it or not. Check."

"What did I do?"

"I used to watch you and tell myself that's what I want in a man and not what I had. I envied Darika for having everything."

"On the outside looking in you thought she did. Check."

"So true. I saw you put her out a couple of nights ago. She hasn't been back since. Except for when she came to get her things."

"So that's why you have the nerve to come over here and ask for candles and a flash light. You knew she wasn't here, didn't you?"

They both laughed.

"She had every right to think I wanted you," she said, and smiled. "Look at you, what woman wouldn't. Me and three other ladies in the neigborhood have a book club and we all talk about how sexy you are. They don't know I watch you every morning when you take your run. Check. You didn't run this morning, why?"

"I didn't feel like it, but I thought you were out of town the majority of the time?"

"I am but when I'm here I watch you."

Keith was flattered but he wasn't impressed. He's never looked at her twice. She was tall, big boned and far from his type. Even in his drunkeness he wasn't finding her attractive. He didn't know how to respond to her so he somewhat let what she was saying go over his head.

"Check," Keith said, and waited on her to make her move.

"I hope I'm not scaring you with all of this."

She wasn't but Keith wished she would stop with the crazy looks she was giving him and all the talk about how she likes him because she was making him feel sober. And besides he wasn't feeling her in anyway other than a friendly neighbor.

"No, you're not scaring me by telling me that you watch me every morning and I helped you get through your divorce and I have no idea how," he chuckled. "I'm not scared at all."

She laughed. "You're silly and I like it. I tell my therapist about you all the time. I know you probably think I'm crazy because I'm telling you how I feel about you and we've never said more than two words to one another. In four years I haven't been with a man since my husband left me for his bestfriend."

"His bestfriend? Man or woman?" Keith asked.

"Man. I moved here from Atlanta with hopes of making him come back to me but it was too late. They had already gotten a house together and they were in love. During the divorce to keep me from suing him for putting my life in danger because of his affair with this man and AIDS, he had some woman to get on the stands and lie by saying she was his mistress. I knew about the affair. We had stopped having sex four years before he filed for a divorce."

"So you haven't been with a man in eight years."

"No, four of those years I had an affair. If I wasn't getting it at home I needed to get it somewhere."

She and Keith looked into each others eyes while shaking their heads at her situation.

She got up from the sofa and walked over to him and straddled across his lap. She then held his face and kissed him again and again. Slowly her tongue slid into his mouth and the heat was on.

She pushed him backwards on the floor and enjoyed the moment of being on top of him. Although Keith wasn't attracted to her, he was still aroused by her kiss and touch.

"Hold up Wanda, we shouldn't—"

"Shouldn't what?" She asked as she sat on top of him. "Keith, I understand that you are going through a separation and I might not be your type of woman, but tonight I need you and I don't need for you to reject me. I'm a big girl, I understand after what goes on between us tonight there might be no strings attached on your part and that's okay. I just got the desire to want a man again, please don't push me away."

Keith was moved by her tears and her plea for him to want her. "Well, I was about to say we shouldn't be down here on this hard floor when I have a huge bed upstairs."

She hugged him tightly and kissed him. "Thank you Keith."

Darika was happy to see Keith wasn't home. It was the only way she could get the two paintings he had given her for her birthday out of the house without him knowing. He didn't bother to pack them with her things when he so-called moved her out. But now the real problem was whether he had changed the locks on the door or not. She placed her key into the lock and to her surprise it opened. She smiled and felt relieved. All the lights were on in the house and she heard the music playing, and noticed the two glasses and the chess board. She didn't think anything of it. She ran up the stairs and slowly took the heavy pictures off the wall. Just as she was about to walk downstairs with them she heard a noise. She stopped and listen for the noise again and it sounded just like she thought, a woman's moan. She placed the pictures against the wall and listen for the moan again as she tiped-toed toward Keith's bedroom. His door was cracked, and from the candlelight Darika was able to see a woman's silhouette sitting upright rocking backwards and forwards. Her heart sanked and her temperature rose. What the hell, she thought. She tiped-toed down the stairs to the kitchen and looked at the knife but grabbed the broom out of the corner and tiped-toed back up the stairs with the broom in position to knock the hell out of whoever was in her bed three weeks after she was out of it. She slowly pushed open the door and flicked on the light. Keith jumped up and Wanda screamed.

"Bitch, how dare you?" *Whoop, Whoop.* Was the sound of the broom as it went across Wanda's back and head.

"Darika, get the hell out of here." Keith screamed. "What are you doing here, anyway?"

"What is she doing here?" *Whoop.* "I knew you always wanted my husband."

Wanda screamed for her to stop while balling up into a ball under the covers and covering her head with her hands. *Whoop,* was the broom across her behind. Keith grabbed the broom but fail to grab Darika. She jumped on the bed and began kicking Wanda until she kicked her onto the floor. Keith was then able to grab her and allow Wanda to get to her feet.

"Let go of me," Darika screamed, as she tried to break free from Keith's strong arms.

"Wanda, get your things," Keith ordered her. "And get the hell out of here."

Trying to catch her breath and put on her clothes. "What is wrong with her? I thought you put her out."

"You thought wrong. I'll kill you if I ever see you over here again."

Wanda ran out of the house for her life.

Out of the hundred and fifty invitations sent out that many and seventy-five more showed. When everybody found out CiCi Shepherd was getting married for the third time, they had to see the made- for- a- princess wedding she has with every marriage. The Episcopalian Methodist church was filled. Some were even standing. Young girls and single women wished for the day they would walk down the isle in a white dress as beautiful as CiCi. But who in the hell told her she could wear white and she has four children and has been married twice already? Someone needed to have told her she needed to wear black, Beverly thought, knowing black was for funerals. It was a fashion show going on in the church as it is every Sunday, but today everyone who had a head for a hat wore the biggest one they could find. Beverly was one of the best dressed women of the Emerald. And as usual she had all eyes on her. After the wedding, everyone had to complement her on how beautiful she looked and the dresses of the bridesmaid and the bride. They had made her promise she would do their daughters and sons wedding. The compliments made her feel good and she had to admit to herself she had done a wonderful job. Her head was on cloud nine when Odessia ran over to hug her and say hello.

"Hey, girl those dresses were beautiful."

"Thank you. Are you going to the reception?"

"I don't know—I might. I have a very important case I have to write briefings on for Monday, so I was going to go home and do that."

"That comes first," Beverly said. She noticed Keith and he noticed her; he waved and smiled at her.

"Who is that? He's very handsome," Odessia said.

"Nobody girl . . . so I hate you can't come to the—"

"Nobody," Odessia replied. "That's not true, brotha looks too good to be nobody. Is he married?"

Beverly nodded. "He's divorced."

"Then call him over here. Hook a sistah up. Wait a minute, where do you know him from, is he legit?"

Beverly nodded. "He's an architect and he attends the Emerald." And an asshole. she thought.

"Why haven't I seen him there before? Introduce us," Odessia insisted. Beverly reluctantly called Keith over to where they were standing. He walked toward them and both women said a silent prayer that God would give them the strength to stand because he was too fine in his black tuxedo. Their knees were becoming weak. He looked like he had just stepped out of Ebony Man or GQ. He was sexy.

"Hello," he said, reaching to shake both ladies hand.

"Hi," Odessia said, as Beverly mumbled.

"Keith, I was just telling Odessia that you are the one that designed Carl's home and she just wanted to tell you herself how beautiful she thought it was."

Odessia had no idea what she was talking about but she went along with it. "It's beautiful and if I had the money like they do I would have you design mine just like that." She couldn't stop staring at him nor smiling.

"Thank you."

Beverly had turned her back toward him.

"Beverly, are you okay?" He asked.

She nodded and continued to look away. She didn't like Keith at all and there was no need of her faking it. She knew his kind and it wasn't nice.

The time was going by so fast Beverly couldn't keep up. She moved around the kitchen in slow motion with her mind in a daze. Odessia and Keith were supposed to be arriving at three-thirty and she was near finished with the Sunday dinner. She wished she hadn't open her big mouth and invited them over, but Odessia kept hinting around about her wanting a good home-cooked meal. Beverly fingered what the hell she would cook it for her after all she's been through with the operation. But after her cousin Mike called and told her it was true that her father had molested him, all she's been doing is crying and lying down. Her life had crumbled. The only man she had ever looked up to was a sick bastard and he had destroyed an innocent child's life. Mike was upset with her mother for telling her because he knew how much she loved her father. He figured he was just gay anyway from the day he was born. That's why her father had chose him out of all her other male cousins to molest. Beverly bursted out crying. She wished there was something she could do to change his circumstance. She felt obligated to help him get his restaurant off the ground, so she wrote him a check for ten thousand dollars. And if he needed it, she would send him more. After hearing the news, she tried calling Odessia to cancel dinner but there was no answer. She didn't want to leave the message on the answering machine so she tried to prepare dinner as fast as she could. Her hair was standing straight up on her head and she was still walking around in her night gown. She tried to pull herself together but the knot in her stomach kept making her throw-up each time she thought of her father. Calling her mother to apologize and telling her she was right was out of the question. Beverly didn't want to see her gloating although she had nothing to gloat about; she hated her also.

Beverly managed to walk up the stairs to get into the shower, bump a few curls in her hair and throw on some clothes. She no longer bursted out into tears without warning. She had to think of her father actually touching her cousin Mike and his students and doing whatever gay men do with Billy Pain. She screamed to the top of her lungs and bursted out crying. She then began to shake her fist up at the heavens but quickly realized there was no way he had made it in.

Beverly busted out crying and ran out of the room to the kitchen to check on the pot roast that smelled like it was burning.

At a quarter to four Odessia and Keith stood at the door with flowers and a bottle of wine from Keith's winery. He made wine as a hobby. Gene hadn't made it back from the bakery and Beverly had sent him four hours ago. She knew he had stopped by his office to work on that damn computer. She called him and ordered him to get home in the next second, or she was going to see a lawyer first thing tomorrow morning. She had never threatened him with divorce before but she was fed up with his obsession with computers and his drive to be bigger than Bill Gates. Amazingly she needed his comfort.

The pot roast, collard greens, black eyed peas, homemade macaroni and cheeses and candied yams had everyone licking their fingers and wanting seconds. Beverly was glad she invited them over. Their company had taken her mind off her troubles. Gene made them drinks and told his silly corney jokes that were not funny but they laughed anyway. He put on his legendary jazz collection: Thelonis Monk, John Coltran, and Charlie Parker and gave each musician's history. Beverly wasn't in the mood for jazz so she put on her favorite Millie Jackson, Al Green and Earth Wind and Fire. Jazz reminded her of her father. Each of them began to dance when Odessia got up and began to dance. Beverly danced with Keith and Odessia danced with Gene. There was a party going on. They called Jabari down to put on some of his rap because they were trying to figure out why all the children were so in love with it. To them rap was nothing but a bunch of talk and loud noise. Odessia offered Jabari five dollars to show them the latest dance but he refused and went back upstairs. Keith wasn't a bad dancer at all he could dance to the rap music and stay on beat. The others moved like old folks.

Ten thirty p.m. had crept up without them noticing the time. Gene had pulled out the card table for a game of spade. Gene and Beverly was beating the socks off Keith and Odessia. Odessia didn't know the first thing about playing cards but she tried. Keith had to explain the game to her as they played and he seemed somewhat annoyed. He thought everyone should at least know the difference between a jack of hearts and spades. Odessia knew nothing. The arrogant pompous attitude Beverly thought Keith had was gone. She had grown to like him out of the couple of hours they've spent together. She had gotten his measurements and had agreed to bring him two of her double breasted suits from her fall men's collection. She felt bad for assuming he was one way when he was another. He was actually more down to earth than any of the people who had told her. He was arrogant. Beverly hoped he had a lot of interest in Odessia because she surely had a lot in him.

Beverly felt sorry for him as he told them the story of his ex-wife leaving him for another man and a young one at that. She could hear the sadness in his voice. To Beverly he was a good man because he wanted children and his wife couldn't give them to him and he stayed with her anyway. Beverly thought most men would have left a woman for that reason alone. She tried to help Odessia put a face with Darika's name after Keith told her she attends the Emerald on a regular basis.

Maybe it was the alcohol that made Odessia tell Keith she had a hysterectomy and she couldn't have any children. Once she becomes sober again, she would regret she had ever opened her mouth, Beverly thought, that was no ones business but hers. Beverly knew how some men were with women who had to have their uterus removed.

They no longer thought of her as a woman. That's how Odessia thought of herself and how Beverly would think of herself if she had ever had to have her breast removed.

Keith put his strong arm around Odessia and lay her head on his shoulder. He tried to understand her pain. The encouraging words Keith and Beverly used to console her, she could not accept. They didn't know what it was like to have the very essences of a woman's makeup removed from their bodies. And because of it, not have a natural sexual desire without taking hormonal pills. Her crying made Beverly think of the crying which she had been doing all day about her father so she began crying and told everyone why. She could tell by the look on their faces they were disgusted with her father which made her cry worse. Gene began asking a thousand questions like he always does. She tried to answer them as fast as he was asking her but between sniffles and breaths she was loss for words.

CHAPTER THIRTEEN

dessia tried to talk Beverly into going to see her thera pist, because he was helping her get over the fact she is not married at forty-one and will never have any children. She highly recommended Dr. McClinton because he was recommended to her and he has really helped her. Beverly was too embarrassed about seeing a therapist and worried about who might see her. If anyone was going to help her heal her hurts and disappointment in her father, God was. She felt more comfortable with telling him the anger she felt toward her father instead of some stranger who she figured could give less than a damn about the pervert.

She took the blue prints of the new house Gene was going to build her for Christmas over to Keith's office for him to look over them. She made sure her hair was in place, her clothes were neat and she had on lipstick. She had even sprayed on some extra per-fume. For no reason at all she just didn't want to go into his office looking any ole'kinda way. Times she's been around him and Odessia she's notice how he gives her this look to say, you're sexy. And she needed that.

He buzzed her into the office and motioned for her to have a seat in the chair by the window. Instead she sat in the chair in front of his desk. She crossed her legs causing her skirt to rise enough for him to glance at her thighs. He imagined the joy he could feel if he could ever lie between them. She was sexy just as she always is when he's around her. She was breathtaking dressed in her short skirt and heels that amplified her tight calves and round ass. Keith tried not to stare at her but it was impossible. She was a perfect picture of beauty. He couldn't stop staring at her as he sat on the phone trying to figure out if Cathleen was going to renege on the High Point project since he didn't sleep with her. Not that he didn't try but it wouldn't stay up no matter how long she had singed on it. Keith had never been so happy to go limp before in his life. He tried walking around the hotel to get his mind to the point of touching her frail body and just when he did after three gin and tonics with a hard-on for all night her husband was whisking her out of the hotel by the arm. Thank God. Charles had no idea Keith was in the room with her.

Cathleen's secretary came back to the line and told him it was a go ahead and he needed to be in Atlanta by tomorrow morning. Keith was one up on them because he was flying out tonight. He hung up the phone and screamed to the top of his lungs with joy. Before he realized it he had ran over and picked Beverly up off her feet and swung her around the office hugging her tightly.

She couldn't remember the last time she had hugged a man and didn't want to let him go. Keith's body was tight and warm. When she gets home, she was going to make Gene's fat ass join a gym instead of sitting in front of that computer all day every day. If he had a body like Keith's, and Earl's her, assistant she would hug him more often or even make love to him every night. There was no way in the world a gay man could be sexy but Earl had the body. Keith pulled out two bottles of Moet champagne, out of his drawer. He had bought the two bottles to celebrate with his employees but they had all gone home when the phone call didn't come in earlier today at five-thirty.

It was time to celebrate.

Between both of them the two bottles of champaign were empty. Pillow Talk with the Love Doctor was playing in the background and the room was smokey from Keith's cigar. Beverly had become relaxed, her shoes were kicked off clean across the room, and she lay on the sofa in Keith's office feeling very mellow. Keith sat on the floor running his finger around the rim of his glass puffing on his cigar thinking of the next project he was going to tackle. Nothing could hold him back now that he was on a role.

Beverly sighed and began to roll her neck and rub the tenseness from her shoulders. "First thing tomorrow morning I'm going to the spa to get me a mean massage. God knows I need it. I've been working twelve hours days to get my fall collection ready."

"Yeah, hard work makes it all the better. But you know what, you don't have to go to that spa and give them white folks yo'money for no massage I can give a mean one myself."

Odessia had told Beverly several times how his hands would massage her shoulders and breast and they felt like they were touching her insides. Beverly didn't think she would be able to contain herself if he had made her feel that good so she passed.

"So you want to give the white folks the money anyway. Woman, lie there and let me relieve you." He placed his cigar in the ashtray and sat on the edge of the sofa and placed his strong hands on her shoulders and began to massage them. Beverly lay there like a rag doll as he eased the tenseness from her shoulders, arms, fingers, legs and toes even. His hands made love to her body without him touching her where she wished he would. Odessia was right but Beverly knew she couldn't tell her. She knew she wouldn't handle that too well her man touching another woman's shoulders, making her feel more than relaxed, but sensual. Luther Vandross, "If only for One Night" played in the background and Keith and Beverly began to sang along. Keith moved his finger down the spine of Beverly's back. His touch was magic.

What an appropriate song for the occasion, she thought and melted as Luther sang.

"Gene is a very lucky man to have such a very beautiful, sexy wife as yourself. What does he do to keep you when he knows there are so many men that would love to have you?"

Beverly moaned at the touch of his hands.

"If I told you a secret, would you keep it between us?" He asked her.

She looked over her shoulders at him and she felt like rising and kissing his lips to let him know his secret is safe with her.

"Odessia, is sweet but she's not my type."

Beverly swallowed because she knew what was next.

"You're the woman that I want but I know I can't have you because you're married. I thought I would just tell you that just in case you wonder why I always stare at you."

She pretended to have never noticed. However, it was obvious he was interested in her from the first day they met in the restaurant, the day of the wedding when he kept trying to make small talk with her instead of Odessia and when he was over to her house some weeks ago and they danced together. He had sized her up from her toes to her head. Before Beverly could say a word, he had bent down to kiss her. She felt the same warm tingly feeling rush through her body like it had from his first touch.

"Maybe it's the alcohol, and you're just not aware of what you are saying."

"I'm well aware, Beverly. I find you highly attractive." He kissed her again and this time putting his tongue into her mouth. She turned her head away once she realized she was enjoying the kiss.

"I've never cheated on my husband before and I don't think I could do it either. Odessia, she really cares about you. You are very attractive and I'm doing every thing I can to fight what I'm feeling right now."

"Don't fight it." He straddled over the back of her thighs and began massaging her back some more. When his lips touched the back of her neck, it was over. He had won the fight and she surrendered. He lay on top of her and her heart began to pound with fear of Odessia and Gene finding out. But then again she was excited about feeling the good sex Odessia had bragged so much to her about. She had told her how he takes his time and caress her body with kisses of passion. Beverly wondered if he was going to do the same to her. His penis was hard and strong with the strength to rip through his slacks and through her skirt and panties hose and into her vagina. Embarrassed by her forwardness she unzipping his pants, lifted up her own skirt and placed his hands on her hips to pull down her panties. He massaged the inner part of her vagina as if it knew she wasn't getting it at home. He had cast a spell of voodoo on her soul. She was so wet the sounds could be heard as he moved slowly inside her. Never had she ever gotten so excited that she would over flow with passion of ecstasy. She was sure she was coming back. They could sneak around and keep each other a secret and no one had to know. She had thought a list of hotels in her mind where they would meet. She would get a pager that Gene wouldn't know anything about just so Keith could get in contact with her anytime he wants. He was the spice she needed in her life. She couldn't wait for the next time they would get together. Tomorrow couldn't come fast enough.

They had gotten dressed with occupied minds of what the other was thinking but too afraid to ask. It wasn't the question of did they feel guilty or not that's for damn sure. There faces reaped with satisfaction.

"Come to Atlanta with me?" Keith asked her and wrapped his long muscular arms around her from the behind and kissed her cocoa colored neck.

His invitation delighted her but she had to refuse. Trying to explain to Gene about a sudden trip she had to take to Atlanta, wasn't going to be an easy lie. Instead it would be somewhat difficult after he asks to come with her.

"I can't, my husband. What would I tell him?"

He kissed her lips and smiled. "I understand maybe next time." He then called his secretary to make his reservations for the next flight out.

Suddenly as Beverly drove into her driveway and walked to the front door, she felt a heat wave of nervousness. Gene was standing in his T-shirt, cotton boxers and black socks that fitted tight around his muscular hairy calves. He was packing his suitcase. Beverly stood in the doorway afraid to walk in the room. She wondered if it's true what they say about a man smelling the scent of another man on his wife. She had to shower and douche without seeming so obvious.

"Going some place?" She asked him. She walked into the room heading straight for the shower.

"Yeah, remember when I was telling you the job needed someone to train some programmers for the new office in Seattle?"

She nodded just as she felt the guilt fall upon her soul like concrete. She couldn't even undress in front of him, or even look him in the face. The computer magazine that was lying on the dresser she picked it up instead and began flipping through its pages.

"Yeah, you are looking at the new asshole they chose to go to lonely Seattle where there are hardly any Black people. Hell, there is hardly any existing life there."

Normally she would feel some type of joy that she was going to have him out of her hair for a while. With her heart pounding with fear and her stomach doing somersaults, she couldn't feel anything. Nervousness of whether he would be able to tell another man had entered her if he tried to sleep with her before he left, taunted her thinking.

"Why didn't you just tell them you didn't want to go? I'm sure they would have understood. You have a family."

"I know baby." He kissed her on the forehead. "But it will look good when I'm up for my promotion in the next couple of months."

"Gene, you are already Senior Programmer what more do you want."

"Senior VP if I can. I've made that company millions of dollars alone. I need you to take me to the airport I leave out tonight."

"Tonight," she replied. She was now feeling the joy of having her freedom and thinking of away she could get her bag packed to fly to Atlanta to meet Keith without Gene noticing. "That's fine I'm going to go jump in the shower." She threw the book down on the bed and headed for the bathroom.

"Wait a minute," Gene said, as he grabbed her by the hand. "Can I join you for a quicky?"

"No."

"What do you mean *no*?"

"Like I said, no, what part do you not understand. I would like to take a quick shower alone without you on my back."She has always told him no to sex but this time she had a legitimate reason.

"Damn, I'm your husband and you treat me like I'm some damn dirty ole' man. Every time I go to touch you, you pull away. Damnit, Beverly," he yelled. "What is it? I'm tired of this shit. Eight years I've been having to bribe you to fuck."

"Why are you yelling?" she screamed. "I'm standing right here. I can hear you clearly."

"I'm yelling because damnit I feel like it. Normal married couples, who love each other don't have to go through this. With making appointments and me giving you expensive gifts or even taking you on trips to get some."

"I don't have time for this. What time is your flight?" She turned around to walk away when he snatched her by her arm with force.

"Don't walk off from me. That's the problem. You don't have any respect for me."

"I am not your child and you better let go of my arm."

"You are not my wife either. This is what I was telling your mother—"

"And that's another thing. You don't have no business telling my mother anything about what goes on in this house."

"I went to her hoping she would give you some incite on what the hell is going on. I've had it up to here." He indicated his tolerance level by placing his hand over his head. "Your mother seems to know what would drive a man away you seem not to have a clue."

"The hell with you, Gene. I don't care anymore. If you want to go to another woman, be my guest. How do I know you ain't going to her now and you're just telling me you are going to Seattle? I'm not going to let you jump up and down on my body every time your dick gets hard wife or no wife. I don't care if we have been married twenty-five years. I'm not going to do it. And if that's a reason for your fat ass to fool around do it."

"I'm hipped to the fact you've never loved me. I've known for quiet sometime now but I stayed around being faithful thinking and hoping one day you might. Yeah, I'm fat and I don't look as young as you do but you don't have to disrespect me the way that you do either. Talking to me like I ain't shit— like I'm not a man. You want a divorce? Damnit, just tell me, sever me the papers I'll sign them."

The seriousness in his face scared her but then she would be free to do as she pleased. She had Keith to fall back on; he's single and so is she. "I do."

"Fine."

He walked out of the room and she took a deep breath and flopped down on the bed not believing she had just told her husband she wanted a divorce. For a man she had nothing with, other than good sex in his office. She was willing to leave her husband. Without thinking Gene could walk back into the room, she pulled out Keith's business card and picked up the phone to call him. She wanted to tell him what she had done, hoping he would make her feel better about it.

There wasn't an answer at his home or cell phone. She wasn't stupid enough to page him. She slammed the phone down just as it began to ring. Beverly jumped and stared at it before answering.

"Hello," she whispered.

"And why are you whispering?" Odessia asked her. "Are you hiding from someone?"

When she realized it was Odessia, her heart began to pound just as it did when she saw Gene. Hearing Odessia's voice made her think of Keith and what they had done in his office tonight; she knew she couldn't talk to her without cracking up so she had to think of a way to get off the phone quick and in a hurry. "Hey girl. I was just about to walk out of the house to take Gene to the airport he's flying to Seattle for a couple of days."

"That's great because Keith is gone to Atlanta for a day or so and you and I can spend sometime together. What about dinner?"

No way in hell, Beverly thought. "Girl, I would love to but I need to catch up on some much needed rest and sometime with, Jabari."

"I understand that. You go right ahead and I'm going to go to the Emerald for dinner. My love wanted me to fly to Atlanta with him but I needed to be here for this case tomorrow. Damn."

"He wanted you to fly where?" Beverly asked surprisingly.

"To Atlanta. You know he landed that High Point project contract."

Beverly knew she was in the office when he received the news.

"He called me all excited wishing that I would come to Atlanta with him and celebrate."

"And he asked you to go with him?"

"Yeah, is that so hard to believe?"

"No, I just can't believe you didn't go. To be truthful I'm surprised you two are still together being you know what type of man he is." Beverly was angry with Keith.

"What do you mean, all I know is that he's a good man. What are you talking about? Do you know something I don't?"

"No I just heard what really went on between him and his wife." Keith had told her and it was nothing new from what he had told all of them during dinner.

"He say, she say," Odessia sighed. "I don't care. He hasn't done anything worse than those other clowns I've dated in the past. This is the man I want to marry and I can't thank you enough for introducing us."

"I didn't introduce y'all you introduced yourself." She chuckled and crossed her legs. "I don't want you blaming me if it doesn't workout between you two."

"Stop talking so crazy this is going to workout we have too

much in common for it not to: He's successful, he has goals, a sense of humor, we are physically attracted to each other and the sex is terrific," she screamed with joy.

"I just don't want you to put your trust in him and he breaks your heart."

"Don't you worry I have this all under control." Odessia assured her.

Beverly sighed and felt like dying. "I guess you do. Well, I need to be going now I have to get Gene to the airport."

"Okay, call me tomorrow maybe we can get together for lunch."

"I'll do that."

Beverly sat staring at the phone before she blanked her eyes or moved from the spot in which her ass was glued. She was angry and humiliated that she had fallen pray to Keith's trap. She had done the unthinkable: sleeping around on her husband, now considering divorcing him. She didn't think of Odessia as a close friend so she wasn't guilty about that. There was no one to blame but Keith and her on weak emotions that had gotten the best of her. He had played her to the end. She jumped up from the bed to go and douche and take a quick shower. She had to put it all behind her and make up to Gene before it was too late.

She put on one of Gene's T-shirts he likes to see her in and walked downstairs. He was sitting in his recliner staring at the screen of the television but not really paying attention to what was on. Beverly sat in his lap.

"I'm sorry," she said. "I do love you and I've always have. You're the best husband any woman could ask for. I know I hold back on the sex sometimes but I haven't completely gotten over what happened to me as a kid." That was her famous excuse and he fell for it every time. "It has nothing to do with you. It's all me. A divorce is out of the question just understand what I'm going through a little bit better." She held his fat round face in her hands and kissed his lips. "Do you forgive me?"

He nodded and slid his hand between her legs under the long T-shirt.

"No," she said grabbing his hand. "Upstairs." She pulled him out of the chair and guided him up the stairs.

CHAPTER FOURTEEN

ain leaked through Darika's roof and flooded her kitchen floor after last night's forecast mentioned nothing about rain. The weather man's words exactly were "sunny, sunny, sun." Darika had been meaning to have some work done on the two year old condo but she never took the time out to call a repair man. She figured getting repairs on a two year old property serve her right for going against her better judgment and moving into a subdivision built just for blacks by blacks. "We cheat each other every chance we get," she screamed as she mopped up the floor and placed several buckets around the floor. Normally August would be the month it would rain cats and dogs but for some reason October had gotten the most rain. Darika was up at her usual time drinking one of her three cups of coffee before leaving the house, smoking her cigarette and watching channel 2 morning news. She hardly ever ate breakfast during the morning but this morning she had a taste for some waffles, eggs, and bacon. She talked back at the anchor woman when she said congress had passed the bill to raise the taxes on cigarettes, which meant a pack of cigarettes were going to cost her three dollars and fifty cents. If there was a committee ready to march on Washington she was ready because she couldn't see paying an extra $1.50 to get lung cancer. She knew she would have to really kick the habit. It was getting too expensive. She was now up to smoking two packs a day.

She stuffed a piece of bacon and waffle into her mouth and commenced to chew it slowly to taste the flavor of the maple syrup when Gail Baylor announced tragedy had struck the family of one of D.C.'s prominent black businessmen, John Stewart. He was found shot to death on the side of the highway. All of Darika's blood rushed to her head and her food came flying out of her mouth onto the wall as she screamed. She ran over to the T.V. to turn it up Gail said that police believed it to be a carjacking. Darika disagreed. She knew Antonio had killed John.

She tried calling Cookie several times but there was no answer. The answering machine didn't even pick up so Darika got dressed and drove across town to her house. She knocked on the door *"bam, bam, bam."* And still no answer. There was no way she could tell if she was in the house or not because her garage door didn't have windows. Darika was afraid Cookie might have given Antonio the go ahead. She ran back to her car to try and call her again as one of the neighbors walked over to her. He said he hadn't seen Cookie in a couple of days and he was wondering if she was alright. He had heard about John and he wished the police would find the bastard that shot him five times in the chest, robbed him of three hundred dollars, took his car and left him dead on the side of the road. Darika busted out crying, threw her car into reverse and flew over to Antonio's car garage in three minutes, but it wouldn't be open until 9:00 a.m. and it was now seven-thirty. She sat in the parking lot crying and screaming that Cookie would be so stupid to let Antonio talk her into such a thing. She later prayed they wouldn't involve her in anyway. She had too much to lose for only having a conversation with them about killing John.

When she walked into her office, Angela, her secretary met her at the door with a ton of messages and questions. She was in a daze so she heard nothing. Angela took a quick sniff and thought she smelled cigarette smoke so she asked.

"Dr. Jones I didn't know you smoke."

Darika snapped out of her daze. "Because I don't, I had given Keith's brother, Kelvin a ride to work this morning and he smokes. And against my will I let him smoke in the car." She had always knew how to lie and how to lie well. Angela didn't know she and Keith were no longer together.

"How is Keith doing anyway?" she asked with a smile. Just the mentioning of Keith's name sent chills through her skinny body. And if he walked into the office one day she would actually drool. That was the affect Keith had on all women and Darika knew this way before they got married. Angela had always thought Darika was one of the most luckiest ladies alive. Next to Juanita Jordan and Paulette Washington all of their husbands were sexy as hell and seemed to love the ground they walked on. "I haven't heard you talk about him lately and he hasn't been by."

"He's doing fine just busy as always," she said, while shuffling through her messages.

"Good morning, Angela," Eleanor Jackson said, as she scrolled through the office door. She saw Darika when she walked into the office sitting on the sofa but she didn't bother to speak to her. She was still angry at the fact Darika had gotten the principal's job over her. If Angela hadn't brought it to her attention that Darika was sitting behind her, her excuse would be for not speaking would be she didn't see her.

"Good morning," Angela said, looking at Darika and then looking at Eleanor. "Did you hear about that man they found dead on the side of the highway?" Angela asked Eleanor and Darika's heart stopped beating and her legs went numb.

"Yeah, he's the one that owns those Catfish Palace restaurants all over D.C. and Maryland, girl good fish. If you haven't tried it, you need to. I stop by there every Friday. Anyway my girlfriend, girlfriend is a friend of his wife, Velma the new one you know. He left his first wife for her. I spoke with her this morning and she said they were just so torn. Her husband is a doctor and they attend the same country club he does. I think his name was, John Stewart.

"Dr. Jones, aren't you a member of that country club where all the rich blacks attend. Did you know him?"

"No." She had her reasons for lying. She didn't want anyone tieing her into his murder because she once knew him and his ex-wife who wanted him dead because she was bitter about him leaving her for another woman and he wasn't paying her enough child support and alimony.

"To tell you the truth I think his ex-wife had him killed. It's gon'come out anyway."

Darika through the pink slips of paper down and jumped up from the sofa. "How could you say such a thing or even come to that conclusion if you don't even know his ex-wife? It's people like you who don't have a life to the first that likes meddling in someone else's life. Now that family is grieving and they don't need someone like you trying to play police detective. Now I think you have a class you need to be teaching, how to modify verbs and the difference between a pronoun and a proper noun so you don't need to be in here speculating about something you know nothing about. Am I correct, Angela could you look that up?"

Angela shook off her shock and ran over to the teachers schedule board and nodded her head.

"You need to go to your class."

"If you are going to run this school like a slave ship, I might as well turn in my two week notice now. I am not your child."

"Mrs. Jackson, do as you please but for the meanwhile, get to your class."

She looked at Darika as if she could rip her head off and stormed out of the office mumbling slamming the door behind her. Angela stood amazed. She had always admired how Darika ran the school. None of the teachers liked her but they all respected her.

"Angela, type a memo." Angela rushed over to her type writer waiting for the first word to spew from Darika's mouth. "There are not to be any teachers in the office or the teachers lounge unless they are on break. If they are caught any place other than their class during scheduled sessions a corrective action will be given. Per: Dr. Jones. If there are any questions they need to speak with me.

She walked into her office and slammed her door and took a deep breath. A weird feeling as she always experienced just before she starts getting depressed and crying uncontrollably was about to express itself, so she popped a Prozac into her mouth. She was thankful she had a warning before she started going crazy. It was imperative that she see Dr. McClinton so she called him for an emergency visit. She had just seen him two days ago and she already needed to see him again. His secretary liked her so she penciled her in for eleven- thirty, although Dr. McClinton's schedule was booked and it didn't seem like he was going to have any cancellations.

There was a knock at her door. It was Angela. She seemed a little bit off her rocker to Darika but she was a hard worker and she looked up to Darika. Each morning she would bring Darika a cup of coffee and spill her guts about her boyfriend. She couldn't leave although she know he's fooling around on her and he's only with her because she's paying all the rent. Darika didn't feel she could give her any advice because she too was caught up in some voodoo love type shit. She knew deep down Keith didn't love her like he should but she kept thinking there was a chance he might wake up one morning and decide he doesn't want any other woman besides her. And that's how she had stayed in a no- win situation until she just grew tired. There was no way she could tell Angela to leave Mario when no one could tell her to leave Keith not even her mother and her mother had gone through the same thing with her father some odd years ago, and know one could tell her to leave. She knew the situation wouldn't get any better unless God intervened. It took her father to suffer a stroke and be confined to a wheel chair before he was able to love only her mother. After then, her mother didn't want his love. But when she kept praying and asking God to make him love her and only her, God was telling her some things are not worth having and love from a man that doesn't love you is not. Her mother wasn't ready to accept that answer from God so she stayed, hoping her father would change. He changed the minute he needed her and all his other women had forsaken him. If her mother would have left along time ago, she never would have had to change her father's shity depends and wait on him hand and foot after his stroke. Some other woman he was cheating with and probably would have married would had to have done those things. God would have never allowed her to enjoy a healthy man she had taken from his wife and family. Darika yelled for her to come in.

"Have you had your cup of coffee this morning?" Angela whined and placed the hot cup on Darika's desk and sat down in the chair. Her voice was annoying to Darika but she had gotten used to it by now. Angela had been her secretary for four years. She was a pretty girl, and she knew it: tall, cute figure, light skinned, long hair and smart but she didn't think she was pretty enough to get someone other than that low-down Mario. "You are going to be proud of me. I put Mario out this morning. I have just had it. I'll be able to provide for Sergio and myself. If I stay with that man another day, I'll go crazy. Believe it or not I was staying with him because I wanted my son to grow up with the father I never had but it's not worth it."

Darika wasn't moved by her sudden burst of independence. Angela has been claiming to leave Mario every since she had met her. First she claimed she was staying in the relationship because he had helped her through so many hard times and they were supposed to get married. Second, she claimed because of her son needing a father. It was something about that man that she loved even if she did find the receipts where he had bought another woman Victoria's Secrets and has help another woman pay her rent. He could never hold a job from what she had told Darika and sometimes he had a way with verbal abuse but that still wasn't enough to make her leave. Darika would have to see it to believe it but she would give her the support she needed anyway. "And you are right you do deserve better. You'll find a good man that will love you and accept Sergio." Darika could see herself in Angela.

"I know that but Dr. Jones I don't want another man right now." She leaned forward and whispered. "I haven't told any one this but I've been seeing this therapist Dr. Mark McClinton—I'm not crazy but sometimes a woman needs someone other than her girlfriends to talk to about the bullshit—excuse my language— that is going on in her life."

Darika felt no obligation to bond with her and tell her she was seeing the same therapist. "So is he really helping you get through this thing." Because he had really helped her.

"Yes, and I really enjoy going to my sessions every Tuesday and Thursday."

Darika had nothing to worry about because there was no way they would run into each other her sessions were on Mondays, Wednesdays.

"So what time is your appointment today?"

"After school. Mario couldn't believe it when I told him to get his shit and get out. He thought I had lost my mind. I know I've said plenty of times before that I was leaving him but believe me when I say Dr. Jones I'm out of there. A woman just has to get to that point in her life when she's tired and just can't put up with no more. I really do appreciate you listening to me complaining about how Mario treats me and you never told me to leave other than that time you thought he was beating me. You let me make that decision although you knew I was with a no-good man and I wasn't going anywhere. You still listen to me talk about the same thing: me leaving that man alone. Well, I'm leaving now for good. I want a man like Keith is to you I deserve that."

Darika wouldn't dare comment because it was obvious she didn't know what type of man Keith was. He was identical to the man she was trying to run away from. Angela had come to a couple of their Christmas parties and she had witnessed what she thought was true love from Keith to Darika but it was apart of his big front and Darika's plea to him not to embarrass her by acting distant and flirting.

"And Dr. McClinton told me to speak it and believe it every-day that there are good men that know how to love me. Being with that man had killed my self-esteem."

Corey walked into the office and stood in Darika's doorway not saying a word to her or Angela. Darika noticed him but she did not acknowledge his presence. Angela finally took a breath from talking to notice him standing there. She jumped up and apologized to him for her running her mouth and not noticing him sooner. She had always felt the teachers problems came before hers with Darika. She was only the secretary. She excused herself and went to sit at her desk. Darika gave Corey a look that probably would have killed him if it were a knife. He walked in and closed the door behind him. He meant nothing to Darika now that she had accomplished what she wanted but she didn't mean for it to come out the way it did. She wanted Keith to find out but she didn't want him to leave her. She was thinking more on the lines of him being jealous.

"So you went back to him? I thought you were so finished with the nigga and I don't hear from you for a couple of days. What did he tell you, that he loved you?"

Darika could see Corey was allowing himself to get a little too deep in what they had.

"Hello, how are you. First of all, do not come in here questioning my whereabouts, second of all, I don't owe you an explanation and third of all, who do you think you are coming to my office as if you run shit."

He sat down and chilled out real quick, he was no stranger too Darika's wrath of anger and her smart mouth that could make him feel two inches tall. She had to curse him out before for trying to keep up with her. "I just haven't heard from you in some days and when I come to the office you're always on the phone whispering or you are not in."

"I'm doing my job and if you would spend more time in your classes with your students you would be doing yours also. Corey, I can tell you now it was a mistake for us to have ever gotten together. We are two different people. I don't have to be with you every night to say I care about you."

"What are you talking about, so you only used me so that you could get over him?"

She compared the time on her watch to the clock on the wall.

"Well, I need to be going. And look at it this way, you used me too I practically wrote your thesis for you."

"You know Darika, you are full of shit."

"Watch your mouth I'm still your boss."

"Yeah, right." He whisked pass her and stormed out of the office.

"What is his problem?" Angela asked Darika as she stood in the door watching Corey walk out. "Men and their attitudes some times I think they have periods.

"You are so right. Well, I have an important meeting I must go to so I'll be out of the office for about three hours. If my girlfriend Cookie calls, please, get a number where I can call her back."

"Roger captain."

Darika thought she had made it clear to Corey along time ago that they could never have anything. She was his boss and thirteen years older than him. What they had was sex and companionship. Nothing was supposed to become of them. Corey had just moved to D.C. and he didn't know any one and Darika was only trying to get back at Keith. She had know idea he was getting his feelings involved or she would have ended it a long time ago.

Since she was not scheduled for a regular visit, she had to wait thirty minutes. Dr. McClinton was happy to see her but he couldn't understand the urgency until she told him she knew who killed John. At first Dr. McClinton thought she was talking about that voodoo hogwash. He thought she was going to tell him she had seen his killer in a dream but when she told him she had sat down with Cookie and Antonio and they had discussed it he became all ears. He didn't advise her to go to the police which she wasn't going anyway because her best friend was involved.

"I told her along time ago to leave that bum alone. Now he has killed her ex-husband."

"I'm not trying to scare you but do you know you are an accessory to the crime because you were there while they were conspiring to kill him and you didn't go to the police."

"How the hell you figure?"

"It's the law, Darika."

"I tried calling her to find out for sure if he did it or not. All for damn insurance money." She began to cry. "I can't get in contact with her. She's nowhere to be found. Maybe he's killed her too. I know Cookie, she would have never gotten involved with this bull. Antonio did it all on his own. If she would only call me." Darika rushed over to the phone on Dr. McClinton's desk to try and call Cookie again but still there was no answer, so she called her job and they told her she hadn't been in all week. Darika didn't realize it had been a week since they last talked. She really became nervous then. Maybe Antonio had taken insurance out on her and later killed her for it, she thought. All types of thoughts were going through Darika's mind, and she felt she was going to have a nervous break down if she didn't get some answers.

The session only lasted an hour and Darika drove to Antonio's garage on her way back to the school. His partner James who looked just like Antonio, dirty, and didn't know water was also for bathing told her Antonio hadn't been in all day and he hadn't even called. He himself was wondering if everything was okay. Darika's knees buckled and she felt like falling flat on her face. There was something up for sure now, she couldn't get in contact with Cookie nor Antonio hadn't been into work, they were in it together, she thought. She drove around town because she was too nervous to go back to the office just in case the police was waiting on her there to question her. She turned on the radio to see if the police had made any latest discoveries about the case, like arresting a suspect. Dr. McClinton was right, she's just as guilty as the bastard that pulled the trigger. She had to tell someone other than Dr. McClinton, he was no help at all. She picked up her cell phone and with tears rolling down her cheeks she called Keith's office. Darika needed to hear his voice if nothing else. He was always her strength when things weren't going right for her. His secretary, Pam told her that he was in Atlanta visiting with a client and he wouldn't be back for a couple of days. Darika's heart sank to her feet and she began to sob like a disappointed child. She didn't need for him to be in Atlanta, she needed for him to be right beside her telling her that it was going to be okay. She sat in the parking lot of McDonald's crying her eyes out trying to decide what to do when her cell phone rangs. It was Cookie asking her to meet her in Food Lion's parking lot. She had been crying.

When Darika drove into the parking lot, she had to circle it several times before recognizing Cookie's car. The store was busy as always. There was no park beside her so she had to park between two trucks and discreetly walk over to Cookies car without anyone noticing her. She felt like she was in a movie and she knew some important information and then she felt guilty because she did know some important information she knew who had killed John. She jumped into the car and sighed while trying to catch her breath. Cookie busted out crying and they hugged each other tightly.

"John, is dead," Cookie informed her as if she didn't know. The news has been on the television and the radio all day long.

"I heard this morning. Was it worth it?" Darika asked her while looking her straight in the eyes for an answer.

"Girl, what are you talking about?" Cookie asked as her hands gripped the steering wheel. "I had nothing to do with it I was in Virginia at my mother's. I hated John but I never would have had him killed. Tony, called me this morning and promised me that he had nothing to do with it either and I believe him."

"You believe him? He's a damn thug who will do anything for money, he killed, John."

"Don't say that Darika. Zoria, called me screaming she was staying with John for the week."

"O'my God. We need to go to the police. He did it."

"I will do no such thing. After we had that conversation that evening and I told him that I wasn't with it, he never brought it up again. John has been over since then to pick up Zoria and Antonio has talked to him about his car."

Darika sarcastically grinned. "Are you foolish or just pretending to be? Accept it, he killed him, or he had someone to do it. You and I are guilty because we had the conversation with him and we didn't turn him in to the police then. He discussed insurance money, he discussed killing John."

"Tony just told me to keep our mouths closed about what we

discussed that day. I don't know nothing you don't know nothing. As far as the police is concerned, it was a carjacking. Whether you believe something else damnit, Darika, keep it to yourself. If you go running off your mouth it could harm all of us. You and I have too much to lose."

"I didn't pull the trigger. What about his wife? She's over there with a newborn, bills and the pain of losing her husband."

"Damnit! What about me? He left me with a child too. He left me for that bitch. She has insurance, she'll be taken care of. Knowing John he left her well off. I don't get it. What in the hell do you care about him or her? I'm your best friend. I hate to think this but was there something going on between you two? You are always taking his side no matter what. I hate that he's dead but I didn't have anything to do with it and neither did Tony but sometimes pay back is hell."

"What did he pay for, for Tony to have shot him five times in the chest. I don't give a damn if he left you seven times over and he had a million dollars in insurance."

"You know what, you don't know who you are dealing with, so please don't go running your mouth off about something you know nothing about or you might pretty well find yourself just like John."

"Excuse me. I don't believe you just said that to me, this man has you under some type of spell to where you don't know what the hell is going on. He has killed your ex-husband, your daughter's father, making us an accessory to the crime. I'm not going down for nobody I have too much to lose. I don't know what he has on you but it's not normal. I don't know you anymore, Cookie, we grew up together. Since he's been around you don't call, you're always sending your daughter away and now you are trying to cover up for him for a murder. Thank you for warning me. I'll watch my back." Darika stepped out of the car and without looking back, she got the hell out of Dodge.

She rushed home and locked herself up in her house checking every door and window to make sure it was locked. Darika was still insecure so she hammered nails into the windows and cut off all the lights and turned off the phone. The only light visible was the fire from her cigarette. She sat in her oversized chair staring straight ahead at the dark walls. She had given up on Keith returning any of her pages. She knew she had burned her bridge between them and he would always hate her for that. She could have called Corey but he couldm't comfort her the way Keith could. Keith knew the right words to say, he knew how to stroke her back to the point she would purr, he was her husband and he would always be.

She had fallen asleep in the chair.

The funeral was packed with businessmen and politicians. You would have thought someone important had died the way the people packed the church to pay their respect to John and his family. Some of the people that were very close to him were thinking the same thing Darika, that he didn't look anything like the handsome man they knew but of course he was dead now. His body was swollen and his eyes were sunken in and his light skin had turned a dark brown. The undertakers had patched up the holes in his chest so they weren't visible for anyone to see. People just pictured them in the back of their minds as they viewed the body. Some of them treated Cookie as if she was still his wife by walking by and kissing her on the cheek. Darika thought, what shock they would be in if they ever found out she had something to do with the death of their beloved friend and her estranged husband. She wore her black and screamed and hollered as if she loved him and she was going to miss him but Darika knew the deal and she prayed that she would shut-up. It was always said a guilty dog will holler. And that's what the police was looking for, a guilty dog. Antonio sat beside her with his arm draped around her shoulders acting like he was her support but counting dollars in the back of his mind. He noticed Darika sitting in back of them and he gave her a look of terror. The look caused her stomach to turn and her body heat to rise. He had actually frighten her. The ball in her throat developed as she tried to hold back her tears of fear for her own life. She wasn't going to say anything and she wanted Antonio to know that before he paid her a visit and make it look like a carjacking. She spotted Keith sitting in the pew across from her and she said hello by nodding her head. She hoped he would notice her saddened eyes and ask her what's wrong so that she could tell him and he could protect her as he has always done. He looked at her and shook his head from side to side and rolled his eyes. He could give a damn. She dropped her head and began to cry.

Zoria and Velma stood at the casket to view his body one last time before the pallbearers closed the casket for good. Without him what were they going to do when both of them relied on him for so much. After he had gotten remarried, he didn't have too much to do with Zoria but he was still her father and she loved him in spite of the horrible things Cookie would tell her about him. Velma stood like a zombie as she watched him lie in his copper- colored casket trimmed in gold. She rubbed her hands over his face and hair as if he was only sleeping and he could wake up any minute. Everyone knew she had no clue on how to live her life without him. Her life revolved around John and now he was taken away from her. Ushers tried to pull her away from the casket after she nearly knocked it over by trying to get in it.

Darika scanned the room and her heart began to race when she noticed two white men dressed in polyester jackets, worn-out slacks, dingy white shirts and out of date ties. They stood in the back of the church looking around. Darika knew they were police detectives by their shrewd hardened look. Anyway there was rumor the police detected foul play but she didn't know how true it was. But she did know a funeral would always be the place to realize a suspect like Cookie who cries the loudest and faints. Darika watched them out of the corner of her eye and she prayed to God they weren't coming for her, Cookie or Antonio because he didn't seem like the type of niggah that would go down alone. Of all days and places for the police to handcuff their suspect with hundreds of people around, they chose the deadman's funeral. If they came up to Darika, she would just faint and they would have to carry her out of the church. She doesn't want to see anyone staring at her and she doesn't want to hear their whispers. The detectives looked around the church as if they were looking for someone so Darika slid down in the pew hoping Cookie and Antonio would turn around to notice them and do the same. The pallbearers had closed the casket and the preacher was ending his eulogy by saying the doors of the church are open. That's why she didn't attend Baptist churches. She wished preachers would stop trying to get people to join their church because their closest friend lie dead in a casket. If they don't know by now, there's a hell and a heaven and one day they might die and probably end up in hell if they are not saved they are not going to ever know, she thought. Today is not the day to get people saved. There are hungry policemen standing in the back of the church ready to close this case by arresting the first person that look suspicious and that person might be her because she was nervous as hell.

Finally, the preacher said his last words after no one walked up to the pulpit and every one was dismissed. By this time Darika didn't give a damn if Cookie and Antonio hadn't seen the detectives, she had, and she wasn't going to wait around to inform them. She mingled in with the crowd that slowly walked toward the church doors. When she reached outside, she sprinted across the street to her car. The minute she got home she ran to the bathroom and began shitting bricks.

Against her better judgement she went in to work. Something had told her over and over again to stay at home in the bed with her pack of cigarettes but she wouldn't listen. She thought it was her depression coming down and she was determined to control her on life and moods without Prozac's help and eventually without Dr. McClinton. Depression was all in her mind, she thought. If she stopped going to work now, when the detectives decided to come to her for questioning they would want to know why the sudden change in her work habits when she's been going to work everyday. It was no longer a rumor, the police did suspect foul play but they didn't have a suspect. They questioned the people closes to John such as his associates, Velma, and Cookie. Cookie had actually held up, she was at her mother's during the time of killing. Darika felt off the hook. She walked into the office with a smile saying hello to all the teachers that where in there checking their boxes but none of them said anything back. Not even Angela she had even looked the other way. What was her problem she thought; they were friends if no one else was. She knew she wasn't liked among the teachers but they didn't have to make it so obvious all the time. To be truthful she hadn't done anything to them but be their boss and they hated her for that. She wasn't on a power trip, she just wanted them to do their jobs and that was to stay in their class rooms and teach the students. Instead of the black teachers embracing her they caused her the most hell with their monthly petition to get rid of her. It was the white teachers that stood by her side on every decision she made for the school. She was always told by her father the higher she goes up the ladder in life the harder her own would try to knock her down. She knew if she was light-skin or white they wouldn't have a problem with her

"Good morning, Angela." Darika said, as she waited for her to respond. "Are you okay?"

"What makes you think she isn't okay? Are you? Huh. We knew we would get something on you one day and you would fall down. Walking around here like you Ms. High Powered telling everybody what to do," Mrs. Fielder, the English department head said. "And you were sleeping with Mr. Brown. So that's why he always got new material when nobody else did."

Darika looked at Angela for an explanation and she gave it to her.

"Mr. Brown, filed a sexual harassment suit against you. He said that y'all had an affair for the last six months and when he tried to break it off, you had threaten to fire him."

"What." Darika wasn't believing her ears. This was all a part of a joke she prayed. "Where is he?"

Angela pointed toward her office. "How could you do this to Mr. Jones?"

"You did it. I know yo'kind," Mrs.Washington yelled. "You act like you got it all and you so happy with your husband— walking around here bragging and you were sleeping with a young boy like Mr. Brown. Couldn't you have picked on someone your own age like Coach Ramsey."

They all cackled like hens.

"She shouldn't have been picking on nobody. She's the principal. She knows better than that," Mrs. Jackson said.

Tears swelled up in Darika's eyes and they rolled down her cheeks. Mr. Baldwin the school superintendent walked out of her office. "Dr. Jones, I need to speak with you."

She walked behind him into her office with her head staring down at her feet and tears hanging from her chin.

CHAPTER FIFTEEN

Atlanta was Keith's home away from home but this time he wasn't enjoying his trip. His mind was back in D.C. where he needed to be trying to find out what the hell was up with Beverly. He hadn't heard from her for a week and a half since he got there and she told him she was going to call. And while he was home for John's funeral she was nowhere to be found. She had every number possible to get in contact with him and still no word from her. He knew Gene was out of town because Odessia had told him when he asked about Beverly on the sly and she hadn't heard from her. Keith sort of understood why he hadn't heard from her. Sleeping around outside her marriage was hell no matter how unhappy she was. He had never felt guilt during all the times he had fooled around until he actually tried to do right by Darika so he knew how the guilt could eat away at a person's heart and mind. Guilt is a bitch at times. He just wanted to hear the voice that he heard that night. She gave him a whole new feeling about love. Several times that day he called her studio and left several messages but she didn't return any of them.

The beautiful skyline of downtown Atlanta had him hypnotized by its beauty. And he regretted not making it his home but he was pulled to D.C. for the money. His pager went off with an unrecognizable number but he returned the call anyway.

"Did someone call 555-2410," he asked.

"I did. It's me. Beverly."

"What's up, lady?"

"What do you want?" she asked bluntly.

"What do you mean what do I want, I haven't heard from you. I was a little worried."

"About what?"

"Well, you said you were going to call and Odessia hadn't heard from you."

"Is she there?"

"No. And where are you now?"

"Home." There was a slight pause. "Gene is out of town for a couple of days."

"Then come here. I'll have my secretary book you on the next flight out of there and you just pick up your ticket at the airport."

"I don't think that's a good idea."

"Why?"

"Keith, what happened between us shouldn't have. I'm a married woman and you are involved with someone who considers me as a friend and who is very much in love with you."

"Where is all this coming from? Earlier today you were all for us seeing each other and spending some time together. What made you change your mind?"

She paused and sighed. "Odessia. It seems like you wanted her to come to Atlanta also after you found out I wouldn't be able to. She told me you asked her to come and celebrate with you."

"She asked me could she and I told her no. And not because I thought you were going to change your mind and come. Like I told you today Odessia and I are two different people and we have nothing in common. Unfortunately you are married and we have a lot in common. I've never slept with a woman and gotten up feeling like I had to have you, see you every moment—making me smile. You do that to me, believe it or not."

She couldn't tell him she was feeling the same way because she didn't know whether or not to believe him. She had made the mistake of believing him in the beginning and she had nearly ended her marriage. "But I'm married."

"It doesn't matter to me."

This time there was a long pause between them before another word was said.

"I would like to have you here with me if you would like to be," he told her.

She took a deep breath and smiled. "It will take me twenty minutes to pack and fifteen to get to the airport."

"Yes, Lord," he screamed. "I'm calling my secretary now to make reservations and I'll call you back with the information." He hung up the phone and did a dance.

Odessia was fed up. "I tell you one thing, she is really getting on my nerve," she said, leaning across the table whispering to Beverly. "Either she's calling or paging 'em every damn minute and I'm tired of it. She just can't get the picture that he doesn't want her. Thank God that divorce will be final soon."

A short caramel-complexioned woman walked into the supper room of the Emerald and they stopped talking to stare her up and down to see if she met the description Keith had given them of Darika. But she didn't have the small pointy nose or the long weave Keith had described. Both of them were now ready to see what she looked like. Beverly couldn't really see her at the club the night of CiCi's bachelorette party. It was too dark.

"She's a principal you know, and she was fired for having an affair with one of the teachers. The same damn teacher Keith caught her cheating on him with turned her in and she admitted to them having an affair. Girl, but I tell you what, if he doesn't stop her from calling so damn much I'm going to—"

She was going to be quiet that's what she was going to do, Beverly felt like telling her. Who is she to be giving someone an ultimatum if Keith was only with her because he felt pressured. Beverly already knew everything Odessia was talking about; Keith had informed her personally and she was there with him in the hotel. When Darika called him crying and begging for him to come back. But she wasn't the only one begging so was Odessia. She kept hounding Keith about a relationship.

"Does he ever call her back?" Beverly asked.

"Hell, yes, he said something about she gets depressed and he doesn't want her to do anything stupid like kill herself. And he told me to stay out of it because he knows what he's doing. I say let the heifa do it, she's just miserable anyway because she realized she let a good thing go for a young buck that turned around and burned her ass. I don't get it— he says he doesn't love her but why does he sits on the phone and talk to her every time she calls. These men and their ex-wives I can't handle it."

"I don't think he loves her. I just think he's trying to keep her happy until the divorce is final."

"If he lets her kill herself he doesn't have to keep her happy until the divorce."

Beverly laughed. "She's kinda crazy but not that crazy." Keith had already informed her of his plans because she too wondered why every time Darika called he talked to her like there was a chance for them.

"Yeah she's crazy all right. He told me about how she used to call his female clients and curse them out because she thought they were sleeping together. I tell you one thing, that bitch has one time to call me and she's going to wish she hadn't when I finish with her. I'm not letting him go so she can hang it up."

"She doesn't know about you two does she?"

"Who cares? But no."

Gene walked over to the table hugging Odessia and kissing Beverly. He had been in the Lamda Alpha frat room talking with some of his frat brothers. "Have y'all ordered yet. I'm starved."

Beverly looked at him and realized what a slob he was compared to Keith's body. The body she had hugged all night. "Baby, just wait awhile, we're trying to give Keith time to get here."

"What time is he getting here?" Gene asked and rubbed his round stomach.

"Well, his plane landed," Odessia said, looking at her watch. "About forty-five minutes ago. He said he was coming over right after he leaves the airport."

Beverly couldn't wait to see him, although she had just left him in Atlanta this afternoon. She prayed that she could contain herself and not let their secret be known with her obvious love for him. They have been seeing each other secretly for a month now and twice she had gone to Atlanta with him. She craved him when they were not together. He made her feel like a woman with his gentle touch and his soothing words that captivated her heart and soul in a way that she was mesmerized. It was hard for her to sit and listen to Odessia talk about how much she loved Keith and how he made her feel when he made love to her. Although she was married and she had gone to bed with him, she didn't want Keith to go to bed with any other woman besides her. That's when she felt she was selfish and falling in love with him. The guilt she once had for what happened in the office that night and its consequences was gone. She was finally happy and that was all mattered. Odessia and her weren't really friends before Keith and at this point she didn't care if they weren't after him. They just talked on occasions and had lunch together once or twice. She only called her after her surgery because she was trying to rally up individual sponsors for her Sistah's Against Domestic Violence Abuse campaign but it was Odessia who went off into her surgery and she thought Beverly was calling her to check up on her. Beverly knew nothing about the surgery. It was unexplainable but her relationship with Keith had somehow made her marriage more exciting to Gene. All she knew was that she could stand to be around him now but she still didn't want his sex.

Keith entered the room and both women gleamed with excitement. Odessia a little more than Beverly because she didn't have her husband sitting beside her and she and Keith weren't secret lovers. Odessia jumped out of her seat and greeted him with a hug and a kiss on his lips. Beverly stared while wishing she could hug him also.

"How are you doing, Keith?" Gene asked him, and shook his hand. "I just want to thank you for turning us on to that Milton guy. I tell you I was over at the house the other day and it is beautiful. They are building it so fast. I told Bev by Christmas she should be moving in. We will be having Christmas in the new house."

"That's great." He looked at Beverly and smiled. "How are you doing. I heard you went to New York. Did you enjoy it?"

"How did you know that, I didn't tell you?" Odessia asked him. Gene looked at him for an answer.

Keith's heart sank and it seemed like Beverly's did too from the worried look on her face. His palms grew sweaty and his heart started racing. He didn't mean to put his foot in his mouth. He was only trying to cover their tracks with extra cement. Now how in the hell was he going to get himself out of this one.

"Beverly, I'm not good at these type of things. I can't keep it a secret any longer."

Beverly looked at him in disbelief that he would be so careless. No, so stupid. Yes, she told him she wasn't happy with Gene but she was not ready to leave him just yet. Things had gotten better between them for some reason or another. She could stand for him to touch her. She watched Gene out of the corner of her eye for his reaction to whatever Keith was about to say.

"Not this way. This isn't the place," Beverly blurted out.

Keith looked at her and smiled while shaking his head. He then turned around and looked into Odessia's eyes. "I knew your birthday was coming up and I'm your typical man, I had no clue on what to get you so I called Beverly and one of her assistants told me she was in New York. So I went with my own heart and got something that I hoped you would like." He pulled out of his coat pocket a box wrapped in red shiny paper with a white bow tied around it and handed it to her.

She tore into the paper like a child on Christmas morning and screamed with joy before she knew it. "O' thank you," Odessia sang as she hugged and kissed him. "Isn't he so sweet? But my birthday isn't until next month, baby."

"That's just one of the gifts."

She flashed the beautiful five karat bracelet that Beverly had picked out for herself around the table for Gene and her to see it.

Beverly couldn't speak, she just smiled with her mouth wide open. Because of Keith's big mouth, he nearly gave her a heart attack and now he had to give Odessia her bracelet. Keith looked at her and smiled to ease her fear; he knew he had scared her.

"I didn't know you were going to New York for a fashion show. So that's where you were when I called you last night?" Gene asked and motioned for a waitress.

"It was a last minute thing. I let Earl talk me into going," Beverly said, as she gulped down her wine and ordered another glass to relax her nerves and heart. "Well, I would like for you all to excuse me while I step to the ladies room."

Keith watched her out of the corner of his eye as she strolled through the french doors. She was the sexiest lady he had ever seen and he was pleased. Of course Odessia was beautiful, but she wasn't sexy. Beverly had elegance and fitness on her side and to top it off she was beautiful. He had never seen that in any other woman and it was strange. He had dated a lot of them in his life and none of them had what it took to keep his attention and his attraction to the very essence of their soul longer than after the sex but Beverly had it. It wasn't because she was married and he knew he couldn't have her but it was something he couldn't explain. Like her, he didn't feel guilty about their relationship. He blamed Gene for not knowing how to be all the man she needed and he didn't give a damn about Odessia anyway. She was just someone to past time away. When he was with her, he thought of Beverly like he was now. Each day he couldn't wait to meet her at their spot and she lie in his arms after they made love so beautifully. He didn't want her to leave. He wanted to ask her to stay but he knew she had a husband to go home to and she still had a commitment to him. How lucky Gene must be to have such a lady, he thought.

He excused himself by saying he was going to talk to a friend he had seen on his way in the door. He waited by the ladies room door for two minutes but she hadn't come out so he walked out on the patio. There was no one else out there because of the windy fall weather of November but she was standing there with her arms folded in all of her beauty waiting on him.

"Hi, sexy." He wanted to kiss her but afraid someone was watching. She thought the same.

"I thought you would never come. I'm new at this but me having to go to the ladies room was only a cover up."

He smiled at her innocence. "I knew that but I was just giving it time so that it wouldn't seem so obvious. You forgot a pair of your panties back at the hotel."

She smiled. "What did you do with them."

He pulled them out of his coat pocket and put them up to his nose and inhaled. "Kept them right under my nose."

She chuckled. "You are silly. Give them back."

"Not on my life. That's my way of making sure you don't go anywhere. You've heard of voodoo haven't you?"

"Yes, my husband has it on me and Darika has it on you. We can't leave them for some reason or another."

"Darika and I are not together."

"She's there. She's in your heart; just face it."

He knew she had no idea what she was talking about because Darika had never had a place in his heart."Can I see you tonight?"

"Odessia is going to want to be with you tonight and Gene is going to want to be with me. There's no way we can get away from them."

"There's a way, I'll page you tonight around 12:30 a.m."

"And my reason for leaving the house at midnight. Gene, will be wide awake, baby. There's no way I can do that. I'll see you tomorrow."

He finally gave up on convincing her. "Well, meet me for lunch in the plaza tomorrow at noon."

"Anything you want," she said, just before she walked back to the table before Gene began to wonder where she was.

Her salad and wine was waiting on her. Gene looked at her as if he could eat her instead of the New York strip steak on his plate.

Keith walked back to the table minutes after she did. Beverly smiled because his timing was perfect. Odessia was just about to go looking for him.

Finally, their curiosity was settled. Darika stormed over to their table. Odessia and Beverly stared at her, barely smiling or saying hello. Keith introduced everyone.

"Darika, this is Odessia, Beverly and her husband Gene."

Darika only spoke to Gene. "May I speak with you?" She asked Keith and rolled her eyes at Odessia and Beverly. Keith walked her into the lobby.

Odessia's eyes followed them until they were out of her sight. "You see, that's what I'm talking about."

Beverly didn't say a word. She just nodded her head and took a sip of her wine.

"Let that man handle his business," Gene said, while wiping the corners of his mouth. "Just because they are divorced doesn't mean they have to hate each other. They could still be friends. That doesn't mean he loves her."

"He shouldn't be disrespecting me by walking off with her."

"He's not disrespecting you, and he's not going to disrespect her by not talking to her. After all she used to be his wife."

"Beverly, do you mind?"

She nodded her head no because she too wanted to tell him the same thing. Gene had a habit of putting his two cents in where it wasn't needed.

"Shut up, Gene." Odessia jumped up from her chair, grabbed her purse, and stormed out of the room without saying good-bye. Beverly smiled feeling Odessia wouldn't be around for long because she was just like the woman Keith was divorcing:very jealous.

Gene didn't find anything funny. He had noticed how Beverly was looking at Keith with something in her eyes she had never shown him and that was lust. He wasn't trying to read into anything that wasn't there but it was obvious something wasn't right. Beverly had been around Keith a lot since he had been seeing Odessia and she had even gone to his office and they had talked on the phone. Gene didn't think anything of it until tonight when he noticed the attraction in Beverly's eyes. Gene wasn't afraid to admit it, Keith was a nice looking man and he knew Beverly wasn't in love with him the way a wife should be with her husband. So with Keith being all the things he wasn't, his wife was bound to fall for him. He couldn't bare the thought of losing his wife to another man so he pushed his plate away and gulped down his drink and announced. "Baby, I'm about to get sexy for ya'. I'm joining the gym."

She looked at him and chuckled while wondering what brought that on. "Good."

It was two o'clock and Keith was still waiting on Beverly's call, she told him to be expecting it around twelve thirty so that he could meet her at their room. Keith had paid the room up for a month since they had no other place to meet. Meeting at the park in a parked car was for someone who had no business being se-cret lovers because that meant they couldn't afford a hotel room. His house was off limits because Odessia had a tendency of just dropping by and so did Darika and some of the people in the neighborhood were members of the Emerald and they knew Beverly and Gene. Their room was at the Budget 8 hotel a hun-dred miles outside of D.C. to keep from running into anyone they might know. It was a mom and pop type of joint hidden behind woods on a dirt road but they didn't expect to see anyone they knew there.

Two weeks had gone by since they had seen each other last. With Keith's busy schedule flying back and forward from D.C. to Atlanta and Gene not letting Beverly out of his sight, it had been very difficult for them to get together. Every time Keith had asked her to come to Atlanta she couldn't because Gene wanted to go with her to New York to pick out fabrics. Beverly had begun to think he knew what was up between her and Keith.

Beverly was deep on Keith's mind and he hoped she could find a way to see him but no love lost if she couldn't. She was a married woman and he had to see her when he could. He knew how the game was played.

Relatives he hadn't seen in ten or twelve years crowded his

house. They were thankful for the invitation he had extended to them for Thanksgiving dinner. His mother, Aunt Jewel, and Cousin Weedia were in the kitchen cooking every thing possible for that day's feast. Aromas he only smelled twice a year during Thanksgiving and Christmas were tempting his taste buds and he couldn't wait to eat. Most of his cousins didn't give a damn about the aroma of a smoked turkey and dressing, ham or collard greens and black-eyed peas as long as they had an alcohol beverage and music to stomp their feet to. And Keith had provided it all for them. Today was their day to enjoy themselves and they were more than grateful to him for that. They tried to be extra careful not to spill anything on the hardwood floors or plush cream carpet or knock over what seemed like expensive sculptures and vases. But Keith told them to relax and make themselves at home, that everything they saw could be replaced or cleaned. Keith wasn't the only successful cousin that had made it in the family but he was the only one they liked. Their cousins Eddy, who was a football player, and Jody, who was a doctor, were married to white women and had disassociated themselves from the family but they broke their necks to keep in contact with Keith. He didn't have two words to say to them. The whole family looked up to Keith as if he was a superstar because he had been in magazines and he lived in a house they had only seen in the movies and on videos. He was the relative they could tell their friends about and be proud of.

The phone rang and he was sure it was Beverly. He was ready to meet her in hell if she had asked him too. Or maybe that was exaggerating his love for her but he was ready to hold her and tell her what had been going on in his life for the last two weeks. She always seemed so interested and enthused about his life. He answered the phone through all the noise in his knee-buckling sexy voice. "Hello." He waited for her to respond with a sexy sigh and a smile as she always did but she didn't this time because she was Darika crying and feeling lonely and depressed. He pulled the phone away from his ear and rolled his eyes up to the ceiling and sighed with frustration and disappointment.

"Darika, what do you want?"

"I'm just lonely and I need to talk to someone. I need to talk to you."

He sighed. "My family is here. Why aren't you with yours, or with Corey?"

"So you are getting a kick out of me being down, aren't you? You are just as low as I thought you were," she told him.

"Darika, you are the low one and it's showing. You played a game that you weren't good at and you lost." He was just about to tear into her but he remembered the nicer he is the less she will ask for during the divorce. So he gave her hope. "Baby, I don't have time to see you suffer. I care about you and I hope we can get through this thing. We don't know what tomorrow may bring for us. Of course I'm hurt right now, you are hurt and we are dealing with our emotions, and because of that, a divorce is an option, but it won't keep us from being friends."

"Do you mean it? Because Keith, I love you. I didn't mean to hurt you. I just thought you didn't love me anymore. No," she snapped. "You never loved me, Keith. What was I a part of, keeping it real? That was why you married me. You went after the darkest woman out there—me, and I fell for it, knowing you couldn't possibly love me. Believe me I've paid for that lie I told ten years ago. Do you know why I lied and told you I was pregnant.?"

"Not now, Darika my family is here and we are about to have dinner. What you and I are talking about really doesn't matter now, baby. You hurt me. I fell for what you told me about that low self-esteem shit, but I had to wake up and realize I'm not your savior. I've tried to be for a long time not realizing you are beyond saving."

She began to cry. "But I loved you and I still do."

He became angry when he heard those words because that's why he never believed she would cheat on him. "So that's why you slept with another man." He hung up the phone and thought nothing of her.

Finally, dinner was ready and three generations of uncles, aunts, nieces, nephews, cousins and grandchildren sat together eating, drinking, reminiscing on childhood memories, and griping about life's defeats because they weren't white.

Keith's pager vibrated his hip to let him know he had a message. It was Beverly finally. The message read. "I am sorry I'm just now calling you. There were too many people around for me to call sooner. I can't meet with you tonight because Gene wants to take me to the movies to see Titanic but tomorrow I promise you, we will be together." He didn't let his disappointment show although he was feeling like a bullet was in his chest. He clamped the pager back onto the waist of his slacks and fell back in his chair. His appetite was gone.

With aluminum foiled wrapped plates and staggering out of the door, his cousins walked to their cars with a smile on their faces that Keith wasn't so high and mighty that he couldn't invite them to his big pretty house. Keith watched each of them drive out of his driveway down the street to the stop sign until they were out of sight. Just as he was about to walk into the house he noticed Wanda getting out of her car. He hadn't seen her since Darika beat her with the broom. He walked over to her. "Hello, I haven't seen you in a couple of weeks. How are you doing?"

"Fine," she said, while getting boxes from her trunk.

"Is there something I can help you with?"

"No."

"I've been wanting to come over and apologize about what happened that night but I've been so busy. So now that I'm here I'm very sorry, Wanda. I had no idea Darika was going to come over that night."

"Apology accepted." She couldn't bring herself to look at him. She was too embarrassed than angry. There was no way she could explain to her oldest son when he unlocked the door why her hair was sticking up on her head, and she was naked with a sheet covering her. All the boxes were out of the trunk but she still acted as if there were more.

"You don't hate me do you," he asked as he walked to the back of her car. "We're still friends aren't we?"

She looked up at him and smiled. His voice sent a warm sensation through her body and his cologne danced around her nose like incense. There was no way she could hate the man she had fallen so deeply in love with just by watching him through her window and sleeping with him one night. "I couldn't hate you. You taught me a lesson and you brought a side out of me that I thought I never had. You gave me my self-esteem back. The only man I've ever desired touched my body and made love to me in a way that it caused me to blossom into what's standing here before you. Have you noticed I've lost weight?" She twirled around slowly giving him time to examine her.

She looked the same to him but he didn't want to hurt her feelings so he lied. "Yeah. And you are looking good. Keep up the work." He hugged her tightly, said good-bye, and he walked back into the house. The phone rang and it was Darika for the fifth time.

"Can't I come over and we just talk. Keith we don't need to be enemies. You won. Is that what you want to hear? I lost—I lost everything a wonderful husband and a friend."

"It's getting late, Darika, and I'm getting sleeping."

"Who is she? Is she there? Is she the little light-skin bitch I saw you with at the Emerald. I saw you walk her out to her car Monday morning and you took her out to lunch that afternoon."

He chuckled. "Are you following me?"

"Maybe, maybe not. Why do you hate me so much?"

"Have you been drinking, Darika?"

"I thought I would spend the night with you tonight for old time sake."

He nodded. "No, we don't need to go there. You have some-one and so do I."

"You what?" she screamed. "You're making love to her?"

"I don't have anybody. I need you tonight. I know what I did was wrong."

"Let's not go there. I'm getting sleepy and it's not a good idea for us to spend the night together."

"So you are going to be faithful to her and out of ten years you've never been faithful to me. I was your wife. Can I at least sleep in one of the guest rooms."

"No."

"What, she's coming by and you are afraid she might see me there?"

"Good night, Darika." He hung up the phone.

After his shower, he did his routine fifty sit-ups and push-ups and jumped into bed. He fell asleep thinking of about how he was going to hold Beverly in his arms and not let her go tomorrow when he saw her. She was the first married woman he had ever fooled around with and he didn't like it because he couldn't stand being second in any woman's life. Now the feeling of love was real. He found himself needing Beverly to be lying beside him in his arms, to be faithful to only her, for her to be his wife, to have his child. They needed to be together.

CHAPTER SIXTEEN

Darika screamed and cried to God for the pressure of the world to be lifted off her shoulders. There was no way she could take it any more. Corey had gotten away with a lie which caused her to lose her job and the divorce was final today and Keith walked away with everything and she had nothing. He had even had a smirk on his face after they walked out of court and he asked her not to call him anymore. He used her up until the divorce was final. He pretended to hurt and be disappointed in her as part of his plot to get her not to ask for anything more than what he was going to give her out of the settlement and she fell for it. She believed he had paid off her own attorney not to advise her to fight. Now all she had was a two hundred thousand dollar condo, a car, and a hundred and fifty thousand dollars. Also she believed the Prozac she had been taking every day to keep her from going crazy had her so spaced out she couldn't fight him in that courtroom if she wanted.

She walked into Dr. McClinton's office, lay across the sofa and began to talk. He was surprised to see her so comfortable.

"Take me off of these pills, they are making me into a walking zombie. I just let that bastard get away with millions of dollars because of them. Because of these pills," she said, reaching into her purse and slamming them on the table, "I couldn't see through what he was trying to do. He pretended to still love me and I believed that one day we could get back together. But he walked out of court with everything. And that damn imbecile of an attorney I hired let him do it. I gave that "MF" ten thousand for nothing."

"Hello, Darika, how are you. Is that what you do, just walk into a place and start talking about yourself before even saying hello?"

She looked at him with spacy eyes. "That's what I pay you for isn't?"

He smiled and shook his head from side to side. "So the divorce is final?"

"Yes, and he won like he always does. I found out who this other lady is he's supposed to be dating. Her name is Odessia Jackson. And she's light skin. But I'm not going to go into all of that today. Tell me, Dr. McClinton, does this depression mess get worse as time goes on? Why am I depressed every day? I can't do anything unless I make myself take those damn pills. Yesterday I refused to take them and I couldn't get out of bed. All I did was cry. This hasn't happened to me in awhile. I was out of control if I must say so myself. I feel real strange right about now like some one might have some roots on me. I feel like someones watching me."

"Roots. Someone watching you? Feeling depressed is a part of the disorder until you start taking your medicine on a regular basis."

"It's making me go crazy, not the depression."

"When are you going back to work?"

She shrugged her shoulders. "I don't know. I'm a little too embarrassed about going back into the school system. Everyone knows what happened. That bastard and his lies."

"What are you going to do for money?"

"Money is no problem to me. I'm going to sell the condo in Atlanta, I have several bonds that will mature in the next couple of months, interest from some money markets and my savings. I probably won't go back to work. I think I might become an event coordinator. I have the style for those type of things."

"So how do you feel about the divorce being final?"

She twisted her mouth upward and began to ponder. "To be truthful I don't know. I brought it on myself. I've realized that much. He's moved on with another woman and I have no one but these damn pills. With Keith, although we were married, we had a voodoo type of love."

"He had roots put on you or you had them put on him," Dr. McClinton asked her as he waited for an answer.

"Voodoo love is when you intertwine with a person for all the wrong reasons. I intertwined, meaning, loved Keith, because I thought he could save me from all the hurts I was feeling from being hated because of my dark skin. And the voodoo come in because I couldn't break free of him no matter how hard I tried. He was the beauty in my life. And to be truthful I felt I was beautiful because he was with me. But I wish him dead now." She exhaled the cigarette smoke into the air.

"You don't mean that do you?" Dr. McClinton asked her while trying to fan the smoke. "I thought you said you loved him."

"I did until I realized he has hurt me time after time and why should I keep loving him. Death is waiting on him because he's so low-down. You know that's what happened to John. He had done Cookie very wrong and she was feeling just like I'm feeling now, that he would never get his payback until he dies and have to meet his maker."

"What is going on with that situation? Do you still think Antonio had anything to do with John's death?"

"No, the police has two boys in custody now."

"That's good. Have you spoken to Cookie since—"

"No, her and that bastard are out spending insurance money like people who have never had anything. Between you and me, Antonio killed John. Cookie is just to in love to see it or maybe she had something to do with it."

Dr. McClinton wrapped up their two hour session with his observation. "Darika, the way I see it if you keep believing Keith won then he has. You said you've realized how you needed him to make you feel beautiful and how he never loved you. Whether you've realized this or not the divorce was the best thing for both of you. Just as he has, you need to move on. Don't sit around wasting time by wishing death on this man. He'll out live you and everyone else he's hurt and betrayed."

Darika began to cry because Dr. McClinton was right. She slowly rose from the sofa, grabbed her pills from the table and walked out of the office without saying good-bye.

She cried all the way home and some when she got into the house. Tomorrow she would take her first step of moving on but today she had some things to get off her chest and off her mind. As she sat slouched down in the chair by the window, she started on a new pack of cigarettes. She read over the divorce decree and her stomach turned into a knot because she had let him play her for a fool. She dialed Keith's number and waited for him to answer.

"Hello," he said.

"You low-down bastard. You knew what you were doing all along."

"Darika, didn't I ask you not to call me. You and I have nothing to talk about. Everything you wanted to say to me you should have said in court today and so should have your attorney but money keeps people quiet."

"A hundred and fifty thousand dollars out of millions, Keith?"

"My millions. You never helped me build what I have today because you were so crazy thinking about what everybody was saying about the black-ass Darika. That shit is old."

Her heart sank to the bottom of her feet when he called her that. Keith had never talked to her the way he was. She knew Odessia had something to do with it.

"You and me both would have been dead if you would have walked out of that courtroom with half of my life. Please, do not call me. We have nothing more to say to each other."

"It's her, isn't it? She's turned you against me. She has some-thing on you."

"Godamit, Darika, don't call me." he screamed and hung up the phone.

Darika wanted to call him back but she decided against it and called Odessia instead. She had gotten her number through the club's directory. Odessia answered the phone in a chipper mood.

"Bitch, you really think you are special because you have my husband's nose wide open. I know your secret."

"Who is this? Darika? If you weren't in the court today, Keith is no longer your husband. The divorce was final today and he would like it if you not call him anymore or me. Don't you have anything better to do besides calling and harassing us. Have you forgotten you cheated and was caught? Yeah, you know my se-cret it's not to be stupid."

"Bitch, you don't know nothing. I loved Keith and he hurt me. Just wait he'll do the same thing to you."

"Darika, you brought that on yourself. And how did you get my number anyway? I would appreciate it if you don't call me anymore. If you think this is going to make me leave Keith, you are greatly mistaking. He is mine and he's going to always be mine."

"You bitch," Darika screamed.

"Call me what you want. I love him and he makes me happy and I make him happy. Why don't you go and fuck some other young boy and leave us the hell alone."

"You listen to me and you listen to me good," Darika said through clenched teeth. "Do you actually think you are the only one, do you actually think he could be faithful to only you? Keith Jones has never loved any woman and I should know after being married to him for ten years. I've had women come to the house claiming him to be the father of their bastards. I've caught him coming out of the shower of his intern. Now you tell me what makes you so damn different? He's going to continue to hurt people. The spell he has on you is that strong. I'm telling you now to break free while you can."

"Darika, you are not only crazy but you are stupid just like Keith said you were."

"So now he wants to degrade me for your sake. You fear me, go ahead and say it. You know that I'm not out of Keith's life for good. The ex-wife will always have a place in her husband's heart. You are the stupid one because you actually believe that man doesn't care about me."

"I know he doesn't care about you, so you are no threat to me."

"That's what you think." Darika began to laugh and Odessia slammed down the phone in her face.

Darika was now through a pack of cigarettes and a pot of coffee. Her hair stood straight up on her head and her clothes draped her body like potato sacks. She had lost weight again. Unopened mail for days or maybe weeks sat on the coffee table but she didn't have the energy to reach over and open it. A rerun of Matlock was on television, her favorite show, but she wasn't paying it any attention. Her mind was on the day Keith would pay for the pain he had cause her. The day she would win and be able to laugh again. Reaching into her cigarette case for her lighter, she came across the card of the voodoo lady Phillis had given to her. Darika read the red bold writing on the card over and over before laying the card down. "Voodoo Love is some times the only way." Darika read the card again from the table and picked up the phone and began dialing the number. The phone rang three times before someone answered.

"Hello, Madam Ruth, how may I help you?" A lady asked with a Haitian accent.

Darika sat quietly with the phone up to her ear.

"I said hello may I help you."

"Yes, may I speak with Madam Ruth please."

"Speaking. What do you want?"

"Help," Darika said.

"Help for what, lady?"

"My husband. My cousin gave me your card and told me that you could help me if I ever needed it. Can I come and see you?"

"Surely, do you know where I'm located."

"Yes."

"Get here."

Darika hung up the phone and sat in disbelief. She couldn't believe she had called. Knowing what she knew about roots, it had never crossed her mind to have one worked on Keith. Root working was dangerous and if she was careful it could backfire on her but it could also bring her husband back. She went upstairs to get the pair of underwear Keith had packed in her bags by mistake just in case Madam Ruth needed something belonging to him. Having Madam Ruth help her wasn't meant to destroy Keith but to only clear his mind and free him from all other bondage such as Odessia who seems to have a strong hold on him as far as what Darika could see.

She grabbed her keys and purse and headed to S.W., D.C..

Madam Ruth was doing business out of the basement of her house, hidden behind rows of trees. Dogs barked and snarled at Darika with the intent to bite her if they ever got loose from the chain around their necks which was nailed into the hard ground. When Darika finally got out of her car after checking out her surroundings, she slowly walked up to the door, more afraid than anything. The house looked old and in desperate need of a paint job. The screen on the windows were out. There was no grass, just dirt and gravel. The screens on the screened in porch were torn and tacked up by nails. Darika didn't see the worn out sign above the door bell that told her not to ring it so she laid her finger on it and pressed it. The door swung open and Madam Ruth was there with fury in her black eyes and a sweet smell. She yelled, "Can't you read?" And she pointed at the distressed sign. "Don't ring the door bell."

"I'm sorry I didn't see it."

"Then you not only need help you need glasses. Come in, child."

The inside of her home looked nothing like the outside. It was furnished with the finest Louie the VIII furniture, shiny polished hardwood floors, and expensive crystal all over the place. Darika was amazed at the difference and Madam Ruth noticed.

"It's not what's on the outside that matters but it's the inside that counts. Have a seat."

Darika sat down on the hard red sofa covered in plastic wondering if Madam Ruth had any idea on how to work a root. She didn't look anything like the root workers she had known back home. Instead of Madam Ruth having ritual paint covering her entire face and a wide-eyed erie look about her, she was a pretty older woman in her late fifties with long salt and peppered colored braids pulled back into a ponytail, wearing an African gown and sterling silver jewelry.

Madam Ruth poured both of them a cup of hot tea. Darika didn't bother to drink any of hers, afraid she was drinking a root. A root that would keep her in bondage to Madam Ruth.

"Tell me something about yourself, where are you from?" Madam Ruth asked her.

"Does it matter?"

"Yes it does, child. Now where are you from and what do you do?"

"I'm from Louisiana."

"Say."

"And I don't work."

"I know. Fooling around with that man wasn't the best decision you could have made, now was it?" She asked her as she looked deep into Darika's eyes.

Darika's heart pounded with fear. "What are you talking about? How did you know that?"

"I know you. So tell me lady why do you come to me for help?"

"How do you know me?"

"I know every one that walks through those doors."

"I want my husband back, but we're divorced and he's with another woman. I believe she has roots on him and me."

"Give me your hand." She grabbed Darika's hand and placed it inside the palm of hers.

"Odessia Jackson."

"What is your husband's name?"

"Keith Jones."

"Do you love this man?"

"With all of my heart, but he doesn't love me and I don't know how to make him see that I'm the woman he needs to be with but with this other woman around he's not seeing anything."

"What do you want to do with her?"

"Nothing. I want her out of his life."

"Well, she has not roots on him nor you. This Keith, he's a root worker himself. His voodoo is charm with the ladies. He's a user and a manipulator. When is his birthday and how long had you been married to him?"

"October 5, and we've been married ten years. Our divorce was final today."

"I can help you. I can clear his mind but it's not going to happen over night. It's going to take some time so you must be patient. In the meanwhile you'll know his mind and I give you the ability to know his mind for a reason. Everything that he thinks, you'll know; everything that he sees, you'll see. You are a part of this man now in more ways than one. He's now your husband again. He has hurt you in the past and I don't understand why you still love him but you do and I will help him find his way back to you. But for those women he betrayed you with, now is their time to pay. Every woman you knew about and every woman you knew nothing of will pay."

"What about that bastard Corey Brown who betrayed me with his lies."

"What about him?"

"I want him to pay for destroying my life. I hate him."

She nodded. "Done. Now that will be five hundred dollars."

"Five hundred dollars. Are you kidding me? For what? Is that it, are we finished?" Darika asked and reached into her purse and pulled out the pair of underwear. "You don't need his underwear? I don't get a jar with a piece of paper in it with Keith's name written in blood and ashes. Where is your red carpet bag with the peacock feather on it. Aren't you supposed to put these underwear in there."

"My child, there's more than one way to work voodoo. I'm

bringing him back to you, I'm not killing him, and even if you wanted that, there are other ways and it would be more than five hundred dollars. Trust in me and my abilities."

Darika reluctantly pulled out her check book and wrote Madam Ruth a check for five hundred dollars. Madam Ruth took the check and tucked it away in her bra.

CHAPTER SEVENTEEN

Beverly sang along with Lenny Williams' "Cause I Love You" while she whipped up some eggs and poured them into the hot skillet. What she was feeling was really love and it was all because of Keith. Jabari walked in, grabbed a plate and sat down at the table waiting for her to serve him.

"What are you doing? Why aren't you dressed for work?" She asked him.

"I'm off today."

"You just got the job, what are you doing off already?"

"Hay man, tell me what's going on with this cat that keeps calling here," he said, as he poured himself a glass of juice and gulped it down in one swallow.

"What cat, Jabari?"

"The niggah that's been calling here every night around the

same time since Gene's been gone. The niggah you've been talking to on the phone. You're creepin? My mama. Only sluts do that to their husbands."

Her reflexes caused her hand to fly up and back hand him right in his mouth and dared him to jump up at her.

"What's wrong with you?" he asked with his voice going up ten notches. He held his lip and checked for bleeding.

"No, the question is what's wrong with you? No, matter what I'm doing I am your mother and the adult and, niggah, if nothing else, you are going to respect me or I will personally kill you. Do you understand me?"

He jumped up. "Man, you can't be hitting on me like that I'm grown."

"I will kill you, Jabari, before I let you disrespect me in any way, be you grown or a child. Now what I do is none of your business. If you paid this much attention to getting your life together, you would be better off."

"Why are you doing this? Gene, man, he's cool people."

"It's not about Gene. I'm just not happy and I've never been. This man I'm with, he brings me joy; he's awakened parts of my body that had never lived. I understand you love Gene. I love him, too, but I'm not in love with him, not like a wife should. Sex with Gene—"

Jabari covered his ears and walked over to the stove and began piling his plate with food. "Nawh, man I don't want to hear that. Not about my mama getting her groove on."

"I hate for Gene to touch me, Jabari. He and I married for all the wrong reasons. I wanted you to have a daddy and I just wanted to be married so that I could have someone else to help me carry the load. Gene is a wonderful husband and a good father to you. I want you to continue to respect him and I will too, but I'm in love with another man."

"Does he know?"

She looked at him. "Jabari if he knew—"

"Just don't get killed over no shit like this."

"Jabari."

"Mama, everybody curse. Didn't you just called me niggah."

"That was only to put emphasis on what I will do to you if you ever disrespect me like some little slut on the streets."

He smiled and kissed her on the cheek. "I'm sorry. I love you."

"I love you, too."

Beverly's eyes grew as big and bright as the moon when Keith walked into the studio. She wanted to run up to him and wrap her legs around his sexy body for the two weeks she hadn't seen him but her employees wouldn't understand . They knew Keith to be Odessia's man and Gene to be her husband.

"Well, hello, Mr. Jones," she said, putting her hands on her round hips and smiling.

"Hi." He leaned against the drawing table and stared into her dark brown eyes as she stared into his. "So how was your Thanksgiving?"

"It was beautiful but it could have been better if you know what I mean." She smiled and placed her short hair behind her ear.

He chuckled and stuffed his hands into his slacks and began shaking his left leg. "I know what you mean."

They both laughed.

Matty and Julie, her color coordinators stared at them both wondering what was so funny. Beverly noticed and rolled her eyes at them. Two things she hated onions and nosey women.

"So what made you stop by?" Beverly asked playing his visit off from their nosey audience.

" I'm out doing a little Christmas shopping and I have no idea what to get Odessia so I was wondering if you would loan me your style and show me what a woman likes. I haven't the slightest clue."

"My style, do you think I have style." She smiled and walked from behind the table and did a quick spin in her white cotton shirt and stone washed Versace's.

"You have a lot of style." He looked at her as if he could kiss her. "And I like it, so what do you think I should give her."

"Well, she's been talking about this tennis bracelet in Tiffany's," Beverly said smiling.

"Bracelet, is that all, I was think more of a trip to France with a shopping spree. I don't know, maybe I'm old fashion."

"You are not old fashion," Matty blurted out. "I would love for my husband to take me to France for Christmas."

"You are not even married,Matty," Julie said, and laughed.

"Neither one of you are, now get out of my conversation." She grabbed Keith by his arm and pulled him over to the side out of their view.

"Since you are talking about France," Beverly responded. "I guess we better shop for my departure outfit if anything." She ran into her office to grab her purse and coat. They walked outside to the car whispering to the other how much they were missed.

Keith didn't open up the car door for Beverly as he usually does because she didn't want any one to think anything was up between them. The way Matty and Julie was all in her mouth she was beginning to wonder if they knew. Her cover was blown with Jabari because Keith had been calling the house like she's a single woman and today he drops by the studio. Matty has answered the phone once or twice when he's called and so did her assistant Eric. But he wouldn't dare say anything. It was Matty and Julie she was worried about.

Keith drove quickly out of the parking lot five blocks down from the building just so they could breathe without being under the watchful scope of her nosey employees. He couldn't contain himself. The sweet smell of her perfume and the essence of her beauty enticed his soul so he reached over and gave her a passionate tongue-tying wet kiss.

She was flattered. After their kiss, they sat staring into each others' eyes regretting they had married Darika and Gene ten and thirteen years ago. They wished they would have met instead. Beverly had gone so far to say she wished he would have never met Odessia. Not because she considered Odessia to be a friend and she was sleeping with her man behind her back. She hated hearing Odessia brag about the love Keith gives her and the love she gives him.

They drove around town listening to the Oldie but Goodie station and singing along with every song while trying to figure out where to have lunch without being seen. With living in a city as large as D.C. not being seen wasn't a problem but they didn't want to take any chances so they drove to their Culpepper, Virgina spot. Gene had her afraid for her life. She would rather they go to the hotel and order take-out, but she didn't want to turn their relationship into a sex thing so she said nothing. Although they had sex every time they got together and it was fine with her because she wasn't getting the satisfaction she needed at home, and she was also not getting the love. She stopped singing and watched Keith with a smile on her face wishing he could read her mind. But like the man he was, he hadn't matured to that level of knowing a woman yet. So she would have to initiate what she wanted. She began to rub her hand up and down Keith's thigh getting both of them aroused. Keith still hadn't caught on. She was beginning to wonder if he had drained all of his energy on Odessia just before he came to see her. An attitude had come down.

"What's wrong?"

"What do you mean?" He asked, and turned down the radio. "You haven't said where you want to eat."

She looked at him and smiled. "At the hotel, naked, lying beside you, eating take-out."

He chuckled. "Why didn't you say so." He bused a big U turn in the middle of the road to hit highway 95 South.

"I shouldn't have to."

"Baby, I can't read minds."

"I see."

He laughed and began to massage the back of her neck. And within an hour they were pulling in the driveway of their usual hotel and racing up the stairs to their room. They tore away at each other's clothes and held each other's naked body in their arms.

During the course of their lovemaking, Beverly felt it was time she told him what she really felt about him. She couldn't keep her feelings hidden like she had taught herself to do when she first felt the meaning of l-o-v-e for him. Keith smiled and without nervousness because she was married and he knew he couldn't as big as Washington there was a slim possibility that they would be seen. Still, Beverly didn't want to take any chances. So they have all of her, he told her the same. He had loved Darika at one time but not how he loved Beverly now. He had never loved any woman like that, as a matter of fact, now that he looked back on it. Being with Beverly made him feel whole and complete. He could be with her every day if he could but they both have other obligations. There were times Keith wished Gene would just find someone else and call Beverly and tell her he was not coming home. Keith would be right there to shield her heart and comfort her. Then they could be together without sneaking around. He would then end it with Odessia. Now they were limited to what they could do and where they could go. Taking meaningful walks through the park and having dinner in beautiful restaurants and she waking up in his arms every morning were out of the question. She was afraid someone might see them and she had a husband to go home to. Keith was now ready to show her what being with a man she loved was all about.

At a hotel like Budget 8 room service wasn't an option so Keith and Beverly drove to a nearby restaurant for a quick bite to eat. They were sure they wouldn't run into anyone they knew at the small mom and pop diner a hundred miles out of D.C. so they sat by the front door in front of a window feeding each other ice cream. Keith told jokes and Beverly couldn't stop laughing and he talked about his project in Atlanta and she was all ears, even asking questions. Gene wouldn't dare start talking about his megabytes or his programming; she would just walk out of the room.

William Feldon walked into the diner with Ursula Smith and Beverly nearly fainted. Both of them attended the Emerald and they knew she was married. Her paleness caused Keith to look over his shoulders. He knew William but they had never spoken to each other before but he had seen him at the club's golf tournaments. William and Ursula smiled and waved as they walked over to a corner booth where Beverly wished they were sitting. But listening to Keith tell her they would never run into anyone they knew in Culpepper, Virgina she felt comfortable with sitting at the door. Beverly began to feel hot flashes. She was sure Ursula would tell CiCi and Cici would tell Darlene and Darlene would tell Odessia and Odessia would tell Gene. She was busted. Keith tried to calm her down by reminding her William and Ursula were married and they were just as afraid of her telling their other halves as she was of them telling Gene. It was true but she didn't want to listen.

"Why are you over reacting? That's what makes us look suspicious. Besides, what do you care if he finds out? You said you don't love him anyway. If it's the new house you want, damnit, I can build you a new house. Money I got. And happy you will be, finally."

"You don't understand, it's not about the money or the damn house. It's about my life."

"Your life. What are you talking about?" It was Keith's first time hearing of her fear.

"Gene knows. I know he does. I wouldn't put it pass him that he's hired some detective to follow us. He knows something's up between us or if it's not us he knows I'm seeing someone else. He made the statement if he ever found out he would kill me, the man he caught me fooling around with and himself. He said he couldn't bare the thought of another man touching me."

Keith laughed. "Every man says—"

"No, he was serious. He said he had given me too much of himself for me not to love him."

"So he has you frightened into staying with him?"

"Yes." She jumped up and stormed toward the door when Ursula ran behind her and tapped her on the shoulder. "Are you leaving? I thought you and Keith would join us for awhile since we are all here doing the same thing." She chuckled and sized Keith up from head to toe. She had always thought he was sexy but Keith never looked at her twice when he saw her. And he wasn't looking at her now.

"The same thing? What are you talking about," Beverly said, while trying to play dumb. "Keith and I are here looking at some property that Gene and I are going to buy to build our new home. Keith is designing it."

"Keith Jones," William said, as he slapped Keith on the back.

"Are you getting ready for this year's golf tournament?"

"I'm not participating."

"So how is Odessia, Keith? She talks about you all the time," Ursula asked him.

"She's fine. And your husband?"

"He's fine."

"And, William, what about your wife?"

"Couldn't be better."

"Great. Well, we need to be going because we need to get some work done at the office. I'll see you two around." He turned to walk out of the door.

"Wait a minute," William said. "This is between the four of us isn't it? We all have too much to lose if it every gets back to anyone."

Keith and Beverly looked at each other. "We never saw you here," Keith said, grabbing Beverly by the arm and walked out of the door.

Beverly was upset and it showed by her facial expression. The trees and blue skies outside the window had most of her attention. Keith had no idea what to say but he knew he needed to say something to break the silence between them. Telling her everything was going to be all right wasn't the words she wanted to hear. She was terrified of that fat fuck of a husband of hers and it showed. The best for her would be a smile and he knew how to bring it out of her. He began to sing along with The O'Jays, "I Guess You Got Your Hooks in me," on the radio. He didn't know all the words so he hummed them and sang the chorus.

"Why are you messing up that song?" She asked him and began to laugh. "You are just adding your own words. It goes like this." She began to sing.

"Thank you. I knew you would smile sooner or later." He grabbed her hand and kissed it. "You know I have a taste for some good gumbo but you can't get good gumbo in D.C.. The only place you can get good gumbo is in Louisiana."

"Of course, but when are you going to Louisiana to get gumbo."

He smiled and she fell in love with him all over again. "Tonight. Let's jump on a plane and fly to New Orleans for gumbo. There's no reason why you can't go. I'll have Pam book us a flight on the next plane out of here."

She was so overwhelmed with his spontaneity. "Don't we have to pack?"

"No, we'll shop when we get there."

"I love you."

"And I love you." He picked up his cell phone and called Pam. Beverly called the studio and told Eric she was gone for the rest of the day.

They arrived at the airport around a quarter to four at the Delta "F" gate flight 1621 just in time for take off. The flight was two and a half hours.

When they arrived at the New Orleans airport, there was a chauffeur waiting on them at the airport door with a dozen of roses and a sign that read, "For my special lady, Beverly" Women walked past him snickering waiting for that lucky woman. Keith stood behind Beverly motioning for the chauffeur to come over. The chauffeur stopped her. "Excuse me, ma'am." He rolled out a strip of red carpet and handed her the roses. Beverly fell into Keith's arms crying with joy.

Everyone stood by clapping.

"What am I going to do with you, spoiling me like this?"

"Whatever you want to do."

She held his face and kissed his lips.

After they drove around town shopping, the chauffeur took them to the restaurant. It wasn't what Beverly was expecting. The restaurant looked more like a pool hall tavern than any restaurant she had been to. People were waiting outside in a line to get in as if they were going to eat at a buffet. There was no linen table clothes; they were plastic. The table were pushed close together which meant they had to share their table with the couple sitting next to them. It was pitch dark with only a small light coming from the candle on their table.

The dredlocked waitress showed them to their table and handed them their eating utensils wrapped up in a napkin. Beverly had already made up her mind that she was not going to eat there.

She leaned across the table. "We flew all this way for this?"

"Baby, don't let the appearance of this place fool you. The food is swang'en. I've been here several times."

"I don't want to eat here, Keith, this place looks like it needs to be closed down."

He placed his hand on top of hers and began to assure her by rubbing her hand gently. "Don't worry, baby. The food is great."

"O' my God," This is not my cousin with someone other than her husband rubbing her hand."

Beverly slowly moved her hand away from Keith's.

"Creeping, aren't we. Who is this nice looking son of a man anyway?"

"What are you doing here, Brenda?"

"Teddy and I," she said, pointing to him over at her table by the door," are here for the hair show. And what are you doing here? And I know it ain't to pick out no fabric. Hellooo...," she said, reaching out her hand to shake Keith's. "My name is Brenda, I'm Beverly's cousin."

"Hello, Brenda nice to meet you. I'm, Keith Jones."

"Nice to meet you. And what are you to Beverly? Last I knew Gene looked nothing like you." She smiled and sat down waiting for Keith to answer.

"I'm a friend."

"Brenda, stop acting stupid."

"So this is why I haven't heard from you. Between being a wife and fooling around you just don't have time for lil' ole me. Who's been doing your hair? I know I haven't?"

"Brenda, isn't your dinner getting cold?"

"No, but I get the picture." She got up from the table smiling. "I'll talk to you when we get home."

Beverly watched her until she was seated at her table.She let out a long frustrated sigh. "So much for the gumbo."

"I'm sorry," Keith said.

"Can we please leave?"

"Sure." he helped her up from the table and they walked outside to the limo.

Once again Keith didn't have the words to make things better.

Beverly was so upset she had fallen asleep on his shoulder on the flight back home. He couldn't understand what she was so upset about. It was her own cousin who they ran into, not a stranger, not anyone they should be worried about.

When they got back to D.C., he drove her back to the studio and she got out of the car without saying a word, not even good-bye. Which made him furious that she was taking everything out on him. Hell, how was he supposed to know her cousin was going to be in New Orleans. She slammed his car door and he drove off not even waiting for her to get into her car.

There were no words that could explain how upset Beverly was with Keith for leaving her in that parking lot. She had thought about calling him and cursing him out for being so silly but she didn't feel like going through the trouble of letting him know it bothered her. That was rule number one: when having an affair do not let your emotions get involved she remembered Brenda telling one of her clients and she had never thought of it until now. Now that she was deep in the shit and had no way of finding her way out. She had already told him she loved him and she couldn't turn away from his sex if she wanted too. She was hooked— voodooed. Here she was married and he was involved and they knew they could never be together but she couldn't break free of this man even if he came today and told her he wanted out. She had never known love like this before. It was like this if he didn't call her every day or at least come by. She would catch an attitude. She was in love.

The phone rang and she was hoping that it was Keith calling to apologize but instead it was Gene calling her for the fifth time today questioning her whereabouts.

"Where were you? I've been trying to call you all day, I even called the studio and they said you were gone for the day." Gene told her.

"For what, Gene?" she snapped. "If you weren't able to reach me that meant I wasn't at home. I have better things to do besides sit around this house waiting on your damn calls all day." Her anger with Brenda had caused her to be angry with Keith and her anger with Keith had caused her to be angry with Gene.

"Did I call you at the wrong time, baby, because I don't know where all of this is coming from. I just asked you a simple question. What's wrong? Did the distributors not get your orders out in time?"

She sighed and dropped her head. "I've just had a bad day and I'm tired."

"I understand. Go ahead and get yourself some rest and I'll call you first thing tomorrow morning. I love you."

Although she was far from feeling the same these days or any day she said it anyway. "I love you too. Bye." She pressed the release button to hang it up and she called Keith immediately. When he answered she hung up. She had thought about it, what she had to say had to be said in person and not over the phone. She snatched up her purse and keys and headed for the door. Every thing she was going to say to him she had thought about it in her mind as she drove to his house. She didn't want to call the relationship off but if he couldn't be a little bit more understanding of her feelings and situation she would. Odessia had told her he sometimes could be a bit self-centered and now she was beginning to believe her. Keith knew before they became involved she was married. Hell, yeah she was unhappy but she didn't want to throw their relationship in Gene's face or Odessia's.

She knocked on the door and to her surprise Odessia answered, which made both of them stand and stare at each other in shock.

"Well hello, Ms. Thang, how did you know I was here?"

With her heart racing and her body temperature rising, she thought of something quick. "I called your house several times and there was no answer so I knew you had to be at your second home."

Odessia laughed. "Girl, com'on in. I was just fixing Keith a sandwich."

"Baby, where is the wine opener," Keith yelled from the kitchen.

"Look in the drawer near the refrigerator, sweetie."

Baby, sweetie, Beverly thought she was going to be sick with all the love they were showing each other. For Keith not to care about Odessia as he said he didn't, Beverly couldn't tell, because as far as she was concerned, you don't call just anybody baby if you don't care for them.

"I don't see it," Keith said, as he walked out of the kitchen. He was startled by Beverly standing there but he tried not to make it so obvious. "Beverly, how are you doing?"

"Fine, I thought I would come and steal my friend for a couple of hours since you always have her. I don't have anyone to talk to over the phone anymore."

"Girl, what are you talking about? We talk everyday almost."

"Baby, could you go and find the wine opener and pour me a glass."

"Sure. Beverly, do you want anything to eat or a glass of wine. It's from Keith's own vineyard."

"Of course let me help you."

"No, sit down," she ordered her and walked into the kitchen.

Keith eased into his recliner and lit his cigar and made sure Odessia was out of sight before he began to speak.

"How are you? Are you feeling much better now?" He whispered.

"You have some damn nerve leaving me out there by myself. Anything could of happened to me out there. So I make you mad and you run to her. You are full of shit, Keith, and I'm not going to be a part of this any longer. I thought you said you didn't care for her?"

He sighed and got up from his chair. "Baby," he yelled to Odessia in the kitchen. "I'm going to show Beverly some of the wines in the cellar if you get a chance come down."

"Okay."

They walked down the stairs to the cold cellar waiting until they were behind closed doors before they said anything.

"Every time I look around she's over here cooking you dinner or knitting you a damn sweater. Tell me the truth, Keith, what do you feel for her?"

Damnit, Beverly, you tell me not to leave her so that we can continue to see each other and not look suspicious and now you are asking me what I feel for her."

"Tell her to leave and I'll come back and we spend the night together. You know I've never spent the night in your bed."

"I can't do that."

"What in the hell do you mean, you can't do that? You don't care about her or do you?"

"If you are so frightened that Gene has someone following you, what are you doing here tonight? I don't need the stress of trying to hide from people or worrying about if any one sees us and you getting upset with me when they do. I understand that you are married and I wouldn't do anything to mess that up. When I told you I loved you, I meant it."

"You are beginning to love her also, aren't you?"

"Don't do this to yourself. You know what's going on with Odessia and me. You know why I'm still with her."

"Then tell her to leave."

He was shocked at what she was asking him to do. He would never ask her to do something so cruel. She had her chance to be with him that night and she blew it by acting stupid because of her cousin. He paused to listen out for Odessia to walk down the stairs. "I can't do that."

"Then the hell with you damnit." She swung open the thick wooden cellar door and stormed up the stairs.

He shook his head wondering if she was on something. He had never seen her act so strange. When he walked up the stairs Odessia was waiting on him.

"I was on my way down there. Where is Beverly?"

"She got a page from Jabari to come and pick him up from his friend's."

"So that means we can have this bottle of wine to ourselves, and I can make love to you right here on the floor in front of the fireplace if I want?" She wrapped her arms around his waist and kissed him.

"If you are up to it."

"All night long."

They kissed and it was on.

CHAPTER EIGHTEEN

No matter what excuse Beverly tried giving Odessia as a reason why she couldn't meet her for lunch, she came up with several why she should. Beverly wanted to stay as far away from Odessia as possible. As Odessia cried to her about Keith and the possibility of him cheating, Beverly sat across from her trying to find the right words to console her but there were no words.

"I thought he was different. After all I told him I've been through, he turns around and put me through it again. I know there's another woman."

"How do you know? Have you seen her? Or them together?" Keith didn't tell Beverly Odessia supected him of fooling around.

"No. Keith is just acting really strange. We hardly do it anymore and we never spend anytime together. Do you know when the last time I saw this man." She pondered. "Hell, it's been so long I can't even tell you. I love him Beverly and I believe he loves me too."

"Has he told you?"

"No, then don't assume. Ask him and tell me what he says." Beverly had to know.

"From the times you've spent around us, do you think he cares for me?"

Beverly sighed and rested her elbows on the table. "There's a possibility. But you have to understand men, and Keith is a man. He's been hurt and showing love is probably the last thing on his mind."

"I hate his ex-wife for all the pain she's caused him because now I'm taking the rap. Bev, I would do anything for this man. I love him and I want us to get married."

"It could happen. But why do you want to marry him if you think he's a dog and he's cheating."

"I'm telling you he's a dog but I really don't mean it. The cheating phase he'll grow out of it. I'm not really sure if he's cheating. I'm just assuming because he's never with me any more. He's a wonderful man, Bev. It's about time I'm happy. I'm forty-two years old and I've never been married. He's the man I want to grow old with and cook breakfast for every morning and make love to every night."

"You really do love him."

"I do and my family is crazy about him. There's another woman and I can feel it. I can't lose him, not when I'm doing every thing right. Has Gene ever fooled around on you?"

"No."

"Then you are lucky. So many women have had to share their husbands and it's unfair. I've dated a married man for ten years so why shouldn't Keith fool around on me? What goes around comes around. That crazy Darika told me he was going to do it."

"Don't pay her any attention."

"A woman knows her husband."

"Ten years and he never left his wife?"

"And he wasn't and I dare not to ask him to. I got pregnant by him several times and I aborted them all."

"My God."

"Yeap, I call on him in the middle of the night when I'm awakened out of my sleep by nightmares of dead bloody fetus remains but God doesn't answer me. My pay back for all those abortions was this hysterectomy. Now I can't have any children if I wanted to and my pay back for messing with a married man, ten years of my life wasted. I never had a man of my own when he died. He left me nothing because I was a secret and his wife got everything I couldn't even go to the funeral."

"Why, did she know you?"

"No, she doesn't know until this day. At least I don't think she does. We were very secretive. Do you know if I would have kept those children I would have five of them. Thank God, I'm not an alcoholic behind the drama in my life."

"You didn't tell Keith these things did you?"

"Sure. I don't believe in keeping secrets from the man I love."

"Some things you just don't tell a man."

"That's how I know Keith loves me. When I told him, he hugged me tightly and each night I have those nightmares he puts me in his arms and hold me the whole night. I want to get married and be like you and Gene,happy. Keith and I are not to old to adopt a child. He thinks it's a good idea."

"If he's cheating now, what makes you think he won't cheat during the marriage. For ten years, he's cheated on his wife."

"Darika was crazy and I'm not. Beverly, I want that man and I'll do whatever it takes to keep him."

Beverly played over her food and glanced around the crowded restaurant. "So you think Gene and I are happy?"

"Yeah, aren't you?"

"He is but I'm not. Haven't been in thirteen years but I can't do anything about it but grin and bare it."

"But he doesn't cheat and he takes care of you. He gives you whatever you want. How could you not be happy, you have love."

"Voodoo Love, it isn't real love. I'm in love with the things he's given me and what he's done for me. I'm not in love with him. That's why I could never leave him. He's given me so much. I'm going to let you in on a little secret. You know how you talk about how wonderful Keith is in bed?"

Odessia nodded and took a sip of her tea.

"I envy you for having a man that makes you feel like a woman. And as sexy as Keith."

"You think he's sexy."

"He's very sexy." And Beverly meant it.

They both laughed.

"I envy you for having a man who loves you and only you. I could never have that," Odessia said.

"If you did, you'd find other things you don't like about him."

"What is it that you are not happy with Gene about?"

"Well," Beverly said, falling back in her chair. "We are two different people and I knew this before we got married but I ignored it by thinking things would get better. The mistake was getting married because all of my friends were married. I married the wrong man. I needed financial help at the time and Gene was there to give it to me. Jabari's father was out of the picture—dead that is. I wanted the best things out of life for me and my son and Gene could provide those things for us. I didn't have a college education and I was working as a bank teller for minimum wage. A rich man driving a Mercedes walks into the bank, pays me some attention, tells me I never have to work another day in my life and I married him. And I've been unhappy since."

"Damn, so you've tipped out before."

"Not until now."

"Who is he?" Odessia asked.

"It doesn't matter I don't kiss and tell. I just told you my problems to let you know you're not the only one unhappy. But I am happy now and I've never loved this way before." She thought of Keith and smiled.

"Does Gene have any idea that you are unhappy the way that you say you are?"

"Maybe he does, but he can't fix it. The man that I'm seeing he's sort of what Keith is to you. He makes everything right and I love him but I want leave Gene for him."

"But you're not happy."

"I know but I just can't leave, Gene."

Ursula walked over to their table and Beverly nearly choked to death.

"Bev, are you okay?" Odessia asked her, while patting her on the back.

Beverly nodded and reached for her glass of ice tea.

"Hello, ladies." Ursula singed and hugged Odessia. "Girl, I haven't seen you in some time. Where is that sexy man of yours?" She asked her and looked at Beverly out of the corner of her eye.

"He's in Atlanta on business," Odessia solemnly.

"Why are you sounding so dry there's another woman already." She chuckled.

Odessia forced herself to smile. "Why are you so crazy? How are the children and your hubby."

"Chile, we divorced months ago but the children are fine."

"Divorced, I didn't hear about that. And you didn't tell me."

"Yes, I'm apart of the divorce club once again but I'm not worried about it life goes on. Now I'm just enjoying my forty something age and his alimony."

"Who are you here with?" Odessia asked her, while looking around.

"No one. I'm meeting Darlene and CiCi for lunch we haven't spent any time together since God knows when. With everybody tending to their own lives." She looked over at Beverly. "So what's been going on in your life lately Bev, how is your husband."

"He's fine."

"Ursula, why don't you sit down and join us until Darlene and CiCi gets here."

"Girl no. I have a table over in the corner. But I want to tell you, that man of yours, don't let him stress you out. He's not worth it. I learned along time ago if you think he's cheating, he's cheating and you better believe it's with who you least expect."

"What do you mean?"

Beverly's heart pound with thrust and her shame wouldn't let her head come up from her plate. She knew Ursula was hinting around to her and she couldn't stand her for it. If she knew she could get away with it, she would just bow her right in her mouth for trying to be so damn smart and sound so stupid.

"She could be as close as your best friend."

"No, Beverly wouldn't do that," she said, and looked at Beverly and smiled.

Beverly couldn't smile back. Best friend. How the hell you figure? All I did was call you a couple of times after your surgery, she thought.

"Ursula, what is your point," Beverly asked her and rolled her eyes. "Did your husband sleep with your best friend or did you sleep with his best friend?"

"No," she said, looking deep into Beverly's eyes the minute they came down from rolling out of her head. "Like I was saying, Odessia, men are dogs and women are back stabbing whores. Friends and all."

"I love Keith," Odessia told her.

"And he could love you if this other woman wasn't around."

"What other woman? Do you know something and you are not telling me? Please, don't hold out on a sistah. I love this man, Ursula"

"Why, because he's cute, rich and good in bed?" She asked and chuckled.

"How do you know he's good in bed?" Beverly asked. Keith had told her how she used to try and get him in bed but he never took her up on her offer.

She chuckled. "Because he looks like it. Haven't you just seen a man that looks like he knows what to do in the bedroom; he's that type of man."

She and Odessia laughed while nodding their heads in agreement. Beverly agreed with them in her mind.

"I don't want to see you hurt. But the truth whether he's fooling around or not will come out sooner or later. So don't stress yourself out with trying to figure out if he is or not."

"I won't."

Ursula bent down and hugged her and walked over to her table.

Odessia leaned across the table and whispered. "Girl, Ursula is a nut. You know her husband before the one she just divorced was sleeping around on her."

"So you consider me as your best friend?" Beverly asked her. "Sure."

Beverly's pounding heart stopped beating as it sank down to her feet. One of the reasons she really wasn't feeling any guilt for seeing Keith, was because she didn't consider Odessia to be nothing more than someone she knew. Someone she talked to every now and than. Their friendship had no meaning, especial not a best friend meaning. Damn.

"Don't you consider us to be best friends?" Odessia asked her. "Out of all my years of living, I've never had anyone I could call a friend until I met you. I feel I can trust you and I've never felt that way about anyone."

Beverly dropped her head and looked down at her sweaty hands in her lap. The guilt she was feeling was unbearable. She tried holding back her tears but they forced themselves through her tear ducts anyway. A strange feeling came over her to be up front with Odessia and tell her the truth about she and Keith but she ignored it. She wasn't stupid. Telling Odessia the truth wasn't the noble thing to do right now or any time. Out of all her years of living she's never had a woman she could call her friend and trust. And here is a woman who feels she's a friend. Tears rolled down her face slowly. Odessia noticed.

"Bev, are you okay? What's wrong?" She asked, while handing her a napkin.

"Nothing—I just never had anyone to consider me as a best friend," she said, and wiped her face. Which that was part of the reason why she was crying. The other reason she dare not to mention. She had already broken rule number one as far as friends were concerned. Never back stab for a penis.

"Girl, friends are hard to come by and when they do keep them."

Even when she thought Gene was on to her and Keith she wasn't trying to end their relationship she was just going to be a little bit more careful and discrete. Now for the first time she's thinking about ending it because of Odessia. She couldn't wait for Keith to get back into town so that she could tell him. Or maybe she would call him tonight and break it off. That way she didn't have to see his facial expression when she tells him.

During the remaining of their lunch, they laughed and cried about their childhood and their crazy family members. Beverly's who beg her for money every other month and Odessia's who are all so-called recovery alcoholics but they still wrap their lips around a cocktail every chance they get. There was a since of closeness among them. Beverly still couldn't give Odessia solid advice about Keith but she sure as hell tried without exposing their relationship.

Beverly had finally gotten Odessia to get her mind off of Keith at least not to talk about him. They had planned to make a day of pampering themselves, so Odessia made an appointment at the Spa for both of them, her treat. Beverly paid for their lunch and had no regrets about ending her fling with Keith.

Just as they handed their waitress her tip and Odessia said her good-byes to Ursula and Darlene and Beverly rolled her eyes at them, Keith strolled through the door with Kathleen. Odessia grabbed Beverly's arm for support as her knees buckled and she took two steps backwards. By Keith's facial expression he was just as shocked to see them as they were to see him. Beverly was pist but she remembered not to let her reactions show or Odessia would surely know what's up.

Ursula and Darlene laughed while they looked on.

"Hey Baby," Keith said, and kissed Odessia on the forehead. "Hello, Beverly."

"Hi," she mumbled. "I thought you were in Atlanta, when did you get back?"

The question Odessia should have asked but Beverly asked it instead. "And who is this?"

"O,'" he said, as if he had forgotten Kathleen was standing behind him. "This is Kathleen Wright, she and her husband are over the High Point Project I'm working on in Atlanta. Kathleen, this is my girlfriend, Odessia Jackson and her girlfriend, Beverly Hayman."

"Hi," Kathleen said, smiling and reaching out to shake Odessia's hand. "He's told me so much about you."

Beverly knew she was lying and she wished Odessia would

realize it too and stop smiling in the bitch face like she's telling the truth. She's sleeping with her man. And hers.

"You know there's a designer name Beverly Hayman. I wore this beautiful gown of hers to a Gala in New York and I got so many compliments on it."

"This is her," Odessia laughed. "My best friend."

"Nice to meet you." She shook Beverly's hand once again. "I wish you two didn't have to leave you could join us for lunch," Kathleen said, as she ran her fingers threw her hair.

"Well, we've already eaten and we are on our way to the spa."

"Enjoying your day aren't you?" Kathleen asked.

Keith stared at Beverly from the corner of his eyes as she turned her lip up at Kathleen and rolled her eyes at him.

"Dessia, I'll meet you out in the car," Beverly mumbled and walked out of the restaurant.

Two minutes later Odessia stormed out of the restaurant to the car and slammed the car door shut as hard as she could with steam exhaling from her nostrils.

"They really thought I was stupid."

"Yeah, because I did."

"What would you have done Beverly if that was, Gene? Was I supposed to act a fool and start cussing and screaming like some mad woman because my man was with another woman? I learned along time ago that doesn't get you anywhere. Do you think he's sleeping with her?"

"I don't know and I don't care. I got a husband to go home to if he wants to fuck every thing with a hole he can. Here I go thinking he's in Atlanta—"

Odessia looked at her and Beverly realized she had stuck her foot in her mouth.

"You know what I mean— you thinking he's in Atlanta and he's out with some white woman having lunch. Hell no, you don't deserve this." Beverly yelled.

"Girl, don't get so upset I'm not taking it that hard and he's my man," she chuckled, and put on her lipstick. "I knew he wasn't ready to settle down when we first met, he told me."

"So what is he doing with you, just putting miles on your

body?"

"We hardly every have sex anymore. Now I know why."

Beverly knew that to be true because Keith had told her.

"He's getting it from this other woman he's seeing and she's not the white woman either. Keith doesn't like white women. She's a sistah and she's not his ex-wife. That fool would have let me know along time ago if they were still sleeping together."

"Don't worry about it. It won't last for long." She was sure of that because she was going to end it.

"Maybe. Or maybe he'll leave me for her."

When Beverly arrived home after her relaxing day at the spa where she had her body wrapped in green seaweed, chilled in the sauna, and dipped her body in a soothing milk bath while listening to jazz, and sipping on a glass of Crystal, Gene was at home cooking dinner for her to continue her pampering. He handed her a glass of wine and a long stem rose every ten minutes which exemplify how much joy she brought him. He had her favorite singer, Betty Wright bumping through the speakers of the house as he ran around the kitchen in her apron trying to prepare her favorite meal, shrimp Alfredo. While whipping up the Alfredo sauce from scratch, he singed to her.

"So what did I do to deserve such royal treatment. Does somebody want some loving?" Beverly asked.

Gene laughed and kissed her hand. "No. You are such a beautiful queen and you are my wife and I love you." He sat her down and took off her shoes and began to massage her small feet. "There's a bath waiting on you."

"Sorry the spa already gave me a milk bath."

"Damn," he said, and handed her another rose.

She sniffed the rose and sighed. "I wasn't expecting you home until next week sometime."

"Things change. I realized I need to give you more of my time, so I'm here."

"Sure you are just not trying to check up on me?"

"What are you talking about Beverly? I fly all the way here to spend the night with you and there's a reason other than what I told you. Why should I check up on you, are you doing something you shouldn't? Look, I don't want to argue with you. You are my wife and I love you. I'm only here for tonight and I fly out in the morning if that makes you happy."

"Don't try to change it around, Gene."

"What, how am I supposed to fucken please you—to not give a damn. Is that what you want Beverly, for me to just say fuck it?"

It was getting harder and harder for her to cover up the fact she really didn't love him. Any other woman would have been pleased to have a husband fly hundreds of miles to romance her but Beverly wasn't impressed. She didn't want Keith anymore and she didn't want Gene. She got up from the table and walked upstairs to their bedroom. Her face nearly cracked when she saw the lingerie from Victoria's Secret lying on the bed covered in rose petals. She began to feel bad for how she treated him but she didn't feel sorry for him. She walked back down stairs to apologize just for the sake of apologizing.

"There's no need Beverly just forget I'm here. I'll check into a hotel."

"You don't have to do that, Gene."

"Yes, I do. Things between us are going down the drain and I can't do anything about it."

And she didn't expect him to either. The love has never been there for him no matter how hard shes tried to pretend.

Gene took off the apron and walked upstairs to pack his bag. Beverly didn't try to stop him either. She finished up the sauce he started, she poured her another glass of wine and danced to the beat of her own drum. The phone rang and luckily she answered it on the first rang. If Gene would have answered it and discovered it was Keith, Beverly would have died.

She whispered through clenched teeth. "Gene is here."

"I want to see you. Meet me at the Ritz Carlton room 415 within an hour."

"I can't." she said, as she looked out for Gene to walk back down the stairs.

"Yes you can. I need to see you, we need to talk."

"I don't want to talk to you," she said, as she tried to listen to the music that he was playing in the background. "It's over, Keith.

You go your way and I go mine." Finally, she could make out the song and she smiled but remained standing for what she wanted. The words of the BlueMagic's "What's Come Over Me" hit her soul and she sung along in her mind. That was her and Keith's favorite song. She smiled. She had a favorite song with a man she had only known for a couple of months and didn't have one with the man she had been married to for thirteen years.

"What in the hell are you talking about woman? You love me and I love you we had a good time together last night. Where is all this coming from?"

"Gene, is here I can't talk to you right now," she said, with annoyance in her voice as she kept walking back and forwards to the steps.

"Tell me you'll come to the hotel or I'll come there." He chuckled. "Now you don't want that do you?"

Gene walked down the stairs and Beverly nearly jumped out of her skin. "Girl, I enjoyed myself at that spa. Now we need to get together and do that more often."

Gene paid her no attention. He grabbed the half gallon of Hennessy Cognac from behind the bar and walked out the door.

Beverly took a deep breath and waited for the garage door to open before she started breathing again. Keith laughed.

"You even sound suspicious. If he had any sense, he would have known you were faking it."

"Well, he didn't so what does that say?"

"Come to me."

"No. Odessia and I had a long talk and we are friends. Why aren't you with her anyway tonight or that white woman you walked into the restaurant with this afternoon. It's enough I had to share you with Odessia. I am not going to share you with some stringy head white woman too."

"Is that what this is about? You think me and Cathleen are seeing each other. That white woman was about business nothing else. Every time she and her husband put up a mall I'm the designer and the builder. Come to me."

His voice sent chills over her body. He did look cute in his thick turtle neck sweater and jeans, she thought.

"No. I never knew Odessia considered me as her best friend. You heard her."

"And."

"Do you love her?"

"No, do I love you, yes, so come to me."

"We have to end this before she finds out."

"So now that you two are best friends you won't out just like that? Fine."

"You never told me she suspected you of cheating."

"And. As long as I'm not under her every minute of the day I'm cheating. You do what you want I'm not going to try and talk you out of it. I don't understand but I'll try. I had some things planned for us here tonight but since you now feel guilt I won't worry about it."

"What do you have planned?"

"Can I see you for one last time. I just want to taste your lips and hold your body. I want you near me."

She thought about his kiss and how nice he looked today and almost said yes. "I have to get off the phone now."

"Beverly?"

"Bye." She hung up the phone and flopped down in the chair at the kitchen table feeling proud she was strong enough not to subcoma to his temptation.

She sat around by the phone waiting for him to call pleading with her to see him but she knew that wouldn't happen because he wasn't that type of man to beg for anything. Not even love. Thoughts of regret began to run through her head. She felt she wasn't fair to him for ending their relationship the way she did. Who was going to make her laugh now that he's gone, who could she talk to about her deepest feelings and fears and who was going to make love to her? Time and time again she picked up the phone to call him but she decided against it when she thought about Odessia and her love for him. Beverly was confused and guilty.

Just when Beverly fell deep into her sleep after being depressed about her dilemma to choose friend or man, she was awakened by Gene. He laid across the foot of her bed sobbing like a child.

Beverly was startled. She jumped up screaming and switched on the lamp.

"Gene, what is going on, are you okay?"

He looked up with sorrow in his eyes. "I love you."

"Why are you crying?" She asked without sympathy. "It is three o'clock in the morning."

"What is going on between us, baby?"

"What? I'm going back to bed. Gene, I don't have time for this." She turned off the lamp and stormed toward the bedroom door to sleep in one of the guest rooms.

"I needed you but you weren't there so I turned to her. She's been there for me and damnit, Beverly, I get lonely too," he blurted out before she could reach the door.

Her heart sank to her feet which enabled her to take another step. She slowly turned toward him with her eyes rolling into her head and her nostrils flaring. "What in the hell did you just say?"

He dried his tears and sat down on the floor with his head in his hands almost afraid to speak. "My conscience wouldn't let me live with it. She was a friend that I confided in about us and we had gone out for drinks and that's when she told me that she loved me."

Jealousy she didn't think she had hit her soul to open her eyes and realize the man that was sitting on the floor was her husband and another woman loved him. "You bastard. How could you?"

"I couldn't because I kept thinking about you. She couldn't understand after I told her about the problems we were having. How you and I never make love any more and we argue about every thing. She stood nude in front of me and I kissed her neck and breast but I couldn't do anything else."

"You disgust me." She was truly speaking with hurt in her voice. "Why in the hell didn't you fuck her if she stood naked in front of you and I never fuck you. Do you expect me to believe that shit. Do I look like a new fool to you, fool? You can come in here crying and I'm supposed to believe that you are so sorry."

"Nothing happened you can even call and ask her."

"What? Who in the hell is she?"

He sighed and with hesitations before he called out the

woman's name. "Joanne."

Beverly's knees buckled and her temper exploded. "That woman never did like me and you were discussing our business with her? At every Christmas party I've gone to that your company has had, she never speaks, she's always rolling her eyes. She told you herself she would never wear my designs."

"Because they don't fit her right—hell I don't know. When we nearly slept together, I didn't try to do it because I knew she didn't like you and you didn't like her. If you ask me the shit is childish."

"Childish, I tell you what my childish ass is about to do, pack my things and get the hell out of here." She grabbed her over night bag out of the closet and stuffed it with clothes, underwear, and a toothbrush.

"Beverly," Gene said, while trying to stop her.

"Get off of me." She yanked her arm away from him and tore off her night gown. "So when things get bad between us, you run to another woman?" She pulled her jeans up her short legs and pushed her head threw the small turtle neck sweater. "She was naked and you didn't sleep with her? And I'm supposed to believe that?"

"I didn't."

"Well, you should have because I'm gone." She threw on the black fur he bought her for Christmas last year.

"Where are you going?"

"Don't you worry about it I got a place to go to. That's why you've been watching me like a hawk because you were screwing around with Joanne flat ass, no neck having ugly behind. But let me let you in on a little secret. I've been—" Something caught her tongue and she thought before she spoke. "Forget it." There was no need to bring Keith and Odessia into this.

She stormed down the stairs out to the garage to her car and speeded out of the driveway. She was hurt but she couldn't cry. She was too shocked to do so. She had underestimated him he wasn't as gullible as she thought. If pussy was put before him, he would fuck it whether he said he loved her or not. Keith came to the forefront of her mind and she needed to be with him. There was no doubt in her mind her hurt and shame.

Odessia wouldn't understand so she refused to let herself consider her feelings or their friendship.

She searched for her cell phone in her purse to call him. Her heart screamed with joy that he was still checked in the room. The front desk clerk rang her through. And on the second rang Odessia answered the phone in her sleepiness. A lump developed in Beverly's throat and a tear fell down her cheek.

CHAPTER NINETEEN

Keith was waiting on Beverly to come back to her senses but he never thought it would be when she caught Gene cheating. When she called him crying after Gene told her another woman stood naked in front of him but he didn't touch her, Keith laughed so loud tears came to his eyes. It was funny just as it is now as he lie in bed thinking about it. What man won't touch a naked woman unless she's Cathleen pale ass or he's gay, he thought. Keith had tried to tell Beverly if she wasn't giving Gene any, some other woman was but she didn't want to believe him. She was so sure Gene loved her and only her too much to creep. Which Keith assured her he did or he never would have put up with her shit as long as he has or even told her he came close to sleeping with another woman. Knowing that Gene betrayed her and she was hurting, was the perfect time for him to persuade her to leave Gene and come to him but he couldn't. Only because he didn't try. He loved her and he wanted to be with her for the rest of his life but he wanted her to come to him on her own. He didn't even try to sleep with her when they met at her hotel room. He simply consoled her which any mature man knows works better than sex. Without saying a word about her new found friendship she and Keith were back together again.

Things were beginning to be a little bit more complex than Keith had anticipated. He was now dividing his time between two women who was beginning to need him a little bit more than he was willing to give. If he wanted to just be alone there was no more time for that; one of them had to be around him. He truly loved Beverly but he was also beginning to love Odessia. No matter how hard he tried not to, she had won him with her kindness and pampering. Her persistence wore down his resistance to care for her. He had found himself more than once feeling guilty for blowing her off to be with Beverly and he had even blown Beverly off to be with her. He had some faults with her. For instance, she wasn't independent enough, she needed to be under him every minute of the day, the popping bones from her bare feet every time she took a step made his skin crawl, the mud facial she packed on her face before bed scared him and the fact he was in love with Beverly didn't make it any better. He enjoyed having Odessia around when Gene was in town and Beverly had to be with him pretending she missed him. Keith couldn't bare being alone and Beverly hugged up with Gene. They had spent every day together since Gene had been gone and their love for each other has grown stronger. They had even talked about letting Gene and Odessia in on their secret. Keith was ready to be with her for the rest of his life. She knew what it took to make him happy and it wasn't just sex either. It was her words that comforted him and her touch that soothe his soul. That was what made her such a beautiful woman. She was his friend and not just his lover.

More than what he can say for what he and Darika had but for some reason she had been on his mind lately. A month out of their divorce and he was thinking of memories of their marriage. Those memories seemed beautiful and everything about her was right. It was strange for him to be awakened out of his sleep thinking of her and longing to hear her voice just to see how she was doing. Although he was trying to fight his desire, he called her anyway, and to his surprise, their conversation was pleasant. Why weren't they together again, he had almost forgotten. Having feelings for Darika to resurface wasn't the only strange thing happening to him lately. He had had this feeling that someone was watching him. Maybe Gene did have a detective following him and Beverly.

Tonight was Keith's and Beverly's first night in weeks that they hadn't been together and Keith felt lost. He hadn't heard from her all day and he was actually angry. He couldn't believe how he was tripping and in love with her. It was the first time Keith had gotten angry because she was married and her husband could enjoy her in public and in privacy. He thought she could have at least left a message on his pager to say hello or even to see if he had made it back safely from Atlanta. Damn Gene. Keith knew there was a way for her to break away from him and get to her cell phone or even driving to the corner pay phone to call him. He needed to hear her voice.

Odessia was different from Beverly and he was beginning to care for her. Which would be easier because she wasn't married, he didn't have to share her with any other man as far as he knew and material things and money meant nothing to her. Not that it meant anything to Beverly but it was a factor. Keith was sure if he didn't have a dime, it was no doubt in his mind Odessia would still love him because of how he made her feel. And then again he believed the same about Beverly, but she was married. Odessia was like a woman with a purpose in life—to love a man and be his strength. Her words were comforting too but they just don't touch Keith's soul like they would if they came from Beverly. A weekend with Odessia didn't mean going to the movies or sitting in some fancy restaurant or having drinks at the Emerald. It was as simple as a walk in the park and her cooking dinner and renting a movie from Blockbusters, as long as they could be together. Beverly enjoyed those things also but he couldn't go to her house and she couldn't come to his and walking in the park holding hands was out of the question. Not while Gene's detective was on their trail.

When Keith came home today from work, she was lying around the Christmas tree in her royal blue satin panties and bra with a red bow tied around her slim waist. A picnic was spread in the middle of the floor with the fire place going. Keith acted surprised and enthused but he wasn't because Beverly had done the same thing a week ago. He then knew they must talk about him. Odessia had to tell Beverly she was going to surprise as he being his gift around the tree and Beverly saw to her doing it first. She was much sexier. Odessia lying around the tree did not give him that same affect he got when he saw Beverly's body stretched around the tree but he made love to her anyway. He was more attracted to Beverly than he was to Odessia. He was beginning to feel guilty when he would blow her off to be with Beverly because he knew she cared for him a little more than he cared for her. And it showed. So on a couple of ocassions he had blown Beverly off to be with her but he lied and told Beverly he was working. She wouldn't understand.

Keith couldn't sleep so he got up and fixed himself a sandwich and went down into his cellar and manually pumped wine into bottles. He had an automatic pump he had spent thousands of dollars on, but he didn't feel like using it. It was very seldom he had time to waste and to himself so he just felt like doing things the manual way. The thoughts of Beverly had his mind occupied and the feeling was strange because he had never known love like this before and he had been married for ten years. The floor of his cellar was covered with plastic jugs that contained fermented grapes and other fruits that had turned into wine. The smell was strong and Keith took deep breaths to inhale the joy of his hobby. The sweet aroma of his favorite dessert wine, StrawCot, a mixture of strawberries and apricots, ate away at his soul. The smell reminded him of Beverly after she would take a sip of the wine and it would stay on her breath and Keith could taste it as he kissed her. Keith had planned to stay in the cellar and pump the wine into bottles all night.

It was sad that his family had no established tradition on Christmas Eve of gathering at someone's house and exchanging gifts like Beverly was doing with her family. Half of his family members were screaming broke even to giving their kids gifts and they had called him to borrow money. He knew he would never get it back but he loaned it to them anyway. Keith had done about four bottles already: two dinner wines and two desserts. He wondered what Beverly was doing or if she was thinking about him like he was thinking about her. They had exchanged their gifts a week ago when they spent the weekend in his cabin in the mountains of Colorado. He left several messages on her pager reminding her that he loved her. There were no expectations of her to return any of his calls with Gene being in her face watching her every move. With her pager being under the seat of her car she couldn't get any of his messages anyway. Her pager was a secret and Keith's way to call her when Gene or Odessia was around.

By five o'clock a.m. Keith had done four more bottles of wine in between tasting a bottle of merlot he had stored away three years ago and dozing a couple of times. He was pleased with the taste but not too pleased with his progress. He had only labeled eight bottles in the eight hours he had been in the cellar. On one side of the cellar he had five hundred bottles of wine and on the other side was his processing plant. He wanted to have a hundred bottles ready before Valentine's Day because several of the black-owned florist had agreed to sale them in their stores.

Keith developed the hobby of wine making when he was just ten years old from his grandmother and grandfather out of Harris County, Georgia. Like some people would take a vacation to get away from it all he would just close himself up in his cellar and smell the fermented fruit as he tasted the years aged wine to make sure it stroked his taste buds.

For some reason Keith began to wonder if Beverly was telling him the truth about how much she hated being married to Gene. He told her he almost slept with another woman and she still didn't leave him. Keith couldn't understand. An unhappy woman doesn't stick with a cheating husband. In the beginning before they started seeing each other she appeared happy and so did Gene but now all of a sudden she was unhappy and she wanted out of the marriage but she hasn't attempted to go anywhere. If she didn't love him and never had, why was she still with him, Keith wondered. She was talking about being afraid of him killing her; that was bullshit. Beverly didn't scare easily. To be truthful Keith couldn't picture Gene as being some crazy person like Beverly said he was. To Keith, he looked like a damn nerd and a pushover who did every damn thing Beverly told him. If Keith were her husband there was no way in hell he would have had her a house built for six hundred thousand dollars, if she treated him the way she treated Gene.

Keith hoped Beverly wasn't lying to him to justify her reasons for having an affair or just to keep him around. He had done the same lying to too many women but they were too naive to decipher the truth. He had no intentions on leaving Darika but he still gave the women hope that one day he would by telling them that he and Darika were drifting farther and farther apart by the day and he was counting the days that they would call it quits. They had no idea he wasn't sleeping on the sofa or not being able to stay in the same room with Darika. He even gave his reasons for not leaving her as he was afraid she might kill herself. But of course that wasn't the case at all. He was afraid that if he left her she would try to take half of everything he worked so hard for. And that was the case with Beverly. She was not worried about him killing her. She was worried about if his so-called detective got pictures of her adulteress acts, the judge wouldn't award her shit in the divorce.

Keith knew the game, he had played it. But he wasn't going to be played. He loved her and he was willing to take care of her but he wasn't going to share her any longer. She needed to make a choice.

Keith had managed to walk up the stairs and had fallen asleep on the sofa in the den. Odessia woke him with the smell of breakfast and singing. He had had only three hours of sleep, which did him just fine. Since childhood he had never been a person who needed much sleep. He did his usual five mile run and came back home to have breakfast with Odessia. She was prancing around the house in the black fur he had given her for Christmas, wearing only her panties and bra beneath it.

When the phone rang Odessia was pushing Keith out of the

door because they were already late as usual but this time it wasn't her fault. Keith was the blame. Odessia ran back to answer it, thinking it might be her parents, but instead, it was Darika.

"Hey, girlfriend." Darika said and laughed.

"Damn," she muttered and rolled her eyes.

"Who is it?" Keith asked her.

"What do you want, Darika?"

"Damn," Keith muttered. "Hang up the phone." Two weeks or so had gone by and he hadn't seen or heard from Darika. He was beginning to think she had gone on with her life.

"We are on our way out of the door and don't have time for this today. Today is Christmas."

"I don't give a damn if it's Easter. Let me speak with Keith. I have something to tell him."

"He's outside in the car."

"Why are you lying? I thought you and I were better than that.He's standing right there in the door."

Odessia ran passed Keith to look out the door for Darika's car. "Where are you?"

"See, you are worried about the wrong thing when you should be worried about where is Keith. Odessia, you are a beautiful girl and you've had your share of men. I heard you used to fuck everything that would fuck you, even old grey-head Walter, Cassandra's husband. Isn't he your daddy's age. No, isn't Cassandra one of your closest friends? If she only knew just as if you only knew. Now let me speak with my husband, bitch."

She held the phone away from her ear shocked at the fact anyone knew about her and Walter.

"What's going on?"

"It's your wife." Odessia handed him the phone and walked outside to the car.

"Don't you have something better to do than call us every minute of the day? It's Christmas."

"I know that. I just thought I would call you and wish you a merry one. We are still friends, aren't we, in spite of everything you've done to me."

He sighed. "Merry Christmas, Darika."

"Thank you. Did Beverly enjoy her Christmas gift from you?"

He chuckled. "What are you talking about? What Christmas gift?"

"The one you gave her up in the Colorado mountains. You told me you sold that cabin and you and that bitch went there a week ago. She's a married woman. But I'm sorry I'm mistaking you as a man that gives a damn. So you really don't want Odessia. You just want that slut Beverly Hayman. Her friend."

"Bye, Darika."

"You better not dare hang up this phone. Her husband doesn't know and neither does Odessia. I'll be the first to tell them."

With a devilish grin he shrugged his shoulders giving less than a damn. "Be my guest." And he hung up the phone.

It took everything in Beverly not to curse Brenda out and hang up the phone in her face. She was annoying just as she was when they were kids. Nothing about her had changed. She was a manipulative bitch who cared about no one but herself. Four weeks had gone by since she saw her in New Orleans and now all of a sudden out of the blue she calls Beverly asking questions.

"Does he have a brother because he was nice looking. I can tell he likes you and you like him too."

"Brenda what are you talking about?" Beverly asked her while she was on the look out for Gene. He had a habit of sneaking up behind her and now that he was suspecting another man he had really been tip-toeing around trying to find out something.

"Girl, I'm yo' cousin. You can tell me. You see I need one of those rich men too. Shit I'm about to lose the shop if I don't come up with seven thousand dollars for back rent. He's rich isn't he? I can tell from those shoe. You know what they say about a man and his shoes. You always get the rich men—Gene, and now— what's his name again?"

"Don't worry about it."

"I tell you, that man I got ain't hitting on shit. Girl, he can't help me buy a can of beans if I needed it. He lost his job a couple of weeks ago. If I could get me something rich on the side or just any man on the side I would do it because this one man, shit, ain't working. I can't lose my shop. I've worked too hard for it. And if I tried to go up on the prices, those broke bitches who come to me every week will stop."

"Well, you have to do what you have to do and if going up on your prices is going to help, do it."

"That's easy for you to say. You design clothes for a living and for the rich at that, so they don't give a damn how much you go up on your clothes. But those broke bitches I deal with, they care. Chile, they'll drop my ass like a hot plate. The bank won't loan me a cent. I still live in an apartment, don't have no collateral to give 'im.""

"Why are you calling me with this, Brenda?" she asked her as she flopped down on the sofa and raked her short hair behind her ears. It was now in the growing stages and she didn't know whether to wear it over her ears or behind them.

"So you couldn't invite me to yo' lil' Christmas party last night. I'm yo' family, too. More family than Mike is."

"So is that what this is about?"

"What, do you think I'm gon' tell Gene I saw you in New Orleans with some other man." She chuckled. "Chile, we are family and that niggah means nothing to me. What you do is yo' business and what he doesn't know won't hurt 'im."

Beverly laughed out loud. "You are something else, Brenda. So if I tell you no, what are you going to do then?"

"Why would you tell me no, Damnit," she yelled, getting very frustrated with Beverly. "Bev, you have all of that damn money over there and you've known for months that I'm close to losing my shop and you've never offered to give me one dime," she yelled. "You know the damn bank ain't trying to lend me the money. Why did you give Mike $10,000 anyway. That sissy don't know how to cook. You and I grew up together."

"Why do you have that broke niggah around anyway if he can't help you?"

"He has nothing to do with this and you know it."

"If you didn't have to take care of that so-called man of yours, you would have the money."

"See bitch, that's yo' problem. Always trying to tell some-body else about their life. That's why we can never get along because I'm not gon' let you tell me shit. I'm grown just like you."

"Then why do your grown ass want my money? You and I can't get along because you are a manipulative little bitch. You saw me with Keith and now you want to hold that shit over my head. Hell yes, I'm fooling around and Gene knows."

"You are a damn lie. Gene doesn't know shit. But I tell you what, I'm not losing my shop for nobody."

"So you are trying to tell me you'll tell him if I don't loan you the money? Right."

Brenda didn't say anything.

"How much do you need?"

"Seven thousand."

"And you need it by when?"

"By next Monday."

"Blackmail is a bitch isn't it, but I never would have thought my own cousin—"

"Beverly, I don't want to hear that shit."

"But I tell you what, you can tell Gene any damn thing you want. I'm not giving you a penny. I'll just deny it. Do you actually think I'm going to let you mess up my marriage? Brenda I'll beat your ass before I let you do that."

"I can't lose my shop," Brenda cried and screamed.

Beverly hung up the phone without saying another word. She told Brenda that she didn't care if she told Gene when in reality she did. A prayer was sent up to God that Brenda would just forget about the whole thing. But there was no way of that hap-pening. She needed the money and if Beverly didn't give it to her things might just get ugly. It would have taken Beverly nothing to write her cousin out a check for over seven thousand dollars but she hated the way she had gone about asking her for the money. Blackmail was the low of the lowest.

She was used to her family coming to her for a fast loan every time they got in a jam. Not that she loaned them the money because she realized a long time ago when dealing with family there is no such thing as a loan. They always find a way not to pay her back, which she doesn't mind, but she didn't want to get in the habit of being the family's personal bank. Gene's family had never asked them for one cent but her family had no pride when it came to asking them for money. In the past she had helped stop foreclosure on homes for her Aunt Janice and Uncle Herb and the first time she said no to giving them money to send their daughter off to college she was called a stuck up bitch and they didn't even invite her to their son's wedding. Then they had the nerve to get upset when she didn't send him a monetary gift. Brenda was right she had never offered her one red cent for that shop and her reason being, Calvin, Brenda's boyfriend who she insisted on holding on to. He could never do anything to help her. He was young and all he did was sit around the house all day while she stood on her feet from 9a.m. to 11p.m. doing hair. Beverly wasn't going to help her when she couldn't even help herself by getting rid of that twenty-five year old piece of dick with no other purpose but to fuck her.

Brenda would have been more than welcome to come to Beverly's for Christmas dinner but after she had run into her and Keith in New Orleans Beverly didn't think it was a good idea. Her cousin couldn't hold an ounce of alcohol in her system without acting a fool and showing out and it would have been Beverly's luck that she show out on her and Keith by letting Gene and Odessia and everyone else who had no clue as to what was going on between them find out that she had seen them together.

Beverly got up from the sofa and walked into the dining room to set the table with her best Lenox china. Anita Baker's "You Bring Me Joy" came to her mind and she began to sing it word for word. Each word she sang was for Keith. The joy he had brought her over the last couple of months was unspeakable. She loved him and she could love him from now until if he would let her. Her heart began to pound when she thought about seeing him walk through the door smiling. His smile alone touched her body and soul which caused her to tremble inside. No one noticed her blushing every time he said a word or looked at her. Her love for him had grown deeper. She was now getting to the point of telling Odessia to be quiet when she talked to her about their sex life and all the great things Keith was doing for her. She didn't want to hear that shit. She was talking about the man she loved. She was beginning to feel jealousy and sometime hate for Odessia because she had to share him with her and she was enjoying him. She too knew how wonderful he could make her feel with words, how passionate he could kiss her neck and body and how he could lay inside of her, pulsating her inner love with hardly no movement at all, and she would call out his name with abundance of passionate juices flowing from her love onto his. Beverly couldn't tell her that all she could do was listen to her brag about having a God-sent man. She got somewhat of a rush when they were all together and no one knew she and Keith were talking in codes and looking at each other with love in their eyes waiting for the next time they could lay in each other's arms after making love.

She was happy Gene was out of town and she couldn't wait for him to go back. There was nothing he could do that could make her feel the way Keith was making her feel. Making love to him was now even more difficult and she had become disgusted just by thinking about him touching her. But she had no other choice. She was still his wife and imagining he was Keith lying on top of her.

CHAPTER TWENTY

efore dinner, everyone had gathered in the living room to exchange gifts. It was just an ideal Christmas: four inches of snow covered the grounds outside, The Temptations "Silent Night" played in the background, the egg nog had just enough brandy in it, the tree was fully lit with beautiful decorations and so was everyone else. Jessica, Gene's cousin from New York, called out the names on the gifts and passed them around. She and Gene kind of resembled each other by their huge fat heads and round short bodies. Something wasn't right about her husband Wayne. He kept staring at Keith and his stares were making him feel uncomfortable. When Keith would stare at him back, he would have this silly smirk on his face. A smirk that told Keith, Wayne was on the fruity side. Damn. So Keith pressed his back into the sofa, swelled up his chest with one deep breath, crossed his ankle over his thigh, raised his left eye brow and gave Wayne a stern hard look that said. "I'll put a bullet in your ass instead." Wayne got the message quickly and turned his head the other way.

Beverly had all of Keith's attention, damn Odessia, who was looking just as beautiful in her baby blue velvet dress that hugged her petite body. Beverly was wearing the red suit Keith had bought her while they were in New Orleans and she looked beautiful in it. She called herself flirting with him on the sly but Ella and Gene's mother, Roberta had noticed and both of them rolled their eyes at Keith. He wished Beverly would stop but her alcohol had taken control. Ella had made her way over to Keith as she singed and danced to the Temptations.She tapped Keith on the shoulder to follow her into the kitchen. Keith was surprised by her tap and he was wondering what it was that she wanted because he had never met her before.

"Yes, ma'am?" He asked once he got into the kitchen

"Sit down," she ordered him. "What in the hell do you and that chile of mine think y'all are doing coming in this man's house lusting over each other in front of his people. Are you stupid or just pretending to be? What are your intentions for my daughter if her husband leaves her? Are you just around for the sex or the long haul, the love."

"Mrs. Cook what are you talking about. I don't understand."

"Don't play me dumb I know about you and my chile. Her cousin told me all about it. Gene is a good man and she's willing to mess it up all for you. She's drunk now and don't know what the hell she's out there doing. Dancing and flirting with you with her breast sticking all out."

"I love Beverly, Mrs. Cook."

"She's married."

"And unhappy."

"Unhappy my ass. Do you think she would have stayed married to him thirteen years, hell no. She might not be getting it like she wants it sexually but what the hell is sex. He ain't gay and he's a good man."

"What is going on in here?" Beverly asked as she walked into the kitchen looking at Keith and her mother for an answer.

"Talk to your mother." Keith got up from the table.

"Wait a minute Keith, mama what's up?"

"I tell you what's up. You and this man need to be ashamed of y'all selves."

"Mama look, what are you talking about."

"I know about you two and so does his mother while you are out there dancing around the room flirting with him. Gene is a good man and how dare you bring this man in his house."

"Mama you don't know what you are talking about. Keith is my friend."

"You are sleeping with him because your cousin told me she saw you two in New Orleans together hugged up."

"So what."

"So what," she repeated. "You are married."

"It never stopped you."

"Your daddy was a fruit cake and I told you that."

"I think I better be going," Keith told them.

"That's a good idea," Ella said.

"No, you are not going anywhere. If anybody gets out of here, it's going to be my mother if she keeps this shit up with trying to run my life."

"Run your life. I'm trying to help you save your marriage."

"My marriage is over I love Keith."

"Then why don't you tell him instead of hurting him the way that you are. He knows that you are fooling around he just doesn't know that it's Keith. He told me."

"Fine."

Ella sighed. "I hope you know what you are doing because I don't." She walked out of the kitchen leaving Keith and Beverly staring at one another.

"Merry Christmas, handsome," Beverly told him and walked out of the kitchen. Keith flopped down at the table and thought about Beverly really being unhappy for thirteen years.

While Odessia and the others had gone into the entertainment room to look through Gene's record collection Beverly stayed in the living room and made her way over to the sofa where Keith was sitting. She pretended she needed him to help her bring up her box of Motown records from the basement her father had collected for her, since James Patten and his wife, Betty was looking in her mouth. James was Gene's co-worker and best friend.

Beverly lead the way down the stairs to the dark basement. There was no time to waste. Gene would be back any moment now and both of them were taking a chance. But hell, it was worth it. Beverly had pushed Keith against the wall and shoved her tongue into his mouth. It was a soap opera kiss that seemed like it had been rehearsed time and time again because it had so much passion and Keith's large thick hands caressed her body and breast. The passion lead them to begin taking down each other's pants with no thought of any one coming down the stairs. Any one like Gene because he had gone to his office for a couple of hours to work on a program. Beverly's legs were wrapped around Keith's waist as he tried to find somewhere to lay her down or sit. Boxes were all over the place and there was very little light for them to see. She held on to him with faith he wouldn't drop her as he stumbled over his pants to the chair in the corner. The thought of them taking a chance while both of their lovers were upstairs with a house full of people was somewhat frightening but exciting. Beverly tore away at Keith's back with her finger nails as he tore away at her insides as if it was a small tight tunnel he was trying to force himself into. The feeling made her scream out his name to the top of her lungs. She knew no one could hear her because the basement was underground. Suddenly Keith heard silent footsteps of someone easing their way down the stairs. He made Beverly aware but she was still whispering in his ear to make love to her. The footsteps seemed closer but neither one of them would pull apart. They were about to reach a climax neither one of them had ever experienced in their lives. The feeling was so unreal they couldn't stop pumping and moaning. A voice called out.

"Baby, I'm back. Are you down here?"

"O' shit," Beverly and Keith whispered once they noticed the footsteps and the voice belonging to Gene. Keith immediately snatched himself out of her while releasing his seed of offspring inside her. She jumped up off his lap leaving him in the corner and ran over to put on her panties and pants. She ran her fingers through her hair and met Gene at the bottom step.

"Hey, baby," she said, and kissed him on the cheek. "Did you finish?"

"Yeah, what are you doing down here?"

"I came down here to get my Motown collection for Julie and Keith to listen to."

"I didn't see Keith up there."

"Are you sure, because I just talked to him and Odessia."

"Did you find it?"

"No." She closed the door and began to walk up the stairs.

"Because it's upstairs in Jabari's room. He's been trying to sample them. Remember he asked you last night if it was okay if he borrowed them."

"O'," she said smiling, "I forgot. Jabari," She screamed as she ran up the stairs.

Keith hid behind the chair trying to catch his breath and waiting for the coast to clear. He managed to slip outside through the side basement door without anyone seeing him. His heart was beating and racing with fear. For the first time he believed Beverly when she told him Gene would kill them if he caught them together. And he knew the judge would determine it as a justifiable death because he had no business fucking another man's wife in his own house. He leaned up against the door taking three deep breaths making up his mind to end it if she didn't make the right choice. When he walked through the front door, Gene was there to greet him. Keith immediately looked down at his hand to make sure he didn't have a gun pointing at his chest.

"Where have you been?" he asked and blew the smoke of his cigar up into the air. "Odessia and my wife have been looking all over for you."

Keith could have sworn Gene put emphasis on the word wife.

"Outside. I ate a little bit too much," he said patting his stomach. "And I had to walk some of it off." He walked into the living room with the others and he felt Gene's eyes stabbing him in the back. No wonder they haven't even eaten yet.

Beverly handed Keith a glass of Hennessey while singing along with Smokey Robinson's "Tears of a Clown." Keith looked over his shoulders for Gene and he was nowhere in sight. "I need to talk to you."

"Sure." They walked over to the box of records pretending to be looking through them. "You are the best and I love you," Beverly whispered. "Yesterday I wanted to call you but you know Gene was in my face."

He nodded as if he understood but he really didn't. He figured if she really wanted to call him she would have found a way.

"Gene will be going back Monday after New Years and we can go back to the way things were. I know this place—"

"Not until you make a choice," he muttered between his teeth. "I'm not good at being in love with someone and they have other obligations such as a husband. You said you didn't love him so I'm asking you to make a choice."

"A choice between what? You and Gene, my husband? Baby, I thought everything was going fine between us. You can't just expect me to just tell 'im I'm leaving him." Because she wasn't going to do it. She had a good husband in spite of her not loving him; he loved her. She had seen women leave a happy home for a man they thought would bring them happiness. She couldn't use her mother as an example anymore because she had her reasons for leaving her father but the other women she knew had no good reason other than they were voodooed and thought they were in love when in reality it was an effectuation. For the first time she began to examine their relationship and the love they say they had for each other, now that he was coming to her about leaving her husband. She will not be gotten by the game. "Do you know what he would do?" she asked him.

"Nothing. Do you love me, Beverly? Do you want to be with me? Yes or no? I can't handle sharing you with him."

She sighed and chuckled. "He's going to take everything if I leave him. Half of my company will be his and I can't let that happen."

"And. It's not about the money, isn't it, Beverly? Is having this damn house and money that important than being with a man you love. When I say I love you, I do."

"Jabari."

"What about him. Jabari is twenty-one years old. He'll get over it. You are not happy and I'm pretty sure Jabari knows that."

"What will every one say. What about Odessia?"

"You don't care about Odessia so don't worry about that. I'm giving you until next week to make up your mind. I know tonight is too soon for you to make a decision so I'm not asking you to."

Neither one of them noticed Gene standing in the doorway staring at them.

"If you don't give me the right answer, I can't stay around."

"You're kidding me, right?"

"Nope. Make a choice, Beverly, it's not that hard. I'm here to rescue you from all of this."

Rescue her from what she felt like asking. It wasn't like Gene was abusing her or mistreating her in anyway. She had forgiving him for his so-called affair with Joanne. She couldn't believe he was pressuring her to make a decision between him or her husband. But it wasn't going to be hard. she had too much at stake to leave her husband for a relationship that might not last longer than a week after she packed her things. "I can't do that."

"Even if I'm willing to marry you to assure you that I love you and we are meant to be together."

"No. I can't. Keith, we've only been seeing each other for months and we have to come to a point where we ask ourselves is it love or an effectuation?"

He grinned trying to understand what was going on. The first woman he had ever loved didn't love him. Love and it's consequences. "Effectuation?" he replied. "Is that what all of this was to you?"

"No, it was something special but maybe we are a little confused between the two. I'm a married woman."

Fine. It was nice." He got up from his knees and walked over to Odessia and put his arm around her. He was sure Beverly would jump at the chance to be with him and now that she didn't he was hurt but he couldn't let it show.

While everyone else was mingling, Keith and Odessia were hugged up carrying on their own conversation with each other.

Beverly was becoming sick to her stomach and she couldn't take her eyes off of them. Her temper boiled with anger and every time Odessia tried to talk to her she would cut her off or ignore her. She didn't care if she noticed or not. There was no need for her friendship any longer because she and Keith were over. Keith knew how she felt about him hugging on Odessia and he was doing it anyway in her house in her face. She didn't know if he was trying to make her jealous or if he was seriously in love with her just as she had suspected. Gene had tried to touch her and she nearly cursed him out for doing so. Her stomach was in knots and she felt like crying.

"Get the fuck out of my house," she screamed and didn't care who heard her.

"Why?" he asked calmly.

"How dare you throw her in my face, hugging and kissing on her as if I'm not standing here."

He chuckled. "Beverly, you are married and unhappy. I gave you a chance to go to another level with this and you chose not to. We can walk out there now and tell everybody. I don't care I just want to be with you."

"It is not that easy, Keith."

And he knew this but his confidence had been shattered when she refused to leave her husband. "I love you but if you don't want anything with this neither do I. Odessia is a wonderful lady."

"But you said you didn't love her."

"Things have changed."

Tears came to her eyes and she wiped them before they fell.

"You said you didn't love Gene but you are willing to stay with him and I don't understand that. You feel something for him. It's best that we go our separate ways. I admit I became a little bit too involved to come in here and tell you to leave your husband. What we were supposed to have didn't involve love but somehow we went against the odds and fell in love anyway. No one knew about us so between you and me we have the memories. "

"You bastard."

"No Beverly, this is your choice." He walked back into the living room grabbed his and Odessia's coat. And motioned for her to come on. They told everyone in the room good night and a Merry Christmas.

"Where is Beverly?" She asked while looking around the room. "I have to tell her good night and thank her for inviting us." She went looking for her until she found her in the kitchen. "Hey, girl." She noticed Beverly had been crying.

"What's wrong?"

Beverly nodded her head because the lump in her throat wouldn't let her speak.

"Keith and I are getting ready to leave and I wanted to thank you for having us over. I don't know why he's in such a rush to leave. It's still early so I guess I'm going to go and give him a warm bath."

"Odessia, excuse me if I might seem rude but I don't want to hear about that tonight."

"I'm sorry," she said, and hugged her. "It's Gene is it? It'll be all right. Well, let me get out of here. Mr. Impatient is waiting on me and you know how he is. See you New Years Eve."

Beverly watched her walk out of the kitchen and she cried even more. Why was she staying with Gene? Was it all in her mind that he had someone following her and that he would kill her if he ever found out? She didn't love him and it wasn't fair to her or him to stay in the marriage and be unhappy and in love with someone else.

Maybe she had analyzed their relationship to make it seem like it was nothing, and now that he was gone and she was missing him like crazy, an effectuation had nothing to do with it. It was pure love. A week to think about him and miss him had caused her to regret ever letting him walk out of her life and take her heart and happiness with him. And it was now too late to change things because he did not want to talk to her. With no place to sneak away to after work and no phone calls to sneak and return, she was back to her usual depressed unhappy self. She took some days off work because there was no way she could design anything under these conditions. Several times during the week she had paged Keith and called him but he would never return her page and he was too busy to talk to her. And she had given Odessia the same treatment when Odessia had called her. There was nothing they had to talk about as far as she was concerened.She had picked out her platinum sequence short strapless dress to wear that night for the New Year's Eve Ball at the Emerald. She and Gene were going to meet Keith and Odessia and she couldn't wait. She missed having him around. She hoped they would be able to talk things out and perhaps start over. In that short time that they were together he had become a part of her life in a very special way. Beverly had tried to turn the love she had for Keith into love for Gene but it just didn't work. He wasn't Keith and he was far from it. His words meant nothing and his touch had no affect. With him being home he was making things worse instead of better. She had gotten used to dealing with him over the phone some thousand miles away. It was better that way.

Keith had put the thought in her head not that it wasn't there already but there was a place and a time for her to do it. Earlier that week she had come close to telling him that she wanted a divorce but she decided against it when she thought of him killing her and himself. She had even rehearsed how she would say it one morning after they woke up.

He would be sitting at the kitchen table reading the paper and she would walk down and standing in the doorway she would say "I've thought about this for along time and it's about time I tell you, Gene I don't love you and to be truthful I never have. You are a wonderful husband but you are not for me. I knew this thirteen years ago but I couldn't bring myself to tell you, afraid of what you might do to me so now I'm telling you that I want a divorce. I'm in love with someone else."

"Who? Who is he, Beverly?" She imagined him asking.

She thought about saying his name really fast to get it over with or not saying his name at all but she knew Gene wouldn't let it go at that. He would have to know who she had fallen in love with so she would tell him. "Keith."

He would slam his paper on the table and fall back in his chair. "I had always thought it but I prayed that it wasn't so. I've noticed how you two look at each other and talk in codes as if you are getting away with something." He would get up from the table with tears in his eyes walking over to her. "I love you, Beverly, and I wished that you would love me too."

He would walk upstairs and load his gun and walk back down stairs and say "But if I can't have you neither can he." And shoot her in the head and then turn the gun on himself.

She was just killed for nothing. She shook her head at the thought and decided against telling him.

As the time grew nearer for them to head to the Ball, Beverly bubbled over with joy. She rushed Gene to tie his tie and put on his shoes in the car and said yes to everything Jabari asked her not paying attention to any of it. But of course he was lying and asking her while she was rushing out of the door.

Beverly hadn't seen some of the people that were speaking to her in awhile. She spoke with them for a couple of minutes to find out what had been going on in their lives since the last time she saw them. As usual she had all the attention for her beautiful dress. She looked around the room for Keith but there was no sight of him; she hoped that he was still coming. As a matter of fact, she prayed that he would walk through the door any minute now. It was eleven thirty p.m., thirty minutes before countdown to 1999. Gene had gone to the bar to get them a drink. Now was the perfect time because they could talk. She turned around to say hello to a couple of ladies she knew and there was Keith walking down the stairs into the room with Odessia on his arm. Beverly smiled inside and waved for them to come over to the sit she had saved for them. Odessia rushed over and hugged her tightly and Keith spoke without even looking at her. As usual he looked like he had just stepped out of GQ magazine.

"Girl, I've been trying to get in contact with you all this week," Odessia told her. "Keith and I flew to New Orleans the other day for Gumbo,"

She quickly glanced at Keith and rolled her eyes.

"And I wanted to see if you and Gene wanted to come along. Let me tell you, that was the best gumbo I had ever eaten," she said smiling as she looked across the room and noticed her brother and his wife."Baby, there goes Winston and Patricia, wave." They both waved and she walked across the room to talk to them.

"Why haven't you returned any of my calls?" Beverly asked Keith. "I still have my pager you know."

"Cause there's no need to and you need to return that as soon as possible because I'm having my secretary have it turned off. Everything we needed to talk about, Beverly we talked about it Christmas night." He put his hand in his pocket and looked down into her eyes. "When I thought we were loving each other, you were thinking it was only an effectuation. I loved you damnit and you tell me it meant nothing. I didn't expect you to leave 'im right away but as long as you knew I wasn't going to sit in the background while you play the cheating wife. Do you know how many times the word effectuation played in my head?"

"I."

"You don't need to call me. Like you said, you are a married woman and I'm happy with Odessia—"

"No you're not and I won't let you tell me that you are. I miss you like crazy, Keith and I don't even know what to do with myself. To be truthful I was afraid of what I was feeling for you. I'm married and I fell in love with another man. It wasn't supposed to happen like that."

"I was only supposed to fuck you because your husband wasn't, right? Please, let me try it again I'll guarantee you I'll do just that. Beverly your mother made good sense to me. You are not unhappy you just wasn't getting any. I was the fool to fall in love but no damn more. Do you want to try this thing again I'll fuck you and not feel a damn thing for you."

"Must you be so cruel?"

"As long as you are. You knew all along you weren't leaving.If I would have been cruel in the first damn place I wouldn't be the one looking like the fool here."

They both got quiet when they spotted Gene walking over to
"Hello, Gene," Keith said, and extending his hand out to shake his.

Gene looked down at his hand and looked at Beverly before shaking it. "Hello."

"You two have a nice night." He walked across the room to Odessia. Gene and Beverly stood staring at each other.

"Excuse me I'm going to the ladies room." With tears in her eyes she rushed out of the ballroom doors down the hall to the ladies room. She flopped down at the vanity making sure a tear didn't fall by dotting her eyes with the handkerchief.

"Who are you fooling? You don't love no one but yourself and I'm beginning to believe you don't even have enough heart to love yourself."

She looked into the mirror at Darika standing behind her and rolled her eyes.

"You're cheating on your husband with your best friend's man. Now damn if that's someone who cares about anybody I'm fooled. He doesn't want you. Let me tell you something about Keith, he's no fool and neither is Gene, but Odessia, yeah, you have her fooled, because that fool has no clue that you are a backstabbing bitch."

"Is that hurt talking or jealousy that I had your ex-husband who you were married to for ten years loving me in four months and you couldn't get him to love you out of ten years. Damn, what does that say about you? You're the fool if anybody is—you just won't give up will you?"

"Two minutes before the countdown." A voice yelled into the ladies room.

Beverly fixed her makeup and got up from the vanity and warned Darika. "You don't want to mess with me."

"Why not? Before it's all over with I'm going to mess with you, Odessia and any other woman that just insist on coming between me and my husband."

"What? You are not over it yet, honey, please. The divorce was final some months ago. Were you not in the courtroom?" She asked Darika and chuckled just before she walked out of the ladies room looking over her shoulders to make sure Darika didn't act out as crazy as she sounded.

It was one minute to countdown before 1998 became a part of history and 99 became the present. Beverly held tight to Gene's hand hoping for a better year than last. Not that 98 was any trouble for her but hoping for a better year was always a part of her prayer for New Years. She counted from the top of her lungs "5,4,3,2,1, Happy New Years." She hugged Gene's body and kissed him as if she felt love for him. She spotted Odessia and Keith standing behind her. Beverly opened her arms to Odessia and hugged and kissed her. Then she opened her arms to Keith. They hugged tight enough for their souls to embrace knowing it would be their last.

CHAPTER TWENTY-ONE

Keith sat on the edge of his bed staring down at the floor trying to think of a way to tell Odessia it was over between them. He watched her as she slept peacefully which made it hard for him to wake her with such hurting news. He didn't want to hurt her but he had to be honest with her and himself and be with the woman he loved.

"Odessia," Keith said, trying to wake her. "Odessia."

"Baby, just give me a couple of minutes."

"No, it's not about that I need to speak with you. It's something I need to tell you."

"What's going on?" She asked as she sat up in bed. "Are you alright."

"No, because there's a lot on my mind and I need to talk." He stood up and walked to the front of the room. "You are a very wonderful lady and one day you'll make a man a good wife."

"Keith, what is going on?"

"I haven't been honest with you and I don't blame you if you think I'm a dog or even low-down. I didn't know how to tell you because I saw how much you were in to me and you wanted this to work. I did too but it can't."

"Who is she?"

"I love her. I've always loved her and I want to be with her."

"Who is she, Keith."

"I know this might come as a shock to you but not to me because this woman will always have a place in my heart. I love Darika."

"You what? You are joking right. You two are divorced. She slept around on you. She hurt you, right. That's what you said, right. She's crazy how could you love her. Is that who you've been sleeping with all this time? Darika?"

"No."

"It's been someone else."

"No. The feelings just came back since she and I been talking. I've fooled around on her and she only fooled around on me to get my attention. He meant nothing to her just like the women I slept with meant nothing to me."

"I don't believe what I'm hearing. This is a dream, right?"

"No. I do love her."

Odessia began to chuckle and then cry.

"Why are you crying? You knew there was a possibilty of us getting back together. You knew you and I weren't where we needed to be."

"But I never thought it was because you still loved that bitch Darika."

"Things change and so do people. I've changed and so has she. We were both hurting and the divorce should have never happened."

"What do you mean it should have never happened, are you crazy or something. Have you forgotten? You caught another man with his hand between her legs. She told you that she fucked men in your bed—in your house." She wished he would get where she was coming from and wake the hell up.

"We both have done some fucked up things."

"I don't believe this."

"I need for you to pack the little things that you do have here and leave."

"You need for me to do what? Just like that. Fine." She jumped out of bed and threw on her clothes. "I hope you know what you are doing. I tried so hard to make you love me and it was all in vain. You never cared for me. You just used me."

"And how did I do that? I told you I didn't want a relationship. We hardly had sex. How did I use you."

"You bastard," she said and flopped down on the bed. "Beverly told me you were a lying, cheating asshole."

"The hell with Beverly if you really want to know the truth." He came close to telling her the truth but decided what they had was only an ex-factor and he didn't want to end their friendship or Beverly's marriage. "She just didn't want you to be happy because she wasn't happy. Gene had her ass fooled. While she's up here thinking his fat ass wasn't fucking, he was doing his secretary."

"You don't know what you are talking about. Gene would never do that to her. Only you are the low-down whore who can't keep his pants up. And just to think, Darika told me you would do me like this."

"Do you like what? I'm going back to her, she's my ex-wife. People divorce and get back together every day. You and I enjoyed each other but we weren't meant to be."

"Fine. You don't have to tell me twice." She walked over to the closet and packed up the couple of things she had hanging and walked down the stairs. "I hope you're happy now. What did tonight mean to you? We brought in the New Years together, we said we loved each other. What did that mean?"

"Darika needs me."

"I need you."

"It just won't work. When I saw Darika last night and we talked and laughed, I saw beauty and I felt love for her. I need to give this thing another try."

"Did you tell her you were going to break the news to me tonight? I guess she just can't wait."

"No, she doesn't know."

"Well, it was nice," she said standing in the front door. "I had it coming. By-bye." She walked out of the door without looking back.

Keith slammed the door and ran over to the phone to call Darika.

"Hello, Darika, we need to talk,and we need to talk now."

Keith felt like a new man as he whipped up eggs and squeezed fresh orange juice with a smile as big as Texas on his face. If there was a cow outside he would have milked it for fresh milk because Darika only deserved the best. Between them talking and making love all morning they had little time for sleep. But it wasn't missed, they enjoyed each other's company and touch and if they slept they were afraid they would miss a moment. The way they carried on, it was as if they had never separated. Darika welcomed Keith back into her life with open arms and he made himself right at home.

"Baby do you still like your eggs over-easy?" Keith asked her as she poured both of them a cup of coffee."

"Yes, do you still drink your coffee black or with cream."

"Black like you."

They kissed and laughed.

"My husband is back." Darika screamed. "And I love him."

"Baby, do you want sausage or bacon."

"Whatever you're having."

"I'm going to be having you in a couple of minutes."

She wrapped her arms around his waist. "We never should have left each other but it just made me see how much I loved you. I can't believe you are here with me. I thought they had taken you from me.Odessia was so sure you were going to be hers."

"Let's not talk about that. I'm here with you and that's all that matters."

"And you're damn right," she said and kissed him. "I have a taste for some gumbo."

"New Orleans got the best gumbo. What'cha say about us flying there for lunch."

"Dinner. We are going to sleep through lunch."

It took every thing in Beverly not to cry when Odessia told her the news. Now she wished she would have slapped the hell out of Darika in the bathroom last night when she called her a backstabbing bitch. She hated Darika's black ass and she felt sorry for Odessia for whatever that was worth. She was willing to live with him loving Odessia but Darika. She felt like Darika had won.

"You have to be kidding me. He woke you up out of your sleep and made you get out. He didn't even have the decency to wait until the morning? Let her have him. He's not worth it. After all that talk about how she hurt him, that bastard had the nerve to go back to her. Girl, he's forty but he has a lot of growing up to do. You didn't need him anyway." She pushed her plate away and fell back in her chair.

"But I love him."

"You still do, after he's dropped a bomb on you such as this? Excuse my french, but fuck him." She was really angry but she could still understand Odessia's love for him because she was feeling the same and glad she wasn't the only one.

"What's up with you and Keith anyway? Last night I detected a little animosity toward you from him and now I'm detecting the same from you. I thought you two were cool."

Because I wasn't a fool to leave my husband, she thought. And now she was glad she didn't if he was going to go back to his wife. "Girl, because I began to realize he wasn't shit along time ago."

"Why didn't you tell me?"

"You were in love. You probably wouldn't have listen anyway "I learned along time ago you don't give advice if it's not asked for."

"I asked you," she said, after taking a bite of her sandwich.

"Yeah, you did but it just wasn't my place."

"He's never talked about her before last night. The news was a shock to me. Here I am thinking there's some other woman and it was Darika."

"They were sleeping together?" Beverly asked.

"He said they weren't but I know that they were. I'm not a fool What they have was something in the making."

"No. I know for a fact they hadn't been sleeping together. Unless it just happened recently."

"How do you know?"

"He's never talked about her in a loving way. She has something on him."

"Something like what."

"Voodoo. All of the signs point to it. Him waking up in the middle of the night and wanting to be with her and only her. She had him fixed."

Odessia laughed. "Girl, do you believe in that mess?"

"Sure I do. I was raised in Georgia. Women worked roots all day long to keep their man. Keith didn't want to have anything to do with her a couple of months ago and now all of a sudden he's in love with her. I bet she cooked him some dinner and put it in his food."

"Beverly, no."

"Yes. She's crazy like that. Keith wouldn't have wanted her any other way. Voodoo is powerful. It controls the mind, soul and heart."

Odessia laughed out loud. "Well, Keith must have it on me because I can't let him go no matter what he told me last night. I love that man and I've never felt this way about anyone."

Beverly shook her head because she understood.

When Keith walked into the supper room of the Emerald, both of the ladies broke out into a sweat.

"There he goes," Odessia told Beverly. "Keith."

"Don't call him over here."

"Hush. Keith."

He walked over to them while looking around the room. "Hello, ladies."

"Hi, how are you?" Odessia asked and got up to hug him. "Having lunch alone?"

"No. Darika will be joining me she's in the ladiesroom."

"No, Darika is joining me, she's in the ladies room."

"She's here? Why are you doing this to me?"

"Because he's a self-centered bastard who doesn't care about anyone but himself," Beverly told him. "You like hurting people don't you? You get a kick out of it."

"Have a nice day ladies." He turned around and walked over to Darika and hugged her.

"Damn. She got him," Odessia cried and runs out of the room.

Beverly looks at Keith and Darika and rolls her eyes. Her stomach is sicken with the both of them.

"Now isn't that ashame, he left both of you and went back to his wife," Ursula said, laughing when she walked over to Beverly.

"Go to hell." Beverly said, as she got up from the table and stormed out of the room.

Darika sat at the bar in the Emerald sipping on a glass of sweet tea as she waited on her TAE BO class to began. She felt good about herself and her life. She and her husband was back together and they were in love. She didn't care if he didn't come back on his own as long as he was back and loving her that's all that mattered. If she would have waited on God or for Odessia and Beverly to take their claws out of him she would have been waiting forever. Keith and her belonged together and by his mind being clouded with other women he never would have realized she's the only woman for him. She was enjoying having a second chance at being the wife she should have in the beginning. Every night she cooks him dinner. She cleans the house and gives him sex every time he's ready. But since she's reached her prime it's been the other way around, they've been having sex every time she's ready. She's been meaning to call Madam Ruth to tell her the good news but she's been so busy with other things such as being a wife and in love. She wished she would have met her along time ago and a lot of things between she and Keith could have been avoided such as him being unfaithful and the divorce. Keith asked her last night to remarry him and she accepted. This time they were going to have a huge wedding and she was going to have Beverly design her dress. Darika did find time to call and thank Phyillis but made her promise not to tell any of her other family members she and Keith were back together again. Darika did not want to hear them talk. Especial when she tells them she and Keith plan to be remarried. She and Keith were doing fine and that's how she wanted it to stay. As long as her family wasn't involved, there were no other women and Madam Ruth knew voodoo things would stay fine between them. She didn't even tell Cookie.

Darika was trying to figure out what she would cook Keith for dinner when a man around in his late forties walked pass the door carrying his golf clubs. He glanced at Darika and smiled. Darika didn't have a chance to smile back for trying to make out whether he was smiling at her or not. She had never seen him around the Emerald before and she wanted to know who he was. She got up from her chair and ran over to the window and waited for him to walk across the patio to the golf course so that she could see him again. She waited and looked for him but he never came.

"Are you looking for someone?" He asked as he stood behind her smiling.

Darika turned around very quickly feeling very embarrassed. "No, I thought I saw someone I knew."

"I'm sorry we've never met before, I'm Richard Grooms." He extended his hand out to her to shake.

"Hello, Richard I'm, Darika Jones."

"Nice to meet you." His smile was beautiful but he wasn't all that attractive as Darika thought when he walked pass the door. But he still had Darika's attention and he wasn't even light skin.

Corey wasn't light skin either but he was the only thing she could get her hands on to hurt Keith.

"I noticed you as you were getting out of your car in the parking lot and I wanted to introduce myself then but you seemed like you were in a hurry."

"I was trying to get to my TAE BO class but little did I know it was cancelled."

"Good because you don't need to work out your body looks like it is in perfect shape."

Darika smiled and pulled her T-shirt down over her wide hips.

"I've never seen you around here before, are you new," Darika asked him.

No, I've just never had time to come. I'm busy with work, and raising two teenage daughters. So while I'm on vacation I just decided to come here and play some golf and take a couple of laps around the pool."

"Are you raising your daughters alone?"

"Yes. And I never thought it would get the best of me with them wanting to wear the lates fashions, boys and curfew."

Darika smiled. "Those are teenage girls for you."

"Do you have any children?"

"No."

"Are you married?"

Without thinking twice she answered. "No, divorced."

"How long?"

"Recently. And what about yourself."

"My wife died a year ago of lung cancer."

"I'm sorry to hear that."

"You remind me of her. She was a beautiful dark-skin woman just like yourself."

"Thank you." Darika said, smiling.

"You have a beautiful smile also. If you don't mind me asking, would you like to join me for lunch right now?"

"Sure."

He signaled for a waitress. They sat at a table in the middle of the room.

"I haven't dated since my wife—"

"I understand trying to find a woman to fill her shoes can be hard. How long were you married?"

"Twenty-two years."

"A long time."

He stared at her and smiled. "You are too beautiful."

"O'stop it. I'm not that beautiful."

"Yes you are. You are so beautiful I can't keep my eyes off of you."

"You're very sweet to say those things."

"But it's true. Dark skin women are so beautiful and sensual to me. Light skin women can be also. So you are a divorced woman, how do you feel about dating again, or are you dating already?"

"I would love to remarry."

He chuckled. "I said date. You women skipping the dating game jumping right into marriage."

"I'm sorry. I would love to date."

"So would I. I'm not your typical man, I see what I want and I go after it, I move fast. When I walked pass that door and saw you for a second time I wasn't going to let you slip through my fingers. I might find out later over conversation that a relationship with me, is something you don't want but right now I know that I want you."

Darika smiled at his forwardness which turned her own. She's never had a man to approach her the way that he was. She wondered what was his motive other than trying to get her into bed. Every now and then a con artist comes through the Emerald and take a couple of people for their money. Richard didn't look like a con but he was saying too many of the right things for Darika to believe he wasn't.

"So what is it that you do?" Darika asked him.

"I'm a cardiologist, have been for seventeen years. I'm from Oregon. I've been in D.C. for ten years. I lost my wife as I've already told you to lung cancer because she was a smoker. Smoked a pack a cigarettes a day. You don't smoke do you?"

"No."

"Good. I never thought about dating another woman because of my daughters but I realized they don't need a mother because they are sixteen and seventeen old enough to take care of themselves but I need some companionship. Darika, I'm lonely."

That still didn't answer her question whether he was a con or not. She was happy he wasn't looking for a wife to be a mother to his daughters because she didn't think she could deal with raising some other woman's children but she still needed to see some credentials on whether he was a doctor or not.

"I would love to meet your daughters."

"That will be great. Why don't you join us for dinner tonight at my place and maybe I can pull them from their boyfriends long enough to meet a beautiful woman such as yourself."

She smiled as she's been doing the whole time he's been sitting across from her. It was something about his looks, smile and words that made her feel sexy all over. "You know how to say all the right things to make a woman smile, don't you?"

"I try to. A woman is so precious and beautiful she needs kind words from a man to keep her that way."

He sounds to good to be true, Darika thought.

"What time should I be over tonight?"

"Seven-thirty. I have to call Winnie and let her know you are coming."

"That's one of your daughters."

"No my daughters names are Keshia and Alicia. Winnie, is my housekeeper."

"Teenage daughters don't cook nor clean and neither do I."

Darika couldn't wait to see Richard again. She was going to rush over to Keith's house and perpare dinner for him before he got there and she was going home to get ready for the night. She couldn't believe Keith didn't cross her mind as she sat talking to another man about dating. She was interested in Richard but she wanted to make sure he was for real and not out to get her.

When she pulled into Keith's driveway there was his car. Damn, what is he doing home so early, Darika asked herself as she threw her car in park and thought of a quick lie in order to cook dinner and leave. Darika walked into the house smelling the aroma of fried chicken cooking. She walked into the kitchen where Keith was.

"Home so early?" She asked Keith.

He turned around smiling with flour on his face and apron. "Hey, baby I didn't hear you come in. Have a seat and I'll pour you a glass of wine. How was your work-out?"

"It was cancelled." She remained standing.

"I rushed home to cook dinner for you but I see you decided to cook dinner for yourself."

"No, this is for you. I got out of the office early just so I could pamper my baby." He walked over to her and puckered up for a kiss. "I wasn't expecting you until another hour so I haven't had the chance to run your bath but go upstairs anyway I have something for you up there."

"What is it?" She ran upstairs to the bedroom and Keith followed her. There were three big boxes beautifully wrapped on the bed with a single red rose on each of them. "Which one do I open first?"

"Either one you would like but only one for right now." She placed the stem of the rose between her lips and tore into the green wrapped box first and dug through the paper until she felt a small box the size of a ring box. She opened it and screamed. "O' my God." Her eyes gleamed and cried as Keith walked over to her and placed the 5ct. diamond onto her finger.

"I know I asked you this last night but it wasn't done right so I'm going to do it with a little bit more class. Darika, will you marry me?"

"God, yes!" She hugged him as tight as she could, kissing him all over his face. "Thank you, Keith. Thank you"

"We are going to make this thing work, baby I promise you that."

"Yes we are."

They kissed and began to consummate their engagement. When Darika finally woke in Keith's arms the time was six-thirty. She jumped up out of the bed and began putting on her clothes.

"Baby, what's wrong. Where are you going?"

"I'm going to be late. I have to meet Cookie."

"I have things planned for us tonight I'm cooking dinner and you have these two other gifts you haven't opened."

"I know baby but I have to meet Cookie this is very important she'll kill me if I don't."

"And I'll be upset if you walk out that door. Call her and tell her that you can't come. I just asked you to marry me and you, take the ring, fuck me and leave."

"What are you talking about, Keith? I have to meet Cookie, she's going through hell with that bastard Antonio and she needs my help right now. She's afraid he might try to kill her if she leaves him, she needs to talk to me."

"She just doesn't want to leave him, she's not afraid he might kill her. All women who are voodooed use that same damn lie."

"Voodooed, Keith? That dumb bastard don't know nothing about voodoo."

"Those are the ones that do."

"Baby, I need to be going."

"I want you home by ten."

She looked at him and then the clock. "You got it." She rushed out of the house to her car, out of the driveway and home to get dressed.

CHAPTER TWENTY-TWO

"My life couldn't be better Dr. McClinton and I didn't have to take any of those damn things," she said pointing at the pills on the table she had placed down when she walked into the office. "Do you know when the last time I popped one of those crazy pills? Three months ago after my divorce was final which was the last time I was here to see you."

"So why are you here today?" he asked.

"Just to let you know how my life is going because I thought you just might want to evaluate my change. I told you that I didn't have that damn bi-polar crap. I'm fine because I realize I control everything in my life. If I want to be happy, all I have to do is smile and remove anything that might not make any sense in my life which tries to destroy my happiness. About two weeks ago I met me a wonderful man by the name of Richard. He's a doctor, divorced with two wonderful teenage daughters that he's raising and they love me and so does he. We have a wonderful time to-gether."

"Good, You've caught on to something I've been trying to tell you for months. You control your happiness and not Keith or anyone else. So you are dating again that's wonderful."

"Yes. I thought it never would happen but it did. But I'm also back with Keith."

"You're what? So soon."

"Yeah, but I don't love him not like I used to."

"So why are you with him?"

"It's a long story. To break it off with him, I believe I'll have to kill him or he'll kill me. We're supposed to be remarried in a couple of months I'm trying to find away to end it before hand."

"How did all of this happen from the last time we spoke?"

"I thought I needed him. I didn't want her to have him. Now Dr. McClinton, I don't give a damn who have him. I'm happy and I don't need someone like Keith who makes me unhappy."

"But you two are going to be married how is he making you unhappy?"

"He says that he loves me and he's sorry for the things he's put me through. Everything is going right in my life and I've found love. And I'm not going to mess that up with Keith and his changes. The minute the spell is off, he'll go back to his old self."

"Isn't he seeing someone?"

"Not any more. They broke up, the three of them. I knew that wouldn't last." She lit a cigarette. "Do you know that little bas-tard, Corey."

Dr. McClinton tried to figure out who she was talking about.

"You know Corey, the one who accused me of sexual harass-ment because I didn't want to see him anymore. Let me tell you how good things are going in my life. Not only do my husband want me back but Corey finally got what was coming to him."

"Yes, the young man you had an affair with."

"Well that low-life got what was coming to him all right. And I wasn't having an affair with him, I was just trying to make Keith jealous. Do you know Dr. McClinton, pay back is hell? If you don't believe me ask him; he hit the bottom of the bottom. One of the students accused him of trying to come on to her. So when they went before the school board it was his word against hers but since she was the student they believed her and he had to resign or be fired. Doesn't that sound familiar. But in his case he lost everything and had to move back home with his mother. His name is shit in D.C. He can't get a job in any school district here. He lost his home, and his car. The last I heard he had become an alcoholic all in a couple of months. It always comes back seven time worse."

"How did you hear this?"

"I have my sources. And you know that tramp, Andrea, I was telling you about who I caught Keith with a couple of years ago in her shower about three or four years ago?"

He nodded and continued to write his observation of how Darika was gloating about Corey's payback.

"That little tramp," she laughed, and blew cigarette smoke into the air. "She has one of those STDs. I believe it's Herpes. You can't get rid of that can you?"

"No, I don't believe you can."

With a smirk on her face she blew more smoke into the air and crossed her legs. "What goes around comes around. She knew Keith was married and she slept with him anyway and had the nerve to laugh in my face about it, well who's laughing now? I am, because I don't have the pussy sores that she has. The way I understand it her husband—the slut had the nerve to get married after she realized Keith didn't want her. Anyway her husband was out there sleeping around and he contracted the disease and brought it back to her but the strange thing about it they can't find a trace of it in him. See what if Keith would have brought me something back after fooling around with her? But he didn't. Her husband did."

"That's sad don't you think? Her life is ruined and she didn't ask for such a thing."

"Yes she did, when she fucked around with my husband."

"You still have animosity toward her from three years ago?"

"You're damn right."

"Have you ever heard bitterness will consume your soul before your enemies do?"

"Not in my case, Dr.McClinton, it is my bitterness that has consumed them."

"Why do you believe that?"

"I'll tell you later. I'm going to give her your number. She's going to need you and some of these pills to keep her sane."

"Darika, I see a change in you. Have anyone else told you that you've changed?"

"For better or worse? Don't answer that," she said, and chuckled. "Dr. McClinton, I've been hurt by these people and because I'm happy and they are now hurting I've changed?" She sighed and pressed her back to the sofa and continued to gloat. "Now you remember me telling you about that Marissa, the one who came to our anniversary party and danced all night with Keith as if I wasn't standing there. I believe they slept together also but it doesn't matter now."

Dr. McClinton tried to remember all of the names she was throwing at him.

"Well she can't dance or stare at him or anybody else anymore. Come to find out she fell over her daughter's skates, broke her hip and hit the back of her head on the stairs which caused her to go blind."

Dr. McClinton threw the pad and pencil on the floor and fell back in his chair and laughed. "Are you making these things up?"

"Why would I?" Darika asked him as she put her cigarette out and sat at the edge of the sofa. "Dr. McClinton, like I told you before, I'm not crazy and I'm sure as hell not a liar."

"But these things seem so—"

"Unreal. Funny what love and voodoo will make you do."

His laughter disappeared to seriousness. "What do you mean, love and voodoo?"

"You don't believe in voodoo, Dr. McClinton, so you will never understand. Do you believe in God?"

He nodded. "No,"

" None of you white liberal, Republicans do—none of you white people period believe in God, but I do and I believe in voodoo."

"So if you believe in God, why do you need voodoo?"

"God was taking too long to answer my prayers and I wanted those people to hurt and suffer the way I did."

"And Keith? He hurt you, didn't he? Why didn't he fall down some stairs or get run over by a bus?" He asked and laughed. "Darika, this is ridiculous. Don't believe in such tales as voodoo. It was just an ironic coincident that all of the women Keith slept with at one time or another ended up having misfortunes."

"Voodoo has Keith's mind clear and he realize that I'm the only woman for him. He loves me again and he's going to always love me."

"So did you use voodoo to get Richard?"

"Didn't have to."

"Why aren't you taking your pills? This is nonsense. I don't want you to get hurt by living on this edge. You are bound to fall off. What happened to those people are coincidences. You or nobody had anything to do with their down fall."

"I didn't expect you to understand."

"Because I don't. So you are using voodoo to clear up his mind; he'll never love you on his own."

"I don't care but he'll love me. Beverly broke his heart when she told him she didn't love him. I made her say that because I knew he loved her."

"Beverly."

"That's the married woman and Odessia's best friend. He was seeing both of them. But not anymore. Beverly wouldn't leave her husband for him and he never liked Odessia so he told her that it wasn't working out to come back to me."

"So they didn't happen to hit rock bottom or maybe trip over a pair of skates?" he asked and chuckled while shaking his head.

"It seems funny to you. Things worked out just the way I wanted them to between them. All of them went their separate ways."

"Does anyone else besides those people you've named have some type of spell on them?"

"No, not really. My cousin, Phyllis hipped me to Madam Ruth, she's from Haiti."

"And Madam Ruth is—"

"My friend who's helped me in this."

"She's the voodoo lady." Dr. McClinton asked.

Darika laughed. "If that's what you want to call her."

"So now that you have Keith to yourself what are you going to do with him?"

She laughed out loud and blew smoke into the air. "I don't know—I don't know if I even want him now. I like Richard and he likes me."

Fifty minutes had come and gone and Darika was on her way out of Dr. McClinton's office. She was going home to get prepared for her date with Richard. Tonight she was going to meet his parents for the first time but she was afraid. She was afraid that his mother wouldn't like her. Out of all the men she had dated from high school to college up until she and Keith were married, she had never found favor with their mothers and she couldn't understand why. She was respectful to them, she laughed at their mother-son humor and she had even called them mother to have that sense of closeness but they never felt it. Before the end of their dinner, eyes were rolling and they were referring to her as she instead of Darika. And on her way out of the door there would never be an extended invitation for her to come back. No matter how hard she tried to figure out what she had done wrong nothing would come to her mind but her skin tone that black people have been so prejudice against since she could remember. All of the men she had dated in her life have had mother's damn near white or if not white. Darika's main attraction were toward light skin men. With her being dark there was no way she could date a dark skin man. She didn't find them attractive or even sexy. Two dark skin people together were sure to draw attention to themselves her mother had always told her. That's why she always made light skin girls her best friend. Cookie was light but she wasn't dark either. Darika thought having some one beside her that was just as dark as she was made her look even darker. But now she's with a man who's just as dark as she is and nothing else matters because she would rather be with him than anyone else.

Richard was close to his mother and he valued her opinion and Darika felt if she didn't like her neither would he. So she had to do something about it and Madam Ruth was her only solution. She had helped her solve all of her other problems.

There was no answer when Darika called Madam Ruth and no one answered her door. Darika had no idea on what to do. She was terrified of meeting Richard's mother and without Ruth's help, she was going to postpone their meeting until tomorrow. She rushed home to call Richard and tell him that she had come down with a cold and she wouldn't be able to meet him for dinner tonight.

Just as she was pulling into her driveway so was Cookie and Antonio in a brand new 1999 gray Mercedes. Darika's heart sank to her feet and her temperature rose to a hundred and something degrees. She hadn't heard from or seen them since the funeral four months ago. Cookie had received a check for Zoria of two hundred and fifty thousand dollars from the insurance company and she had her man, so she had no reason to call Darika. Although the police had someone in custody who they thought pulled the trigger, they could easily come to Cookie as the mastermind behind the whole killing if she started spending the insurance money like a person who's never had anything. And from what Darika heard through gossip that was exactly what she was doing. Being stupid is the first way most people get caught for murder, she thought. Darika stepped out of her car.

"Hi, girl." They hugged and kissed each other on the cheek. "Hello, Antonio." Darika shook his hand looking him in his eyes that were glassy and dilated.

They walked in behind Darika and took a seat on her sofa.

"So I see you have a new car." Darika told Cookie, as she fixed both of them a drink.

"That's Antonio's. I bought it for him for his birthday."

Darika stopped pouring and rolled her eyes up in her head. "What a nice gift, girl. Where did you get the money to buy such a beautiful expensive car?" she asked.

"I have my ways to do for my man." She giggled and Antonio's skinny arms hugged her fat shoulders tightly.

"That's my baby, Darika."

"Cookie, or the car?" Darika asked him.

Cookie and Antonio laughed. "Girl, you crazy. Do you like it," he asked her.

"I love it. So when was your birthday?"

They both laughed and looked at each other. "Five months from now but he couldn't wait."

Darika rolled her eyes once again and handed them their drinks. "So where is Zoria?"

"Girl, she's been spending a lot of time at Velma's. She stole my husband, now she's trying to steal my little girl." She dropped her head and Antonio put his arm around her to comfort her. "So how does it feel to be a divorced woman?"

Darika flopped down in the chair by the window and lit a cigarette. "Great."

"What's so great about it? You didn't get shit but a condo and three hundred and fifty thousand dollars out of millions. The bastard won again."

"Not really."

Antonio shouted, "Shitttttt. You know that nigga got'ta pay for what he has done to you." He gulped his drink down and handed Darika the glass for a refill.

"Darika, girl, how did he manage to only give you pennies."

Darika shrugged her shoulders and put her cigarette out. "I don't know and I don't care."

Antonio dumped the ashes of his cigar into the ashtray. "If he doesn't get what's coming to him, what are you going to do then. If he continues to win every battle you two fight what are you going to do? You see, Darika, Keith is a smart niggah. For years he's played with your emotions by building you up just to let you down. He made you think he was the only man that wanted you while you sat back and let him cheat. You are beautiful. I was asking Cookie on our way over if it's all right if we invite you over to the house and introduce you to my brother."

Darika twisted her weave up in a ponytail and placed the clamp on it that was lying on the table. "I have someone but thank you."

"You got to be lying, why haven't you told me?"

"Because I haven't talked to you since God knows when."

"You really don't know what type of power you have do you?" Antonio asked Darika and she giggled knowing well enough about her powers.

"You have the power to stop that nigga right in his tracks and walk away with all the money and the smiles you deserve."

"Let me stop you because I know where you are going with this and I'm not interested. Killing him is out of the question. I have Keith right where I want him and I didn't need your help."

"Darika, why are you getting so up tight? He's only trying to help you."

"Suggesting that I kill someone is your idea of help?"

"This man has hurt you. He's engaged to some other woman now."

"No, he's not. And if he is he won't be for long. There will never be a wedding. Not if I can help it."

"What can you do? You don't have any powers on what that man does."

Darika shrugged her shoulders.

"Tony," Cookie pleaded. "She's fine."

"No she's not fine, you got what you wanted. Let her get what she wants and that's everything she should have gotten in the divorce. He's laughing at her and I can feel her pain. I could feel your pain while he was over there living with Big Willie and you were losing the house and had no money. She doesn't need to go through that."

"I'm not going through anything, Tony, believe me. I'm happy."

Cookie walked over to her and put her arm around her shoulders. "And I'm happy for you and this new man you never told me anything about."

"What do you care about this new man of hers? That ain't none of yo' damn business. I'm trying to take care of business here."

"There's no business for you to take care of, Tony. I'm not interested in having anyone killed."

"What about the policies you have on him?"

"What about them? I don't remember telling you anything

about any policies."

"When do they expire?"

"That's none of your business and I don't want to talk about this anymore."

"Tony, baby, just leave it alone," Cookie said, handing Tony a drink. "So, Darika, I gave myself until April to lose thirty pounds, starting next Monday. I'm going to the gym every day and I'm going to run—well in my case, walk every morning."

"That's good. Go for it, girl."

"My baby don't need to lose no weight. I like her just the way she is—big boned."

Cookie laughed and planted her lips against his. "Baby, I need to lose a couple of pounds. Darika, doesn't Keith still run those five miles every morning."

Darika nodded. "He's been doing that for eleven years faithfully every morning at five o'clock."

"Damn, what a healthy man he must be. No wonder he had time for all those women," Antonio said, and chuckled. "He had stamina for days." Then Antonio asked, "So he runs from his house through the park?"

Darika nodded and lit another cigarette. Antonio was making her very upset.

"About how many of those do you smoke a day?" Antonio asked her and she rolled her eyes at him.

"So the two boys that they have in custody, who are they?"

He shrugged his shoulders and gulped down his drink. The power of the cognac woke up his insides and burned his chest. "Just some niggahs that were in the wrong place at the wrong time."

Darika looked at Cookie.

"Darika, why don't you go and get yourself cleaned up and join us for dinner at that new restaurant everyone is screaming about-Apples and Crickets. I believe it is. I hear they serve the best french cuisine in D.C."

Darika put out her cigarette and immediately lit another one; she was nervous. "Not tonight. I'm going to meet Richard and his mother for dinner."

"So Richard is his name? And he's introducing you to his mother. It must be serious."

Darika nodded. "Could you please excuse me for a second?" She had forgotten she needed to call Richard to cancel for tonight. She ran quickly up the stairs to her bedroom. Knowing Antonio had something to do with John's death made things a lot clearer for her and she was a lot more afraid of him. It wasn't going to make her go out and do something stupid like turn him in to the police because that meant Cookie would be tied in with it some way, even if she didn't give him the okay and some how Darika would be involved.

Richards's mother answered the phone and Darika disguised her voice to sound as if she had a cold. She was talking out of her nose. "Hello, is Richard in."

"He's in the shower. May I take a message?"

"Hello, Mrs. Grooms I'm Darika—" She said talking through her nose

"Darika, hi. How are you? You sound like you have a cold."

"Yes, ma'am, I woke up with it this morning. So I was calling Richard to cancel for tonight. I feel pretty bad."

"Poor baby. Well, he's in the shower right now. I'll tell him as soon as he gets out."

"Thank you. Now you get into bed and get some rest."

"I will." Darika was pleased at how well she had pulled off her disguise. She hung up the phone and headed back down stairs to get Cookie and Antonio out of her house. They were beginning to depress her and she hadn't been depressed in awhile now.

When Darika walked back down the stairs, she didn't see them, which scared her, with all of Antonio's talk about killing for insurance money, and God knows how many times he had gotten away with it. Darika called out Cookie's name but there was no answer. She ran over to the window and their car was still parked outside. She stood in the middle of her living room wondering where they could be when she heard a noise come from the kitchen. She slowly walked toward the door and burst through it, only to discover the shocker of her life. Antonio shooting heroin through Cookie's veins.

"What the hell are you doing?" Darika screamed.

"Damn," Antonio muttered and dropped the needle.

"Darika," Cookie said, jumping up and nearly tumbling over as the heroin relaxed her. "Is everything okay."

"Hell no. Cookie, you're doing drugs and this sorry bastard is pumping your veins with them?" Cookie dropped her head and stared down at her shoes and the black and white squares on the floor. "You sorry bastard." Darika screamed and took off her slipper and began beating Antonio with it.

"Get this bitch off me," he cried as he tried to protect his head with his skinny frail arms.

"Bitch, you don't hit my man." Cookie slurred while trying to pull Darika off of Antonio. "You got to be out of your mind."

"No, you are out of yours. Get out of here, both of you. How could you, Cookie? You are ruining your life."

"Don't worry about my life. Worry about your own."

"Get out." Darika pointed toward the door and followed them to it and slammed it shut with no words said. She then flopped down on the sofa and took a deep breath. She was going to see Ruth first thing tomorrow morning. Antonio would be out of Cookie's life for good.

As Darika thought about everything Antonio had said about Keith and everything she remembered he had did and said to her during their marriage she couldn't understand how she had loved him or stayed with him as long as she did. Now that she had a real man who loved her and treated her with respect, she didn't feel like being bothered with Keith. He calls her every other minute crying and pleading for her to give him another chance after she hangs up in his face, but she now hates him. She wish she never would have gone to Madam Ruth but she didn't know she would meet another man and fall in love with him. She thought she would always love Keith for some strange reason. Maybe because she thought no one else would want her. She gave him back his ring, the keys to the Lexus and the ticket to India they were supposed to visit in June. When she told him that it was over, he flipped and nearly tried to kill Darika. They both fought each other like cats and dogs. Darika fought for her life but came out with a black eye and sprung ankle from trying to run away from Keith. Just to hear his voice was disgusting. Finally she now had a chance to see him hurt and cry and beg for her to come back to him but now it didn't matter, because the love she once had for him was gone. And one thing helped her decipher the truth from a lie was the root she had Ruth put on him. She was going to have her remove it first thing tomorrow morning, along with giving her favor with Mrs. Grooms and running Antonio out of Cookie's life.

Darika lie stretched out across her sofa flipping through the channels on the television with the remote, exhaling the smoke of her cigarette when she heard a knock at the door. It startled her because she wasn't expecting anyone. Richard had called earlier to check on her and he was still going to go through with his plans to take his mother out. She tipped-toed over to the door and stretched her eye through the peep hole to see who it was. "Damn," she screamed without saying a word. It was Richard and his mother. Darika didn't know what to do. She was fully clothed and her house smelled like cigarette smoke. She ran into the kitchen to get her Country Breeze air freshener and ran through the house spraying it into the air. The smell was still in the air so she lit three incenses. Richard rang the door bell again and this time laid on it. Darika screamed out through her nose. "Who is it?" as she ran up stairs to tear off her clothes and put on her robe. She walked back down the stairs like a snail and opened the door as if she was asleep.

"Baby," Richard said, with open arms to hug her. "How's my special lady?"

"Miserable," she moaned. "I thought you were going out to dinner?"

"I was but I had to come and see about you first."

"Thank you."

"And this is my lovely mother, Pandora Grooms."

"Hi." Darika smiled and extended her hand out to hers. "I've heard so much about you."

"And I've heard so much about you." Darika looked at Richard and smiled because Mrs. Grooms was just as dark as she was or even darker. Darika knew they would get along well because both of them had something in common—the obstacles their dark skin had brought them in life.

"Is that cigarette smoke I smell?" Richard asked. "Baby, I'm allergic to smoke," he said, while sniffing the air and coughing.

"Cookie and her boyfriend came over to see how I was doing and he was smoking a cigarette." Darika began spraying the air fresher into the air. "Do you smell it now? I told Cookie to light these incenses to drain out the smell."

"Baby, why don't you open the door so that some fresh air can circulate in here," Mrs. Grooms suggested to Richard.

Richard opened the door, took a deep breath of fresh air and was startled by Keith's appearance from out of nowhere. "May I help you?" Richard asked.

"Hell no. I'm not here to see you. I'm here to talk to my wife."

Keith walked up the stairs and Darika rushed to the door to meet him."What are you doing here, Keith? You need to leave before I call the police."

"For what? When all I want to do is talk to you, Darika."

"Darika, what is going on? Who is this man?"

"Who are you? Darika and I have been married for ten years and we are trying to work things out so that we can get back together."

"That's not true. Baby, this is my ex-husband Keith. I have no idea what he's talking about," she explained.

"You have to be kidding me. I love you, baby. Isn't this what you want?"

"You need to leave." Richard told him.

"Richard, honey, don't get involved with this."

"Mrs. Grooms I don't understand what Keith is doing here. We've been divorced."

Keith tried to come through the door as Richard blocked him. "She doesn't want you any more. It's over."

"Richard, your mother is right. Don't get involved. I'll handle this."

"No," he said blocking Darika. "I'll handle this and he's going to leave now."

"This is between me and my wife. I want to speak to her— Darika come outside."

"Keith, you need to leave before I call the police."

"Damnit I love you," he screamed and burst through the door knocking Richard down and grabbing Darika and pulling her outside. Once Richard picked himself up from the floor, it was on. He snatched Darika from Keith and threw her over to the side as if she was a rag doll. And went up under Keith flooring him to the ground and jumped on top of him and began beating him in the face. Darika and Mrs. Grooms screamed for him to stop. Keith managed to get Richard off of him so he straddled over him and began to beat Richard nonstop. Darika ran into the kitchen, grabbed the broom and *Whop, Whop* two times across Keith's back and head driving him off of Richard.

"What in the hell is wrong with you. Why are you hitting me."

"The police is on their way. Get out of my yard and stay out of my life!" she yelled.

Richard's mother helpd him up while dusting him off as if he was a child. By this time all of Darika's neighbors were peeking through their curtains and standing in their front door to get a better view.

"You had no right coming by here," she screamed while pointing her finger in Keith's face. "I don't love you. I hate you. Why can't you get that through your big head? We will never be together again."

"Is that what you feel?" Keith asked her while wiping the bloody cut above his eye.

"Yes, I love Richard."

"Fine."

Darika ran over to Richard to help him. "Come on, let me get you cleaned up."

"I'm taking my son home. I'll take care of him."

"Mrs. Grooms, I had no idea this was going to happen."

"Save it, honey, my son doesn't need a woman like you." She walked Richard to the car as he leaned on her shoulder and limped.

"Richard.." Darika called out.

292

"Baby, let him go. He's a mama's boy anyway."

"You shut up-you, shut up and get out of my life." She stormed into the house and slammed the door behind her.

CHAPTER TWENTY-THREE

At five thirty this morning Beverly woke up cooking a big breakfast and later threw it all up. Silently she stood over the toilet crying with no hesitation about what she was going to do if she was really pregnant. Her breast were tender, she felt like she had to spit and she hadn't seen her period in two months. She was too embarrassed to go to her doctor because she hated to tell him she wasn't going to keep it so a home pregnancy test would do. She ran to the 24 hour drug store around the corner before Gene and Jabari awakened. She crept back into the house heading straight for the downstairs bathroom, peed into the little plastic cup and stuck the stick into it and placed it under the sink for ten minutes. She paced around the house counting down the minutes, waiting to discover the reality she had already suspected.

There were two blue positive signs which meant she was

pregnant. How many months she didn't care to know because she wasn't going to keep it anyway. Her heart pounded and her hands shook like a leaf on a tree as she discarded the remaining urine into the toilet. The sooner she could have the abortion the better. Thank God Gene was going out of town today. She would have time to heal without him suspecting anything or wanting to have sex. She looked through the yellow pages of the phone book to find a doctor to do the procedure but none of the offices were open. It was only eight o'clock in the morning.

It was puzzling to her, out of thirteen years of never being on anything and having sex with the same man, she had never gotten pregnant or even had so much of a scare. There was no doubt in her mind that Keith was the father. She had known a long time ago that Gene was only shooting juice. She even knew the day she got pregnant, on Christmas morning in the basement. She couldn't tell Keith with him being so in love with Darika he prabably would scream and tell her to do something she was already going to do. She sat at the kitchen table staring into space wondering how could this happen to her. At her age she was pregnant with her bestfriends ex-man's baby, who is now back with his ex-wife. She was now living some talk show type shit.

Gene walked down stairs with his bags for her to take him to the airport, not taking his eyes off of her, he asked her where she had been as if he knew something was up with her.

"Nowhere, why do you ask?"

"I heard you when you left."

"And."

He sighed and looked at his watch. "We better be going I don't want to miss my plane."

There was a delay with Gene's plane which was a perfect time he felt for him to put fear in Beverly's heart. He looked straight into her eyes and warned her of any feelings she might have for Keith better end or else he would promise to kill them both along with himself.

"I don't know what's going on between you two but whatever it is it better end. I never could trust that muthafuka but I thought I could trust you."

Beverly didn't know where he was coming from. She hadn't seen or talked to Keith in two months and didn't want to see him.

"But I see now that I can't even trust you, so I'm telling you. If you fuckin like him, you better stop fucken liking him or I'm going to put a bullet so deep in your head they won't be able to find it."

"Gene, you don't scare me," she said, through clenched teeth. "It's just your own damn mind making you think I would want something to do with Keith; he used to date Odessia and you know that." Beverly was frightened and her voice was cracking with fear. She had never heard Gene use profanity or had seen him this angry. She used to lie to Keith about her fear of him finding out about them and killing them both but now her fear has come true. The white part of his eyes had turned blood shot red and the veins in his forehead looked as if they were going to burst through his skin he was so angry.

"You always told me people could pull the wool over my eyes but you can't. My mama told me about you. She always warned me that you were sneaky, but I tried so hard, Bev, to not believe her."

"Your mother never liked me."

"Because she knew you were some fuckin slut."

"What."

"Who never had anything and I came and gave you the world and you fucked me over."

"I don't have to hear this coming from you."

"You're fuckin him. We've been married damn near thirteen years and you are going to let some light skinned- want'a be-playboy come between our marriage." Tears formed in his eyes and Beverly's heart broke into thousands of pieces. She had never seen him cry before. "Damnit! I love you. How could you do this to me?"

"Baby, what are you talking about? Keith and I are only friends and have always been. You've seen me talk to him because he was having problems with Odessia and he wanted me to talk to her. Please, don't accuse me of something I'm not doing." This was her time to find out if he was only assuming or if he had seen pictures of them together. "I know you've hired a detective to follow me around but I haven't been with any man."

"Detective, what in the hell are you talking about, Bev?"

"You have someone following me that's how you know I'm sleeping with him right?"

"No I don't, but that might be a good idea. Instead of my mother assuming because you two were all over each other in my house during the Christmas party and my own instinct and gut feeling that the yellow nigga is fucking you I need to hire a detective. Better yet a hit-man to kill you both if he sees you two together."

The stewardess called for first class to board the plane. He opened his arms to hug her and he whispered in her ear. "I mean it if you fuck around on me, Bev, I swear I'll kill you and that bastard."

The killer instinct in Gene's eyes and the base in his voice had Beverly terrified. She ran out of the airport without looking back. She had no time to waste, she had to find a doctor to perform the abortion today or she was going to do it herself.

When she drove home Odessia was sitting in her driveway waiting on her.

"Hay, girl, what's going on?" Beverly asked her while trying to smile through her terror and worry.

"You fuckin tell me. Why? I thought we were friends and the whole time you two were just using me as a cover up so that no one would suspect anything," Odessia said, with tears in her eyes.

Beverly's heart was pounding. "'Dessia, what are you talking about, me and Keith? Do you think—"

"She might be crazy but she knows what the hell she's talking about. I've watched you two whispering and laughing and I never thought anything because I didn't want to seem insecure. I've watched him look at you with something in his eyes that was more than friendship. Darika told me she saw you two."

"And you believe that nut." Now she knew where Gene had gotten his information from; she had called him also. "She's just upset because he doesn't want her. So she's going to try and lie and tell you something like this. Keith and I, no. That's not true."

"Don't lie to me. So he broke up with me because you broke it off with him. So what did he want you to do, leave Gene. How could you do this to me knowing how I felt about him? Beverly, you are a self-centered bitch." You have a wonderful husband. Why?"

Beverly didn't say anything.

"Why, godamit! I told you everything I ever felt for that man and you were screwing him. So how did it feel to have such a big secret as you, laughing in my face," she screamed. "Gene and I were fooled while you two were meeting up at the hotel a hundred miles outside of D.C., screwing."

"It's not what you think."

"Then what is it, Beverly?"

Beverly turned away from her and walked toward her front door.

"Damnit, don't walk away from me," Odessia screamed, as she grabbed Beverly by the arm. "Was it that much of a good fuck to have stabbed me in the back for it?"

Beverly snatched away from her "This man made me happy, something I wasn't getting here. I'm sorry if I hurt you but I needed him. I needed the joy he was giving you."

"You bitch. How could you? Right under my nose and I thought we were friends."

"We weren't friends. We were associates."

"What? So that's the excuse you gave yourself for doing it?"

"I don't want to talk about this anymore." She turned to walk away.

"What about Gene, how could you do this to him?" She ran behind Beverly, snatching her by the arm once again. "Tell me you're not pregnant by him? She said that you were pregnant."

"That bitch is crazy and so are you."

With her tears falling down her cheeks she threw her hands around Beverly's neck and started choking her. "You betraying slut."

"Get off of me," Beverly screamed. "Get off of me." She threw Odessia to the ground and ran into the house. She fell against the door while trying to catch her breath and then ran to the phone to call Keith.

Pam put her right through to him with no questions asked.

"She knows," Beverly cried. "She knows that we've been seeing each other and so does Gene. That crazy bitch told her every thing."

"Wait a minute, Beverly, calm down. What are you talking about? Who knows what?"

"Odessia. She said Darika called her and told her every thing this morning about the hotel—about us."

"And."

"What do you mean and? I'm married and Gene has already said this morning that he is going to kill us both and this damn baby I'm carrying."

"What baby?"

She had opened her mouth too soon.

"What baby, Beverly? Are you pregnant?" He asked her.

"I'm not keeping it."

"No. You have to, please, tell me. It's mine, it has to be mine."

"I can't keep it. Gene will blow. He'll know that it's not his."

"Do not do this, Beverly, I love you, you know that I do and we can get through this. We belong together. We've already established that much. That is our child you are carrying. If you kill that child, you are only thinking of yourself."

"I am not. I'm married and I'm thinking of the consequences and the pain I'm going to cause a lot of people. What are people going to say once they find out?"

"Damn those people. That child you are carrying is mine. It was conceived in love, and whether you want to leave Gene and be with me or not is besides the point."

"It was a mistake damnit. I'm married and you are with Darika."

"Have the baby, Beverly, and give it to me to raise. Darika and I are going to do it together."

"What? Are you out of your damn mind?"

"No, you got to have the baby. This is my only chance to be a father."

"Bye, Keith." She slammed down the phone and began to cry.

Keith was right about Beverly being pregnant might be his only chance to become a father but then again it might not be the best thing now that he and Darika are trying to work things out. He felt they didn't need any new obstacles standing between them. It was bad enough he had hurt her in the past by cheating. There was no way he could put her through the pain knowing she's not able to have children. He picked up the phone and called Beverly.

"Hello, Beverly. You are right. Do what you know is best. Right now me having a child isn't. This would only hurt Darika worse than I've hurt her in the past."

"Are you out of your damn mind? Have you fallen and bumped your head? When did you start thinking about her again?"

"You wouldn't understand. Darika and I love each other just like you love Gene. No matter how unhappy you are with him. you're not going to leave. It's almost like voodoo that has you trapped there."

"And that's exactly what she has on you, I can see it."

Pam interrupted his call with a message that he had a visitor. "Well, I have someone here to see me. I trust that you'll do the right thing because having that baby isn't you, and I have too much to lose. And if I never talk to you again I hope that you take care."

Burn in hell, bastard," she said, and slammed the phone down in his face.

Keith walked out of his office to greet his visitor."Who's here to see me?" he asked Pam and her eyes led him to the woman sitting behind him. He turned around and stood agape at who he saw. "Tammy."

"Hi—"

He held out his arms for a hug and she glided into his arms. "Long time no see. What brings you to D.C.?

She said nothing.

"I see you are still looking good."

"In spite of the extra weight I've gained over the years," she added.

"How long has it been, two years?"

She smiled and nodded. "You still look the same."

"Yeap, running five miles a day helps."

There was a long silence between them. Keith was looking down at his shoes and Tammy looking up at the ceiling. "So you never said what brought you here."

Pam stopped what she was doing to hear Tammy's reason.

"Keith, there's someone that I want you to meet."

That was Pam's cue to jump up from her desk and walk into one of the vacant offices to bring back a beautiful two year-old little girl wearing a pink and white dress. Keith's knees buckled as he stared at the spit and image of himself. His heart exploded with mixed feelings leaving him feeling faint and confused. A child. Pam handed her small hand to him and he stared into the little girl's eyes which were the same color as his.

"Tammy, I need to see you in my office." He handed the little girl's hand to Pam and stormed into his office with Tammy following. "What the hell is going on? What are you trying to do."

"What do you mean? I couldn't tell you two years ago because you were married."

"Why are you telling me now? Is she supposed to be mine?"

"Well, look at her, she looks just like you. I never would have come here today if she wouldn't have asked about you."

"Do you know what this could do to me and my marriage? Darika and I are trying to work this thing out and you come with this surprise two damn years later. I can't accept it and Darika won't accept it either. You're damn lucky I didn't have a heart attack out there in front of her."

"Forget I even came. I just wanted her to know who you were since one of her parents might be dead in a couple of months and I didn't want her to feel alone. Three weeks ago, Keith I was diagnosed with breast cancer and it's spreading as we speak but I begged my doctor to let me come here and introduce my daughter to you. That's fine, Keith, you don't have to accept her." Tears came to her eyes.

"I can't. I love Darika and I don't know how she's going to handle this. If you could just give me some time to explain it to her."

"Forget it." She stormed out of his office slamming the door behind her snatching Alexis's hand away from Pam and storming out of the office to the elevator. Pam ran behind her.

Keith tried calling Darika for the fifth time that morning but she had blocked his number out. Pam came rushing into his office.

"How could you do that? For years I've watched you be a low-down bastard and I've covered up for you and apologized but no more. It hurt my heart to lie to Odessia to tell her I didn't know about you and Beverly but I didn't want to see her hurt anymore than what she was. I told her. That was your child that you sent running out of here not knowing you anymore than she did when she came in here. What does Darika have over you— the same woman you caught with another man not too long ago and you are talking about you love her. All of a sudden. It's obvious that she doesn't want you. I haven't heard her calling here for you and she has another man. Your days of womanizing is over, Mr. Blackanova, your own wife doesn't even want you a woman you thought would eat your shit if you let her."

"Darika and I are not up for discussion. Don't you have some work you need to be doing?"

"No, because I quit."

"You what? Fine."

"All of a sudden you want to be this righteous man when you've hurt so many people. Tammy has cancer and all she wanted was you to know your child and you didn't even have the decency to do that."

"I had my reasons, Pam. Darika and I—"

"Ain't shit because she doesn't want you. Go and get yourself checked somethings not right. You running up behind some woman. How did this change come about? The child that you've always wanted is here."

"But what about Darika?"

"What about her?"

"I love her and I can't go another day without her."

Pam looked at him in disbelief while shaking her head in pity for his soul.

In the meanwhile while Keith was trying to call Darika she

was at Madam Ruth's pleading with her to lift the spell off of him. She was willing to pay her whatever she asked to make Keith leave her alone, to make Mrs. Grooms like her and to run Antonio out of Cookie's life. Ruth was pleased with her last two requests but she laughed at her first one and explained to her that it wasn't that easy to lift the root off of Keith. The root was now a part of Keith's soul and it had to work itself off. Darika couldn't handle it. She needed something done. What was meant for good was ruining her life in the meantime. Ruth took her down to her dark basement, lit candles, drew a circle on the floor backwards in white chalk, put Keith's name inside the circle, pour candle wax over his name, and began to chant while Darika stood over the circle with her eyes closed, praying that when she opened them she wouldn't see the devil standing across from her. She opened one eye just to make sure. Ruth chanted for about five minutes before she told Darika it was okay to open her eyes. Darika slowly opened them and noticed Keith's name had been erased out of the circle and she knew Ruth didn't do it because she was walking around lighting candles. Darika's heart pounded with fear.

"What happened to his name?"

"It was lifted as the spell was reversed. Will he remember any of this?"

"Yes, his friends will remind him but he'll never believe them. And as for Mrs. Grooms, she's prepared a special dinner for you. And Antonio, he'll be leaving real soon."

"Thank you."

"Five hundred dollars."

This time Darika wrote her a check with no hesitations.

Just as Ruth said, Mrs. Grooms invited Darika over for dinner and she was considering her as the daughter she never had. Darika thought she was in there. With Richard's daughters liking her and his mother. She was finally accepted and loved. But little did she know Richard was going to like her anyway, regardless of what his mother thought. But after what happened yesterday things had changed. He didn't want to get involved with her unresolved relationship with Keith, no matter how much Darika tried to tell him it would never happen again. At first Darika had laughed at his attempt to break it off, because he would be changing his mind as soon as she talked to Ruth. Then she figured, what the hell. It wasn't worth it after she had tampered with Keith's mind and she didn't want him afterwards. So she let him go without a broken heart, or any regrets.

Keith laced up his sneakers outside his front door and stretched his body as he prepared his body for his routine five mile morning run. He darted down his driveway at full speed. When he entered the park he noticed two thugs leaning against a tree. They looked pretty rough in their hooded sweat suits but they didn't scare him. The closer he got to them the meaner they looked. Their stares were cold. They were sent there to do a job and they were going to do it for the money. They pulled their stocking caps over their faces and stepped out in front of him to stop his run.

"O' shit," the thug in the blue-hooded sweat shirt whispered. He dropped his head and began to act nervous.

"Excuse me," he said, as he tried to go around them.

"Niggah, you ain't going nowhere," the tallest one said and pulled out a .45 caliber pistol.

Keith threw up his hands. "I'll give you whatever you want, just don't shoot me." There was a voice he heard inside his head just before he left his driveway telling him to take another route and he heard it again as he approached the park but he figured it was nothing.

"Yo, man, I got to dip on this one."

"What the hell—"

Keith recognized his voice. He had heard it before several times. "Jabari?"

"You know this cat?"

"Damn, I didn't know it was going to be him. I can't do it."

"Jabari, what in the hell is going on?" Keith asked him.

"I don't give a damn, it's five thousand in this for me. Yo' family got money. I ain't got shit."

"If it's money you want, I'll give it to you, just don't shoot me."

"Let's forget this, man," Jabari said.

"Schooter said, If we fuck this up it's our ass. So the way I see it, it's his ass or mine and I got the gun. I don't give a fuck about this nigga. He ain't a friend of my family and he ain't a friend of mine."

"Who put you up to this, Jabari?" Keith asked him.

"I'm outa here." Jabari turned around and took off running.

Keith screamed. "Jabari." And there was a shot that brought on darkness.

He heard the doctors screaming you can make it and he tried to open his eyes but they wouldn't bulge no matter how hard he tried. He saw the light that everyone talked about but he didn't see any familiar faces or angels standing behind it. The light was so bright he couldn't stand to look at it so he dropped his head and tears rolled down his face. They were tears of sorrow. From the day the doctor handed him to his mother until the day his life ended from a gunshot wound near his heart he could see his life flashing before him. The pictures moved so fast before his eyes but he could remember all of them. He had lived his life and it wasn't right.

The light turned into darkness and he heard a nurse scream, "We're losing him." He then began to plead with God for another chance. He heard the long drawn out beep and a nurse screaming, "flat line." It was too late. He was dead although they tried to resuscitate him.

He screamed, "God please." And he felt his soul enter his body like a gush of wind. His eyes slowly opened with tears running down the corners of them.

"Mr. Jones," A doctor called out. "Can you hear me?"

A twitch of Keith's finger informed him that he could.

Finally Keith was out of surgery and in his room recovering. He lay hooked up to tubes and wires while staring up at the ceiling reflecting on his near-death experience. His brother stood over him calling out his name but Keith wasn't yet ready to answer.

Darika rushed into his room as soon as she heard the news, with Odessia and Beverly rushing in behind her. Keith's nurse informed them that only one visitor could be in the room at a time. Kelvin walked out leaving the three women to make their own decision on who was going to stay or leave. Each woman stood looking at the other waiting for them to leave until finally the nurse had to decide for them. Since Darika was the first to walk in the room, she was allowed to stay. Odessia and Beverly had to wait in the waiting room. They rolled their eyes and stormed out of the room.

Seeing Keith so helpless lying in the bed and the thought of him almost dying caused Darika to cry and she was regretful for ever dealing with Ruth. She called out his name while standing over him.

"I'm so sorry I hurt you. I just wanted you to love me. You were all that I thought I needed at the time, but when you didn't want me—I'm the blame for this. Now I wish it could have been me instead of you. Look at you, so handsome, and you were my world."

Keith opened his eyes and gazed around the room. "Where is Pam?" He whispered.

"I believe she's in the waiting room."

"Get her in here now."

Darika ran down the hall to the waiting room to get Pam.

She rushed into the room crying as if he was dead.

"Pam."

"Yes. Please don't die. I didn't mean any of those things I said. I'll come back and work for you."

"Get my daughter here."

"They flew back to Atlanta last night."

"I don't care get them back here now."

"Consider it done." She ran out of the room to the pay phone.

"Daughter." Darika replied.

"Don't worry about it."

"I won't I'm just glad to see that you are doing fine. When your brother called me, I nearly fainted. I love you Keith."

Keith sat dazed not paying any attention to Darika and she noticed.

"Well, I better be going I guess you'll be more interested in the other two women you have in the waiting room waiting on you." Darika walked out of the room and Beverly entered.

"Hi," she whispered.

"What are you doing here?" Keith asked her.

"I'm here to see you, silly."

"When are you having the abortion?"

"Tomorrow."

"Good. I guess it hurts that he didn't kill me."

"Who, did you see the killer? The police is out there asking us questions."

"You wanted me dead, didn't you? For what?"

"What are you talking about, Keith? I wanted who dead,you? I don't understand. I was upset with you about going back to Darika but I didn't want you dead for it. I loved you and I still do."

"I loved you. It was a mistake that we became involved but it happened and I'm sorry that it had to end this way."

"So am I, but why do you think I wanted you dead? I understand why you want me to have the abortion you and Darika are back together and she wouldn't understand."

"Darika and I are not together and we'll never be and neither would you and I."

"Why are you carrying on so?"

"Where is your son? Did you put him up to it or did Gene?"

"Put him up to what? Are you crazy. Look, I guess it was a mistake that I came here today. You are talking crazy and I don't understand where you are coming from. I'm having the abortion like you asked. I'm out of your life like you asked, now what more do you want."

"For you and your son to burn in hell for what you've done to me. They tell me that I might not be able to walk again." Tears swelled up in his eyes. "I didn't deserve that."

"Let me get this straight, are you saying Jabari had something to do with your shooting, my son. Is this how you want to hurt me by trying to place this on my son."

"I saw him. I heard his voice."

"You must be out of your mind. Why are you trying to destroy me?" She grabbed her purse and stormed out of the room.

CHAPTER TWENTY-FOUR

G ene stood in the foyer watching Beverly wipe the windows clean of any dust or residue. From the behind she looked like she had gained weight. Her ass had spread, her arms looked thicker and her breast were fuller. He didn't want to believe it but he had a feeling something wasn't right with her and he knew he had nothing to do with it. He walked up behind her and began kissing her neck and massaging her breast with roughness.

"Ouch," she screamed, and pushed him away from her. "What in the hell is wrong with you."

"You tell me, you don't want me to touch you. We don't have sex anymore. I look at you and you're getting thick everywhere. What is it?"

"I'm just eating a little bit more than normal. Depression."

She hadn't told anyone Keith had accused Jabari of his shooting.

Tears rolled down Gene's face and he whispered, "Don't lie to me, Beverly. How could you do this? It wasn't good enough for you to just fuck 'im, but to get pregnant by him."

Her body temperature rose and she felt faint. "What are you talking about?"

"Your breast, your ass and you sleep all damn day. Why they didn't kill 'im, I don't know," he yelled, and punched a hole in the wall big enough for him to fit through.

Beverly began to cry. "I'm not going to keep it, Gene. I'm going to have the abortion tomorrow."

"Damnit, why did you do it?"

The phone rang. It was Ella screaming. Gene answered the phone. "Hello," he yelled.

"Ella, what's wrong?"

"Jabari,"

Beverly's heart sank and she immediately thought the worse. "What about Jabari." She jumped down off the ladder and snatched the phone from Gene. "Mama, what about Jabari?"

"They got his picture all on the news saying he's responsible for your friend's shooting that happened in the park."

"O'my God," she cried and ran down to the television. "This is crazy." She yelled for Jabari.

"What is going on, Beverly?" Gene asked as he watched the news. "Jabari? A suspect. That's bullshit." Gene ran upstairs to check his room but there was no sign of him. Beverly screamed, dropping the phone. The doorbell then rang. It was the police and a detective. Gene ran downstairs to answer the door.

"Yes."

"Is Beverly Hayman in?" the Detective asked.

"Yes, but I'm Jabari's father. I can help you."

Beverly came to the door.

"Mrs. Hayman?"

"My son didn't do it? He's a good boy," Beverly proclaimed.

"Mrs. Hayman, we're placing you under arrest for conspiracy to kill a Mr. Kenneth Jones."

"You have to be kidding me. Is this some kind of a damn

joke," Gene asked. "You are not taking her anywhere. This is some kind of a mistake. My wife had no reason to kill that bastard."

The detective began to read Beverly her rights as the officer placed the handcuffs around her wrist.

Beverly began to scream. "Gene, tell them this is crazy. Officer, how did you come to this conclusion. Where is my son?"

"He's still at large along with Reginald Brown, the second suspect."

"My baby isn't a killer and neither am I," she said, just before they walked her outside.

Beverly held her head down praying this was all a dream as she was greeted by the vultures of the local television stations and newspaper reporters standing on her front lawn trying to ask her questions and take pictures. With all of the commotion her neighbors had come out to be spectators. Beverly felt more ashamed. How would she ever live this down, she thought.

"Baby, I'll have the attorney meet us down at the station. Don't say a word until we get there. You have rights. This is ridiculous. I'll have your job for this." He told the detective as he jumped into his car.

Beverly sat in the back of the police car crying and professing her innocence.

Within five minutes after Beverly's arrest Jabari walked into the police station to turn himself in after seeing his mother on television taking the blame for his crime. The police immediately placed him into handcuffs and under custody. He did exactly what Gene had informed him of when he called him to let him know he was all right and he was going to turn himself in. He made no confession until the family attorney arrived and with the presence of his attorney he told the truth. Killing Keith was supposed to put five thousand in his pocket to buy studio time for the album he was trying to release. He gave the name of the man who approached Reginald to do it for five thousand dollars.

A chill went through Darika's body when she received the call early Tuesday morning from Kelvin telling her Keith had been shot and the doctors didn't think he would make it. She didn't know what to do with herself and she immediately thought of Antonio but called Ruth. By having Ruth lift the spell, she didn't think it meant killing Keith and remove Antonio out of Cookie's life by having him arrested for Keith's murder. She needed Ruth to explain to her what was going on but there was no answer. But now that Keith told the police it was Beverly's son that had something to do with his shooting, Darika didn't need an explanation. It was all a part of the plan and spell to run Beverly out of Keith's life for good.

She lit a cigarette and turned on the television only to see Cookie and Antonio being carried out in handcuffs for the attempted murder of Keith. Darika threw the remote on the sofa and ran over to the television to manually turn it up. Her heart sank and fear came over her as she knew the police would be knocking on her door next.

The detective that was interviewed described the case as a complex one. He had exposed the love affair Beverly had with Keith and her pregnancy which she had miscarried once they took her into custody. Her son was hired by the boyfriend of the best friend of the ex-wife. Motive for the murder was insurance money. The case read like a mystery novel. Darika had no doubt that the police was coming for her next so she dialed the number of her attorney while wiping her tears and lit a cigarette. Before she acknowledged who she was, she assured she had nothing to do with either of the murders.

"I'm sitting here watching the news and I was wondering when you were going to call. I'll meet you at the station."

Just as Darika hung up the phone there was a knock at her door. She took one last long drag from the cigarette before putting it out. She wiped her face clean of her tears and opened the door.

"Darika Jones, I'm Detective Ryan and we are here to place you under arrest for the murder of John Stewart and the attempted murder of your ex-husband Keith Jones." The detective placed the handcuffs on Darika and she burst out crying while pleading her innocence. She held her head down from the television reporters and her neighbors as she was carried to the car.

The battle was finally over and Odessia was the last one standing so the reward went to her. She felt she deserved the reward, and she hated to have had to fight for it, but she loved Keith. Now she had the man she loved just as the power of voodoo told her she would. She kissed Keith on his forehead and rolled him out of the hospital.